LOVE UNCHARTED
LOVE'S IMPROBABLE POSSIBILITY
BOOK THREE

LOVE BELVIN

MKT PUBLISHING, LLC

book 3

by Love Belvin

Published by MKT Publishing, LLC

Copyright © 2013 by Love Belvin

All rights reserved. This book may not be reproduced, scanned, or distributed in any printed or electronic form without written permission from the author. Please do not participate in or encourage piracy of copyrighted materials in violation of the author's rights. This book is a work of fiction. Names, characters, places, and incidences are fictitious and the product of the author's imagination.

ISBN: 978-1-950014-67-5 (Hardcover)
ISBN: 978-1-950014-16-3 (Paperback)
ISBN: 978-1-950014-12-5 (eBook)

MKT Publishing, LLC
First print edition 2013 in U.S.A.

Cover design by Marcus Broom of DPI Design

CHAPTER 1

That was as forward as it got. She wanted Azmir. The emotions I felt were some that hadn't eclipsed since I was a kid going through the drama with O and Keysha. The distant memory from the pain of betrayal was still acute.

I reached up and returned the phone to the nightstand and immediately started experiencing hot flashes. My armpits excreted sweat, and my heartbeat picked up. Azmir opened the bathroom door, and I practically jumped out of bed in search of a few toiletries before hitting the shower myself.

As much as I thought I'd improved on my responses to unfavorable situations, the familiar urge to shut down, run, and protect myself was too tempting—too easy. I was quickly slipping into self-protection mode, a place where Azmir wouldn't survive.

The elevator ride down was in complete silence, and I found my eyes glued to the floor, trying to quest through my ruminative thoughts of the Dawn Taylor intrusion. I'd slipped on a pair of black leather cropped leggings, a retro Run DMC white off-the-shoulder sweatshirt exposing my left shoulder, and a red shimmery scarf, double wrapped around my neck. I paired the ensemble with pony hair, buckle booties.

Azmir bought the booties for me a few weeks back and, finally, I thought to wear them. I prayed he'd be impressed. After all, I was trying to prove to him I was warming up to his desires to splurge on me. A few times since leaving the suite, I had the urge to ask him about the texts from Dawn, but didn't have the guts to do it, feeling I had no rights to him.

"Hey... You, okay?"

His question startled me out of my private thoughts, causing me to slightly joggle. He looked delectable standing there in his crushed velour, smoke gray sweat suit with the hood covering his head. This was his relaxed look, much to the contrary of the designer suit he had worn the night before.

"Yeah...yeah." I sighed. *I* didn't even believe me.

"Are you sure? You've been a little distant since you got out of bed." He paused, but I wasn't prepared to answer. "Was my conversation too heavy for you...or was *I* too aggressive?"

I knew he was referring to our sex from earlier when he mentioned aggressive. Though he *was* aggressive, I relished every moment of it because it made me feel desired and wanted. I could get used to that.

I swallowed. "*Ummm...* No. You were great. No paw marks this morning." I attempted humor. I had to get the spotlight off me. "I'm a little tired from waking up so early. I guess my body is on its weekday schedule." I gave a mirthless chuckle as I adjusted my scarf, trying to sound convincing and distract from my disingenuousness.

He moved up from behind me, pulled the back of the scarf down from my neck to expose my skin and whispered into my skin, "You can wake me up anytime of the morning or night with *that* type of restlessness. You were *sooooo* good last night...and this morning. I can't wait to get you home to return the favor." He kissed and then sucked on my neck, causing a stir deep down inside of me. I didn't want it; I couldn't handle it at the time, but I had no will in me to tell him to stop, my body would betray me. It always did for Azmir.

"I love your look today. It's urban and classic. You're killing those *Monolos*," he sang in between kisses into my neck until the elevator rang its arrival at our destination. As the doors opened, it had caught me gazing deep into his eyes, feeling aroused, but also full of questions and doubts stemming from those texts from Dawn Taylor. He let off of me and with a quick jerk of his chin, prompted me to lead us out of the elevator. It was hard for me to break my gaze deep down in his honey brown irises. Once again, I was lost in the rapture of Azmir.

As we entered the designated section of the restaurant, I was so happy to see Kim. My heart warmed at the sight of her nestled next to Petey, demonstrating a rare display of affection in public. I really had hoped they'd work things out. I held no judgment in my mind if Kim still wanted to be with him, nor did I hold contempt in my heart towards Petey for his transgressions. I was just happy to see two people who had been together so long persevere. I wish I'd had the same endurance.

As we approached them, Petey stood with his hands in the air and shouted, "Damn. I thought you two wasn't gon' come, man! What 'chu doin' to my man, Ray?"

I shot him an expression feigning offense to his carnal allegations and popped him on the arm before hugging him. He returned the enfold with adoration.

"Hey, baby girl! Good to see you again."

"Hey, Petey," I sang before leaving his embrace. I didn't forget about his deceptive orchestrations the night before, but until I had proof, I couldn't react.

I went over to hug Kim while she was seated and then sat next to her.

"Hey, girl! You look cute."

"Thanks, Kim. I appreciate that." I gave a graceful blush.

"You're glowing. Is there a baby number five in the oven?" I teased to her delight.

"Girl, no! I would love another child, but my ass is too old. How 'bout you carry it for me and then I'll take over."

"Deal!" I acceded and together we giggled like life-long buddies. "Where's everybody? It's almost one o'clock."

I looked around the private room of the restaurant, landing my eyes on the buffet table the wait staff was assembling. The food smelled delightful. I was starving.

"Man, that food smells good! I am hungrier than a runaway orphan. Azmir didn't feed me last night," I joked.

"From what I heard he was too busy tryna' feed from yo ass!" Kim bit out with humor.

I scrunched my face with a smile. "What are you talking about?" I asked, knowing full well what she meant.

"You know them bitches can't keep their mouths closed for shit. On the way back to the room, they was talking about how they hooked Divine up by setting up a whole bunch of candles in y'all's suite and shit."

Showing poise, I smiled with a closed mouth. "Oh, so that's who did all of that. It was a nice scene." I nodded. She laughed at my discretion. "So, what's going on with you? You seemed a little unlike yourself last night—not with me, but you didn't socialize with the other girls."

"Girl, dem bitches ain't shit. I'm too old to call phony foes friends," she snapped.

I gave her a playful pout. I didn't know how else to respond. It would have been deceitful of me to ask for details when likely I had gotten them all from Chanell. I didn't want to get involved. They all had a history; I was the new chick.

Speaking of Chanell, she flew into the private area with the local girls in tow. I braced myself, not knowing what type of vibes I'd be getting from them during this function. I looked over in search of Azmir to find him in the corner talking to Petey. I put my purse in the seat to the left of me to reserve it for him, though I doubted anyone wouldn't have already known it.

Chanell waved at me from across the room as she talked to the wait staff. I could only imagine the lack of etiquette in that exchange. I loved Chanell with all my heart, mostly because of her rawness and sincerity, but I was fully aware of her dearth in the class and decorum department. What was more interesting was how they used her as a front man for coordinating this weekend's events.

"Where's Syn? Why hasn't she been involved in the planning for this weekend?" I nodded my head toward Chanell.

"Shit. Syn's ass is doing what Syn know how to do best. She been drunk since she got here. She drove down with her cousins because her dumb ass got into it with Kid when Petey was booking our flights and rooms down here. It got to the point where he said, *'fuck her'*, and told us to book without her. So, she packed her cousins and friends in two cars and came down drunk as hell. Kid was so fucking mad. I keep telling Syn she fuckin' up with him. She just don't know how to express herself, then get mad, get drunk, and fuck up everything."

Hmmmmmm...

"That's too bad," I sympathized and couldn't help but to wonder what her problem was with me.

Kim cut her words short because the girls started taking their seats at the table. Kid glided into the room without Syn, and we all shouted birthday greetings out of sequence. He smiled and waved. I noticed his oversized *Versace* shades to, likely, disguise his hangover.

"Hey, party people," he greeted.

By this time, Azmir and Petey had returned to the table and gave Kid birthday dabs the way manly men did. Almost immediately after, Syn wandered in about a half dozen deep with her girls. Kid sat across the table from Kim and me. Syn took her rightful place to the left of him, placing her directly across the rectangular table from Petey. Kim sat face to face with a recovering Kid.

Syn didn't acknowledge me at all but took on a heavy conversation with Kim. I chalked it up to her simply not liking me and certainly wouldn't allow it to damper my mood. In all truth, I'd much prefer not to share space with her either but had no choice.

We were all seated and eating at the table. Conversations flowed, everyone seemed to have been engaged in one. The spread was great with an assortment of traditional breakfast and lunch menu items, none of which my diet called for, so I did the best I could to exercise self-control. Azmir offered to order me a vegetable omelet, but I whispered my adamance of not wanting to draw attention to myself at Kid's birthday celebration. I stuck with eggs and fruit.

I caught Syn gawking into my profile and could see from my peripheral view when she shoved the girl next her who automatically looked at me. I could tell she'd spoken about me to them beforehand. I simply shook it off as I always did.

Azmir seemed to be relaxed while Wop and the other *Clan* members weren't shy of stories filled with doltish gossip from the neighborhood. At some point during the sit-down, the waiters served us all mimosas to my dismay, and Wop stood and tapped his glass, trying to make an announcement.

We all quieted down, giving him our undivided attention. "X'cuse me, er'body. I just wanna show sum love to my dude who done took me under his arm and showed me sum love over the years. He make sure I keep gettin' money to feed my son. He don't hate. He always got my back. And...dis is from me to you, playa."

Wop pulled out a massive square gift wrapped case and handed it to Kid. After the unwrapping, it revealed a bright, clustered diamond chain with a humongous diamond encrusted cross. It was every bit of what you see your average rapper wearing. *So them*. But I could appreciate the sentiment behind it. From the sounds of it, Wop was gifting his mentor and it was admirable within itself.

"Thanks, man. Love you, man." Kid beamed, giving him some special handshake I'd seen of this *"Clan"* and pulling him into a bear hug.

What type of work did Wop do to earn the money for such a piece of jewelry? I could only imagine the expense. Kid slid the chain over his neck and the girls' clicked pictures on their phones.

"Dat's stacks on stacks right there on ya' neck, playboy!" Wop shouted as he sat down. The girls at the table *oooooh'ed* and *ahhhhhh'ed* in amazement of the bling.

Petey then stood and gave a few words.

"You know, playboy, you my strong peoples. Over 'da years my respect fa' you done grown more than I eva' thought it could. I remember you from snatching chains 'dats about forty-nine stacks cheaper than da one you wearin' right now." In unison, the table burst into laughter. It was clear they all had history. "I remember my dude, Rock, tellin' me to watch out for 'dis light skinned kid who was robbin' fa' jewels. Memba 'dat, Divine?"

Azmir nodded his head and smiled, apparently at the recollection of it.

"Yeah, 'cuz, I told Divine and 'dem, *I'ont give a fuck how young he is, I got sum heat fo' 'dat ass if he run up on me or my duke!*" Petey shared in laughter, referring to Azmir. He always protected Azmir. I quickly surmised after meeting him, it was his role. As if it were more than a friendship, like an assigned position of some sorts. "Well, Im'ma just say happy thirty-fifth birthday and give you 'dis. I got mad love for you, homie. You been a strong soldier in da field."

Petey handed Kid a smaller wrapped gift. Upon opening it, we learned it was an eighteen karat rose gold *Audemars Piguet* watch —*or in this case*—timepiece. I was floored. I knew the brand of watch *without* diamonds could run about fifteen to thirty grand, but when you add in the bling, I was out of my league.

Can Petey afford that with his strip club earnings?

Everyone clapped and affirmed the value of the gift as Kid reached across the table, giving Petey the same dap he had just given Wop minutes ago. I could tell Kid was overcome with emotions, *as he should have been.* These were extremely profligate gifts! *What next?*

Petey motioned to Azmir, and I was beside myself in anticipation of what he was going to say and give. Azmir stood.

"Kid, you're a solid soldier, far surpassing my expectations. I'm not a man of many public pronouncements, but I will say you've done well and are a vital piece to *The Clan*. May your loyalties remain true, and your belly stay fat. Happy birthday."

Chanell squealed, breaking my attention away from Azmir. That's when I noticed the heavy anticipatory expressions across the table—I mean, I saw mouths open and some even looked as though they were holding their breaths. I turned to see Azmir had pulled out a five by seven sized wrapped case and was handing it over to Kid.

More jewelry? Is that Kid's thing?

Kid seemed to have taken forever to open the box, and I realized I wasn't the only one to feel this way when one of Syn's girls yelled out, "Hurry the fuck up, Kid!"

To be honest, a nervy side of me, brought on by the mimosa, shot her a look of, '*Shut the hell up and stop acting like a damn hood rat!*' because I knew much of the reason for her suspense was due to *Azmir* being the benefactor. Shoot! Even I was on edge in anticipation.

Kid opened the box and discovered a car key fob with a huge emblem on the ring that I wasn't familiar with. He read from a piece of paper, barely audible to those at the table. That was until he screamed, "A fucking *Aston Martin One-77*?"

The table went up in a roar. I was frozen at the table, steeling in my seat, unable to move.

What in the...?

"Holy *shiiiiiiiiiit!*" Wop screamed and jumped his five-foot seven-inch frame from his seat at the opposite end of the table from me.

The other *Clan* guys were right behind him in their shock, approval, and envy of this over the top gift being bestowed upon Kid. I really didn't know much about the dynamics of this group, or *The Clan* for that matter, and felt it was an odd phenomenon.

I swear, I felt like I was at the table of an organized crime family with their interactions, but knew the thought was silly and didn't wrestle with it long.

Honestly—you're living with the man, if there was anything illegal going on you'd know!

I recalled some of the things Chanell told me in Puerto Vallarta about Azmir being the leader of *The Clan*, but I never thought to ask what the mission behind the group was. I suddenly questioned where all the money was coming from. Things started feeling weird—cognitively and *physiologically.*

Azmir, tenderly rubbing my shoulders, hurled me from my ruminative thoughts. He took to his seat next to me. I peered over and found him searching my eyes for answers.

"You okay, Ms. Brimm?" he whispered in my ear so low I doubted if even Kim to the right of me could hear.

"My stomach's feeling a little queasy, but I should be okay." I was telling the truth. My stomach had begun bubbling, and I couldn't figure out why. *Could it be the eggs?*

"We'll be leaving soon enough. I'll have you home resting."

I gave him a slight smile, trying to force politeness. I also noticed Syn all in our faces. I may have even cut my eyes at her. *I don't know.*

Eventually, everyone resumed their individual conversations. I saw Kim turn toward Petey. Kid was looking down the table, chatting with Wop and the other guys. Azmir bent his long upper torso down to my ear and continued to ask me about what I was experiencing and offered to order me ginger ale. I obliged, feeling like the sensation wasn't slowing down. He ordered the soda and took to his phone—the personal cell, which was his *iPhone*.

Chanell blurted out, "Yooooo! Was that private party dope as hell or what on Thursday night, yo!"

"Yeah...yeah! Yo, Chanell, man, you did yo' thing!" Wop yelled in concert with the other guys.

"Yeah, good looking, C! 'Dem bitches was right!" Kid blurted before freezing under Azmir's cautionary glare, apparently signaling him to use discretion, and I'm sure because they were in front of mixed company.

"Oh, my bad," Kid mumbled apologetically. "But for real, Chanell, that was dope of you. Good lookin' out!"

Syn narrowed her eyebrows, mad. *At what though?*

"Oh, nah! That was all Crack over there. I just held him down," Chanell shouted, attempting modesty.

Kid reached across the table and gave Petey dap.

"Divine, did you get a lap dance at da party?" Syn brashly quizzed Azmir.

All eyes went to Azmir and then to Syn. I swear, I'd never seen dynamics like I was witnessing among this group. I guess it was out of order for her to ask him such a question. I could see how it was inappropriate, but why was Azmir revered in this manner with these people? It was as though he had the presence of a king or someone of royal priesthood.

What the...?

"Nah, Divine wasn't there. He was working," Chanell answered, trying to circumvent Azmir addressing Syn.

"Oh, cuz I know he like 'em," Syn proclaimed. At first process, I was thrown by her statement. It took a minute for it to penetrate. "Ain't you a dancer, sweetheart?" My head jolted back when I saw she was looking me square in the eyes, expecting an answer. It was clear Syn was drunk. *But how, so soon?* We were barely into the afternoon.

I felt Azmir's hand grab my thigh underneath the table. *And here it begins.* Honestly, I thought I'd be able to make it through this function without any production from Syn seeing all the men were with us. I'd guessed her liquid courage mixed with the padded comfort of her family being present gave her the audacity. I wasn't afraid. I didn't easily scare—especially from someone of Syn's mentality and non-threatening stature. I just didn't want Azmir and *his family* to see me in *that* element—an element they were all too familiar with and subscribed to, no less. If I could get just ten minutes alone with Syn, I'd acquaint her with the soles of my *Manolos*. She wouldn't have to worry about upsetting Kid or Azmir, I'd make sure of it.

With fortitude, I chuckled, much to myself before speaking. "If you mean in the *pole* sense, no. I practice the artistic form of it. No dollars involved," I explained calmly, yet directly.

You could hear a pin drop. *Lord, keep me from snatching this broad from across the table!* Syn was probably only a hundred and five pounds—soaking wet. I knew I could drop her quickly.

"Man...Syn, shut the fuck up before you find yo' ass in sum shit you 'on't wanna be in," Kid barked, giving her the look of death. Syn, unmoved, slowly rolled her eyes and sucked her teeth.

"I'm just saying," she hissed, suddenly ruffled by Kid's verbal discipline. Her girls giggled in the background. I'm sure it was at my expense. Azmir's face was set in a scowl. I really didn't want a scene.

"What da fuck is you sayin'—Divine girl is a fuckin' go-go dancer? Is you crazy! Don't fuckin' try to come up in here fuckin' up the cipher and embarrassing me. You can take yo' trick ass friends...or cousins and drive y'all ass back up to the Watts!" Kid was obviously livid, and it made me incredibly uncomfortable.

I didn't know where the thought came from, but before I knew it I announced, "This brings me back to an idea I'd already had. I would like to invite you to my show next weekend. It's a fundraiser and all proceeds will go to dance lessons for underprivileged children by my dance coach. It would be great if you all could join Azmir."

I knew Azmir wouldn't approve because he was almost as private a person as I was when it came to our relationship, but I didn't care. I felt like I had something to prove at this point. This was clearly Azmir's inner circle, and I was attempting acceptance on both sides—mine and theirs.

"Rayna, you don't have to prove anything to anyone at this table. One of us seems to have lost our manners, but that'll be handled immediately. I'm sure of it," Azmir vowed, looking directly at Syn whose face was ashen in fear. He was trying to give me an out.

"No," I shook my head. "This is your family. I'm very comfortable with them and I would like to allow them to get to know me better," I murmured, piercing into his examining eyes before turning my attention back to the table. "Please. You all are invited."

"I can't let you invite all these knuckleheads here, but some of us'll roll through," Petey accepted, being sure to inform *The Clan* they all were not allowed to oblige even though I'd put the invite out there.

Kim nodded her head in agreement. I could tell she wanted me to know I had her support against Syn's foolishness. She wasn't a woman of many words, but her presence had always been strong.

"You know I'm in 'dat mufucker, Rayna!" Chanell championed. I smiled at her enthusiasm.

I shot my eyes across the table. "The invitation is open for you, too, Syn. Maybe you can gain a little...culture, aye?"

I had to clap back at her for her unexpected jab at me. She never looked at me, just kept her head in her plate. But the act of her rolling her eyes and letting out an exasperated exhale didn't miss me. I had no idea what her beef with me was. *I mean— seriously!*

"Now if you good people will excuse us, I have to get the little lady home and rested for tomorrow," Azmir bode in much of a snarl as he rose from the table. "Peace-Peace."

His hidden brash scared me. I could tell Syn's words did not sit well with him. I was just glad things didn't get out of hand.

One by one, everyone—with the exception of Syn, her crew, and Chanell's girls—got up and exchanged farewells with Azmir. Kim gave us hugs while Petey hugged only me. Petey and Azmir exchanged a few brief and muttered words before parting ways.

We then took off for the airport.

The ride there was a little thorny. My stomach hadn't improved, and my head began to throb. Azmir kept a watchful eye over me during the trip to the airport and while on the aircraft. I tried drinking more ginger ale, but at some point, I couldn't ingest anything. I just wanted to sleep, which was finally possible when we were seated on the plane.

I was so grateful for the first class seat. I needed the space and the comfort of the larger seats. Azmir kept his hand on my thigh the entire flight which, fortunately, wasn't long at all. He was concerned but decided not to go the prodding route with repetitive questions about my sudden ill state. The sickness progressed. My stomach groused, and my head started to spin.

As Azmir was gathering our carry-on luggage from the overhead compartment, I felt the bile threatening to rise from my belly. I tugged at the hem of his sweat jacket, trying to inform him of my need to make a dash to the bathroom. Suddenly, unable to wait, I sprinted past the captain and the flight attendants who were alarmed by my urgent fleeing.

Once out of the gate and into the airport, I searched frantically for the nearest restroom. Luckily, it was just ahead of me. I burst through the stall door and barely made the toilet, vomiting my guts out. Within seconds, I felt a strong hand on my lower back.

"Brimm, baby, are you okay?" I recognized Azmir's firm voice, laced with hidden fret.

"Is she okay?" was another unfamiliar voice.

I couldn't speak, neither could I believe Azmir had followed me into the ladies' room. Another round of vomit came up. My abdominal muscles ached, and I used the stall walls to balance myself. Azmir rubbed my lower back, and I didn't know if it was soothing or annoying from moment to moment.

"Was it something she ate?" a male yelled from outside the bathroom. I'd guessed he wasn't as bold as Azmir to enter the ladies' room.

The female voice just beyond Azmir spoke again, "I hate to be so personal, but is she pregnant, sir? It would help to know how we can best help her."

PREGNANT?

God, no!

That shocked me into some level of stability, and I thought to stand so I could clean my face and get out of there.

"I just ate something that didn't agree with me, I'm sure," I was able to weasel out, on my way to the sink. I washed my hands and rinsed my mouth.

Someone ordered a wheelchair, which was the best idea because it felt as though my ribs were cracked. I was handed another ginger ale I could only bring myself to hold in my hand while being wheeled out to the car Ray had waiting. Azmir helped me inside and it took me a while to find a comfortable position in the back of the *Bentley*. I decided on one allowing me to lay my head back.

It had become clear that I had been holding my stomach because Azmir reached over and pushed his big hand underneath my arms, resting it over my abdomen, "Is it your stomach? What do you feel?"

With one eye, I found his concerned face and breathed, "My head and stomach. I didn't know what it was specifically I ate. The eggs or fruit, maybe."

His eyebrows were knitted, and delicious mouth set in a grim line. He didn't say anything. We just rode home in silence. When we were on the ride up in the elevator at the marina, the bubbling in my stomach was joined by abdominal spasms told me I needed the bathroom and right away.

We were barely inside the apartment when I sprinted to the closest bathroom to the front door. I slammed the powder room door behind me, hoping Azmir would get the *do not enter* hint.

He yelled through the door, "Can I get you anything? Do you want me to call your doctor?" It was more a shriek, and I could tell he was concerned. My body worked hard to expel whatever foreign object managing to invade it, scarcely leaving energy for me to speak.

"No!"

I screamed, not to be rude, but forcing the word out which otherwise wouldn't have budged. Immediately, I regretted opening my mouth because I felt *it* coming up. I quickly jumped on the toilet, looking for a receptacle when I found a trash can with a fresh bag—not that it mattered. I hurled inside of it.

Oh, my god! It's coming out from both ends!

I heard a bang at the door. "Rayna, I'm coming in there!" Azmir yelled.

"Don't you dare!" I screamed and discharged again—*from both ends*.

I was miserable. I felt weak and sleepy! I had no idea what I'd eaten to throw my body into such a fit. I was deathly desperate for relief. Once the stomach spasms and head spinning had stabilized, which was nearly twenty minutes after being in there, I cleaned myself up and found comfort on the cool marble floor. When my face met the chilled tile, I sighed in relief.

Minutes later, Azmir was back at the door. "Rayna, I can see you're on the floor. Do you need help up?"

How can he see me!?

It then hit me how the entire apartment, with the exception of the master suite, was monitored through a surveillance system. *How embarrassing!* Azmir could see my bare backside plopped up in the air.

Where would my dignity lie with him after this experience?

"No! Leave me alone. This is horrible! I don't want you to see me like this, Azmir...please—"

With that, I jumped up, feeling another round of spewing, forcing me to take my seat back on the toilet and to shove the garbage can back to my face for dumping.

This went on for the next two hours. Azmir respected my wishes; I didn't hear from him again. It was the most miserable physiological experience of my life.

When I treaded out of the powder room, I could see the sun setting on the marina from the balcony and floor-to-ceiling windows of the living room, across from me. I was woozy, sore, and completely spent. I closed the door behind me just as Azmir charged towards me, lifting me up into his hard arms. I slapped him weakly because I had no strength.

"I stink. Please don't! I'll walk."

He didn't respond. He marched toward the back of the apartment; we entered the master suite and then the bathroom. He sat me on the chaise and walked over to start the shower. When he ambled back toward me, he began removing my booties, tossing them into the corner before grabbing the hem of my shirt and pulling it over my head. I had little resistance to his quick movements. I was that weak.

"Stand," he ordered while he held my waist to assist. I did, but when he went for the elastic tip of my leather leggings to remove them, I panicked.

"No! I'll do this. I smell horrible."

"I haven't smelled any foulness yet. Don't be so prideful. You're weak and damn near trembling. We're adults here."

I shook my head. "But you're no nurse who is accustomed to body secretions of the waste type. No. Go out and I'll take it from here," I spoke in susurration.

Azmir sighed heavily in exasperation. "Rayna, I take advantage of your body for pleasure, I can take care of it when it's ill, too. Let me help."

His broad shoulders sunk in disappointment and frustration. He was earnest in his desire to take care of me. While the thought was hugely endearing, my body's odor was not. There was no way I was exposing him to the ugly of it. Menstruating was something we could work around; defecation and vomit we couldn't survive —*I couldn't survive!* I respected Azmir's willingness to cross this boundary in our relationship, but I was not prepared. This was god-awful and exceptionally embarrassing.

I shook my head with a sulking expression. I had no energy to fight with him, but there was no way I would forfeit my appeal in his eyes. Azmir worshipped my body—I had to give it to him. I was not willing to compromise that. This was all too much. I couldn't even look him in the face. I just extended my arm, telling him to go.

"You have two minutes to disrobe, or I'll be doing it for you," he hissed before walking out of the bathroom, leaving the door opened.

I held on to the pillar mounting a fern planted pot as I pulled off my bra, leggings, and underwear. I kicked them into a corner and slowly sauntered to the shower. I was winded at the door of it. Azmir's shower could comfortably fit five people and stuff seven. There were at least a dozen jet nozzles in there, so I knew I'd catch water somewhere, but looking at the massive space inside overwhelmed me. I didn't have the strength to wash. No sooner had the revelation hit, Azmir was right back at my side, placing my shower cap on my head, lifting me into the shower, and setting me on the bench.

I eventually noticed he was naked and gathered he was going to wash with me. As much as I was discomfited by my torpid state, I was relieved he understood my needs without me having to express them. It was as if he'd read my mind. Azmir was always good at anticipating my needs. He knew much of them would never be lodged if left to my own devices. I was not yet programmed to reach out for assistance. It was now clear to me he understood this.

He took his time washing me until I adamantly told him I would take care of my private parts and he had to turn his head. He then began washing himself, providing me privacy. I knew the task would require no sensitivity, but a thorough and aggressive sweeping instead. When we were done, he dried himself off, returned to turn off the shower and carried me out to the center rug and dried me off. I sat back on the chaise when he hurried out of the bathroom and quickly returned, holding a short silk slip in one hand and one of his clean white tank tees in the other.

"I figured you'd need easy access in case you're not done and will need something cool to help with the hot flashes." He gave a soft smile.

He was being sensitive to my disgusting situation. If I wasn't so sick, I'd lick him from head to toe. His body was still dewy, exposing his stony abs, masterfully sculpted shoulders, and muscular arms. He wore only a Supmia towel, also affording me a view of his strong columnar legs and bare feet. Azmir was a work of art, worthy of the highest bid.

I opted for his tee, seeing nothing sexy about this ordeal and therefore the slip should be spared. He helped me with it on. As I brushed my teeth, he stood close behind me, slipping on his boxers, basketball shorts, T-shirt, and black ankle socks. I couldn't ignore the muscular contour of his lengthy frame. I was beyond content with his mildly slender, yet solid physique. Azmir wasn't bulky like body-builders but was cut up so well with nearly every muscle defined.

Once out of the bathroom, he led me over to the sitting room. I insisted I'd walked no matter how slow I had to wander to get there. He gathered pillows to set up a comfortable spot for me to rest in. As he handed me the remote, he stood over me to assess my disposition.

"I'm starving and I know you need to eat something, too. I saw you had leftovers from Chef Boyd's meals this week in there, so I can find enough scraps to make myself a meal. For you, it'll be BRAT."

He must have read the perplexity in my face. "Bananas, rice, applesauce, or toast. I called a physician friend of mine and gave him a rundown of your symptoms. I assured him it wasn't likely pregnancy since you're still within your normal cycle."

What the hell? How does Azmir know my cycle? Did he count days? Even I wasn't that good! I was too shocked by his sheer confidence in my bodily schedule to ask.

I continued to listen. "He says by the sounds of it, you have some sort of stomach virus and can be miserable for the next twenty-four hours, at least. So, that's probably about all your system can handle right now. And the biggest challenge is going to be keeping you hydrated." Azmir paused for my selection.

Errrrrrrr! "Toast."

"Dry," he informed me before leaving for the kitchen.

Twenty minutes later, Azmir returned with three pieces of wheat toast for me and a huge plate of delectable food for himself. *God, my guy could pack it away without consequence!* He set up a tray for me. It included water and ginger ale and sat across from me on the L shape sofa. It took some time for me to consume the toast, but I got at least one slice down before I gave up on eating all together.

Just as Azmir put down his tray and mounted his laptop onto his lap, I had the urge to go to the bathroom. I practically jumped from my seat and made a dash back to the powder room, out near the great room. Azmir was on my heels until I left the room. He watched me from the door of the master suite down into the hall. I stayed in there for nearly forty-five minutes, dispelling the toast and liquids I'd just eaten and drank, causing me to feel dirty all over again. My ribs throbbed all over again, my mouth reeked of foulness *all over again.*

I made my way back to the suite and stopped at the door in exhaustion from the commute. Azmir sensed my presence and quickly jotted from the sitting area to the en suite bathroom and started the shower process *all over again,* yet again reading my mind.

Once we were done, he carried me to the bed, but I explained I didn't want to spread my germs to our coveted resting place and I'd preferred sleeping on the floor, next to the bathroom instead. Azmir graciously made a huge pallet of plush blankets for me on the floor in the region of the master suite between the bed area and bathroom. I didn't need all the space but didn't question his kindness. I eventually learned the extra spot was for him when I felt Azmir crawl under the covers, next to me when he came to bed. His kissed the back of my neck as he always did before falling asleep. I couldn't understand how he was still able to express adoration after my disgusting illness today.

The night was spent in complete restlessness from me getting up a half a dozen times to visit the bathroom with the last being just before six in the morning when Azmir was up at his usual rising time. He helped me shower again and set me up on the sofa in the sitting room where I finally slept for nearly four hours and more restfully than I did the night before. My body was completely depleted from being internally overworked.

When I had awakened, it was almost noon. I challenged myself to walk and discovered though I was still weak, my head didn't spin, leaving me to find my equilibrium unlike the previous day. I slowly walked the hall in search of Azmir who was in his office, working at his computer. I stopped and rested against the door frame. He had a pencil in his ear and writing with a pen in his hand while checking something against the computer. His head rose almost immediately, landing his beautiful eyes on me.

"You're up." His expression was like a deer caught in headlights. "How are you feeling?" I was so appreciative of his attentiveness to me over the past twenty-four hours or so.

I smiled softly. "I've seen better days."

"I think it's time for you to try to eat something...at least drink something. You look wan. Let's try you on some broth...maybe with tofu or something with substance. I'll call and order it from the Japanese spot."

"Okay," I nodded. I felt embarrassed and vulnerable. "Did I keep you from something?" I asked as he made his way towards me. "...like work?" I hated to be a bother.

With his eyebrows furrowed he scoffed, "Don't be ridiculous. I'm just glad this went down on my watch. I would've gone crazy knowing you were here sick while I was out of town." He reached for the small of my back and softly kissed my forehead.

"I just hate to be a burden and keep you from work or anything you had planned this weekend," I muttered apologetically. It was true. I now, more than ever, understood how busy a man Azmir was. He was responsible for and depended on by countless people.

He looked me in my eyes. "You were my weekend agenda. You are always my weekend agenda, Rayna, unless *you* plan otherwise." He was annoyed, according to his tone.

He strolled to the kitchen. *Had I managed to piss him off again?* I followed him at a reserved pace, crawled into a chair at the kitchen table, and watched as he placed the order for the resident concierge to pick up and deliver to our door.

The broth was gentle on my stomach, and I could assess the virus was easing up on me. We spent Sunday relaxing, watching television, and Azmir got some work in. My trips to the bathroom came to a halt by the afternoon. I even felt up for a walk on the marina. It was a beautiful evening breeze out on the water. Azmir continued his quest to learn more about the woman I was before moving out to California. I answered his questions to the best of my trusting abilities. I'd even gotten more information on his childhood. We talked about his current business projects, and he offered to have me travel with him.

The following morning, after having Chef Boyd serve me toasted croissants to spruce up my breakfast considering my dietary restrictions, Azmir hesitantly left for work and insisted I stay behind to get some rest. He was right. Although my bathroom needs had ended, I was slightly dehydrated and needed to take it easy for at least one more day. I called in and let the staff know I'd be available via telephone should they need me. Chef Boyd left around nine in morning and informed me he'd made a special broth soup for me considering my bug. I returned to bed after seeing him out.

I didn't sleep much after Azmir left for work. My body was officially thrown off its daily program. Once resigned to the fact of sleep not happening, I pulled out my laptop to return e-mails and worked from home. At around twelve thirty, I was still on my laptop in between working and shopping for a thank you gift for Azmir when I got a new e-mail notification. I soon discovered it was from Sharon, furnishing me with Azmir's weekly schedule. I'd totally forgotten about this tradition. We'd been doing it for months since he suggested it, believing it would make us more "in sync," but I never really took advantage of it. Perhaps for the first few weeks I felt like a *lucky* girl to be the recipient of the *Great A.D. Jacobs'* weekly itinerary, but as time progressed my anticipation of it had dulled. And when I'd moved in with him, it had really become useless as he often shared much of his whereabouts with me, for the most part, by way of conversation.

Just like in the morning, before he left, he informed me he was headed to a staff meeting at *Cobalt*, followed by a disciplinary meeting for one of his bar managers there. Then he'd be making his way to the rec center. I decided to match his itinerary against what he shared with me earlier out of pure boredom. After a few clicks, I started at the top of his day, confirming his aforementioned plans until I got to a twelve forty-five luncheon with *Bacote & Taylor Public Relations Team* there at the rec. The name Taylor struck me. It had to be that Dawn Taylor.

I gasped.

Azmir didn't announce that this morning!

Not that he had to. Azmir owed me no previews of or explanations of his affairs—work-related or otherwise. I was not his... *girlfriend.*

There.

I'd said it to myself. *Ugh!*

That quickly, I'd forgotten all about Dawn and her crushing on Azmir. I recalled Azmir being surprised by their visit to the West Coast that Friday night in Vegas and how Dawn said they decided to fly out at the last minute. *So, when was this luncheon planned?* I checked the time again and thought it was fifteen minutes before their scheduled meeting. My head spun and my heart raced.

Out of all the women who presented as competition for Azmir's attention, Dawn made me uneasy, heck—JEALOUS! I couldn't figure out why. Azmir had a constant and dedicated legion of women who fawned over him—in my presence even. Maybe I viewed her as a strong rival, *but why?* I knew nothing about her other than she was possibly from Atlanta *and that she was rather good looking.* I felt light flutters in my belly, and they weren't related to my recent illness. I panicked and grabbed my phone to text Azmir.

Hey...what are you up to?

Within seconds, I got a ping.

About to go into a meeting. How are you feeling? Are you okay? Have you eaten lunch?

He was still concerned.

I'm fine. Can't wait for you to come home later.

I knew I was running game. For the first time, I'd referred to his place as home.

Me too. I'm exhausted. I'll warm up dinner. You just rest. I gotta go.

It was clear our conversation was over, and I didn't like it. I wanted to intercept his interfacing with Dawn *Desperado* Taylor. She was practically salivating in Vegas at the club when she ogled Azmir.

I had to do something. Devious and insecure thoughts began invading my mind. I dashed into the closet in search of something to throw on—something appropriate for the occasion. I had to fight with my dirty hair to pull it up into a bun on top of my head. Then I took to the vanity to apply makeup. I wore very minimal makeup unless I was going out socially, but today was all about deliberate tactics, also I didn't want to look as sick as I'd been and needed to color in the recent paleness of my skin.

Twenty minutes later, on my way to the door, I gave myself a once over in the full-body mirror in the master closet. My black sleeveless, skin-tight cat-suit, with a yellow blazer, blue hidden double platform suede *Red Bottoms* and red clutch completed my look. I did a soft blue smoky eye to match my shoes and nude lips. I headed out the door for the LBC.

En route, I called Peg to ask for Azmir, knowing she'd tell me he was unavailable. But I hoped she'd give me the keywords of his unavailability I needed to locate him.

"He's in the cafeteria in a luncheon meeting, Ms. Brimm. I can tell him to call you when he returns," her tone just above rude. She was warming up to me, though not at an expedited rate as I'd wished.

Pissed they were eating in the same place where he initially pursued me, I pushed down on the accelerator even more to get me there faster. As I walked into the rec, I was relieved to see a familiar face at the desk so I could just whisk past to the elevator to head down to the cafeteria. The café was rather large and because it was during the lunch hours the place was pretty packed.

It took little time for me to locate him in the corner—*for privacy?* Azmir wasn't alone. He was with Brett and Shayna. Azmir wore a lavender dress shirt and his smoke gray suit jacket hung on the back of his chair. He looked tired, but delicious. That man totally did it for me no matter what he was wearing. My awareness of his heart-stopping Adonis revved up my competitive gene several notches, reminding me of my mission.

I started my amble over to their table, and just when I was a few mere feet away, he sensed my presence and gazed over to the exact vicinity until his eyes landed on me.

Let the games begin.

I slanted my concealed droopy eyes and pouted my otherwise pale lips—*thanks to my bug.* I could tell he was completely surprised by my impromptu visit.

Good...now we're even!

When I approached the table, he didn't rise as he typically would. But he did breathe, "Ms. Brimm?" as if I was the woman of his wet dreams.

Brett looked up and Shayna, who sat across from Brett at the table seating four, turned around to see what caught the guys' attention. A wave of relief settled upon me seeing this wasn't an intimate meeting between Azmir and Dawn Taylor.

I stood, smiling softly while clasping my clutch in front of my pelvic area. I didn't know my next move. The perpetrator was nowhere in sight. Obscurity had descended over me. This *so* wasn't what I'd expected to walk into.

"Hi, Rayna!" Brett sang with gleam in his eyes, furthering my guilt.

He appeared genuinely happy to see me while I, on the other hand, was on a *Destroy Dawn* mission. I often wondered about Brett's thoughts of Azmir and me. He knew so many personal details of our relationship because he was usually the one arranging them.

"Afternoon, Brett," I greeted softly.

"Wow! I see you're feeling better. You look great," Brett

observed, without making the words sound inappropriate. I took it as though he appreciated my efforts. *Now, let's see if Azmir does, too.*

"Thanks, Brett. I'm feeling much better. I've had wonderful medical attention."

I vaguely flirted with Azmir, who I had now locked eyes with. He had been gaping at me the whole time, now it was my turn to return the attention.

"I was coming to show my gratitude by surprising a special someone for a lunch outing, but I see he's indisposed."

My eyes never left Azmir's as our gazes danced with each other in search of answers; mine of his meeting with Dawn and Shayna, and his of me leaving my sick bed for a surprise visit. I then noticed Azmir's eyes slowly transitioning past me. Instinctively, I turned, only to find Dawn standing there, sharing a similar reaction to my company as the rest of the party.

We locked eyes for what seemed like minutes. I even shifted in my stance, hoping to grant her a better view of my person, silently communicating marked territory until I heard Azmir calmly chime in, "Ms. Brimm, you remember Dawn Taylor, don't you?"

With a slight squinting of my eyes and wrinkling of my forehead—*that should have garnered an Emmy*—I finally say, "Vegas?"

Knowing full well I'd just encountered her only three short days ago. I didn't care, I was playing hardball. I was still confused by my drive to do so with Dawn Taylor, but I certainly acted conscious-free as I continued to peer straight into her masking eyes.

"*Rag and Bone*," she acknowledged approvingly, referring to the designer of my blazer.

Oh! So, you are about your diva!

"*So Kates*," I replied, referencing her *Louboutin* patent leather pumps as if I didn't start wearing the designer in recent months when Azmir flooded my closet with them.

I knew those because I had them in leather and made a mental note to never wear patent leather shoes unless they were *LouBou*'s.

They went well with her form fitted, plaid midi dress. Her hair was in the bouncy curls I'd seen in Las Vegas, framing her ebony face. She looked good!

She didn't greet me beyond that, and just like in Vegas, I followed suit, turning my attention back to Azmir whose eyes were alert, but his expression was otherwise inscrutable. He just sat there with his elbows resting on the table and hands clasped together near his chin, calmed and self-possessed. *Always.*

"Did I miss something while in the restroom?" Dawn asked in a slick manner.

The smirk she wore as she took her seat back at the table— *directly across from Amir! So, you can get a clear view, huhn!—* confirmed my feelings regarding her mask. She flashed a cunning smile over to Shayna who, for some strange reason, I could tell didn't share Dawn's sinister persona.

"Oh...oh, nothing at all. We basically reiterated the cons of the proposal and agreed on the need of a follow-up date for answers and solutions," Shayna shakily mumbled to Dawn. Brett obliviously nodded his head.

"Ah, yes! And we hope that date won't be projected," Dawn spoke suggestively, flashing a stealthy smile over to Azmir. I wanted to choke her.

My attention returned to Azmir when he spoke. "Brett, did you not send my weekly schedule to Sharon?" he asked while searching my eyes, inadvertently making it clear to me he was not committed to their conversation.

Crap! What the...!

"Uhhh..." Brett stalled while typing on his *iPad*. The girls looked over to Brett, trying to figure out what was going on with the question. "Yes, sir. First thing this morning, sir."

Crap! Crap! Crap!

Then Azmir smiled at me, but not with his mouth, with his eyes. "Uh-huh. Well, we'll need to see to it that Sharon forwards them in a timelier manner, now, don't we?"

He didn't force me to lie and say Sharon hadn't forwarded me the itinerary yet—and boy, was I grateful for that pass! He knew my pop-up visit was motivated by a surreptitious agenda.

"Ladies, we're just about done here, aren't we?" Azmir spoke to the table, but without his gaze leaving my face. His thumbs wrestled each other as his long fingers were intermingled contemplatively. Through my peripheral I could see all eyes on us. "I was just telling Brett before lunch to clear my schedule for the rest of the day. I have lots of preparations to complete before my departure tomorrow."

For some strange reason, at the announcement, my attention turned to the table. Shayna's eyes shot nervously over to Dawn as she sat up in her chair.

"Uhhhhh...ummmm, yeah!" Shayna fumbled over her words as she looked over to Dawn for guidance. She was stalling for her girlfriend, demonstrating she knew her friend was after Azmir.

It was now known that Azmir was contemplating leaving soon. So, I shifted in my stance again, causing my blazer to open, exposing my spandex clad figure in the cat-suit.

I could play dirty with the best of them. *For Azmir.*

I saw Brett turn beet red and Azmir's smile descended from eyes down to his beautifully sculptured, luscious lips. My libido had just returned.

"Okay, we have the dates and a preliminary agenda. Brett will be sure to do the follow-up. We'll be in touch, ladies. This looks great," Azmir instructed at an even pace, clearly preoccupied, as he pulled his jacket off the back of his chair, draping it over his arm before standing.

He rose from his chair the same way and shook hands with everyone before rounding the table. It appeared rather odd. What was even more overt was how Dawn expected a different type of parting expression from him. Her face fell into a disappointed puckered brow.

He kept her at arm's length as he traveled over to me and

muttered, "I'll just grab my things from upstairs and meet you in the car or you can come with me."

Before I could answer, I heard Dawn call out, "Mr. Jacobs, a word, if you don't mind."

A word? For what?

I could have decked her. I gave Azmir a slight nod, excusing him, though I genuinely wasn't feeling that diplomatic. He walked back over to her, and I noticed the *cat that ate the canary* smirk she bore as he approached her. She had twenty seconds of my patience, or we were going to have scene in the middle of Azmir's cafeteria. I couldn't hear what she said, but I could tell Azmir wasn't as involved in the exchange as she was, and Dawn was trying to buy time.

I did hear him say, "I'll go over the proposal and give you my deliberations as soon as I can." on a chuckle. She was flirting with him, but he wasn't prepared to reciprocate. My fists clenched at my sides. *Some women have no dignity!*

With that, he started back over to me and placed his free hand on the small of my back, warming me as we walked out of the cafeteria. I couldn't address Dawn's childish attempts at his attention, I wasn't prepared to play the role of the jealous girlfriend without actually being *the girlfriend.*

"Are you okay? Why did you rise so slowly from the table...and since when don't you wear your suit jacket after rising from the table?" After dispersing my words, I recognized them as the typical nagging girlfriend's jargon. *Ugh!*

Without skipping a beat, he lowered his mouth to my ear and whispered, "Since you walked into my place of business wearing *that* and causing *this.*" He partially removed his suit jacket from his abdomen to reveal his massive erection through his pants. I gasped and tripped on the way out of the door. Azmir politely caught me with his free arm, helping me regain my balance, nearly seamlessly. I studied his impassive profile while trying to keep up with his stride. "Don't worry. If you go to the car and give me a minute out of your presence, it'll go away. I'll meet you in the parking lot."

En route to the apartment my stomach was still uneasy, but likely because it was time for me to eat. On our way back, Azmir picked up an order of rice from one of my favorite authentic Mexican restaurants. I loved the way they seasoned even plain white rice.

We were sitting at the dining room table and Azmir was feeding me from the container. He raised the spoon to serve me more rice when I shook my head.

"No?" he asked in disbelief.

I shook my head again.

"We agreed on ten spoonsful."

"We said I'd try to get to ten spoonsful. I can't fit anymore in after six."

He glared at me with suspicious eyes. "I understand you're sick and all—"

"...was sick," I interrupted him.

"...*was* sick, but this is all you've eaten since I left you this morning," he protested. "C'mon, Brimm. I need you healthy again."

"I am fine. I've been toilet-free since yesterday morning. The worst of it is over. I'll start focusing on my hydration." I took a sip of my bottled Evian water to placate him. "See?" I gave him a wink, awarding me a sexy smile.

"So, what now?" Azmir tapped his fingers leisurely.

"What do you mean? You said you left work early to start preparing for tomorrow's trip," I quizzed.

He scrunched his eyes and shook his head as he scoffed. "You're incredulous, you know that?"

"What do you mean? You *did* say that in the cafeteria."

"Yes, I did, but even the simplest of men would know I was referring to you. I wanted to make sure *you* were well or at least in stable condition before I travel. So, you—you were my preparations. I wanted time to observe you in case I needed to cancel the trip." He sounded slightly annoyed.

I felt as though the joke was on me. I didn't know he was so thoughtful. I was still processing his good deeds over the past forty-eight hours.

"Azmir, you would cancel business for me?" I didn't recognize my own voice. I couldn't begin to accept his care. I didn't know how.

Shaking his head again, he mumbled, "I can't believe this." But he spoke louder when he asked, "If I were not here and you were one hundred percent well, what would you be doing?"

"*Hmmmmm*... I realized how dirty my hair was when I got dressed earlier. It definitely needs a wash before my trip to Adrian on Saturday morning. Ewwwwww!" I cringed as I scratched my head.

He let out an exhale. "Come on."

Come on? Where? I followed him to the bedroom where he removed his pants and started unbuttoning his shirt. I scratched my head in confusion, "What are we doing?" It disturbed me to be getting turned on by the mere sight of his smooth skin.

"We're going to wash your hair. You typically do it in the shower, right?"

"Yes..."

"Well, come on." He walked into the bathroom, and I swallowed the abundant amount of saliva collecting in my mouth. I started peeling off my cat-suit—*my lucky cat-suit*. I gave myself a smug look in the mirror. I had scored with Dawn Taylor. Next time I want to totally eliminate her.

Azmir yelled out from the bathroom, "Your shampoos are in here, correct?" breaking me from my reverie.

"Errr...Yeah," I replied.

A part of me was apprehensive about getting into the shower with a naked Azmir. What if I got aroused as I always did by it? Would he turn me away after having seen *and smelled* me over the past two days? I could never survive rejection from him. I decided it was too late, there was nothing I could do at this point, so I went into the bathroom to step into the shower.

The bathroom had started to steam, but I could still see his tall chocolate frame, standing near the toiletry rack where he held my shampoo bottle. I nodded my head in agreement, and he waved for me to come nearer. My heart rate accelerated and instantly I had no doubt my sexual appetite had returned.

Azmir's hands were divine on my scalp. He massaged it firmly, but not too rough. A few moans escaped during his treatment. Even Adrian's miracle hands had nothing on Azmir's. He washed my hair twice and then applied conditioner. I couldn't believe he even went the length of combing the conditioner through before rinsing it.

"Turn around," he commanded after he was done with the comb. I regrettably knew it was time for him to rinse me and this unbearably pleasurable experience would be over. I turned to face him as he asked, and for the first time since the initial shampoo application, I opened my eyes. As Azmir's arms were extended, working his deft fingers in my hair, I saw his chest muscles flex at every movement. His abdomen muscles were perfectly pronounced. I could never tire from experiencing the sight of him in the nude. Immediately, he caught my ogling, making me self-consciously embarrassed for sneaking a peek at him. He flashed his coochie-creaming smile, and I was done.

"Somebody's excited," he sang teasingly, gesturing to my hardened nipples, causing me to cover them with my hands.

Why did I suddenly feel so shy? I guess it was because usually when Azmir and I were naked in front of each other it is well known that we're going to make love, but on this rare occasion it wasn't expected. I was afraid to be forward, fearing rebuff. Then, I thought if Azmir was so disgusted by me, he wouldn't put himself in a situation to be naked *with* me. As he rinsed my conditioner out, he massaged the back of my head, firmly gripping my lower skull and thumbing behind my ears. It reminded me of what he did when I went down on him.

Suddenly my modesty felt silly, and I dropped my hands from breasts. I was surprised when I hit his very long, very thick, very hard, and very erect penis. My mouth dropped as I instantly lost control of my breathing and my eyes shot up to his face.

He didn't look me in the face when he coolly and slowly murmured, "Calm down, Brimm. I am a thirty-seven-year-old man. I can't help my reaction to you, but I can certainly control my actions. You're ill. I would never take advantage of your weakened state."

How did he know I didn't *want* him to take advantage of me? At this point, I was prepared to take advantage of him!

"I am going to wash your body now. Okay?"

My words failed me, and all I could do was nod my head. He took his time scrubbing soapy bubbles over my body including my now sunken belly. *I really need to step on a scale.* Although I'd still experienced pain in some areas, the nerve endings embedded in my skin were overly–sensitive to his gentle contact. It was as if his touch dulled the pain. When he was done, I asked to wash him, returning the favor, but he wasn't too keen on the idea.

"Brimm, I'm not sure I can handle that. You're still fragile. I could feel your wincing at my trace." Little did he know those winces were of pleasure.

"No. I want to do this," I demanded, grabbing his cloth, and lathered it up.

I started with his broad shoulders and extended out to his arms. Next was his carved chest then muscular abdomen, leading down to his silky trail. I dropped down to his perfectly molded legs and started washing at the thighs but kept hitting my head on his erection. It was so long and heavy I couldn't avoid it. My insides quivered, and I was happy he couldn't hear my moan over the sounds of the cascading water. I didn't know how long I could spend washing his legs, it really wasn't a complicated body part. I was trying to steal time to talk myself out of what my body yearned. I just couldn't deal with rejection. I gave up and rose to my feet, bumping my head against him once again.

How embarrassing!

Once fully standing and facing his chest he whispered, "Thanks," with a generous smile.

I grabbed my washcloth and began washing my private parts, unable to look at him. I heard my labored breathing rushing through my head. I was so sensitive down there as I rubbed to wash and rinse. Azmir stood against one of the wall faucets, allowing the water from it to spring into his lower back. I knew he was waiting on me to finish so we could leave the shower together.

I couldn't resist anymore, I walked over to him and pushed my head into his chest, feeling exhausted from my internal battle. I couldn't tell him I wanted him desperately but feared his indifference. He pulled me into an embrace, and without knowing for sure what it meant, that was all it took for me to take to my knees once more, slowly as my body still ached, and hungrily took him into my mouth devouring him.

"Rayna...you. Don't. Have. To..." he spoke in laborious breaths.

Something I'd never experienced before overtook me. I became besieged with a raw emotion and unyielding need to communicate something to him. I pulled and sucked with the desperation I felt for him in the moment, for the gratitude I felt, for his gentle care, for the desire I had to claim him against the likes of Dawn Taylor. Beyond anything I needed physically, feelings I couldn't describe surfaced here in the shower. I wanted the opportunity to care for him the way he had me over the past few days. *I wanted to be with Azmir forever.*

Possibilities of being capable of loving and partnering with him for a lifetime flashed through my heart as my head bobbed in his lap. I *needed* his love, suddenly acknowledging I couldn't live without it. I didn't want him up for grabs because I wanted him all to myself. I was longing, almost frantically.

"Gah! Fuck!" he yelped in a way I had never heard before. It was unintended, unguarded, and guttural. Did he feel what I did? He could have by the sounds of the aching in his voice. "Rayna, wait...wait. Wait!" he whispered. But I couldn't stop. I was just as emotionally hungry as I was sexually.

"You're about to make me... *NO!*" he grunted just under a shout when he pulled me up by shoulders, lifting me into the air with his strong and capable arms.

"Can you hang on?" With burning desire pouring from his voice, he was asking if I could straddle him.

So turned on, I panted, "Yes!"

"Are you sure? I don't want to hurt you...or turn you off."

Those were the magic words. I lunged at Azmir and covered his mouth with mine. I needed him so bad. As we kissed so wildly and urgently, he slowly entered me, stretching me and causing me to yelp from the pressure.

"You okay?" he asked anxiously. I was disturbed he had pulled out of me and cradled my trembling frame to keep me in the air.

"No... Go... *GO!*" I screamed.

He turned so I was against the wall and pushed my body into his, pushing into me. His tardigrade movements were unintentional torturous thrusts. I was insanely desperate for him to plummet me. Precipitating more, I threw my tongue into his mouth, hoping he would catch on to me not wanting to lose a second of passion. I wanted his roughness.

"Harder!" I begged, caught up in lecherous fury.

Azmir couldn't be close enough. Couldn't be deep enough. I wanted him so far into me, he could feel my expressions and need of love without me having to speak them. I yearned for that deep of a connection with him. I wanted him to sense my desire of *forever.*

In no time, he pounded into me as though he had an idea of my desperation. Off were the kiddie gloves used in light of my condition and rushing in were the wild slams into my core. He was losing control. I relished every thrust. I could see the muscles in his neck strain as he pumped into me.

The sounds of our bodies smacking were intoxicating, and I knew Azmir was content because he loved the sounds of making love. I could swear the tip of his penis connected with my heart with every thrust. But I wanted more. Needed all of him. Totally. Completely. Permanently.

In no time, I withdrew my mouth because, that quickly, I was on the verge of my orgasm. I leaned back to give him full access to my sex. My body tensed and I held my breath to brace myself. I was too sore to work with him. But it was apparent I didn't have to because the next thing I knew, I was screaming and convulsing from a violent orgasm taking no prisoners on my feeble body.

"Azmir, I want to do this forever. Please love me...forever!" I screamed out in pleasure of his deeds, and at the same time from the fear of breaking into two from the intensity.

Azmir exploded in the middle of my orgasm, crying declarations of insanity. "You are fucking everything. I could... Never. My. Life!"

This was the shortest length of a love making session we'd had at this point. It was as though something bigger than what we could understand was taking place.

And I was the better for it.

CHAPTER 2

Azmir

I walked into the bathroom to check on Rayna. She sat at the vanity cross-legged, combing her damp hair. A part of me felt guilty for having her a few minutes ago in the shower. I had no intentions on touching her. *Shit.* I was able to shower with her twice the day before with very little temptation. She'd been sick, and it had been difficult for me to see her in that condition. She was very forward in inviting me to herself. Hell, she fell to her knees and put her mouth on my cock. What the fuck was I supposed to do—apply the patience of a priest? Not when Rayna was concerned. I'd never have the fortitude to deny her of a goddamned thing.

I was a caring man, but a man with a sexual appetite no doubt. I'd just hope I didn't take advantage of her. Rayna's body had always been tempting to me, what I craved all day. I enjoyed making her come, feeling her clamp around me while I was balls deep inside her. It invaded my every thought. Hearing her screaming my name, begging for forever caused me to lose myself in there. It was exactly what I'd wanted with her. I'd just hoped her plea wasn't just an act in the heat of passion. I was a patient man but hoped all this time we had been building something solid. Something forever. I also hoped I didn't scare her by slipping up with my true feelings of her encompassing my world. My life.

I tapped her shoulder as I watched her in the mirror. "You okay?"

"*Mmmhmm*," she hummed with a satiated smile.

"Are you sure? You were acting like a damn cowgirl in there. I know you like the rodeo and all, but you're still recovering," I reminded her in jest.

"Mr. Jacobs, you got jokes?" Rayna playfully rolled her eyes as she worked on brushing her entangled mane.

My girl's beauty was breathtaking. She wasn't the most diva-ish woman I'd met, and she didn't have to be. Her splendor was so natural it was exotic. I could watch her all day but didn't. I'd already roughed her up in the shower, fucking her like I'd lost my goddamn mind. That's because I felt like I did each time I was buried deep in her. I wished I could navigate into her heart the same way.

"I'm going to warm up dinner. What can I get you?" I forced my mind out of self-pity land.

"Chef Boyd made some concoction for me in there. I'll have that. I'm really not ready to resume my normal diet."

"Yet," I qualified before turning on my heel for the kitchen.

"Huhn?" She stilled in the mirror.

I turned back to find her eyes glued to me through the vanity mirror. "You've lost a few pounds already. I don't like it. Stop burning calories in the shower and allow your body to rest so you can heal and return to your normal eating." I was partially teasing, but very serious about the weight comment.

Rayna narrowed her beautiful brown eyes, but wisely chose to not respond.

For the rest of the evening, we ate and talked about our upcoming week. Rayna reminded me she had a show on Saturday, and she'd invited *The Clan*. I wasn't too thrilled about it but was happy to see she felt comfortable enough to extend herself to my people. They were a major point of contention for Tara and me during our relationship. She never took to them no matter how polite and inclusive they tried being with her. I was grateful to Rayna for accepting this aspect of my life, of me. Syn didn't make Rayna's efforts unproblematic. Her animosity for Rayna was incredibly palpable, you would think they knew each other in a former life. As much as it initially concerned me, it now reminds me how much of a kindred spirit Rayna is. It's as if she's familiar with Syn's kind and therefore manages her without losing her cool and laying a hand on her—*yet.*

And when I think about the tension between Rayna and Dawn, I get uneasy. I was not the type of man who enjoys or encourages my woman's insecurities to flare at the threat of another sniffing up my tree. I knew Dawn wanted me, but so did dozens of other women. I'd been pursued by and on the wish-list of many eager dames in my life. I kept in shape, bagged my swag, and my money took it all to a new level. And even with knowledge of these things, I only had eyes for one woman, whom for some reason could not understand my exclusive commitment to her.

I found it cute how Rayna "popped" up at a business luncheon of mine fiending for betrayal blood. Dawn seemed prepared for her, too, which opened the floodgates for a surge of revelations concerning her. I don't want Rayna losing her cool around Dawn either. She isn't worth it. No one was worth me losing Rayna.

After my time with Rayna, I read through a few contracts and made notes on them. It wasn't long after my time in the office that we turned down for the night. I curled up against Rayna's soft and warm body. Very few times was I able to rein in self-control when she was in this close of proximity—her warmth, fragrance and delicate skin never failed to make my sacs tingle with carnal need —but I managed. I was so damn exhausted I didn't even recall dreaming.

My eyes opened to a dark room. After blinking several times, I realized sleep was no longer on the agenda for me. Not needing to check the time, I knew it was just before six in the morning. So, I started contemplating my day, the length of it and, what it would take to make it successful.

Her scent made it difficult to focus. It wasn't every day I'd awaken to her being so close although she now shared my bed. My throbbing arousal caused a mountain tent on my lap through the bedding. On an average day, I could cope until my shower, but this morning I couldn't and didn't have to. She laid with her back to me, her long, loose hair was splayed across her pillow. The scent from her shampoo and other hair products was aromatic and alluring. I turned onto my side to graze her soft skin. I ached for her. She'd alchemized into my obsession in mere months—owned my every thought, personified my every craving.

Rayna wasn't the type of woman who slept with her arms and legs draped across you. Not my lady. She much preferred her own space in the bed. There were nights I'd lay awake, studying her soft angelic features, giving thanks to Allah for the gift of her in my life, in my home. In my bed. It took a little groveling, but damn if she didn't finally relent, making me the luckiest son of a bitch on the West Coast.

I enjoyed this cohabitation experience more than I initially thought I would. Like every morning, I yearned for her warm morning breath all over me as I reached over her and grabbed her left breast, kneading it through my fingers. *So supple.* Within seconds, she stirred. My hand traveled down to her soft yet firm left thigh, gently pushing her leg back onto mine so I could find her clit, her pleasure control house. In no time, she purred from the slickness I milked between her legs. She was so wet. So warm. Rayna always melted for me. I nibbled on her neck, calling to her awakening.

"Brimm, baby," I whispered out in need of her.

She stirred again in her resting place, bringing her arm up to wipe hers eyes awake. I knew she was still slightly dozed, so I nibbled a little more as I stroked between her legs, two fingers entering in her soaked valley and called out to her again. Her eyes fluttered as she fully roused. She thrust her pelvis into my hand, giving into the stirring pleasure. She twisted her caramel body and turned to me with hooded eyes. Those eyes caused my near explosion as she moved toward me. Within moments and without instruction, she shifted and mounted me.

This was one of a sundry of things I appreciated about Rayna; she was always ready to gratify, fervent in pleasuring. Yielding to my physical needs. Once she was saddled onto my cock, her wild mane cascaded down and around my face, she pulled the blanket up over us and took me for an erotic ride. And my girl did this well. I would fuck Rayna next to a corpse just to get my fill of her, but this morning I wanted her atop. This is her favorite position. Ironically, when she's here, Rayna's aggressive in her desire of me, more self-assured and effervescently feminine. This was how I longed for her to radiate every second of her life—strong, fierce in nature, and exuding self-confidence.

I pulled her face down to mine and covered her lips in a hungry kiss taking my breath away. Our tongues danced with fervor. Our lips locked hard, and I sucked her tongue and each lip one by one. My fingers tangled in her hair until they itched to grip her lush ass. I grabbed a hold of each of her firm cheeks and pulled her into me with dire need. She moaned as she rocked on top of me with delicious plunges.

Fuck!

If she only knew how much I needed this, how much this connection with her now affirmed my being. Like the taut grip her hungry walls had on my dick, she held the source of my control. As though I was her very own marionette, she controlled the strings to my happiness, my destiny. Dictated my world. I can't lie and say I was comfortable with her having said power. I needed to know she could responsibly govern my universe, and yet I couldn't be so sure. But shit, when she put it on me like this, causing my fucking toes to curl and goose bumps to cover my skin—I knew the reality was she owned every part of me. Mind. Body. And fucking soul.

I walked her to the door, sulking internally. Saying goodbye before a trip. This was the part of my job I hated. She smelled delightful in her *Cool Water*. Her ass puffed in a plum pencil skirt and bone *Prada* pumps. Her hair was pushed back into a knotted ponytail, and I suddenly noticed she wasn't wearing lipstick.

"Where's your lipstick or glossy thing?"

Rayna was beautiful. Her caramel skin glowed radiantly without makeup or extra add-ons. Her lips were plumped and a shade darker than her face, helping to create the most alluring smile. Her eyes were dark brown and always kept you guessing what was behind them, making them so fascinating.

"Oh, no!" she sputtered, holding her palm to me. "I'll put that on before I get to work. I knew you'd smear it before I made it to the car." She giggled. She was right. I loved fucking up her lipstick. It's a part of my brutish nature.

"I'm glad you're giving yourself more time before resuming to working out." I stood along the wall adjacent to the door, leaning my head into it like some love-stricken teenager.

"Just one more day. After this morning, I'm reminded of how much I need to stick with my workouts," Rayna shot back. "You were an animal. That should last ya' about a week, I hope."

I smiled, taken by her teasing. She had no idea—I could never have enough of her, in my bed or on my jimmy.

"You gonna miss me?" I asked, unmasking my solemnity.

"Probably a little more than you're going to miss me," she murmured, moving closer.

"How do you know that's possible? Can you measure how

much I miss you?" Goddamn if her sudden proximity didn't arouse me in less than seconds.

"You're the one leaving every week. I'm here...waiting on your return," she murmured soberly. My head slightly jolted back. It was almost as if I'd been jabbed in the stomach. Her eyes widened in reaction to it.

"No! No, I don't mean that in a guilt trip type of way. I just meant I'm here surrounded by *you* until you return," Rayna tried to assure me, albeit unsuccessfully. "It's probably a little easier for you when you have no reminders. You're in a new place...new surroundings all the time."

I exhaled from frustration. I didn't want her to feel this way. It was so far from the truth. "Brimm, it's never easy for me, trust me. Believe me when I say I am looking into ways to slow down my travel." I traced her jaw with the pad of my thumb. She'd become so precious to me in no time. "I didn't mean for us to kick things off like this. I promise, I'm working on a solution." I tried pleading through her eyes. "Keep in mind, you can always tag along."

She gasped. "...and get on your nerves even when you're away working? I don't think so." Rayna shook her head emphatically, bearing a soft smile and rolling her brown irises. "I'll be fine. Just don't forget to come home from time to time—" She stopped, and I could tell something had suddenly come to mind. "Hey! How 'bout we video chat. That could be fun."

A wicked smirk appeared upon her face as she raised an eyebrow. Sensual images ran through my head as quickly as blood rushed to the head of dick. *Goddamn*. I liked the idea immediately and wanted to show her.

"Give me your hand," I ordered, and she did so hesitantly.

I pulled it to my rock hard crotch. Her eyes lit up, and she was about to speak before I pulled her into my chest and placed my mouth to hers, pulling her into a hard and long kiss. The current state of my cock. She moaned and deepened the kiss. I didn't want to let her go; I'd much prefer taking her back to bed and making her scream my name from insane pounding. I wanted to hold her naked body in my arms for hours on end.

"Brimm, you gotta go. I'll call you when I land," I muttered, resting my forehead on hers, breaking our embrace. I heard her heavy panting over my own.

"Text me when you board the plane," Rayna whispered, her voice laced with longing. Her eyes looked heavy, and I didn't know if it was from lust or simple sadness of my leaving. Either way, it made it difficult for me.

After I closed the door behind her, I headed back into the kitchen to grab my coffee from the breakfast table. Chef Boyd broke from his melodic whistling to offer, "You're going to marry that young lady, Mr. Jacobs."

It stopped me in my tracks. I took a split second to consider his words. My concentric and ruminant eyes traveled to his large frame. Boyd was a robust man. He towered me a few inches and his shoulders stretched a bit wider than mine. He'd always been mannerly and prepared with appropriate responses to trivial exchanges as well as formal conversations, which is likely why I entertained his comment.

"If I can slow down my life just enough for her to see I'm a formidable candidate, I just might have a shot," I admitted with candor. "There aren't enough shopping trips able to push her hand in that. Turns out she isn't that type of catch."

"That's very true, sir, but I'm confident you'll find a way. Just know time isn't your friend, it will never be," Boyd heeded and went back to whistling a tune. After several beats of contemplation, I headed to my office for a conference call with a head filled to the brim with *Brimm*.

After my conference call concluded, I made my way into the master suite to wash and dress for my flight. I was in the closet when my cell phone rang. The tone was distinctive, I immediately knew it was the iPhone. It wasn't Rayna's programmed ringtone, *"Nasty Girl"* I had my I.T. guy install some way only techy freaks would know how to do. Instead, it was a generic ring. I crossed the closet over to the island and answered it.

"Peace-Peace," I greeted.

"Divine, my man, long time no hear!"

A wide ass smile splayed across my face, "David. How are you?"

"It's D.J., D. You know I don't like that David shit," I could hear the petulant pouting in his tone. He still had lots of growing up to do.

"David is a strong universal name. I told you to never hide from your legacy. That cool shit is whack. You're twenty-eight years old and are on the road to success. Your name is David. Fuck a D.J.," I recited sternly. My intent wasn't to condescend, but to reaffirm the strengths of his reality.

"Ye-yeah," David sputtered, suddenly sounding lowly. "I know. It's just that I want to be my own man. Build my own damn legacy—"

I cut him off, "You do, and you are. You're making profound strides. Don't trip off the small shit."

"I know, D, man. But every time I hear his name, it makes me feel like a peon."

I could hear ruffled sounds in the background, making me wonder where he was. I'd usually hear from David on a weekly basis and sometimes saw him just as much. He hasn't been to *Cobalt* to visit me in a few weeks. I would have been more concerned if I didn't get him hooked up with a job at the movie theater, I'm part owner of. I'd hoped he maintain his struggle on the straight and narrow.

"Have you been keeping your visits with Dr. Halsom?" I quizzed as I adjusted my pants to zip, button, and belt. I was extremely cognizant of the time. I had less than fifteen minutes to be out the door.

"Yeah, man!" David cried, his voice was high pitched. I knew he was petrified of me losing faith in him, and I hadn't. But I still wanted to make sure he knew what was expected of him.

"And the job. How's working as an assistant manager? Are they treating you right?"

"Y-yeah...yeah, man!" he spoke emphatically. David's a former meth junkie and his voice is always so shaky, but I believed him. I would've heard if he'd fucked up at his sobriety or job. "Everything's all good, bro."

"Good. Thanks for checking in. Next time don't space it out so fucking much," I warned as I grabbed my wallet, keys, and pocket watch from the island drawer.

"You're right, D. I won't. I've just been taking some time to rebuild my life, you know..." his voice trailed off.

I knew this although he'd been clean for a year, David was still fucked up in the soul. I was not sure if it was beyond repair. That was for the therapists he visits to determine. But I knew he needed someone to stay on his ass. Someone he respected. The walks of life we traveled were as polarized as they could get, but we did intersect in the streets—streets I owned, and he fell victim to as he spiraled down a dark hole of addiction.

I didn't know why I gave a damn. I'd been a cold-hearted son of bitch since fifteen, slinging all types of narcotics. My actions made no connections to the lives of the feeble who were crushed in my illegal trade. The arms of my transgressions stretched further than to the patrons of the pipes, leaves, and powder I'd slung; they extended to the loved ones of those users and to those who were made victims in their ruthless attempts to score my shit. These revelations never scratched the surface of my conscience until I ran into David. He held the mirror to my inner-sinister being. There had to be an unrelenting comeuppance in my afterlife.

"But I'm okay, I swear," David pledged, waking me from my introspective thoughts as I zipped my duffle bag, ready to leave for the airport.

"Indeed. I'm on my way out of town on business. Come through *Cobalt* next week and let me lay eyes on you. Maybe we'll catch a bite," I murmured as my eyes scanned a partially opened drawer, I gave a cursory glance in to discover it contained Rayna's birth control pills. Several suggestive thoughts raced in my head in mere seconds regarding those magic pills. I immediately reeled them in, I needed to go.

"Sure, man," David agreed, and I tapped the red *End* tab on the phone as I made my way down the corridor towards the front door.

I flew to Connecticut to meet with a casino whose owners overhead exceeded the business' earnings and had been in the red for a couple of years, barely able to stay afloat. Ironically, Mark and Eric's fraternity was having a convention there. They were *Alpha* men and were due to be in town for a week-long celebration. I hadn't seen them in a while and thought to rent a house we could utilize and meet to catch up. Brett found a four-bedroom home with a pool, outdoor Jacuzzi, basketball court, and a fully finished basement with a pool room and fully stocked bar. It was my treat to them for not having had the time to chill like we used to do regularly.

Right after landing, I headed straight into a meeting, but called Rayna on the way. Her parting words were still fresh in my head. I needed to make her feel a constant connection to me, even if it meant calling her like the fucking love-stricken adolescent I was when I last saw her. I'd do what I had to do.

The meeting was draining. This was a family owned business and according to my partner, Richard, these were the most difficult to resolve because of the emotional attachment and sense of entitlement the owners had to the business. We had our numbers set and they weren't very flexible considering the timing and money needed to save it from an inevitable debunk status. I could tell from the start of the meeting this was going to be long and drawn out.

We were invited to tour the casino in the evening and asked to stay for dinner. They were trying to impress us into believing the business was promising and therefore worth more than what we were offering. This was one of the cons of being a rather new merger and acquisitions firm; if we were larger and more reputable, it would have been understood our decision was based on what's on paper—only their bottom line. But until we were a little more matured in the business in terms of reputation, we had to rely on the art of compromise and negotiation savvy. Needless to say, I was all too happy when the meeting ended.

I walked through the door of the house and was contented immediately by its stateliness. The motif was very contemporary and comfortable enough to be considered family style. I saw the lights were on, and although the sun was going down, I didn't believe they were left on by the property-keeper. Mark and Eric had to have arrived before me. I didn't see traces of them until I dropped my things and made my way out of the foyer and closer toward the massive kitchen area displaying a long white wooden island seating at least six. There was an open door across from the kitchen's entryway, and I could hear boisterous laughter sounding very familiar. I walked down into the basement where I found the two fellows, around the pool table.

"It's me, bitches," I sang as I skipped down the steps.

"Azmir, baby, please let me tea bag you to express my gratitude for this pad!" Eric exclaimed as I approached him and gave him some dap. "Bro!"

"Oh, no! I'll blow him first for the Jacuzzi out on the deck!"

Mark shouted just before I gave him some love as well. "Do you know how many young and firm *AKA*s I can fit in there tonight?"

"I'll exonerate both of your acts of kindness and accept a simple *thanks* instead. From the look of the stubbles on both of you, I'd have carpet burns for a week." I put both my palms in the air, gesturing a no thanks. It was good to see them. They both held whiskey glasses. "So, what y'all sippin' on?"

"Dude! There's a fully loaded bar. I've started off with brandy. This shit is quality. Fuck!" Mark craned his neck back, looking at the miniature glass. I knew the bar was fully loaded, I paid to have it that way.

"You know, men of my refined nature always enjoy scotch. It's delicious, bro!" Eric raised his glass in the air as I walked over to the bar to make my selection.

"So, what does the agenda look like this week for you guys?" I turned my attention back to the shelves, looking for a tumbler. Mark pointed my attention over the sink, and I grabbed a whiskey glass. "What type of Greek function is this?" I poured my *Armagnac* and returned to the cipher at the pool table.

"Our bicentennial. There are supposed to be nearly five hundred confirmed attendees. And I've remembered my rubbers," Mark beamed.

"Last I heard, *AKA*s were predominately sisters. I thought you didn't do them anymore, bruh," I teased.

Eric burst into laughter. "That man is so fucking horny he would stick his two inches into a Cheshire's pussy!"

The liquor had obviously settled into these two. Mark gave a hard dismissive wave. "I still love my sisters, you know. Their bodies are like none other," Mark defended.

"Now, I don't know about that one. I've seen some Asian sisters with tits and ass for miles and would put a Tanika and Kyisha to shame," Eric argued.

"I have a few of my Caucasian beauties who have the bodies of goddesses—tits, ass, ankles, and wrists! At the end of the day pussy is pussy, riiiiight?" Mark stroked the air by winding his pelvis area.

"I bet you can't even see your dick over that goddamn meatball, man! Didn't we talk about you working out? I thought you got a membership at your local gym? Shit, you know you can always come over to rec center and I'll hook you up with one of our personal trainers. The ladies are going to look at you like you're a geriatric pervert, man," I scolded Mark as I was perched on a bar stool, and mostly because he'd lost his dad to heart disease when we were all in undergrad together.

His father was young and so was his grandfather when he had expired a couple of decades before. I didn't like the risk hanging over one of my best friends' head. I could never express it to him that way. Men go the alternative route; we take jabs to express our feelings and fears. It adds pressure and is a manipulative method, but effective, nonetheless.

Mark snapped, "Fuck you, Jacobs! If I had your pesos, I'd fucking look like a damn Greek god, too! You have a goddamn chef who cooks for you, a personal trainer who pushes you in the gym at your beckoning call and a—"

"...a bad ass African American woman who is the epitome of a fucking Aphrodite, complementing his Adonis," Eric chimed in, interrupting Mark's weak ass argument. "Damn, that woman! She still haunts me in my wet dreams. When I think of how she shook her curves on that stage the night of your birthday bash, Jacobs, I get a boner!"

"Oh, fuck you, too, Eric! This conversation is not about me and my affinity for Caucasian sisters. And by the way, Rayna *is* a great catch, Jacobs. But hell, I'd have her too, if I could afford it!" Mark practically shouted. He was getting emotional, per usual. I tried to stifle my laughter but couldn't.

"Why thank you, Mr. Richardson. I appreciate your approval of my pussy," I jeered evenly to Mark who, I knew after just a few more drinks, would become indignant and I was not up to calming his drunk ass down. I turned to Eric. "And to you, Garrity. You can dream about my girl all you like...and feel free to include your palm to finish yourself off, but as soon as you come sniffing around her, I'm crackin' your ass." I gave him a warning glare. Mark toppled over in laughter from Eric choking on his drink. I guess he thought I'd forget about his grievances with his wife, which included her scent a few months ago. "So, when do the affairs begin, tomorrow?"

"No, there's a *Meet and Greek* tonight...fully stocked bar. You should come along, bro. It'll be a nice change of pace for you. You know deep down you've always wanted to be an *Alpha* man," Eric announced with haughtiness. He was nuts.

"Oh, nah. If I *were* Greek material, I'da been a *Q Dog*. I'm too animalistic to be pretty." I threw my tongue out like a dog, just like the *Omegas* do. With a scoff, Mark waved me off and Eric shook his head in contempt. They knew I was joking; I was too wrapped up in the streets to appreciate the benefits and culture of a fraternity. *Shit*, I'd created *The Clan*. I was good.

"I think we should all go and see who comes back with the most numbers," Mark's eyes were just as big as his damn belly in excitement. "Shit! This could be fun like old times, only Jacobs, you won't win so easily with that thick Brooklyn accent. We have *Alpha* brothers coming from all over the country and with all types of swag. So, you won't have the advantage."

"Fuck! I'd beat all your asses out. I've been known to rack up *AKA*s. You know NaTasha's one." Eric raised his eyebrows.

"I ain't fucking with y'all, man," I muttered, much under my breath. "Why in the hell does everything end up with wagered bets between us?" I protested.

"Yeah, Jacobs, like when we bet you could slam Kristen Johnson, the transfer from *Yale*, and we watched from the closet when you had her head hitting the hard ass headboard in the dorm. That shit was awesome!" Eric reminisced at my expense.

"Oh, yeah! Remember when we walked in on Jacobs banging

the shit out of two *Deltas* at the same time in the shower," Mark shrieked, walking up on me while adjusting the glasses on his face. "Do you still get pussy like that?" Eric stopped taking shots on the pool table to wait on an answer.

"Man, fuck y'all." I laughed hysterically. "I am thirty fuckin' seven years old. I don't need pussy like I did when I was nineteen. I'm good with quality over quantity." My phone rang, interrupting my thoughts. I saw it was Rayna calling. As I answered, I informed the guys, "I gotta take this," and walked towards the stairs.

Eric whispered, "Is Rayna quality because she can keep up with your energizer bunny ass or does she have platinum between her legs?"

I flipped him the bird while walking up the steps.

"A.D. Jacobs. How may I help you?"

"Thanks for the *iPad*, A.D." Rayna's voice was calm, a little seductive even.

I grabbed my suitcase from the foyer and made my way up to the second floor in search of a vacant room. I was impressed with the house and having Rayna in my ear put me in the mood to go house shopping.

"No problem. Did you see the inscription?"

"*Ms. Rayna Brimm, property of A.D. Jacobs,*" she read from the back of the *iPad*. "I like that," she hummed into the phone.

"Oh, yeah? What about it?"

"Oh, you know..."

"Ummm...no, I don't. Do tell," I urged.

"My vagina being considered your property. That's the only thing you can be talking about because last I checked, nothing else about me had an owner."

"Fair enough, but you do know wherever your vagina is so are you, right?"

"Correct you are," she quipped.

"So, I can get a two for one'er on that?"

"*Hmmmmm...* We'll see. You can't barter deals from so far away."

"Why?"

"Because I can't read your eyes. I need to see them; they're the entryway into your soul."

"Hence the *iPad*. We could always Facetime from your phone, but the *iPad* will give you a better view."

"Ohhh!" I could tell she caught on to the idea. "Well, let me fire this baby up for a test run. How does ten tonight, PST time sound to you? You think you'll be up for a little Facetiming?" she asked with a hint of promise in her voice.

"Bring it," I egged her on just before checking the time to be sure I'd be ready.

"Okay. I'm going to warm up dinner and feed Azna. I'll hit you up once I'm showered and ready."

"Girl, don't start nothing I can't finish," I groaned.

"Oh. If you need, I'll coach you into finishing."

"Indeed."

"Later."

I ended up at the *Stamford Plaza Hotel* about an hour later with Mark and Eric. The gazebo was nicely lit with heavy energy adding to the ambiance. The early autumn weather was fair, but I kept my blazer on. Fine ass black women of all shades, sizes, hair lengths, and textures, wearing green and pink were all over the place. In many ways it felt like a candy shop.

The *Alpha* men were not as uniformed as the women. I've always appreciated seeing dignified African Americans gathered. I offered to order a round of drinks for me and the fellows, but Mark intercepted, insisting on treating everyone for the evening. I had a keen suspicion he was still hoping for us to implement the bet of getting the most telephone numbers. Even by the way he attempted to buffer the bet by saying I could simply discard them at the end of the night, but I wasn't with the kiddie shit. I just figured I'd come out to extend my time with my friends.

Black women aged so gracefully, so it was difficult to tell who was of what graduating class. I started out making rounds with Eric and Mark and being introduced to their Frat brothers and some of their Sorors as well. I couldn't take Mark's salivating at every woman he encountered and Eric's perverse whispering in every chick's ear, thinking it was appealing. I discreetly backed out of their company and played the bar. I was feeling a little buzzed and didn't want to blow up their spot and embarrass them by clowning them.

As I checked the e-mails on my blackberry, the bartender called out to a guy near me, telling him his drink was ready. The guy couldn't hear him over the music and was walking off, so I pivoted quickly, trying to tap him to get his attention, only I accidentally elbowed a short stocky woman who cursed under her breath. When she turned to catch a glimpse of the perpetrator, as luck would have it, her eyes softened.

"I am so sorry about that. I wasn't aware you were right behind me. Let me buy you another drink," I offered. She stood there motionless, batting her lashes. Then I noticed the woman across from her, frantically wiping the spilled drink from her shoes. *Shit!*

"I'm sorry about your shoes as well. Your next drink is on me," I announced. The second woman was tall, light, and had long shoulder length hair. She seemed more concerned about her shoes to even acknowledge my apology or offer, but the first shortie had begun smiling from ear to ear.

"Thank you." She was all breaths and teeth under dark red lipstick. "Are you here alone?" she asked flirtatiously, looking around me.

"No," spilled out of my mouth without a thought. Her smile

turned upside down and to my relief. Instantly, I decided to get out of here.

My phone rang, giving me the perfect escape from my short-lived conversation with *short and stubby*. I pulled it out, turned back over to the bartender and threw him a fifty spot for their drinks as I answered. It was Rayna, asking technical questions about setting up her e-mail to go to her *iPad*. I could tell she'd started acquainting herself with the gadget. I couldn't wait to get her ass naked on my screen. I gave her the instructions and we got off. I took a final swig of my drink and decided to text Mark and Eric, letting them know I was out when I felt a tap at my shoulders.

Bracing myself for another round with *short and stubby*, I was shocked as hell when I saw Dawn Taylor, standing before me, looking extremely tall with a fitted, hues of pink sweater mini dress and open toe sling back suede emerald *Giuseppe*'s, giving her at least five inches. Her slender chocolate legs were bare, shiny, and toned. Her hair was in its usual untamed curls, and she wore pink lipstick on her puckered lips.

Dawn Taylor was a bad bitch, and she knew it. She had been coming for me and hard, but I'd been ignoring her advances for obvious reasons related to my current relationship status. And also, because she and her girl, Shayna Bacote, who had just launched their new PR firm were actually talented prospects.

I'd been on the market for a PR team for a couple of years to help me out with my brand. I'd hired a few freelancers, but no one impressed me enough to lock into a contract. These girls came with fresh and cutting edge marketing ideas for *Cobalt*, the rec, and even my corporation. They had connections but needed viable clients to build their repertoire and as an entrepreneur, I understood this. However, even if I was single, I wouldn't risk a solid business relationship by fucking an associate. That shit never worked. But I'd be damned if I lied and said she wasn't tempting.

"Ms. Taylor, yet another surprise," I admitted, not so jolly as I am one drink past tipsy.

She slanted her eyes with a sexy smile, "I like when you call me that."

"Call you what?"

"Ms. Taylor."

"Do you now?"

"Yes." She giggled. "It makes me feel sophisticated." She removed a tendril from her eye. I watched as her face went from seductive to pensive. "Are you here alone?"

"Yes and no."

As soon as those words left my mouth, Mark and Eric's slightly drunk asses came my way. I chuckled to myself as I saw they were holding each other up with Mark being damn near a foot shorter than Eric. They were certainly a pair.

"Yo, yo, yooooo, Jacobs!" Eric sang as they approached me. Dawn backed up, startled by their outburst. "Do you know what this prick just did?"

"Easy. Don't you see a lady in our presence," I calmly scolded.

I didn't want them to say anything about either one of them trying to score some ass and embarrassing the hell out of me any further. I loved my dudes, but they were definitely a different breed.

"Oh, my! Well excuse me, my scrumptious chocolate drop. I hope you didn't feel the slightest bit of disrespect. There is no way common men such as us could ever feel worthy of being in the presence of your exquisite beauty. Are you a Soror of ours?" Eric inquired before reciting their Greek chant. Mark followed behind him.

Dawn was cool about it and returned her sorority intone. She turned to look at me, I had assumed, for answers.

"My escorts. Eric Garrity and Mark Richardson," I introduced. She greeted them and then turned back to me with big eyes and lungs filled with air. I cut her off, "Oh. And no. I'm not Greek. Not my thing."

She released the air and seductively twisted her neck, "Well, what is your thing? I've been trying to figure this out for a while now."

In my peripheral, I could see Mark nudging Eric and Eric's mouth swinging open. My phone rang again. This time it was Brett, calling with important information about my travel. I knew he wouldn't be available for long, so I had to take the call.

I answered the phone, "Brett? Yeah, hang on."

I looked over to Dawn and answered her question, "Merging and acquiring at the moment." Her brows furrowed as she chewed on my words.

Then I peered over to Mark and Eric, "I was just about to tell you I'm gonna head back over to the house. I have a few contracts to read over and an important call from the West Coast I have to take soon. I'll have the car come back and collect you two whenever you're ready." I gave them dap. "Thanks for inviting me out, my dudes." I guessed, sensing my sudden flux, they didn't say much outside of agreeing to my plan.

Dawn looked greatly disappointed. I knew better than to keep blowing her off and very soon I would have to give her an ultimatum, but I was hoping to consider their offer and see which way the wind blew me first. I reached over to her and gave her a quick hug and kiss on the cheek before taking my call and walking back out to the car.

Back at the house, I quickly showered and set up my control center in the television room so I could get some work done. I was tired, but anxious to knock out a few pertinent action items before Rayna's called. I'd poured myself a glass of brandy to help me relax. If there was anything able to unwind me, it was work. And if there were an abundance of anything in my life, *it was work*.

Once I was done renewing contracts with a few of my vendors, I pulled out the *Bacote & Taylor's Planning and Public Relations Corporation* proposal. This preliminary contract was to launch the re-opening of *Cobalt*. The earnings of the club were declining. We were riding the initial high wave of the novelty of being a new and trendy club on Santa Monica Blvd, but three other clubs in the vicinity had opened since us and clientele is finicky. People are typically with the hype and if you aren't new or innovative, you weren't hype. I wanted to launch with fresh ideas and mainstay themes.

Taylor & Bacote was very promising. Much of the proposal read as their verbal pitch did, just more in detail. They even introduced suggestions for minor cosmetic upgrades to the bathrooms and bar. They had record label connections similar to mine, only they were driving hard at adding live performances to our identity by having someone there weekly. I hadn't thought of that. I needed to know if it would increase my liability and therefore change my premiums. I made my notes with my infamous green pen, denoting money, when the doorbell rang. I thought it was strange that the guys didn't have their keys, but figured they were too drunk to even know.

I swung the door open, prepared to cuss their asses out, when I found the radiant Dawn Taylor shivering and rubbing her hands against her arms.

I jolted. "Come in. What are you doing here?" I asked as I moved aside to let her through the door.

"Trying to make sure you're a man of your word. I wanted to walk you through the proposal and take any questions you may have on the spot. That's door-to-door treatment for ya." Her lips were quivering, making it difficult to focus on anything else.

"Can I get you a drink? You look like you've just walked out of the arctic. Is it really that cold out?" I asked, noticing she had her own little private focus. I looked down at her eye-level view and realized she was gazing into my chest.

"Pardon me for being indisposed. I wasn't exactly expecting company. Were you doubtful I'd read the proposal in good timing?"

She licked her lips just before snapping out of her lustful trance. "Errrrm...good timing is a subjective phrase. I want the job,

Azmir." Her words seemed to have a double meaning, but I still wasn't prepared to go there.

"How did you even know where I was staying?" I couldn't help my clipped tone. I wasn't too keen on surprise visits.

"Your friends, Mark and Eric, told me." She sucked her teeth and clapped her pumps into the floor while flaunting her bright smile. "C'mon, Jacobs! I promised Shayna that I could deliver on the *Cobalt* launch. Don't make a liar out of me!" It was like a teenaged daughter, begging her doting father for a new car.

Without a smile, I relented, "Come on in." I led her to the television room. "I was actually just working on the proposal and made a few notes. I guess we can go over some seeing that you are so earnest in your pursuit." I didn't think this was the best idea and didn't like being hustled, but I couldn't knock the persistence of budding entrepreneurs. "Have a seat. I'll go slip on something more appropriate to discuss business," I informed as I made my way out of the room.

"Or we can discuss anything calling for your current dress code," she purred slickly and added a wink.

I shook my head and headed to my room. When I'd returned, I noticed she had fixed herself a glass of brandy and was casually sipping it, quite comfortably nestled in the single sofa chair. This woman was dangerous. My buzz had become an inconvenient truth.

We'd been talking for nearly thirty minutes and as promised, Dawn had answered all my questions satisfactorily. I still had more thinking to do. Unbeknownst to her, I had a second proposal that I was expecting in the next couple of days. *Taylor & Bacote Planning and Public Relations Corporation* was ahead of the curb because they acted expeditiously.

"You keep nodding and saying, '*Ummhmm*' but not giving much feedback. I'm going insane over here. Give me something!" she trilled in exasperation, gesturing with her hands midair. Her agenda-consumed smile never left her face, which always concerned me. There was something behind her eyes.

"Poker-face, Ms. Talyor. You should develop one," I murmured before pouring myself another glass.

"That you do so well," she murmured pensively while fixing her gaze on something towards the floor. She licked her lips before speaking again. "Tell me, Mr. Jacobs, why have you been ignoring my texts and advances?"

Bingo! *Though, I was slightly confused.* I didn't recall ignoring any texts, I'd never received any from her.

"The advances can't be ignored, but what texts are we referring to?" My expression was quizzical.

"The ones in Vegas when I invited you to lunch. You never responded." She looked unusually bashful, causing me to believe she was dead ass serious.

"That's because I never got them," I offered, reclining back in my seat, stretching my arms out on either side of me.

"You know lying is such an undesirable trait." Her eyes were squinted and her voice icy.

"This is true, but I'm being totally honest here. I never received a text from you or Shayna. I am a subscriber of two mobile phone services and have been for nearly fifteen years, I can assure you I'm a master at keeping up with both. Had you texted me, I would have returned it in due time. My word." I kept my tone even, though I resented the accusation.

She searched my face for the truth. I had nothing to hide and didn't want to give her the impression I was the type of man who gave a shit enough to have to. I wasn't pursing her, giving me no motive to lie.

"*Hmmmmm*... Okay. I believe you," she spoke slowly while bending over in her seat to retrieve her glass and took a sip. "The question now is how did it get lost in cyber space? Or did your lady of the week intercept me?"

My eyes shot up while I sipped my brandy. I wasn't expecting this. This Dawn Taylor was a damn firecracker. I saw I needed to switch gears to keep up with her.

I chuckled. "That would be a negative."

I didn't feel the need to explain any further, but Rayna would have never touched my phone. She would have to let down her guards long enough to *care* to play the jealous role. I swear, being involved with her was like fucking a woman, but being emotionally entwined with a man most of the times. She still had a problem with expressing her feelings. Shit. Even in the cafeteria, there at the rec center, when Dawn called me into a private conversation to spite Rayna, she didn't react with rage as most women I knew would've. And while her coolness *in that* incident worked to my favor, it was becoming increasingly difficult for me to deal with Rayna's heightened guard when my feelings for her were growing so fucking intensely.

"You sound so confident," Dawn challenged smoothly while arching an eyebrow. I could tell she was a little nervous by how her fingers toiled with the hem of her dress.

"Because I know her."

"How well?"

"Why are we asking, Ms. Taylor?" I snapped, becoming a little ill-patient.

With a tone of righteous indignation she spat, "I'm trying to get to know you, Azmir. It's what someone does when—"

"When?" My tone was pithy as my eyes shot straight to her face.

Who the fuck did she think she was pimping? I had to admit, she was coming strong with her audacity, and it was somewhat appealing, but I wasn't about to lay down my *G* for her to pick up and use against me.

My repositioning tactic worked; Dawn was at a loss for words. I needed to gain the reins of this conversation. Rayna wasn't up for discussion; she was a sensitive part of my private life. If I wasn't emotionally involved with Rayna, Dawn still wouldn't be a strong contender; I would have just fucked her right then and discarded the *Taylor & Bacote* proposal after she left for the night. She needed to be handled properly.

I sat up in my seat, inclined towards the coffee table. "Listen, Dawn, pardon my...apophasis, but if there is something you want to ask me about my personal life, do it with caution. I will answer whatever questions you have no matter what answers I believe you're looking for, but what we will not do is dance around shit under the guise of small talk. When you're negotiating potential relationships, it's best to avow with no filters so in the end if something goes awry, you're not left with the liability." A hint of agita was in my tone, but I didn't give a fuck, she was pushing me to my limits.

There, before me, her eyes filled with some type of emotion, and her cerise lips parted. *Yeah*. Just the way I liked her, fucking consternated. It took her quite a few seconds to collect herself, that gave me time to pack away my things. It was after twelve thirty in the morning. I didn't have a lot of time.

"Well, I've been told," she spoke just above a whisper. "*Ummmm*... I guess I'll be moving along."

"Give me a sec, and I'll walk you out." I tried sorting a few papers.

"No, no need. I think I can find my way to the door." Dawn had suddenly regained her forcefulness.

"Don't be ridiculous," I snorted as I stood to my feet and rounded the table to lead her out. Behind me, she maintained a steady stride to the door. I could hear her shoes click clacking down the corridor and into the foyer. As I grabbed the knob of the door, my mood had started to settle. I didn't know if guilt had hovered in about chewing her out because of my sensitive issues, but whatever it was, I wanted to end her visit on a good note. "I'll have an answer on the proposal by the week's end."

The sound of my voice arrested her tread and her stance settled and softened as she acknowledged my words. She gave a lungful exhale, taking her chin down with it, contemplatively, and immediately brought it back up. Without provocation, she pounced on me, bringing her delicate right hand up to my shoulders and taking the other to pull my head down. Dawn dashed her tongue down my throat with determined force. Her tongue was lithe, and the tasted of brandy mixed with traces of mint along with her unique flavor which turned me on.

Without deliberation, I lowered my head and took her at the small of her back, welcoming her in. Her movements slowed at a rate telling me she had switched from impulsive to cruise control in her audacious move. Her left hand stroked the back of my neck. She was getting comfortable on my person. Not wanting to be overtaken, I flickered my tongue in her mouth seductively, causing her to push out a gut-felt moan. When I let her catch my tongue, she sucked on it and moved her right hand down my abdomen in search for the hem of my T-shirt.

She was aggressive, and I'd suddenly come to the realization it the aggression drawing me to her. I enjoyed her initiative, her fierce nature. She was out on the prowl for my attention and had been making it damn clear. Any time before the present-day it would not have been an issue for me at all; I'd been pursued by countless women and regularly, but that was the one thing I didn't have with Rayna. Dawn lacked indifference. It felt good to be assured of. Dawn's hand brushed passed my pelvic area, sending a tingling sensation down to my groin. This fractured my lewd state. If I didn't stop, I would be fucking her against the foyer wall.

I pushed back. "Dawn, you need to go. We can't do this. It isn't possible right now."

Her eyes were lost on my words. She was hungry. Within the blink of an eye her face crinkled as if reality had finally hit her at the moment.

"Shit," Dawn panted heavily and with both her hands she rubbed the frustration from her face. "Azmir, I hope I didn't fuck anything up." She couldn't even look me in the face. It was probably for the best.

"Don't sweat it. It never happened." I tried to sound as assuring as possible, but I needed convincing, too. I couldn't believe my lack of restraint. I exhaled while holding my head. "Are you going to be okay getting back to wherever you're staying?" My voice was involuntarily calm.

"*Ummm*... Yeah...yeah. *Uh*—I'll be fine." She moved up to catch the handle of the door and took two steps before turning back to me. "I'm sorry for..." She was at a loss for words, something I didn't think was possible.

I shook my head as a means of telling her it all was cool then I watched her leave. My head was spinning in confusion and self-abasement overtook me as I padded to my room. I didn't know how I was going to pull off the upcoming *FaceTime* chat with ol' girl.

I went into the bathroom to splash water on my face, hoping it'd help clear my mind. Hesitantly, I took a furtive glance in the mirror and noticed the red stains of Dawn's lipstick around my mouth.

Fuck!

My chest tightened. Since Rayna, I'd grown obsessed with traces of lipstick on my body. But only from *her* lips. The gloss and matte colors matching *her* divinely soft skin, not another woman's.

How the fuck did I get here?

I mulled over the question as I scrubbed my face and brushed my teeth, ridding myself of Dawn's essence, though I could still smell her. Her fragrance was foreign. I only knew *Cool Water*. It was what my heart responded to. *Then why in the hell did I slip the way I did?* I contemplated the question as I crept toward the bedroom.

Within minutes, my *iPad* chirped, and my heartbeat raced as a direct result of it. I was feeling fucked up before, but now I was... paranoid. I knew I couldn't keep her waiting, so I accepted the call and waited for our connection.

Connecting...

As I read the word, it suddenly took on a new meaning for me. I'd been begging Rayna to connect with me in the most intimate way for months now. And for the most part, she'd been making every effort to do just that. We were making strides, and now... Dawn Taylor. I hadn't suddenly developed feelings for Dawn after kissing her. I was experiencing a bout with guilt for indulging her on Rayna's watch.

Rayna was precious to me, something that I didn't want to fuck up. I had to get a fucking grip on this situation now before it warped into something that could destroy everything I'd been building with Rayna and wanted with her.

My life.

The screen changed, and suddenly I saw a portion of my bedroom—our bedroom—appear. It was the headboard of the bed. Rayna moved the *iPad* down to the lower end of the bed, giving me a full view of her and then laid lazily on the pillows stacked against it. She appeared relaxed, comfortable, and unhurried...*unguarded.*

Fuck!

Her hair was up in a ponytail and her beautiful face was makeup-free, giving her flawless caramel skin a demure and youthful look. Her lips were nude and plump. Her eyes were heavy and hooded. My girl wanted to fuck around.

Damn!

"Heeeeeeey, Mr. Jacobs," she murmured lasciviously, before abruptly picking up on my pensive state. "Is everything okay?" She wrinkled her forehead, causing my stomach to twist.

Get it the fuck together or blow it, Jacobs! I took a quiet deep breath, a fortifying tactic.

"Hey, beautiful. I'm just a little jet lagged. How was my number one lady's day?"

Rayna's face softened and then she stretched her arms out, releasing a provocative moan, sounding so fucking sexy. My cock twitched. I groaned inwardly. I could never have my fill of her. This telecommunications idea of hers quickly became a gift and a curse.

"Oh, blah," she hummed. "It started off sucky..." I know she was referring to my departure. *Shit.* "...and it continued mediocrely. How did your meeting go with the casino family?" My eyes slowly roved over her attire, or lack thereof.

"They were tight...may even still think they're in the lead of the deal, but we aren't wavering." I could no longer hide my amusement. "What are you wearing?" I tried masking my smile with my wrinkled eyebrows.

Caught off guard, Rayna glanced down her body in assessment. Her eyes told me when she processed the situation, and a gorgeous smile eclipsed her face.

With a soft roll of the eyes, she whispered, "Your T-shirt."

"I see." I adjusted myself in my seat, trying to take in every square inch of my screen. "And what else?"

Her sexy chestnut irises diverted down her body again without thought before she sheepishly answered, "Nothing."

Immediately, her eyes hooded again. Goddamn, I loved having this type of effect on her. I swear, I would fuck my way into her destiny if it was my only means there. And she'd enjoy every orgasm I delivered getting me there. I'm fucking confident of this.

"How are Mark and Eric? I'm sure they've been...entertaining," she chuckled.

I followed suit. "Yeah, that's an adjective one could use to describe those bitch—*I mean, cats.*" I almost let my manners slip. I couldn't believe those motherfuckers gave Dawn this address. What the fuck did they think she was asking for—Greek orientation?

"And your mom...when is she due in town?"

"I'll have to ask Brett. He's taking care of all of that."

I bit my nails, still on edge, and even adding horny as a motherfucker to my fucked up state. *I can't believe I kissed that woman.* I was no saint, I'd done some pretty shady shit in my life—seriously fucked up deeds. But never would I hurt Rayna. I could never betray her trust. I couldn't imagine her being disloyal either. I get sick at the thought of her being with another man. Ever. If I had it my way, she would never experience another cock fucking her properly, arms to hold adoringly, tongue teasing her insanely or lips worshipping her totally.

Ever.

"Azmir..." Rayna called out to me, bringing my attention back to our conversation.

"You look stressed. Are you keeping something from me?" Rayna asked in jest as she narrowed her sexy eyes and her luscious lips twitched, trying to conceal a smile. That was the only clue I had of her not being totally aware of my reckless malefactions. My guilt. Before I could respond she purred, "I can help remedy the stress." She lifted a seductive eyebrow.

Suddenly, I decided to push all bullshit concerning things that didn't include making Rayna the happiest woman on this planet aside. She's my right now. My forever. My life. No one else mattered. Not now. Not ever. This was our *bubble*.

I cleared my throat as I inclined myself in my chair. "Sure, you can. You can start by showing me what's underneath that T-shirt," I all but growled.

Without a moment of hesitation, and with the sexiest scraping of her bottom lip, Rayna pulled the oversized T-shirt over her head, and I watched raptly as her arms collapsed back down against her ribcage. Her brown nipples glistened, and my tongue contracted, begging to taste them.

Fucking beautiful.

"Azmir," she moaned, feeling exposed, I was sure. It didn't help I was gawking at her like a hungry man at a T-bone steak. I didn't answer right away. I couldn't help my ogling.

After a few beats, I ordered, "Bring your knees up and spread those meaty thighs I'm addicted to being in between. I'm about to show you how to pleasure yourself A.D. style...but you have to promise me one thing."

Her chest rose and fell visibly, and Rayna's round eyes popped open while her mouth collapsed with impatience. "What?" she panted.

That quickly, Rayna was caught up. She never failed to reveal who her pussy belonged to. It might as well have had my name tattooed on it. I commanded it even from across the country. If I couldn't capture her heart, I damn sure held her body captive. This, I was sure of from the first time I tasted her. She is mine. All mine.

"You don't share this technique with anyone, neither do you attempt it without me. Understand?"

With her mouth hanging open, she nodded, filled with anticipation. Her beauty took my breath away. I used to think that was some corny shit only love-sick fools used to express loose emotions. That was until I became one of those fools. Rayna's presence rendered me speechless. I could now say that I knew what this love shit felt like. It had you thinking and rethinking everything. It had you exploring thoughts and possibilities your mind had never ventured to. It had you transforming into a being you never knew your substance consisted of.

Goddamn, if I wasn't in some shit totally consuming me.

Everything done with and for Rayna was done so with great effort, with everything I had. No challenge was met with unexceptional attempt. She was worth my time, efforts, and resources. I'd put it all on the line for her, even if she didn't quite know this yet. I decided right then and there to take my time with her. Tearing down those stubborn walls made of keloids derived from her past —whatever that represented to her. I would give Rayna my all.

Within five minutes under my adjuration, Rayna was screaming my name so loud and hard, I was sure the entire marina heard her satiated cries.

Her yelps of pleasure were so palpable, I was near explosion my damn self.

Rayna

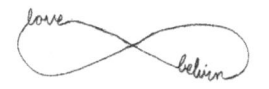

Time blurred pass after Azmir left for business on Tuesday. I'd busied myself with dance class, bible study, and my counseling sessions. Ironically, Pastor Edmondson started exploring the phenomenon of love and how it varied to the wonder of being in love. We had only gotten halfway through it before the session was up and I couldn't get any more questions out, but I'd had a lot of time to think about how it applied to my life.

Usually when Azmir left, I'd longed for him from day one until he returned to me, but this time my endurance was assisted because I had long days and even longer nights due to my show on Saturday. *FaceTime*'ing nearly every night also helped.

The *FaceTime* conferencing started off slow and odd...*yet interesting* the first night he was away, but over the course of a couple of days they had evened. I don't know what it was about the first night, but Azmir had seemed withdrawn. He didn't give me the impression he didn't want to talk however, he appeared peculiar, almost preoccupied. He struggled through it to coach me on how to give myself an earthshattering, toe-wiggling orgasm, something I'll never forget. But something was off.

Toward the end of our *FaceTime*'ing experience, he mentioned he'd just come from a Greek event with Eric and Mark, something I found hilarious considering they actually looked the aristocratic *Alpha* type. Azmir got a good laugh when he asked me if I'd pledged during my academic career and I explained I'd considered it, but quickly realized it wasn't for me, though Michelle went ahead with it and pledged *Delta Sigma Rho*. She was the sole Caucasian on the line and did not care. And I was extremely proud of her.

Thursday came and I'd been preparing for Saturday by keeping the song I was covering in my ears, on repeat every chance I got. I needed it to seep through my pores so I could excrete it through my sweat when I hit the stage on Saturday. Work sped by in a flash and before I knew it, I was at the dance studio with Jimmie who cursed me out every which way he could imagine.

"You're fucking up, The Lost One Found!"

"If you're gonna go this soft, you might as well get "lost" before Saturday, The Lost One Found!"

"Shit, would a drink loosen those stiff ass muscles, The Lost One Found? You need to get the stick from up your ass!"

No matter how hard I tried, I kept missing drops, being delayed for beats, and my kicks were never swift and correctly aligned. I'd started to worry I chose the wrong song. I was embarrassed and pissed to no end. Jimmie all but kicked me out of his studio.

I headed straight to the marina, frustrated and filled with anxiety. I was soaking in the tub, sulking, and trying to figure out what was biting at me. It didn't take long for me to get honest with myself and admit I'd put those texts from Dawn Taylor to the rear of my mind since Vegas, and not to mention her surprise pop up visit to Kid's party had really rattled me. Azmir's distance Tuesday night still haunted me as well.

There was something different about Dawn Taylor compared to Tara, Spin, and all the other women vying for Azmir's attention on a daily basis. Dawn wore a speck in her eyes telling me she was different...dangerous even. I didn't like what my gut was warning me of. I wish I knew if she reached out to him again *or what his response was to the texts, I'd read that morning in Vegas!*

My mind churned until revelation smacked me in the face. I

jumped out of the tub, splashing water every which way until I got to my towel. I didn't bother drying off. I just wrapped my body and went straight for my *iPad* laying on the coffee table of the sitting room there in the master suite. I typed in the web address to Azmir's mobile service provider and clicked on **My Account**.

My heart raced as I typed in a password, I wasn't completely sure was correct, but I had to try. I didn't feel the floor once the screen refreshed to a page reading, "**Welcome back, A.D. Jacobs**." One hundred kilowatts of dopamine coursed through my brain, and I jumped up and down, deliriously enthused by my discovery.

It was the password he'd given me last month when we were having problems with the internet while he was away. I needed to call the provider to rectify it and though I didn't expect for him to allow me to make the call because he usually had staff to do everything, he did and provided me with a password. I had hoped he was like ninety-eight-point nine percent of the population who duplicated passwords for the sake of sanity when they need to call upon them.

I clicked away until I was able to pull up his texting records. It took the hassle of starting my search from present day, all the way back to the day we were in Vegas. And once I was there, I had to decipher the messages to locate Dawn's. Once that was done, I made a mental note of her number and scrolled down the columns until I found it again...*and again. And again?* My heart was ripped from chest when I saw the nauseating amount of times her number appeared. I followed their exchange that started the TUESDAY NIGHT HE WAS IN CONNECTICUT!

Dawn wrote: *Azmir, I can't stop thinking about our encounter earlier. I hope this does not put our business relationship at risk. Shayna doesn't deserve to lose a heavy account because I can't exercise self-control. I am so sorry...well, kinda.*

A few hours later, Azmir wrote: *Like I said, no sweat...shit happens.*

Dawn replied immediately. *Are you upset over it? I really wish* we could have a do over...not that I have any regrets about any of it. I just wish I knew what you're thinking.*

It was just a kiss. No biggie. Sleep on it. Azmir replied sometime later.

Okay. Let me know if you need to talk about it or if something will change between us...professionally or personally. Dawn followed up immediately, and it apparently ended the conversation because Azmir never replied.

The cogs of my mind started rotating—right away, quickly, and hard! *There were a few hours of delay from Dawn's first text and Azmir's response.* I checked the times again. Azmir had kissed her just before *FaceTime'ing* with me. *His delay was because we were...busy being intimate.* Suddenly, I recalled asking Azmir if he would join me in my masturbatory indulgence. He declined, saying that he'd had all the indulgence he needed for the night.

Adrenaline shot through my veins, and I started feeling a myriad of emotions and physiological responses all at once; betrayal, pain, anger, cold chills, self-pity, loose limbs, confusion, an up-rise of bile...*bile...BILE!*

It was rising from the pits of my belly when I took off to the bathroom and hurled face first into the toilet, barely making it. I hugged the frigid porcelain bowl as though my life depended on it. The upchuck didn't last as long as the ones over the weekend, but it was just as forceful.

I blacked out for a minute, consciousness waned. When I arrived back to a cognizant state, I felt cold firmness against my back. I looked around me and realized at some point, I'd reclined against the cobblestone wall of whirlpool with my naked body squatting on the cool floor. I'd lost my towel somewhere along the way to the bathroom.

I wanted to cry so badly, but I couldn't. The tears remained at bay. It furthered bewildered my confused state. Azmir had cheated on me with Dawn Taylor. The woman who I'd sensed was a threat turned out to be my worst nightmare. After a run through the shower and washing out my mouth, I found myself out in the living room at the bar, deciding on which poison I'd choose to help numb the pain of my heart. *The heart I thought was well-protected and wasn't accessible to hurt.*

Azmir had so many decanters of varying shapes, sizes, and colors. I was out of my realm of knowledge. I decided on pouring Azmir's *Armagnac*, I only knew because he drank it most frequently, and I'd asked him about it. The tumblers were just as varied, but I grabbed the one within the shortest distance of my reach.

The first swig was hard to get down. It burned my esophagus so brutally, but the numbing from the subsequent sips made the venture to the amber juice worthwhile. After pouring my fourth glass, I sauntered over to the mammoth sofa, finally able to release the dam of my tears. They would harbor no longer. The croak lodging from my throat was so unrecognizable, it scared the crap out of me. Once again, for the millionth time in my life, I found myself in the throes of pain.

CHAPTER 3

Rayna

I jumped up to a startle. My heart was beating out of my chest. I heard the **THUMP-THUMP** again, but this time in a conscious tense. Someone was pounding on the front door.

Afraid out of my mind, I walked slowly over to the door and as I got closer, I heard, "Ms. Brimm...Ms. Brimm!"

My stride sped up and I looked into the peephole to find Roberto on the other side of the door.

BANG-BANG!

The sound of him banging on the door was more alarming up close.

I swung the door open. "Ay Dios mío, Señorita Brimm!" Roberto cried out as he took a deep exhale. He looked petrified.

"What is it, Roberto?" *A damn fire?*

"Señor Jacobs called. He's been trying to contact you for hours. He is on his way to the airport. He thought something happened to you!"

Crap! What in the world happened?

I grabbed my head, trying to stop the spinning of my cranium. "What time is it?" I asked in my post-inebriated condition.

"Two twelve in the morning, senorita." Roberto's face was ashen in despair.

Double crap! "I'll call him now. I fell asleep in the living room. I didn't hear the phone." I blurted out the first plausible excuse coming to mind.

"Si, I'll go call him, too!" Roberto turned on his heel for the elevator.

I went down the hall to the bedroom to locate my cell and saw the ringer was off. *When did I do that?* I had thirty-two missed calls and seventeen texts, all from Azmir. Suddenly, I realized I must have passed out in the living room and had been out for quite a few hours. I figured I had no time to waste and didn't want him returning early from his trip, so I sent a text to Azmir.

All is well. I fell asleep in the living room. Chat tomorrow.

I didn't wait for a response and kept the phone on silent. When I checked, I saw the house phone was muted as well. *When did I do that?* Memories of my discoveries had begun to flash through my mind, taking me back to my *iPad*. I logged in again as my time had expired from earlier and sat up for the next three hours reading and investigating texts. I didn't fall back asleep again until after five in the morning.

I was in my office, in the mix of my day when Sharon peeked her head in my door, informing of Azmir being here to visit me. I thought it was strange considering I wasn't expecting him back in town for a few days. *Did I worry him that much about not answering my phone?*

I nodded, gesturing for her to let him in. Within seconds, Azmir's tall frame rounded Sharon and gaited in his usual, sexy manner into the room. He was laced in a gray suit with a stalk white dress shirt, sans the first few buttons attached, and black oxfords. His heavenly scent preceded his proximity as he neared the front of my desk. Sharon closed the door shut after dismissing herself, leaving the two of us alone. My heart raced and my mind spun. What was up with this impromptu visit?

Something was wrong. Azmir kept one hand in his pant pocket and the other at his mouth, gnawing at his index finger. This was something he did only with me when he was nervous about a impending topic, which was rare. My gut had proven reliable recently where he is concerned, so I braced myself. This didn't look good. At all.

God, please!

Azmir cleared his throat, preparing me for what was to come. My body had tensed so much, my thighs ached in my stance.

"Rayna," he shrieked, voice devoid of its usual baritone nature. "We need to talk. Some things have come into play, and it's changed the course of our...friendship."

Friendship?

So, I was *just* a friend to Azmir? My limbs gave out on me, and I found my body slamming into my chair, thankfully missing the floor. My chest heaved. My vision suddenly distorted. The weight of my being left me as I laid sprawled out on the chair.

Azmir cupped the back of his neck. Whatever he was about to deliver, it was difficult for him. And yet it was already killing me. I couldn't speak to tell him to get on with it. The suspense chopped at my breathing.

"I guess what I'm trying to say is, I've re-thought this thing and I don't think it's best for us to be together anymore. I thought I was prepared to share my life with you, or at least try it out..." Another pause.

And another death I'd died.

After another tentative pause, Azmir continued. "I think it's best we see other people. And if we're going to do this, it's also best for you to move out of the marina."

My head jolted back and my neck, unable to hold it, snapped it forward. *I knew it!* I knew Dawn Taylor would break me. Her existence marked the death of my holdings in Azmir's life. I no longer held his attention.

"Dawn Taylor," I breathed, unable to find my diaphragm for much sound.

"Yes and no," he murmured on an exhale. "I just don't think you're cut out for what I need. I thought you were, but you've made every indication of being incapable of what I need. I'm sorry, Rayna, but I think it's best for us to end it here and now. I can't wait on a change that may never come. A promise that is a probable impossibility." Azmir spoke in all of his CEO mien as though it was a business we were dismantling instead of my heart being slaughtered. My life being cut short.

"*Uh*—I... I... I—*uhhh*..." I couldn't speak.

I was panting from my stomach instead of my chest. My body suddenly felt empty. Hollow. If I'd ever thought my heart was unavailable, it was nothing compared to my essence being robbed, my soul being snatched right out of me. I could feel nothing, no pain, no chills, no cold sweats. Nothing but air in my head being pushed out of my empty body.

Azmir barely looked at me. I knew this because with panic in my eyes from feeling death was upon me, I cried through them for help. I was quickly losing the ability to breathe. To live. This couldn't be happening. I couldn't be losing Azmir. He was my ray of sunshine. An endless source of strength. Loving arms to hold me up and push me into my journey of learning who I am, how to love myself. He was my next breath.

"Don't worry. You can keep Azna. He seems very attached to you. I could never make such a drastic change for him. I think you'd agree," Azmir paused for an answer. An answer that would never come because I didn't possess the ability to breathe in order to speak.

Azna didn't deserve drastic change, but I did? Why did he deserve asylum I didn't?

"Brett is having your things transported from the marina to Redondo Beach as we speak. Goodbye, Rayna."

I watched his glorious lengthy frame walk out of my office with just as much ease and brisk as he'd walked into my life. The door shut. White clouds engulfed me. I was out. Consciousness concluded, commencing my death.

What woke me from my sleep was Chef Boyd, making his regularly scheduled appearance to prepare breakfast for me. If Azmir and-or I were not out there to place our order by six a.m. sharp, he'd paged us in the bedroom from the kitchen.

"Oh, Ms. Briiiiiiimm!" Boyd's familiar voice broke my daze. "What would you like for breakfast this morning, sleeping beauty?"

I looked around the room, trying to make sense of my surroundings. A rush of relief washed over me at being *home* in Azmir's bed. *Oh my god!* It was *just* a dream—a nightmare. *It wasn't real!* I'd never felt consolation as I experienced it there, nestled in the sheets of A. D. Jacobs.

It was a good thing I didn't have a scheduled session with Tyler, who was away with Azmir this week. Azmir being his most valued client, allowed for Tyler's priority when scheduling. If Azmir needed Tyler, he'd wipe out all his appointments and follow his boss for whatever specified amount of time. Lucky for me, my grueling extended dance practice sessions substituted for my workouts this week, and I decided to workout at the rec alone. I drug my enervated body out of bed to prepare for my day.

On my ride to work, I thought over the various messages I'd read a few hours earlier, no longer able to keep putting off my reality no matter how much I wanted to distance myself from that horrid nightmare. My summation of it was Dawn had been after Azmir *via text* since Vegas. I wondered how far back her face-to-face advances took her. He kept his communications with her brief, which confused me. Why kiss her if you're not trying to at least communicate with her? The remainder of their correspondences were business related.

There were a couple of texts from Shayna, but they were all about some event in the works for possibly next month. I didn't quite get the crux of their conversation, but it wasn't personal like most of those from Dawn.

I saw dozens of texts from Tara and could quickly conclude she was vying for his heart again. So many of her texts had soft touches like, *"Good morning, Azmir"* or *"I just came across* **The Best Man** *on BET and it made me think of Sandra and Paul's wedding we attended and the drama behind it all. Lol. I hope you had a great day."*

None of those he responded to, but there was a heated texting battle, a few weeks back, about him not attending Azina's christening. Apparently, Azmir didn't have an interest in going and it pissed Tara off—majorly. She'd cursed him out seven shades of Sunday, all for him to fire back with silence. I eventually grew bored with Tara's thread and actually pitied her.

Lady Spin had sent a few texts as well. She'd asked to see him on several occasions, most of which he declined. Then I could surmise they did meet, she wasn't happy with him turning down her advances. And just like with Tara, my name was used to blame. And just like with Tara, Azmir would not dwell on me and said his private life was not up for discussion, though he did make clear to Spin I was the lady of his life, and it was best to leave their relationship in the past and move on.

Call me an idiot, but I felt bad for both women.

Though there were a half a dozen more suspect texts clearly from women, they offered no distrustful behavior on Azmir's part. But Dawn, Tara, and Spin's pursuits were hard to ignore. Tara was a done deal, and Spin had never owned his heart, but I wasn't settled on his position with Dawn.

I fought back the tears all morning, even when Azmir texted, asking why I was refusing his calls to the practice. I'd told Sharon to tell him I was with a patient each time she buzzed me letting me know he was on a line. It was unusual for her *and* Azmir. Typically, I'd excuse myself and steal a few seconds to take his calls.

I typed back to him, **Hectic day. Hope yours is better. I'll hit you up tonight after practice.**

I choked back a cry while typing, suppressing my aching tears. It was so intense, it hurt. He didn't write back. *He had gotten the memo.* The knock at my door snatched my attention.

"Come in," I shouted coarsely, still shaken.

Brian Thompson peeked his head through before fully entering. Oddly, his smile thawed my mood. I'd even found myself being taken by his pearly white teeth glistening through his beaming smile. I smiled back.

"Oh, wow! For once I don't feel unwelcomed," Thompson quipped. "Good afternoon, Rayna."

He looked good in his finely tailored black suit, shimmery crimson tie, and nicely buffed oxfords. His hair was its usual close cut, and his goatee was handsomely trimmed. He looked...*suave*.

A soft chuckle slipped my lips. "Oh, stop it." I threw him a short wave of my hand, acknowledging his melodramatic antics. With a full on smile, I continued, "Hello, Brian. How may I help you today?"

"I brought my niece over to the recreation center next door. She's visiting from Seattle, and I heard about the dance classes offered over there. I thought I'd have her check it out. Figured if she liked it, I would enroll her in the summer program when she comes to visit next summer."

This was news to me. I knew Azmir had been developing a plethora of programs over there, but dance?

"Oh, I didn't know the rec had a dance program. That was very...avuncular of you." I snorted, suddenly jovial in my disposition. "Did she like it?"

"Avuncular?" he quizzed with a sardonic grin.

"Joke," I shot back.

"Uhn-hnn. I'm not sure. I'm headed over to get her now." His eyes darted down to the floor as he was preparing for his next words. "I was wondering if you wanted to join us for lunch. We've developed a partiality to *M&M's Soul Food,* and I thought it may be common enough to invite you to, so you don't think I'm coming on too strong."

Hmmmmm...

I wrinkled my nose. "Are you coming on to me at all?"

It was Brian's turn to scoff, only he added a rolling of his eyes. It was *cute*.

"Must we go there?" His head was tilted to the side to express annoyance. *Double cute.* It was a rare moment to not see Thompson's arrogance in full bloom. "Are you free?"

I eyed him from ear to ear, with so many scenarios running through my mind.

"I can't," I sighed. He pushed out groan of defeat. "But!" I qualified a pitch higher. "In lieu of lunch today, why don't you guys come to my show tomorrow night. If she likes to dance, she should be inspired by some of the acts taking place there. It's a fundraiser and should be fun for an uncle and niece date."

"Your show? You promote shows?" Thompson wore an earnest look of confusion.

"No. I dance. It's just a hobby, something to break the monotony of physical therapy." I tried to make clear. "Wait.... How old is she?"

"Seventeen."

"Cool. Some of the material is age appropriate, but it's all artful."

"Okay. What type of dancing are you into?"

"I do a few types; ballroom, hip-hop, jazz and a little tap, but there should be a little ballet and salsa there at the show, too. What's she into?"

"I believe hip-hop."

"Oh, yeah. She should be fine. There will be lots of flavor there to expose her to." I smiled. Thompson was off balance, his face blank of expression. "What's wrong? You don't have to feel obligated to come."

"No... No! It's just that..." I gave him a few seconds to gather his words, eager to hear what was running through his mind. "Never mind. We'll be there," he agreed, dismissing his previous thoughts.

I wrote down the address to the theater and he left. Something was weird about his visit. Perhaps because the temperament of our exchange was lighter for once. Thompson always led with his ego. His aura had always been foul, in my opinion, and met with resistance from me. Today he was humbled. Cute even. Cute in a *stray puppy dog I could feed today* way. Bizarre.

My day continued with little effort. I headed straight to the dance studio after work for a full run-through, which included props and background dancers. There were two skits the entire group participated in: the opening of the show and the closing. My act was somewhere in the middle. I didn't get cussed out much by Jimmie. In fact, I was bestowed several satisfactory nods throughout my number, and for that I was relieved.

That night once I turned down, I tried to get a handle, mentally and emotionally, on what I had managed to force to the rear of rears of my mind; Azmir's cheating on me with Dawn Taylor. As I sat at the vanity in the bathroom, trying to pack makeup for the show, my mind churned with images of Azmir's head descending toward Dawn's mouth. And when my visual got to the point of Dawn's reaction to it, my heart twisted, and my throat closed.

Did he butterfly his tongue with her the way he does with me? I swear, that single act from him, whether it's in my mouth or between my legs, took me places a plane couldn't give access to. *Did it do the same for Dawn?* The tears wouldn't stop. The hard bellow from the marrow of my soul echoed throughout the bathroom.

Call me a glutton for punishment, but I logged back into his mobile phone account. I wanted to see if there was further conversation between Azmir and Dawn. To my relief there wasn't. Torturing myself further, I also scrolled back up to the texts from earlier this week, feeling the need to see it again, to be sure I wasn't mistaken. This part of my recent string of misfortunes weren't just a dream—a nightmare. I felt a trickle of pain I didn't know I was capable of feeling. I logged out, not wanting to find any other heart-wrenching news. I couldn't eat, couldn't think, so I cried myself to sleep.

I was hit with another blow the following morning. Azmir informed me he wouldn't be able to make the show. He'd called first thing in the morning, awakening me from my sleep. I didn't know why I felt the twinge of disappointment I did, knowing he'd cheated on me just days ago. But strangely enough, I did. How could you be thwarted by someone who has ripped your heart right out of your chest? *I don't have an answer.*

"Brimm, you there?" Azmir asked after my delayed reaction to his news.

It also didn't help hearing his voice—his morning voice— awakening my libido. It stirred something deep down in my belly. My insides betrayed me, liquidating. He still had a hold of me, to the core of me. It would make sense seeing he did in fact, steal my heart from its icy chambers. Azmir owned me.

"*Ummm...* Yeah, I'm here."

"I've been trying to tell you since yesterday. I didn't want to text this to you. What the hell's been going on with you? Have you been that preoccupied with preparing for this show? I haven't heard your voice since Thursday morning. You scared the shit out of me the other night!" Azmir took a moment to breathe. "I was ten minutes away from the airport when Roberto called to tell me he'd reached you." He paused again, this time for an explanation.

I had none. *You wanna hear how I discovered you cheated on me with Dawn Taylor that night?*

I exhaled, frustrated about not knowing where to go with all of this. I had literally no one I trusted to share this with. Even talking to Pastor Edmondson was out of the question. I certainly wasn't prepared to deal with it at this point. I'd much preferred focusing all my energies on the show.

Azmir relented. He attempted a cease fire. "Sweetheart, I'm so sorry. These assholes are trying to get over on us and it's costing me flight and other accommodations to get my attorneys down here on a Saturday to let them know the shit ain't going down. I'm not even sure how long this will take or if it will run into my Miami trip next week. I'll make it up to you, I swear."

A tear slipped from my swollen eyes.

"Azmir, I'm good. Go, take care of business. I'll be fine." When I heard how dry that slipped out, I buffered it by saying, "I need to wake up and head over to Adrian's."

"Are you sure you're okay? I wouldn't be offended if you were disappointed—"

"No. I'm fine," I cut him off, rushing out my words in a quick breath. I couldn't manage much more. I was about to break.

"Have a great show, Brimm. I'll be home as soon as I can," Azmir murmured apologetically.

My heart sunk at his words. They were filled with so much sorrow and promise, but it may have been too late. He had betrayed me.

My heart was racing, and my mouth had gone dry. I was on stage, behind the curtain, waiting for my music cue. There was no announcement of names at this type of show, guests had to follow the program to know who was performing. I'd gone to the bathroom for the fourth time before curtain call, so my nervous bladder had no excuse.

The auditorium was quiet as the audience was anticipating the performances as well. I heard the bass drop and instantly, all anxiety had left my body and the memory of my muscles took over.

"I know you don't usually hear me talk like this..."

I'd invited my guests in for a show.

And suddenly no one was in the room, but me and the music. Every word Tamia belted radiated from my core. I demonstrated it from the top of my head to the heels of my feet. My twirls, figure-eight hip sways, leaps, jumps, and flips were all perfectly timed and executed with true passion; passion I'd experienced time and time again with Azmir.

"So, come and get it..."

I gave Azmir total control of my person because of things he commanded from it. The way he brought out a sensual side of me I didn't know existed. How he made my body do things and answer to him in ways I'd never dreamt possible. It amazed me how he knew crevices and soft spots and sensitive locations and could summons responses to his skilled acts of lovemaking. I could never get enough of it. I didn't want to lose it.

Tamia's voice was strong and my male background dancers, who made cameos throughout the performance, were virile and well-coordinated.

Azmir somehow appeared in my mind and suddenly, he and I

were there alone. I had become aroused. I ad-libbed, *"Close the door! I want you!"*

I extended my arms to the floor, inches away from my feet, pushed my hips, and swung my body a few yards the way I did when Azmir caught me practicing in my room a few months back. He loved this move and showed me just how much right then and there. It caused me to push harder in my performance. I was one with the music. So much so, I could swear I'd felt a quickening deep in my canal.

Boom-boom-bap. And one-two-three. Dip - swing - jump. I sang in my head, trying to keep my counts. *One-two-three-four...* "I can't get enough of yoooooooou!"

I ended, lying on my back with my legs behind me, nearly touching my head. I laid there panting hard, trying to come down from the salacious ride I'd just been on. I must have been down there too long because my male dancers, who were not involved at the end of the number, reappeared to help me up. With a wave, I gestured it wasn't necessary. But that's when my ears popped, and I heard the explosive applauses from the audience. I stood to curtsy as I saw them standing in ovation. I was blown away, awakening second by second from my trance.

God, I love that man!

Hopelessly.

Completely.

A surge of pain rocked my chest.

After our collective closing number, which included all dancers, we all dashed off the stage, many of us in a rush to gather our things so we could quickly greet our guests. Jimmie was standing in the wings, singing praises, and clapping his hands like a proud papa...*or mama*. He stopped several of the dancers to give personal evaluations. I'd scrambled out of my costume and into my change of clothes, hoping not to be delayed. Via text, I told Chanell I'd be right out after the last act.

I was able to deliver on my promise and located them with no problem at all, considering we'd just about had a full house. As I approached them, Chanell was chanting my name, "Rayna!...Rayna!...Rayna!" in a deep tenor note.

Kim was smiling from ear to ear, looking as if she was the beaming proud big sister. Kid didn't notice me coming their way and was typing into his phone. Wop stood there looking out of his element, eyeing everyone who walked too close to him. And Petey was chatting on the phone. A small part of me wondered if it was Azmir on the other end of the call, but I stowed my curiosity, figuring if he wasn't here it didn't matter anyway. Once I got to them, I distributed hugs and cheek kisses. The small crowd was full of compliments.

"Yo, Ray! Yo, I ain't know you could move like that! You gotta teach your home girl some shit!" Chanell yelped in her usual enthusiasm. I smiled at her with modesty.

"Oh, please! Chanell, you're the one who taught me how to Dougie," I reminded her of her skills. She laughed bashfully, something I didn't experience often at all from her.

Kid cut between Kim and Chanell with his arms stretched. "That was dope, Rayna. Y'all got some skills up in this bitch. I'm glad I came, yo...word up!" Kid smelled good and looked his usual urban self. He wore an oversized red leather jacket, baggie jeans, a graphic tee with red and black Timberland boots. His hair was neatly corn-rowed to the back, curling at the end of his neck. I couldn't ignore his dime-sized diamond studs, the left one scrapped me during our rapid embrace. I was relieved to see Syn was pleasantly absent.

"I'm glad you came, too, Kid. I appreciate the support," I returned. Kid barely looked me in the eye. I figured it was a sign of respect because of my relationship with Azmir, who was some sort of mentor to him.

Kim followed up with a hug and whispered in my ear so no one could hear, "Girl, how much these classes cost? I need to bring my fat ass down here to help me get rid of this weight."

"He's very reasonable. To be honest, that's one of the many reasons I started. Then I got hooked," I admitted, and we laughed.

"Ms. Brimm!" I heard a familiar voice call from behind me. It was a little alarming because outside of work, only Azmir addressed me by my last name, and this clearly wasn't his voice. I turned to find Brian Thompson standing with his hands over the shoulders of a beautiful adolescent girl with glowing brown skin and hair spilling over her shoulders. Her smile was soft yet admirable.

Thompson looked good in his blue jeans, gray button up shirt and violet sweater vest. He had style. His eyes bounced between mine in elation and wonder. My breath caught. Not only was he a sight for sore eyes, but I had completely forgotten about inviting them. When I extended the invitation, I was so wrapped up in a vindictive web from my heartbreak. Those maleficent feelings I honed in yesterday was now temporarily at bay, seeing all of my supporters there.

"Brian! You...you guys came. This must be your niece, the future dancer," I beamed, extending my hands to her. I didn't realize she had been holding a gorgeous bouquet of flowers for me until she extended her arms for me to retrieve them. Brian's eyes squinted seductively, which told me the flowers were his idea.

"Oh, wow! Thank you. My name is Rayna. What's yours?" I asked the young girl. There was something endearing about her eager and innocent eyes.

"I'm Brandy. Brandy Thompson. You rocked on that stage! I never knew I'd get so much interpretation from that song. It was like watching a video, with the artist performing it!"

"Wow, Brandy. Thanks! It makes all the months of choreography, edits, and additions worth it, hearing those appraisals from you."

"You choreographed that?" her eyes widened in amazement. It suddenly hit me. Seeing her reminded me of Erin. *Oh, how I'd missed her.*

I looked up at Brian, suddenly overwhelmed by her excitement. "*Yuh*-yes...we all choreographed our acts tonight. Only a little help from our instructor."

"That's awesome! I would love to be a part of something like this someday!"

Her animation seemed genuine, so I tried to appease her. "I can take you around back to meet the instructor. Maybe he can point you in the right direction." I gave her a wink.

She bounced up and down on her feet, eventually turning to, without words, ask her uncle's permission, to which he responded, "How can I say no to my favorite little girl." His smile was cool and comforting like an uncle's should be.

I turned to see all inquiring eyes locked on our exchange, it was very unnerving.

"Errrrr...Brian, Brandy, these are family-friends...Kid, Wop, Chanell, Kim and Petey." I smiled, still feeling anxious about the mixed company. Suddenly, the job of hosting these folks posed daunting. "I've never invited guests to see me dance. And what support I have the very first time! I'm feeling kind of lucky tonight." I tried unsuccessfully to lighten the atmosphere. I got a few mirthless laughs, even smirks, but Petey gave nothing. I tried not to show my concern.

"Yo', Rayna, come back here. Should be something for you," Petey basically ordered territorially.

Oh! Not you, too!

Petey and I walked to the back of the auditorium to find a tall man with orange hair dressed in livery, holding a long tan box. I guessed by the way we gaped at him he had an inkling we were the right group to ask.

"Rayna Brimm?"

His eyes bounced around all the females of the group. I didn't look to see if Brian and his niece had followed us back. But I did catch when Chanell pointed to me. He advanced toward me, handing me the box. I thanked him and noticed Petey slide him cash. I opened the card attached and right away admired its rich stationary. It read:

> *Orange roses represent Pride and Fascination.*
> *Congratulations on a job I know was well done.*
>
> *I am all too sorry I wasn't able to be in the audience,*
> *but I'll hold on to my front row experience*
> *a few months ago, at your former home.*
>
> *Forever Missing You,*
> *A.D. Jacobs*

My breath hitched. Surprise, sadness, excitement, *lasciviousness,* and a few other sentiments were felt concurrently in flashes. I was mindful of being watched, so I tucked the card back into the envelope, turned to my small group and, with a smile, thanked them again for their support.

Everyone gave a hug, one by one, with Petey being the last. He looked over my shoulder, causing me to do the same, and I noticed Brian and Brandy leaning against aisle-seats, waiting on me to escort them backstage. Brandy spied the stage while Brian kept his eyes glued to me—and then Petey.

Petey leaned into me, slyly asking, "You gone be okay, Rayna? Did Ray drive you here?" He wore an expression of unease.

I gave him a warm smile and a nudge. "I'll be fine, Crack." I threw him the moniker Azmir would use from time to time. "Thompson is a colleague of mine. I don't socialize with him outside of work and I won't start tonight. His niece is in town and is an aspiring dancer, so I invited them out for inspirational purposes. Don't worry."

Petey cracked a smile at that, something I was relieved to see. I didn't want to stir up any conflicting feelings among Azmir's friends. I didn't invite them to perpetuate the drama I always seem to find myself in when I'm around them with Syn.

"Alright, ma. Divine was fucked up that he couldn't make it. I'm sure y'all will rap about that." His tone was assuring.

I knew he was making a plea for his dear friend, but I wondered was it genuine or because he saw another man there, posing a threat. I also hadn't forgotten about, what I was now convinced was, a cover up operation at Kid's party in Vegas with Dawn Taylor and Shayna Bacote. I gave him a wink, and he promenaded over to his waiting crowd. I waved my goodbyes as they left the auditorium.

The evening ended just as uneventful as I'd promised Petey. I introduced Brandy to Jimmie and a few of the dancers who were still hanging around backstage. Brandy even showed Jimmie a few of her moves. She looked promising as he critiqued and corrected a couple of them. Brian invited me out to dinner with them, and as much as Brandy's zeal from the invitation pulled at my heartstrings, I declined. I was exhausted and really looked forward to worship service the next morning. I'd also missed Azna. With all my time at the studio this week, I really hadn't spent much time with him. He did, however, lick my hands when I cried at nights from my heartache and snuggled with me when I tried falling asleep.

When I stepped off the elevator at the marina, I saw them—all six dozen of them, lined up from across the elevator, against the wall, all the way to the apartment door. They were large clear vases, filled with long stem, fully blossomed orange roses. And to my surprise, when I opened the door, there were more—exactly twelve more—vases, perfectly aligned down the corridor, leading to the master suite.

Azna trotted out from the back of the apartment with his miniature frame, drew up and scratched at my calf. He must have been frightened out of his mind at the ruckus of getting the flowers in here. I'm sure Azmir paid a small fortune for all of them and had

Roberto or the on-duty concierge arrange them like this. The gesture was thoughtful, but the emptiness in my belly reminded me of his infidelity.

I sat on the bed and cried for what seemed like hours until I was startled by the sound of my phone ringing. It was Azmir. I couldn't talk. I wasn't ready to. I waited until after my bath when I had calmed down and my eyes had returned to their normal state and sent him a text saying *thanks* and I would call him the following day.

How long can I get by like this?

It would be some time before I would be able to anchor my feelings. Sorting through them could be difficult when you shove them to the back of your mind, so you *don't* have to deal with the pain from them. Some moments, I felt I wanted to abandon the relationship *that didn't exactly have a category*. Others, I truly believed I couldn't live without Azmir. He had awakened so much life and essential substance deep down inside of me.

Azmir stirred passion in me with his companionship, two things I'd never dreamt of. Two things I didn't think I could live without moving forward, after having experienced them with Azmir. I didn't want to let go of those things and didn't know if I'd find another being I'd let in enough to experience life as I do with Azmir again. I was completely drawn to him. Hopelessly. But I couldn't let him cheat me, rob me of fidelity. Exclusivity. My heart couldn't handle it. He couldn't just lay me down and move on to a new conquest arbitrarily like my father had done to my mother all those years ago. I wouldn't have it. I was an emotional yo-yo. I kept rolling optimism in and rolling it right back out.

Though completely exhausted, emotionally and physically, I had a presentation to prepare for in San Diego. That of course, gave me the perfect escape from my despair. I didn't know where the inclination or the strength came from, but I found myself on my laptop, logging into my e-mail. My heart slammed in my chest when I saw a message from the attorney, I'd hired to help negotiate visits with Erin. I hadn't spent time with her since Michelle's passing. I'd called and texted Amber, but to no avail. She was making her message clear: I wasn't welcomed in Erin's world. Azmir offered his attorney, but I didn't want to bust down Amber's door with guns ablaze. The e-mail was to inform me Amber had hired her own attorney, further demonstrating her resistance to my access to Erin.

Life could be so cruel.

Azmir

I was in an evening video conference meeting in Miami at the *Fontainebleau*. There was a failing company in Canada who wanted to discuss liquidation options. We'd conducted our meeting through a canvas screen, mounted to the wall. My partner, Richard, and I sat at a large conference table facing the projected screen.

It had been a long day. I was hungry and absurdly exhausted. What I wouldn't give to be home in my bed tonight. My mind had been running mad at Petey's report of this clown ass attorney chasing Rayna's ass—my ass. I was feeling mounds of guilt for having missed her show a few days ago. A part of me also felt like I had given Thompson's ass an in. I didn't think Rayna would go for it, but I also realized I hadn't done much to secure her as mine. Yeah, I had her in the high-rise, but if I considered the number of women I'd fucked while they were living with their boyfriends and husbands, I'd be a fool to believe her tipping out was impossible.

All I could hear were Petey's words of advice, "*If you wanna lock a woman like Rayna down, 'da last thing you need is ta' leave her for days, and sometimes weeks at a time. Snatch her ass off 'da market with a ring.*"

I'd already started considering marriage with Rayna prior to his sage advice. My only reservation was her wanting it. What Petey didn't know was how difficult she could be with revealing her inner most feelings. She had been improving, especially now with her joining the church and learning about love and trust. We'd come a long way and I didn't want to push her over the edge. I appreciated her progress. Whatever it took to get her to open up, I was game for.

The church thing was a gamble because those Christians went hard about living together and having sex unmarried, but she hadn't brought it up and I'd been happy as hell about it. I loved having her with me. There's nothing like coming home to a sexy ass woman every night. One who didn't press you about the events of your day or complain about theirs. She was cool. But to a certain extent, a little *too* cool. Rayna had yet to express her desire for marriage or a future. I'd been quite confused.

Either way, I had to man the hell up and take the leap. This clown ass Thompson had to be dealt with. There was no way I'd lose her to his sucka ass. I was no fool. I understood Rayna was an attractive woman, and I was not the only man who is attracted to her. But this dude was a known adversary. There's nothing wrong with having a little competition to keep you on your toes, but I'd fix his ass if he took it further though.

This meeting was dry, and I honestly didn't want to be here. My partner took the lead on it, but the Canadians wanted both buyers there. This was the part of this business I hated. *Your organization is failing. We got the bread to bail you out. Give us a reasonable figure and keep it fucking moving!* I'd been advised this was simply how it went at the beginning. So, I waited in complete boredom.

I played around on my *Mac-Pro* and checked my ever-abundant number of e-mails. Then I saw a video message from "*RayChoppa.*" I chuckled each time I saw her profile name. Why she'd chosen it was beyond me, but it was a testament to her humor. I must admit, I was completely thrilled at seeing this notification. Rayna had been throwing shade for nearly a week. It would be easy to say it was about me missing the show on Saturday, but it started before then. Something was up, yet there was so much I could do from across the country. I slipped in one of my earpieces, not wanting her message being heard by my business associates. I was being rude. However, I was also playing the role of bad cop this evening. So, fuck it.

I hit play and the video loaded. Soon, I saw the ever beautiful and glowing Ms. Brimm with a head full of bouncy curls and a tastefully made-up face, hunched over at my side of the bed, appearing glum. Tamia's *Officially Missing You* played loudly in the background. I knew Tamia's husband from around the way. I'd also seen her live and was a little familiar with her work.

But what the fuck was it with her and Tamia?

This time her music didn't work to my favor. She lip-synced the song as if she was shooting a video. Rayna looked...sad. I guessed that's what the message was all about. She was lonely. She wore my white tank T-shirt, fitting fit her like a dress. From the clear view of her pebbled nipples, I could see she wore no bra. My dick swelled. I looked around, making sure no one had a clue of my private and intimate show.

Damn! Is she wearing panties? I gotta get the fuck home.

Baby girl was lonely and apparently purring. Before I knew it, she sat up to end the video.

Fuck!

My mind began running a mile a minute. I had to get home. This shit could not go down like this. I felt like I was being caught with my pants down and ass in the air—fucking vulnerable! Rayna had gone AWOL on me emotionally a few days after I'd left her for this trip. Initially, I didn't understand why. Our first *FaceTime* session proved to be successful once I got my shit together. But almost right after that night, she began distancing herself from me, not taking my calls and creating long response periods for my texts. Shit. I'd almost flew home, fearing something had happened to her.

When I wasn't able to make her dancing event, her moodiness didn't let up. Hell. I knew it wasn't that time of the month for her. I knew her cycle well enough to know she wasn't menstruating. She'd finally let up last night when I called to check in and she answered. Our conversation was short, but I'd at least heard from her on first my attempt. This shit was driving me crazy.

I checked the time. One thirty-nine a.m. I glanced at the time stamp on the message. She'd left this an hour ago. I signaled my partner before stepping out of the hotel's conference room.

Answer the phone, Brimm. Answer...

She inhaled deeply, "Hello?" Rayna was sleeping.

"It's early."

"Is it? I fell asleep looking over quarterly reports. What time is it?" I assumed she was turning to look at the clock. "Wow. It *is* early. I must be tired...or bored."

Damn. Suddenly, I felt that was my fault.

"How was your day?"

"I've been up since five this morning, training with Ty. Then work. Church. Nothing much to speak of."

"So, we're shortening his name now?" I scolded her about my personal trainer, Tyler, I'd contracted for her a few weeks ago, per her request—or expressed interest, Rayna never asked for anything from me.

Rayna shared there were parts of her magnificent body needing perfecting—something I didn't agree with. Her body was sculpted perfectly, made just for me. However, it was my responsibility to give her the world and if that meant a couple of hours with my efficient trainer, it was nothing to expend. Tyler took her on. She was content. End of story.

"Oh, Mr. Jacobs, please. He is not interested in me. He has enough eligible women swooning over him. Besides, I've got it bad for a man who works around the clock...and the world. When I'm training, I'm building my stamina for you," she advised convincingly.

Damn!

I dipped my head backwards before pressing my forehead against a nearby wall. With eyes clenched, I vowed, "I got your video message. I'll be home soon."

"I know... I know you're busy, Azmir," she murmured on an exhale. "I'm not trying to change who you are. I don't expect you to end your career now that we're... Now, that I'm living here."

She didn't know how to label our relationship. Neither did I. I knew what I wanted it to be but didn't want to scare her away. I knew I had to handle Rayna with delicate hands.

"What are you wearing?" I whispered, though I could give a fuck if I could be heard by passing patrons.

She giggled softly. "You know what I'm wearing. I thought you got my message. I'm wearing you...and your favorite panties."

"Cheekies?" I quizzed.

"In black...lace."

Fuck.

I swallowed hard and in despair, murmured on an exasperated breath, "I'll be home sooner than scheduled." I was panicking inwardly. I had to fix this shit. I felt her slipping away. "Let's go away in a week or so. Just me and you." This was something I'd been thinking about since our return from New York. Now felt like the appropriate time to broach the subject.

"I'd like that," she sighed. "Just get here. I want to be wherever you are. Home just isn't the same."

I took her words in. They tortured me as much as pleasured

me. I wasn't used to this type of connection with a woman—*hell*...a person. I had to make this right.

"I'm gonna do better, Brimm. I'm working on it. Be patient with me," I pleaded through clenched teeth, suddenly feeling angry with myself. Attempting a relationship for anyone is difficult but trying to walk a fine line considering my increasingly growing feelings for Rayna made the task that much more daunting.

There was a pause. A long pause. I wasn't surprised by it; verbally expressing herself wasn't Rayna's strong suit.

"I had better go. Hopefully, they're wrapping the meeting up as we speak."

Abruptly, she called out, "Azmir?"

"Yeah," I quickly responded, previously resolved to ending the conversation.

"I love you."

What the hell did she just say?

Another pause, but this one was brief.

She exhaled deeply before saying, "I went to a counseling session with Pastor Edmondson tonight...interesting session." She let a small wry chuckle escape. "Remember your question to me, back in Vegas, about being in love?" I thought a minute, immediately recalling our exchange about how one knows they're in love. She didn't wait for me to answer before she continued, "I know I told you I was in love with you in The Bahamas. And that was true. But now I know I *love* you...not just the way you make me feel, but who you are—your generous heart, your gentleness, your patience, your tenacity, your independence, your mind, even your solitude," she informed, as her voice began to sound strained.

This was all hard for her to share—that I did know. But I'd be damned if my body wasn't reacting to the context of her message. She went on. "I love that you want to be with me...in my brokenness. I love you outside of what you do and can do for me materialistically. I love you for more than what you can make my body do."

She snorted at that, and my dick twitched in response. "I'm in love with you and... *Man, I love you.*" She exhaled long and deep.

I was speechless.

Suddenly, she ended with, "I need you to know this. There's a difference between the two. I'd love you even if this doesn't work out...because who you are is who you are and... I love who you are. The true essence of Azmir Divine Jacobs."

Another pregnant pause.

I was shocked beyond words. Perhaps this counseling shit was working after all. I couldn't believe what my mind was attempting to process. I almost thought I was dreaming...or was deep in another Rayna Brimm fantasy. *Did she just say she loved me and was in love with me?* Rayna was the most frustrating and complex woman I'd ever encountered. I'd had the most challenging days trying to crack the treasure code, desperately trying to decipher her encryption. And in a matter of words—mere seconds, she exposed her treasure. Her heart. Suddenly, all things concerning our future was made clear. There was no need for further delay. I knew she was mine from our first date, but starting today, I would initiate plans to make her mine officially. Heart, body, mind, and fucking soul. She was mine.

"Goodnight," she sounded winded.

A wide smile eclipsed my face. "That just exhausted you?"

"In your infamous word: *Indeed*," I snickered silently, split faced, full on smile. "But it sure is liberating."

Rayna was forthcoming, but I could swear there was something more behind her decrees. I wouldn't ruin the moment to ask what it was. I just wanted to revel in her candor.

"Aye..." I called sternly, trying to command her attention. "I'll be home—soon," I declared.

"Okay," she murmured softly, with emotion behind her word.

After my conversation with Rayna, I immediately called my assistant, Brett.

"Yes, Mr. Jacobs, sir," he answered somnolently.

"Brett, I know it's late, but I need a flight out of here as soon as possible tomorrow. I don't care the expense. Hell—if you must charter a plane, do it. I need to be home in eighteen hours. Understood?"

"Yes, sir. Uploading flight schedules now. I will forward you the arrangements as soon as they're made," Brett, who was as efficient as they come, assured.

"Another thing, I need an appointment with a jeweler when my schedule permits next week, but before Friday. See if *Schwartz...Lorraine* is available."

"Anything in particular, sir? So I can explain the time you'll need," Brett inquired.

I smiled to myself, suddenly caught in a moment of clarity. "Engagement ring. I'm in the market for an engagement ring." I couldn't believe those words had left my mouth. I felt proud.

"*Shit!*—excuse my French. I mean... Congratulations, sir!" Brett bade, unsuccessfully masking his surprise.

"Thanks, Brett." Taking a break from my authoritative role to absorb what this all meant, I smiled to myself. He had every right to be caught off guard. "Lastly, I need a vacation scheduled within the next two weeks. Somewhere where there's lots of a water and privacy...an island. Sharon from *Smith, Katz & Adams Sports Medicine Center* can send you dates of availability for Ms. Brimm, which should be matched against mine. Feel free to initiate the communication for her schedule."

"Yes, sir. How long are you thinking...the duration of this vacation?" he asked.

"Minimally three days, but as long as our schedules can handle. That'll be all, Brett. But eighteen hours—tops. I need to get home," I urged.

"Of course, sir!" he asserted, sounding far more spirited than he did when he answered. That ended our call.

As I returned to the room, Richard exclaimed, "Perfect timing,

Jacobs. We have come to an agreement I think you'll be amenable to."

As Richard ran down the details, I saw one of our Canadian associates squirming in his seat, extremely uncomfortable. I read their expressions and processed Richard's information, synchronically.

"Smile, Gagnon," I pestered. He's the one who'd pissed me the fuck off the most out of the two partners. I was eager to gloat at his dismay. "You're four million dollars richer...and happier, aye!" He rolled his eyes and sucked his teeth, all to my delight. *Goddamn prick.*

After the video conference was done, I turned to Richard. "Rich, I need to get home. The old lady is at her wits' end, and I need to go placate back into her good graces."

"Shit, Jacobs! Am I that much of an ass I haven't had the balls to say the same? We've been going so hard at full speed ahead, I may not have a home to go back to," he chuckled, and I joined him. "All right. Let's take the next few days to rest and re-strategize *Alco, Inc.*" He paused, suddenly hit with a revelatory thought. "Shit, if we fuck them good, we'll have the rest of those bitches licking our asses. But we must be smart! *Simeon & Dundst* are sweeping up the solar wind industry. Those pussies won't know what hit them. Trust me, Jacobs!" he vowed.

Richard's analogies always made me uncomfortable. I mean, really... What man references fucking other men or having them lick his ass?

"Work on those damn analogies and we can get our hustle on," I gently scolded as I grabbed him by the shoulders while we were making our way to exit the room. He laughed heartily. I'd been advising this since I'd known him.

"What time do you plan on leaving tomorrow? Don't forget about our morning conference call. *Gintz, Co.* is antsy," he reminded.

"Oh, that's a done deal. I'll meet you back down here at nine to seal the deal," I confirmed. I stopped in my tracks and looked at my partner, square in the eyes. "You've done me very proud, Rob. Your mentoring and incredible partnership has changed my direction, man."

Rob's eyes lit up in amazement. "Azmir, you've given me a second chance. Seeing you achieve the American dream has inspired me anew. You're not the only one with a heart of gratitude, my brother! We're ebony and ivory!" he beamed infectiously, with the broadest smile canvassed across his face, referring to his Scottish heritage versus my African American lineage.

As we made our way out the conference room door, he patted my shoulder endearingly. It was a good moment.

The next morning, I was awakened by the blaring sounds of my cell. I reached over to the nightstand to check the number. It was Brett. He was very much awake and refreshed compared to the last time we spoke.

"Peace. Peace," I greeted.

"Mr. Jacobs. Your flight leaves today at two fifteen. I had to charter an aircraft, as all other commercial ones were booked or had layovers. Your itinerary has been e-mailed to you. I should be in touch with you soon about the other things you requested. Good morning, sir," Brett greeted, ending our call.

"Thanks, Brett. Please have a bouquet of pink tulips delivered to Ms. Brimm this morning, if possible." He paused a moment, presumably to check her schedule.

"Mr. Jacobs, according to Ms. Brimm's weekly schedule, she's at her practice's conference in San Diego today."

She didn't mention that last night. But, then again, she spoke about far more important things during our conversation.

Hmmmmmm...

"Well then, this changes a lot, doesn't it?" I spoke introspectively. "I need a flight from here to San Diego and a suite at the hotel she's staying at."

"Already looking into flights," Brett informed, as I heard him typing away with great speed. "Looks like that'll be a lot easier than *LAX*. I'll contact you with updated flight information shortly. Bouquet delivered there, sir?" Brett asked.

"Nah." I figured I'd surprise her.

"Good day, sir," Brett bade, ending our call. It was seven nineteen a.m. Time for me to get up and hit the gym. I had to be back downstairs in the conference room by nine a.m.

At ten sixteen p.m. Pacific Standard Time, I sent Rayna a text, asking her what she was up to.

Having drinks with colleagues at a bar call "Wino's" in San Diego. How apt a name! LOL!

Sounded like she'd had a few and was relaxed. I'd just landed and wanted to surprise her. First, I had to find out where she was. *Mission accomplished. She may be there for a while.* My plan was to stop in and have a few drinks with them perhaps.

Don't want to disturb you. Just wanted to finish our convo from this morning. Hit me up when you're done.

I'd chatted with her earlier about the situation with my mother. I was considering Rayna's offer of Yazmine staying at her place in Redondo Beach.

Okay. But we can chat now if you like. Rayna offered.

No. Enjoy. Hit me later.

Indeed. Cute.

About an hour later, I was checked into my suite. Luckily, I was able to do it without running into to Rayna. *Surely, she must be in her room by now.* I sent her another text.

What are you up to? Hope you're not sleep.

A minute later I get a ping. **Hey Mr. Jacobs! Still hanging out at Wino's. I have to bring you here. LOL!**

I didn't respond. Instead, I searched for the location on my *iPhone* and proceeded to the bar. My expectation of seeing Rayna started to build. I knew she'd be beside herself in delight. And my reaction to seeing her after so many days would be equally elated, if not more. I'd been more than looking forward to her lips, her hands. Her warm reception.

As I walked to the front of the building, I looked through the glass for her. It took a minute before I finally located her. She was dressed in all black. Her hair was full of the small, bouncy curls I recognized from last night's video message. She wore red lipstick, and it was dull, yet still sexy I guessed from a day's long wear. She probably hadn't touched it up in hours. She looked delectable in her black *Tom Ford* pumps trimmed in a little gold. I recalled purchasing those for her a few weeks back. Rayna's beauty was striking, per usual. I took my time admiring her ornaments. It came to a screeching halt by the unpleasant sight of Brian Thompson sitting across from her.

I suddenly saw red.

My lady's drinking with a man who clearly wants to fuck her?

I saw a waiter bringing Rayna what seemed to be a glass of water. *How much did she have to drink?* I wondered if that fucking herb was trying to take advantage of her. And what was worse of all was the fact that I wasn't even supposed to be here.

What would happen if I weren't?

I was so fucking heated I could feel steam coming from my ears. I guess my introduction at *Smith, Katz & Adams Sports Medicine Center's* gala a few weeks back wasn't enough. I knew I should have been more forceful with the motherfucker! Why would Rayna be here with him anyway after his fucking seating trickery?

I walked to the door and coolly opened it. Right away, I saw the waiter who'd just brought Rayna her water walking towards me. I asked for the check for their table. He asked for a few minutes to go ring it up. I told him he had two. My gaze never left their table. I watched Rayna fixedly as she talked with Thompson. My eyes burned with venom. Within a minute, the waiter had returned with their check.

Without removing my angry gaze from Rayna, I informed the waiter, "Your tip will be awaiting you at the table," as I walked over to them. I glanced at the three hundred, twenty-nine-dollar bill while still in my stride towards the table. I quickly surmised the tab was initiated by others who'd left before I had gotten there. *But Rayna saw the need to stay with this motherfucker?*

When I was just feet away, Rayna noticed me and was visibly shocked. She was frozen in place as I slammed the bill on the table. Eyeing Thompson dead in the face, I pulled out my wallet, counted out five hundred-dollar bills and placed them on top of the receipted tab.

I then turned to a trembling Rayna who looked as though she'd seen a ghost and ordered, "Back to the *'W'*." It was more of a roar than I fucking intended.

Wincing, she calmly, and with good sense, gathered her things and abandoned the table. I watched as she headed for the door. I don't think I'd ever seen her so *sensibly* anxious.

I then drew my heated gaze back to Thompson, fighting every urge to choke the shit out of his bitch ass. "Esquire, I am a man as you are. And I can appreciate the sight of an attractive dame. But I can also respect another man's territory." My voice was calm and even as I was bending down, in his face, being sure to invade his personal space. "You're on marked property. Stay the fuck away from her. The name on the deed is A.D. Jacobs. Fucking. Ask. About. Me," I ended, not raising my voice, understanding the Triple L's— *lawyers love lawsuits.*

His eyes damn near popped out of his head before he regained his confidence. Suddenly, wearing a sly grin on his face he quirked out, "I didn't realize she was a commodity and had an owner."

Oh, he has a little heart?

Because of his relationship with her practice, once again I thought it best that I behaved.

"If the walls of her pussy could talk...*to you*, they'd say otherwise. I'll be sure to think about that when she's screaming my name tonight during her second orgasm."

I gave him a sardonic grin and walked off, but not before I noticed his punk ass' appalled expression. Bitchass had better been lucky of the circumstances there or else I would have hemmed his ass up before he could say *civil suit*.

Rayna

I rushed back to the hotel on a dash, red of embarrassment. While having drinks with Thompson, Azmir showed up unannounced and abruptly ended our conversation, demanding I return to my hotel room. I wanted to explain it was just conversation after other colleagues had retreated to their rooms. That Thompson and I were simply discussing conduct protocols for my presentation the next day. But that wasn't the truth. The truth was, subconsciously, my acts were of a vindictive nature.

I was still wounded from learning Azmir kissed Dawn Taylor. He'd been away for over a week and paranoia kicked in several times over whether they were together. I found myself logging into his account far too often for an update. And while I didn't find anything substantial, finding out about the kiss had done damage I hadn't initially realized.

Azmir was so upset when I left him at the bar alone with Thompson. So upset, I feared for Brian. I'd learned since training with Tyler how Azmir was a trained boxer, something he never shared, though it made sense considering his jabs in Puerto Vallarta. For this reason, I'd hope Thompson's arrogance didn't flair with Azmir. We were just chatting over drinks, mostly about work.

If Azmir was going to start having a problem with men who were attracted to me, he was in for a world of trouble. Not to mention how hypocritical it would be considering he'd kissed Dawn Taylor *and* the number of women who drooled over him when we're together. It was ridiculous, but I never complained or reacted. No matter what my arguments were, this was bad—*real bad.*

Upon entering the hotel, I was notified by the concierge of a message for me. It was from Azmir, letting me know he was here in the *Extreme Wow* suite and was out looking for me in case I'd missed him. He instructed me to bring my things up. He'd left a key.

I rushed to my room and threw my things together. My heart pounded in my chest with each passing step. I didn't know how I would face Azmir. All I could see were images of his venom at the bar. Minutes later, I was headed up to his suite. There were a gazillion butterflies in my belly as I approached the door.

I entered to find the living area unoccupied. *Wow!* I immediately got the *Wow* effect. This place was spacious and beautiful! The contemporary architecture was out of this world. Every detail of the suite was state of the art...voguish. The vibrant colors from the walls to the furniture to the décor, blended so well and tastefully. *It's nice to see how the elite live.*

I noticed Azmir's suit jacket thrown on the back of the main sofa. *He must be in the back.* I went to what was obviously the master bedroom because there was only one bedroom. Through dim lighting, I could see a shadow of a man, sitting near a window, next to a huge bed, holstered up on a white platform. The bed area was rounded and partially enclosed.

"I'm in here." I recognized Azmir's husky voice, laced with contempt.

I didn't say anything. I just stood there awkwardly, not knowing what to say or do. For crying out loud, he *did* ask me to join him. *Now what?* I was growing angry by the minute. He had some nerve embarrassing me in front of a colleague for no good reason at all. Now, I'm here standing, waiting on the verdict of his mood like a child. He had some explaining to do. Even with my sudden irritation, my fear wouldn't allow me to display my ire. The atmosphere was too charged.

"Take your shirt and skirt off," he demanded.

In the dark? Really?

But I hesitantly did as I was told. I unbuttoned my blouse, unzipped my skirt and off they both went.

"Shoes and stockings," he quietly ordered, and I complied by kicking off my heels and slowly pushing down my hosiery.

There was an expectant pause.

What gives, Jacobs? Are you enjoying the strip tease?

"Panties."

For heaven's sake, what is he thinking? Minutes earlier he was seething and now he's asking me to strip! This was not of his nature. But I did as he asked. I lowered my panties, stepped out of them and they were discarded into the pile of my ensemble. In the deep silence, I heard the trembling sound of my heartbeat. I swallowed nervously.

Why was I so nervous?

Perhaps because deep down inside you wanted to piss him off?

"Come here."

I walked over to him. He was stretched out on a padded window bench with his back against the wall. I could see his silhouette from the lights outside, piercing through the window. As I approached him, he proffered his hand.

"Come."

What is he going to do? I could still sense the hidden rancor in his voice.

"Place your feet on either sides of my hips and stand over me," Azmir instructed with calm in his voice.

What the hell?

He tugged at my hand, urging me to step up. I placed my right foot on the bench, next to his thigh and slowly lifted my left foot up to do the same next to his right thigh. He held my hand to help steady me. Once rested on my feet, I realized I was straddling his face. My heart began racing a new speed as I felt his nose inhaling my sex. At the same time, his hands were caressing the back of my thighs. He used his long and skilled fingers to trace lines up and down, from the bottom of my cheeks to ends of my thighs.

He grabbed my left thigh and placed it on his hard shoulder, giving himself clear access to my valley. His tongue moved cleverly in between my thighs, causing me to rest my upper torso on the wall from the undulating sensations radiating from my core, rushing to every adjacent cell of my body. It was unanticipated instant bliss. I stood there, hovering over him with nothing but my bra on as he went to town tasting me. It was as if he was trying to lick every inch of me. I moaned, almost on a cry as my body trembled. I used my hands to claw the wall facing me. The grip he had on my backside brought all senses to my pelvic area as I tried to balance myself against this wall.

He eventually used his tongue to do that beautiful sensual dance with my swollen pearl. *My goodness.* This man loved tasting me. For a brief moment during my time in ecstasy, I wondered was this something he bestowed on all his lovers. *He is so good at it.* It must have come with lots of experience. I immediately tossed out that unfavorable theory. He was *just* good at it—period.

His tongue was swift and lips agile. And… And when he got to the point of his tongue rapidly sparring with my pearl, my body jerked uncontrollably when my climax was imminent.

"*Ooh!*" I cried out in undeniable pleasure and...fear. Fear from his disposition. There was something eerily diverse about his execution tonight.

Not even seconds later, at the apex of my orgasm, he hastily grabbed me by the waist, letting me down on the floor in front of him, leaving me abruptly bereft. I climaxed midair and continued there on the floor, *right before him*. My body shivered and knees buckled. He sat there...still and watched intently.

Did he not know I was coming? He wouldn't do that intentionally—would he?

When I was able to gather my bearings after it was over, Azmir jolted up, ushering my body over to the bed. Placing my hands on the mattress, he bent me over, and I could tell he was planning to take me from behind. *Well, good! He can make up for his oversight of my orgasm.* The next thing I felt was the wide crown of his penis ramming into me.

Shuddering, I gripped the comforter underneath my shaky palms. *What the hell?*

Azmir, the most gentle and sharing lover I'd ever known, was rough handling me.

WHAM! Another thrust.

"Arrgh!" I yelped in pain.

WHAM! Another forceful propel.

"Uuuuh!" I whimpered as my feeble body trembled.

I couldn't believe the force of his plunges. They were punishing. *This was anger.* He'd never done this type of rough housing before.

Then, he'd never seen you out with another man since you'd been living together either.

How could I bring him back from this spiteful state?

I started to panic. I didn't like this side of Azmir Jacobs.

WHAM!

"Ahhhhh!" In fright, I grew desperate. "Azmir, I'm sorry!"

Sweat had begun to form on my forehead, underneath my

arms—all over my body. I didn't know how much of it I could endure. Tears began forming in the crevices of my sockets. The pain had emitted to my heart. Azmir was relentless.

Oddly enough, each lunge became less uncomfortable. The discomfiture lessened by each pound and therefore became more pleasurable, but his intent was to punish me, and the sentiment could not be ignored. I could feel him lift his right leg onto the bed to gain him more access into me. He unhooked my bra, causing my breasts to be released and clap. He knew what he was doing. My howls of pain turned into bellows of pleasure. He reached for my head and clasped my scalp in a gripping massage. My head swung back, giving into his masterful grasp.

"Oooooooh!" I belted out. I felt my sex lubricating even more.

Something changed. I felt it in his thrusts. Azmir rolled his hips, thrusting at a new angle and suddenly, I felt the rim of his penis rub against a new wall deep inside of me, a very delicate spot he'd homed in on. The purpose of his impels shifted. As he steadied his rhythm, I joined in with him.

"Oh, Azmir!" I screamed because he felt so good going in and out. My body started to appreciate the punishment at the hands of its newly acquired nemesis.

Abruptly, Azmir bolted out a cry, and I immediately knew he was ejaculating, shooting hot semen against my swollen walls. Though arousing, it wasn't something I'd been used to with him, as he always insisted on me coming first. All of a sudden, my canal tensed as I increased my flexes onto his cock.

I'm so close.

It's here.

I exploded.

"*Oooooh!*" I cried, as the warming sensation overtook me, and my belly detonated with heaps of pleasure my delicate frame couldn't contain.

In the blink of a second, Azmir pulled out of me, once again forcing me to orgasm alone. I stood there, helplessly shivering and erratically breathing. I tried to catch my heart beating at an alarming rate, my head spinning uncontrollably, and my limbs trembling fitfully. My brain was filled with delirium as I fought for my lucidity. *What in the hell just happened?* I gathered the sheets of the bed tightly, clasping them in my hands to help steady me as I let out purrs of pleasure and of wild abandon.

Azmir stood behind me stoically. From beneath my armpit, where I took refuge during the crux of my haze, I could see his lower torso. His long columnar legs were bare, his pants and boxers were pooled around his ankles and his heavy throbbing penis dripped deliciously at the head. I felt him closely observing me. Once I was done shuddering, he walked off into the bathroom. Next, I heard the shower run.

I slowly stood to gather myself, and I could feel his viscid liquids racing down my inner thighs, taking with it the flow my dignity. At a snail's pace, I grabbed my underwear to catch his essence, trying to prevent the juices from hitting the floor. I felt…used. But that quickly, I'd figured out his game. His intent was to level me and he did. I felt humiliated. I wanted to drop to my knees and cry. I just declared my love for this man less than twenty-four hours ago and he goes sexually primeval on me. All because of Thompson.

I'm not interested in Thompson! I'm too busy trying to explore love with you! screamed in my head.

I had to admit, to some extent I deserved it. I knew Azmir must have felt some level of anxiety seeing me with Thompson considering his ordeal with Tara cheating on him with the aspiring rapper. *But what nerve did he have considering he'd just betrayed me with Dawn?* It seemed like a vicious web of trickery—malicious deeds. This wasn't love.

There I stood, naked, feeling awkward. My dignity was left seated at the *Wino Bar*. I choked back on the tears begging for a release, not wanting to give Azmir the satisfaction of seeing me broken. Racing through the events of the evening and processing my recent sex with Azmir, I suddenly felt exhaustion hovering over me. I needed rest or I'd crack.

The shower stopped running. *Good. My turn.*

As I dried off from the soothing shower, I spied Azmir's tank T-shirt on the floor.

Hmmmmm... I'd much rather sleep in this than my own pjs.

As cold as he'd been to me, I still craved every piece of him, even his scent all over me as I struggled to understand the obscurity we were stuck in. I picked it up and gathered it into my face, inhaling the A.D. Jacobs scent. Man, I could do this all day. His T-shirts at home weren't worn. They didn't have his body oils mixed in. I could never get used to his scent.

Why...oh, why are we fighting? Azmir, I just want to be a part of your world. But you betrayed me.

Then I wondered how long this awkwardness would last. There was only one way to find out: take it one moment at a time. I saw no other alternative.

Manage the moment.

Suddenly, sleep was warranted. I slipped on his T-shirt and headed for the bed. He was already in there, burrowed underneath the covers. I nervously pulled back the blanket on my side; I didn't want to disturb him. He pulled back all the remaining sheets, inviting me in bed.

Ah! He's not as upset.

But what he did was wrong!

Ugh! I just want to forget about this Dawn Taylor/Brian Thompson nightmare!

I lay down, finding my comfort in the oversized bed. As I did, Azmir scooted closer to me and found his contentment underneath me. I felt a warm sensation run through me. And not of a libidinous nature either. I felt peace radiating from him. He was at peace and yet I was embattled. Though I was beyond pissed with his actions and still unsettled about his indiscretions, I decided it was a good note to end a long day on.

"Good-night, Ms. Brimm," Azmir whispered.

He kissed my head and nuzzled against the back of my neck, as he always did. It drove me wild. His voice was calm and even. *What just happened earlier?* echoed in my head. I couldn't leave well enough alone. I had to know.

"Azmir, I had two orgasms tonight—*alone*," I informed with my eyes wide awake, awaiting a response.

"I know," he mumbled, softly breathing into my neck.

I tried to hold on to my defensive thoughts and not get swept away by the current zinging through me from the sweet sound and tantalizing feeling of his breath hitting my body—after all, I *could* go another round.

He had admitted it was done on purpose. My heart pouted.

"Why did you do that?" I had to know.

He went tense behind me. There was a tentative pause, and I could hear my heart stammer over the silence.

"I don't know how else to show you what my life would be like if you stepped out on me. It would appear as perfect art on canvas, building up to the best picture any man could create. But my life would be worthless if I had your shell and not your heart and soul. So, I thought the best analogy would be having an orgasm, but with no one to share it." I found myself wrinkling my forehead, desperately trying to find his perspective as he continued. "For some, they'd be happy with the thrill alone. Others, like me, want to share in the experience with that special person...only *one* person." After a brief pause, he whispered, "Good-night, baby. You have another long day tomorrow."

I didn't utter another word. He'd given me a lot to think about. Although sleeping with another man wasn't on my horizon, him fearing it resonated with me. But the hypocrisy in his actions with Dawn went unmentioned. I was so confused. But I could wrestle mentally or emotionally no more. I drifted off to sleep.

The next morning, I awakened to the sunlight blaring through my lids. I turned over and opened my eyes. It took a few seconds for me to recall where I was. I looked at the clock on the nightstand and saw it was eight minutes after seven. Then Azmir's arrival popped into my head and eagerly I searched the bed for him. To my surprise, he was sitting up against the headboard with his laptop, looking down at me, wearing a pleasant smile. I relaxed, releasing the strains of my tendons.

As I rubbed my eyes he murmured, "Good morning, love," flashing his million-dollar smile.

I have to ask if he's gotten any orthodontia done. His alignment was picture perfect. My eyes roved over him, and I couldn't help but take notice of his bare, chiseled upper body.

"Morning," I muttered, trying to shake my sleepiness.

"You're beautiful even first thing in the morning," Azmir charmed.

Remnants of the previous night started to flood my mind. *This is certainly a different man.*

"Are you still mad at me?" I asked candidly.

"I'm still upset—but not with you," he warmed as he rested his laptop on the nightstand.

He then reached down to cup my face and kissed me hungrily. His mouth was cool and minty. *Damn him for freshening up but catching me off guard this morning!* In all honesty, I didn't care. I was so enthralled by this man, nothing mattered—even if he went caveman on me last night. He went out of his way to see me. He wanted me and I, him. His touch was soft and apologetic. What a way to wake up.

He released me, and to my discontentment.

"I was wrong. I overreacted," he poured out while searching my eyes.

I exhaled, grateful for his concession. "Azmir, I'm not prepared to leave you. I meant what I said the other night. I love you," I placated. I wanted him to believe me.

Heck, I *needed* him to believe me.

I still hadn't dealt with the Dawn situation. Or had I? I hadn't come to a resolve yet and didn't know how I would. I just knew how revived I felt when I was with this man. How enlivened I became each time his eyes landed on me. Making a call would be deciding between agreeing to his mediocre commitment to me and losing him totally. I didn't want to lose. But could I live with myself by allowing Azmir to not fully commit to me? This would be me perpetuating my mother's fatal mistakes, which broke our family. I swore I'd never let a man love me arbitrarily. It was all or nothing. Until Azmir, I had no desires for a commitment. Clearly, this had changed, and my world will never be the same no matter what decision I made.

He gazed deeply into my eyes—long and seemingly by design. "I need you, Rayna, more than you'll ever know."

He reached down once again to kiss me tenderly. I raised my hand to hold his face. He felt so good. His hand went for my bare backside. From my movements while sleeping, the T-shirt rose to my abdomen. He pulled up at my thigh, prompting me to rise and I did as we were still enraptured in a passionate kiss. Azmir's lips were soft, and his tongue was hungry. He situated me into a straddling position and trailed soft kisses from my mouth to my chest. My pelvis lunged at him.

"I owe you," he murmured as he continued planting delicious kisses on my torso. "I know this is your favorite position. Now let me see you ride," Azmir growled lasciviously when his busy mouth arrived at my ear.

It was exactly what I needed. I began instinctively grinding into his lap. My upper body was glued to his as my head reclined in the air. I was ready. He pulled down the straps of my T-shirt—his T-shirt and I freed my arms from the sides as he pushed it down to my belly. I'm now virtually naked, body flowing freely. The only thing missing was him inside of me, buried to the hilt.

I anxiously pushed up to grab his boxers. I lifted my body to give him room to pull them down, unleashing his throbbing erection. After kicking them off, he guided my body onto him, nice and slowly. *I don't want slow, Jacobs! I want you—all of you, alive in me now!* I was still achy from his primal behavior the night before, but more imminent was my need for him now.

He felt delicious, fitting himself in me. I moaned like a mad woman. He went for both of my cheeks and massaged them up and down. Azmir skillfully buried his face in my breasts, sucking my nipples until they were fully extended. He bit down on one of them, gently, driving me wild. The currents flashed through my body, and I was caught up that quickly.

Azmir must have felt it because he heeded, "Slow to gain, Brimm," through clenched teeth.

I couldn't help it. "Azmir...Oh...You...Feel...So...Good," I protested as I grinded up and down and up and down.

"All for you, Ms. Brimm," he declared, fighting to maintain composure. "All because I need you."

That was it. I couldn't hold back any longer. It was like he said those magic words to unlock the treasure chest. I exploded all around him. I used his broad and muscular shoulders to anchor myself, and I could see the salacious grin he wore as he watched me climax. He eventually pulled me to his chest as he forcefully flexed his hips into me, extending my orgasmic float.

It was the perfect erotic image—my abdomen pinned to his chest, my head gradually reclined away from him, pushing my breasts in his face. Azmir grinded hard and purposefully. My arms dangled behind me onto the bed as Azmir freely used my body to find his release. Seconds later, he sang my name as he detonated deep inside of me.

I lay in Azmir's arms, exhausted, satiated and out of breath. Our breathing eventually stabilized, though I could lay there forever. I forgot where I was and the nature of my visit until Azmir reminded me.

"We have to get up. You have a long day ahead."

"*Mmmmmm...*" I purred, indicating my desire to stay put.

"Come on, Brimm. You have another presentation today."

"Crap! I do!" I yelped like an alarm had gone off in my head. I sat up on his lap. "What time is it?" I asked, darting my attention to the clock. It read seven forty-one. "Crap! I'm missing breakfast. I guess I'll just have to starve."

I wasn't in the mood to rush through a meal. Most importantly, I wasn't ready to leave Azmir.

"Let's order room service then get you into the shower. You can still be on time for your presentation."

Huhn?

"How did you know I had a presentation?"

This was his second time mentioning it. I hadn't even told him about this conference. I was sure Sharon forwarded my schedule this week to his assistant per usual, but it didn't indicate me facilitating, did it?

"It's my job to know everything about you," he whispered with a sly, yet sexy smirk—his panty-snatching smirk. "Now come on. Up!" he ordered.

CHAPTER 4

Rayna

We rode north on Interstate 5, on our way back to the marina after the conference in San Diego. After stopping for lunch on Newport Beach, we returned to the car to finish the commute, exchanging no words. I accepted the companionable silence and simply appreciated the breeze blowing forcefully through the cracked windows and the majestic oceanside view.

It was seldom I got the privilege of being driven, which is why I loved when Azmir was at the wheel. It reminded me of traditional normal, where the man leads and the woman sits back and relaxes, trusting his navigation—literally and figuratively. It gave me time to think.

As much as I tried, I could come up with no plan for how I would confront Azmir about his kiss with Dawn. I struggled with the fear of him feeling he didn't owe me an explanation because although he'd invited me to live with him, he didn't promise anything beyond that.

When we arrived at the apartment, we ran into Manny, one of the building's concierges, who was as eager as ever to see Azmir.

They spoke vaguely when Azmir asked him about a delivery. Whatever it meant, Manny assured it was received and properly handled. Azmir also asked Manny to arrange for Azna to be picked up from the kennel and brought home, much to my relief. I'd missed my little fur ball. Hearing Azmir bark out orders in his CEO mien reminded me of the lifestyle I'd adapted since agreeing to live with him. Everything was at his fingertips, hugely convenient and at a moment's call. This could possibly be another thing I'd be walking away from.

As soon as we stepped into the apartment, there in the foyer was a concierge luggage cart with a black suit bag hanging from it with an Italian boutique's name displayed on it. On the floor of the cart was a shopping bag with shoes. I quickly turned to look at Azmir who didn't seem as surprised as I was at all.

"It's for you...for tonight. We're going out."

"Out where?" I was confused.

"On a date."

"Oh."

"You should be ready by six thirty. I have some calls to make. Do what you must to get prepared." He walked off toward his office. He continued, "I have to go get a cut in a couple of hours so, I'll have to go back out."

I watched his captivating gait into his office. It was never dull watching Azmir's stride. He was so graceful and confident in his movements. Just so sexy! When the show was over, I turned to the cart and dubiously unzipped the suit bag to find a stunning *Hervé Léger* gold, glimmer, strapless dress. It was a form fitting mini. My mouth dropped at the said two thousand-eight-hundred-dollar price tag... *Azmir didn't have the opportunity to discard,* something he usually did. The urge to tell Azmir how ridiculously over the top this was surged through my veins, but I couldn't ignore the thoughtfulness in his gesture.

This was premeditated. In the bag below were black leather *Christian Louboutin Daffodile* one hundred-sixty-millimeter pumps and jewelry accessories. Suddenly, I felt those overwhelming anxious sensations.

Were these guilt gifts? Did Azmir sleep with Dawn?

Bile ascended from my belly, and I swallowed hard to keep it down. I tried so hard not to dwell on that depressing theory. I employed everything within me to adapt a sanguine disposition for the sake of the evening. I would just have to ride this out until the appropriate time to confront Azmir with what I knew.

Later in the evening, we attended a Trey Songz concert. It was the first leg of his international tour for his latest album, the hottest ticket in town. I'd heard advertisements for contests to win tickets for it. In true A.D. Jacobs' fashion, we had impeccable seats. I could swear I was hit with Trey's sweat from where we stood.

The show was great from start to finish. It really helped me escape my internal stressors, even if only temporarily. Trey sang a few of my favorite hits of his including *I Invented Sex*. I gave Azmir as licentious of a lap dance I could considering we were in public. I could tell he enjoyed me by the way his heavy gaze swayed between my eyes to my backside gyrating meticulously in his lap. He tried his best to keep his hands limited to my hips as I enjoyed teasing him. It was weird to have security with us, though I knew the game, so I dared not complain. I simply acted as though they were not there, just as Azmir did.

After the show, we caught dinner at a small, high end restaurant allowing us intimacy. Azmir talked a lot about his work, something I relished. He mentioned insane stories from when he stayed with Mark and Eric for a few days last week—*the same timeframe he'd kissed Dawn Taylor*. The guys agreed on a triple date event in the near future. I had hoped it was possible.

Dinner was delightful and the drinks complimented the meal. It was hard to ignore Azmir's phone going off. He didn't take a single call, just kept sending them to voicemail. As much as I wanted to believe he was hiding something from me, it was difficult to considering how heavily engaged he was in our conversations. He must have told me how beautiful I was at least a dozen times tonight. It melted my core—literally.

We didn't stay for long after finishing our meal. We were whisked off to a private after party for the tour, which was already in full swing in West Hollywood. It was at an upscale lounge and the line to get in was fairly long. Marcus, our security, jumped out to talk to the guards at door before returning to the car and opening the door for Azmir and me to exit. Ray pulled off as we jumped the line to get inside.

The place was packed, but the atmosphere was relaxed. There were so many celebrities in there and per usual, they were very much acquainted with Mr. Jacobs. He was always equanimous in his interactions with them. Azmir was never pressed to speak to anyone or kissed up. In contrast, he returned greetings and did very little talking, but mostly nodded and smiled. Occasionally he'd introduce me to one, but for the most part he kept conversations brief, promising to chat at another time.

Who was this Azmir Jacobs?

Not even twenty minutes into our arrival did I notice Lady Spin and Britni. They sat in a lounge across the room at a comfortable distance. I saw them whisper and point in our direction and wondered what they could possibly have to say. Suddenly, I felt Azmir's lips on my ear whispering, "I see your friend over there. You should go say hello," sardonically.

I scoffed. "She's with *your* friend. You first." He flashed his panty-snatching smirk and my insides clenched. When we were seated with our drinks I asked, "Do you know Trey Songz?" trying to get a better understanding of him and who he was in the industry.

"We've met in circles...been in the same places...know a few of the same people, but not personally. I don't think he's here. He's probably at a public after party."

"Public?"

"Yeah...this one is private, more for industry heads who want to mingle without the hoopla and fanfare. It's like the listening party, but after the release of the album, for those who may not have attended. He'll come in and greet folks, he may even perform a little. Do you want to meet him," he offered, his face completely deadpan.

"Oh, no. I'm a fan of his music, but not the groupie type." A rush of relief washed over Azmir's face. It was too overt. "Don't get me wrong, if he was like a Charlie Wilson, or a Will Downing or even a Keith Sweat I'd be bum-rushing his security," I joked.

Azmir wrinkled his nose. "Keith Sweat? How could you even place him in the same sentence as Charlie and Will?" He laughed and although it was at my expense, I enjoyed his light-heartedness.

"Are you kidding me? Keith Sweat could beg the sweat off my back effortlessly." Since I was a kid, I'd crushed on Mr. Sweat. He was so hot to me.

"I'll make sure to slip his music in the shuffle the next time I have your ass. If he can make your back sweat, I'll lick it off." Azmir gave a soft grimace. "No Keith Sweat concert in your future, kid." I couldn't read if he was speaking in jest or was serious with his declarations.

Before I could ask, I heard, "Divine, surprised to see you here." I looked up to find Spin standing before me.

"Lady Spin, long time no see. How are you?" Azmir was his usual cool and polite self.

"I'm good. I worked the concert. We aired live." Her brows furrowed suddenly. "You don't do concerts anymore," she was goading him for answers.

"I've been working hard lately…wanted a romantic evening and thought Trey could help set the mood," Azmir shared as he ran his thumb across the start of my spine, causing me to shiver. I'd hope not so conspicuously. I smiled—probably giggled in my tipsy state. That made Spin's spiteful gape shoot over to me.

"Nice to see you again, Spin." I attempted to be civil.

"Hi...?" She pretended to have forgotten my name. I knew in this moment it wasn't going to be a pleasant run in.

"Rayna," Azmir retorted.

"Brimm. Surely you couldn't forget that. You *are* cousins with an old *associate* of mine, and I'm *friends* with an *old* associate of *yours*," with a bright smile I added to the sting.

She silently gasped. I don't think she was expecting Azmir's protectiveness or me to clap back at her.

I've read your texts to him, bitch!

Spin kept her gaze on Azmir. "I'll be seeing you around, Divine. Your assistant contacted me about the fair your rec center is planning in the LBC?" Azmir nodded. *What fair?* Azmir had never mentioned a fair. "I'll make room in my schedule to be there," she forced a sinister smile.

"Good to know. I appreciate that," Azmir nodded again. Not having much left to say, she turned to walk off, but not before rolling her eyes at me.

"Aye, Spin," I called out to her. She stopped and turned to me.

"I look forward to seeing you at the fair. Thanks for helping out. We appreciate it," I took my final jab. She huffed, rolled her eyes again, and turned on her heel.

"You need to be nice, Ms. Brimm," Azmir teased when Lady Spin was out of earshot.

"I am so sick of *your* people picking on me. What is it? I mean— Spin, I get. But Syn I don't."

Azmir hissed, "Syn is a fucking nut case. I was ready to choke her little ass over the table in Vegas. I can only imagine what Kid did when he dealt with her. She is getting bolder with her crassness and her drinking contributes to it all."

"Yeah, Kim mentioned her drinking," I murmured contemplatively, suddenly feeling sorry for Syn. "I didn't know it was that bad." I still didn't get why I was a target but decided to stick with my original plan of simply tolerating her ghetto antics. It's not like I was unfamiliar with her kind.

"Don't pay her any mind. She's not worth your time." His words were comforting even if they weren't necessary for Syn. She really was insignificant in my book.

"I need to go relieve myself," I shared to excuse myself.

"I'll go with you." Azmir sat up in his seat.

"No, Mr. Jacobs, I'll be fine. I've been drinking all evening and will probably have to go several times before we leave. You can't come with me every time." Disappointment settled on his face. "Unless...you wanna explore your exhibitionist side." I raised my eyebrows.

A bashful smile formed on his perfectly sculpted lips. I watched as he made the decision to stay put. He sat back on the sofa.

When I came out of the stall, I headed to the sinks and washed my hands. I looked up in the mirror to check my makeup and noticed the red on my lips had dulled before I came upon gaping eyes. They belonged to Tara. *What the?* She was the last person I was expecting to run into. She looked like a deer caught in headlights.

I casually pulled out my lipstick to freshen up my lips, the way Azmir preferred. Tara was eventually able to move up to the sink and wash her hands. I caught her giving me a once over on her way. She appeared saddened by my presence. The texts she'd sent Azmir came to mind and when I matched it against her current disposition, my heart softened to her. No matter my impression of her, I couldn't help but pity her situation. Yeah, she did her dirt and lost Azmir in the process, but she was now a single parent and, oddly, that was something I could sympathize with.

"Hello, Tara."

Her eyes jumped in surprise at my civility. She took a second or two to plan her response.

With furrowed brows, she tentatively asked, "Rayna, right?"

Why do these chicks think I would believe for one second, they didn't know my name? Heck, they likely knew my occupation!

"Yes, Rayna. And I think you knew that." I tried to quiet my sigh. "Listen, we can at least be cordial. There's no need to be otherwise. Azmir told me you had the baby. Congratulations." I gave her a warm smile in an attempt to lower her guards.

It didn't have the immediate warming effect I was going for, but she did manage, "Thank you." It was a little stiff, but I applauded her efforts.

"You look really good," I tried to end our awkward exchange on a good note. It was sincere. She wore a mini black fitted long-sleeved dress. Boa-like feathers ran from the neck and down both sleeves. She accessorized with a gold plated belt with a chain hanging from the side and the same *Daffodile Red Bottom* pumps I had on.

After looking me up and down she offered, "Great minds."

I knew that would be the extent of her compliments and really didn't have much more to say, so I gave her a final gracious nod and walked out.

On my way out, I found Azmir in the hall, presumably waiting for me. *Could he not have given me a minute?* I could see he was talking to a woman, but her back was towards me. After a few more treads forward, the back of the woman's hair grew familiar. *Oh, no!* It was Dawn Taylor.

Does this chick stalk him? Why is she always popping up? We were outside of the main room of the lounge and the music was muffled, making words audible without screaming over the music. People were moving about the area, either exiting out of the building or going into the main lounge area. I was at an angle where Azmir couldn't see me, and neither could Dawn with her back to me.

Eventually, I was close enough to hear her say, "I didn't see you at the concert. Did you make it? I reserved a seat for you." My body froze in place.

Azmir replied, "I was there. I had seats on hold already."

"Oh, I'd been trying to reach out to you to make sure you knew. I'm glad you at least made it to the after party. I have a few people I want you to meet. I was hoping we could do that and then go grab a drink and chat a bit. I haven't really heard from you since Connecticut," Dawn paused, awaiting lead from Azmir. When she didn't get any, she continued, "We should really sort that situation out."

Her tone made my skin crawl. She was still pursuing him. *Were those her calls he was ignoring during dinner?* I didn't know what to do.

"Dawn, I told you then it never happened. There's nothing to discuss. It's never been my practice to shit where I eat. Let's just keep it professional." Azmir *weakly* tried warding her off.

"I understand but..." She sounded frustrated by her thoughts. "Azmir, I can't... I know I've been a bit aggressive and it's not something I do with men, but with you it...it's like the more I see you the more I want to be around you. I thought at first it was simple attraction, but the more I get to know you and the more I learn about you...your reputation, it's like..." Her voice trailed off. She was at an emotional impasse. "I don't want to compromise business, but if I had a choice between the two—"

Azmir cut her off. "Dawn, I'm not here alone."

"Who are you with?" Without giving him a moment to respond, she asked, "Rayna?" Dawn sounded as if she desperately wanted him to say no.

"Yes. Dawn, perhaps if another time, but right now..." It was Azmir's turn to be at a loss for words.

"Is it serious?" she asked forlorn. "I mean, tell me what I'm up against here." *Oh, my! She IS forceful!*

"Roommate type of serious." Azmir's response was like a jab in the stomach. I could no longer breathe from the blow. There was a pause as Dawn decoded his encrypted words.

"Are you two exclusive?" She was desperately grasping at straws of hope.

"I have to go. I need to find her." Azmir turned to leave.

I did an about face myself and headed back into the ladies' room and into a stall to try to catch my breath and fight the harboring tears. After some time, I heard the door open and some chatter catching my attention.

"Are you okay? What's the matter?" I didn't hear a response.

"Don't cry, baby. What the hell is wrong? Was it something he said? Oh, no! You were so excited to see him tonight. No. No. Don't cry," came from the same voice.

I figured the other party was too distraught to speak. It seemed as though I wasn't the only one with drama going on here. At least this person had a shoulder to cry on. That led my thoughts to my loss of Michelle.

That's it. I need to get out of here before I breakdown publicly.

I flew out of the stall and over to the sink to observe my makeup once again before washing my hands. When I turned the corner for the door out of the bathroom, I saw the two *weeping women* I'd heard from the stall. It was Dawn and another woman I didn't know. When Dawn laid eyes on me it was as if she'd seen a ghost. I was a bit shell-shocked myself. Her eyes were red, and her mascara ran down her cheeks. She was panting out of breath and her red stained lips were parted to assist with her breathing.

Without speaking words, our eyes communicated *well*. Mine told her I hated her for barking up my tree that was Azmir. Her eyes told me she resented me for being in the way. The other woman tried to follow our scowls, confused by it all. I walked out of the bathroom with no words for her.

Flustered from my run-ins of the night, I tried to remember which door I'd originally come out of. Nothing looked familiar. The music had stopped, and I heard someone with a silken masculine voice speak over the microphone system. I figured it was time for the performance and had hoped they didn't start locking doors for security reasons. There were several entrances leading into the main room. I had to try one to begin the hunt. I chose my door without hesitation. When I pulled it open and started in, I immediately noticed I was at the top of the room and had entered into the door closest to the stage.

Crap!

I saw women with their hands raised eagerly and hopping on their toes like toddlers.

What in the...

In a nanosecond, all eyes flew to me, causing me to still in my tracks.

The sleek voice flowed throughout the room again and it crooned, "*Daaaamn*, baby! I remember you from the concert," with a strong southern twang. "Look it here!" it continued. I followed it to discover it was none other than Trey Songz himself...and he was looking in my direction. I instinctively turned to see who he was speaking to then heard him say, "Nah, baby. You in the gold. Is that gold?" he asked. Straining his eyes, he used one hand to block the bright stage lights, glaring in his face.

A brolic figure standing next to the door I'd just come through called out to me. "Miss, he's talking to you." My heart sped in my chest. I looked back up to the stage and pointed to myself.

"Yeah, baby, you. What's yo' name?" he smiled, very much aware of his charisma. His vanity was built into the slant of his eyes.

With hesitance I sputtered, "Rayna."

"Hold up. Let me come down there to get a better look." The crowd cheered and laughed, apparently enjoying the show. My mouth went dry. I was extremely embarrassed and wanted to crawl into a dark hole, but I couldn't. I had too many reasons not to fold—namely three, and they were all females, vying for Azmir's affection. *Never let them see you sweat!*

Trey made his way down and as he approached me, I fought harder to maintain my cool. "*Daaaaaaaaamn!*" he exclaimed, walking just a few feet away. When he got up so close, I could smell his cologne, I felt my legs chilling from nervousness. "You even better looking up close. What you say yo' name is?" he asked as he slipped his arm around my shoulder.

He was quite the performer, and his audience clearly loved it by their outbursts and chants. I chuckled ruefully, unfazed by his undeniable charm.

"Rayna," I repeated.

"Oh, Rayna. That's a sexy name for a sexy woman, baby." He batted his long eyelashes.

I realized he was a lot taller than I gave him previously. I smiled. *Trey, you don't want it with Rayna,* I flirted in my mind.

"Did you come alone? Please, god, say you came with ya' girls!"

The room was filled with laughter. Even I had to chuckle at that one. He was good at this. I shook my head and gave a pouty lip to buffer the blow. I wasn't alone *although at least three women in the room wish I was.*

"Damn," he droned smoothly and gave a deep exhale. My cheeks flushed. "Okay, gorgeous. Just before you burst through those doors and into my dreams—*I mean this room.*" Another round of laughs from the room. He laughed, too. "I was asking someone to pick an old school Trey Songz hit we can kick the show off with. I want to show a little evolution, you know what I mean, baby?" I couldn't get past his accent; it really didn't come across in his music.

I played along with his flirtatious gaze piercing into my eyes and gave it right back to him. "*Hmmmmm...*" Instantly, my contemplative thoughts turned vindictive. "*Can't Help But Wait,*" I offered, suggestively.

His head jolted and he flared the seductive smile that made all the girls go crazy. "Okay, that's a good one." He looked over his shoulder at one of his band members, giving a nod to cue the music. "Damn, I was wishing you'd say something like *Does He Do It*...or *Invented Sex!*" A light chortle slipped, pushing air through my nose. He was a coquettish man. "Alright. I'll let you get back to your date." For my participation, he awarded me a wet kiss on the cheek and then hit the stage to start the song.

I found my way back to Azmir who was sitting evenly with a pokerfaced expression. I sat next to him and right away was hit with all the emotions I'd previously been plagued with before my run in with Trey. I had to confront this Dawn Taylor issue and right away. She wasn't going away easily, and Azmir didn't seem to be pushing her either. I knew we couldn't continue like this. It was making me insecure and paranoid.

"Interesting choice of song," Azmir finally spoke. I didn't know what that meant but decided carefully on my response.

"Not really," I shrugged. "Now, '*roommate*'...that's an interesting choice of words. Isn't that how you termed our relationship to Dawn Taylor?" My tone was even as I trained my eyes to his.

Azmir's eyes narrowed, but he didn't speak. And wisely.

Turning my eyes from him, back toward the stage, I hissed, "Yeah. Let's go." And without giving eye contact, I stood and headed to the door at a non-alarming, but purposeful speed. I knew Azmir and Marcus were awkwardly on my heels.

While we were outside waiting for Ray to pull up, Azmir turned to me and informed in his CEO mien, "I'm not sure what you thought you heard in there, but I can assure you it wasn't anything to be upset about."

I shot him a look of death. Azmir had the inimitable and exquisite ability to bring calm to an alarming situation by calling on his authoritative demeanor. It could be effective in the severest of situations. But I wouldn't give his controlled nature any room. There was too much to unload in public, and I didn't want to create a scene, so I didn't respond.

Our entire trip to the marina was silent just like our trip back from San Diego earlier. He all but slammed the door to the apartment as we entered and roared, "What's the problem?"

I turned, alarmed by his audacity, and muttered, "I can't do this anymore."

"Do what anymore? What did I miss?"

"A whole hell of a lot. Tonight was filled with face-offs with your ex-girlfriends, ex-lovers, and wanna-be lovers. It's all too much for just a *roommate*!" I yelled, feeling my rage rising.

With furrowed brows he asked, "Ex-girlfriends? What are you talking about?"

"Tara was there. Did you not see her?"

"No, I didn't," he muttered broodingly.

I squinted my eyes, studying his telling body language. "You don't sound convincing to me, Azmir."

He cut me an eye, telling me he didn't appreciate my insinuation of him lying. "I saw her *boyfriend* there, so it comes to no surprise." His voice was terrifyingly crisp. But I refused to back down.

"Azmir, why did you ask me to move in? What are we doing here? Why am I even here?" my voice cracked.

"Because I want you here, with me. I want you to share in my...!"

"Again, at a loss for words, just like you were earlier with Dawn," I shot at him, with acerbity. "Have you fucked her yet?"

His eyes shot up at my brashness. He knew I'd sworn off profanity weeks ago. But I was so angry and confused, I'd lost self-control. It was as though all those deprecating feelings I'd experienced when I learned of his betrayal had suddenly resurfaced.

He cocked his head to the side, "Yet? When and why would that be a possibility?" he murmured in disbelief.

"Don't stand here and undermine my intelligence, Azmir! At least acknowledge my dignity. I saw the damn texts from her. *You kissed her!*" My tone was stridulous.

I barked to the point of straining my vocal cords, I had hit a brick wall. My emotions were on high, and it was clearly evident to me at this point. Azmir's eyes widened again in surprise.

"How did you read my text mess—" his voice dropped when the password revelation hit him.

Azmir backed into the wall, there in his foyer, and let his knees give way as he dropped to the floor. He rubbed his face and exhaled in exasperation.

Yeah, even the powerful and fearless mogul is brought to his knees when confronted with the truth!

My stomach jumped to my throat, not letting my words escape, but I fought to push them out. "You betrayed me. I asked you in there..." I pointed in the direction of the master suite. "...the night I moved in, not to hurt me and you did. You kissed *and* did God knows what with her. You were in clear violation!" My words were mumbled from my fierce, yet unsuccessful efforts to suppress my tears. I panted, trying to catch my breath among the pouring tears.

He rose to his feet. "I did not fuck Da—"

I interrupted, "And then you had the nerve to dick slap Brian Thompson, who I have never dreamed of touching. You are such a hypocrite, and I can't believe I told you I loved you! I can't believe I trusted you with my...heart!" Once again, my words were barely audible.

"You haven't trusted me with shit!" Azmir shouted with an unknown emotion glaring in his eyes. Eyes that suddenly didn't peer into me with adoration or desire. I saw frustration. Exasperation. Near brokenness. "You never lower your guards long enough to do it! I didn't know what you felt for me until two days ago when you said you loved me!" Azmir screamed so loud I jumped in my shoes.

His words ripped the air from my lungs. His fury gouged my heart. How could he act as though he had no clue of my feelings for him? We've been together, going full steam ahead ever since Atlantic City—even when we weren't physically together. I felt shattered, completely broken.

"So, you kiss her?"

He won't put this on me.

With his head buried in his hands, he muttered, "It was fucked up and unplanned, but yes. I did." I gasped so deep I felt like my lungs were going to explode. Learning about it was one thing but hearing him admit it was a totally different type of discovery. There was an expectant pause before he continued. "She was clear about her desire to be with me. She was consistent, and even though I felt like shit once I realized what was happening, I knew it was because she showed interest." His voice grew silent with each word, and I knew they were indicative of his true feelings.

There was silence for a while.

"I don't want her."

"But she wants you," I quickly retorted, needing him to know how I read the situation. It was my reality, my doom. "...and she will continue to be clear and forceful in her pursuits and when she finally captures your heart, because I can't give you the type of emotions you say you need, where will that leave us?"

"*I DON'T WANT HER!*" he roared.

Why is he repeating himself?

Then it hit me!

"You know, don't you?" I felt my eyes squint and my mouth drop. "My God, you know!" I couldn't believe it.

He peered at me with perplexed eyes. It was almost intimidating. "I. Know. What?"

"You know she would be a viable candidate should this thing between us fail—if *I* fail *you*." My thoughts extended, pushing my realizations. "You're giving her soft rejections because you know she's falling for you and don't want to ruin that...just in case," I shared just above a whisper. I was shocked by my own revelation.

He scoffed, "I haven't dated her or fucked her. How can she be *falling* without me participating? You sound ridiculous, Rayna!"

"Azmir, she was in the bathroom crying at your *weak* ass excuse as to why you two can't pursue a relationship. That kiss meant a lot to her," The tears started to fall again. "...apparently similar to what it does to me." My body started to tremble, though I fought hard for steely veneer.

"It didn't mean shit to me and neither does she!" he insisted.

I cocked my head to the side, resembling contemplation. "Oh, yeah? Well, why is she always around? Why does she fly across country on the hopes of intersecting with you?"

"She has a PR firm with Shayna Bacote. They are trying to contract me as a client. This is *all* business, Rayna!" His lengthy frame moved into me, roaring as he pushed his index finger toward the floor.

"Then why don't you refuse their business as a conflict of interest? You want me to show more possession over you? Call her... right now and tell her you've decided and decline their offer!"

He tightly closed his eyes and deeply exhaled. "I can't, Rayna," his voice was much lower and calm.

My heart clenched and my body numbed. "Why?" I breathed out.

"Because I've already signed the fucking contract." His eyes met mine apologetically, telling me this was a no win situation.

More silence as I stood there and cried my eyes out.

"We are not going to let my business interfere with our personal life, Rayna. Do you know how absurd this all sounds?" He bent down to force my gaze to his and when I looked him in the face, I gave nothing. I had nothing to give. He waited a beat. "Please, baby, say something," he pleaded through a hoarse throat.

"Why haven't you told her we are more than roommates? Why haven't you told me you love me?" I whispered over my tears.

The look in his eyes made me feel there was more going on than what he was going to share. And this was the cause of my needing to bring this whole ordeal to an end. It was enough that I was in over my head, in love with this man. His robust courting had pushed me to the cliff. And the look in his eyes made the decision for me: I couldn't compromise commitment for companionship. Mediocrity just wouldn't do. I didn't want to give myself to a man who had a plan B. I didn't want to feel I wasn't good enough for complete devotion. For exclusivity. If I died alone avoiding hurt from pseudo-fealty, then suddenly, I accepted my fate.

I was defeated. I was done.

I turned to head back to the master suite, packed two full suitcases, grabbed as much of Azna's things, too and left Azmir in the very same place he stood in his foyer. He didn't chase me or try to talk me down. He tried to help with my bags, but I snatched away, forbidding him from coming near me.

He only murmured through clenched teeth, "You won't get too far. I won't let you."

Manny was on the elevator when it had arrived. He helped me to my car, and I was on my way to Redondo Beach.

It was nearly three in the morning when I arrived at my house in Redondo Beach. The place had a nimbus of abandonment and smelled of vacant dwellings. After unpacking Azna's things to at least get him comfortable, I showered and made my way to my bed. I pulled back the stale covers and crawled in, hoping to fall asleep right away, but when I tried to find comfort on my stiff mattress, my blues started setting again. *This isn't Azmir's oversized, plush mattress. Neither does it smell of him.* I tried tricking my mind into believing I was at a hotel, on neutral grounds. I was not sure if that helped or not, but I did fall asleep *eventually*.

My alarm went off, startling me from my sleep. I jumped from my pillow, trying to convince myself I had gotten more than ten minutes of sleep. The thought of calling out crossed my mind, but I decided not to because it would leave me too much time to think about my breakup with Azmir. I got up to let Azna handle his business while I surveyed my home. Since moving in with Azmir, I'd stopped by from time to time to check on the place and do a little housekeeping. But now that I'd returned, I regretted not doing more. I figured it all had to wait until later because I needed to get ready for work.

Day one of my breakup was painful, however, not as bad as I'd thought. The morning flew by, and my lunch hour arrived quickly, much to my surprise. There was a knock at the door. It was Sharon telling me I had a guest. My heart jumped into my stomach, fearing it was Azmir. I took a deep swallow then gave her a nod, granting permission to let them in. Much to my disappointment, it was Brian Thompson.

"Good afternoon." Thompson looked tense. The wrinkling of his forehead and the squareness of his shoulders told it all.

"Good afternoon. Is everything okay, Thompson?" I dipped my chin in anticipation.

"I hope so. I wondered if I could get a moment of your time and thought the lunch hour would be the most opportune. Is it a good time?" he asked before taking a seat. His apprehensive approach concerned me.

What is this about? I wondered. Then I was immediately hit with a revelation. *Crap...Azmir!*

"Sure," I gestured toward the seat in front of my desk. "Look, Thompson, I apologize for that embarrassing episode the other night. I have no explanation or justification for—"

"I know you don't, and I appreciate your compassion, but I need to know *what the story between you and Azmir Jacobs is*. Is he your boyfriend? Is he the jealous type? Because he was pretty threatening a couple of nights ago."

"Did he threaten you?" The hairs on the back of my neck straightened. I'd become embarrassed.

"Not directly. He seems like the savvy type who knows how to without crossing the line."

I sighed. Azmir was really pissed, so I was relieved. It could've ended much more cyclonic than it did. I didn't forget about Brian's place card trickery and neither did Azmir, I'm sure.

"Again, I apologize. He obviously got the wrong impression of what was going on."

"No, he was one hundred percent clear on what was happening. A man knows when another man is on the prowl."

I squinted my eyes. "Huhn?"

"Rayna, I will admit I am attracted to you and would like the opportunity to get to know you better. It's been on my agenda since the first day I came here to start data sharing. It's taken some time for you to soften to me and now I'm viewing Azmir as a problem. You've never said he was your boyfriend, but by the looks of it two nights ago, he is. Not to mention his abrupt introduction at the charity ball. So, I was hoping to get a straight answer from you, hence my visit."

I swallowed hard trying to process all he'd just said. He did just put it out there, he was interested. As much as I was available at the time, I had no interest in taking on a relationship with Brian. There was something about him that didn't work for me. Thompson was too forward, more aggressive than I preferred. There was something hidden beneath his forcefulness. I'd just never invested the time to figure out what it was.

Too wrapped up in A.D. land.

Well, no more!

"Well, Brian," I hummed, affording myself moments of delay while assembling an answer. "...your question has a convoluted answer...and here it is: Azmir and I had a weird and rare setup. It was serious and exclusive...for me. We've recently decided to take a breather, but even with that—I am in no position to take on a relationship with a colleague." I raised my finger to prevent him from cutting me off again. His scowl in return reaffirmed my issues with his level of aggression "I know you've said you wouldn't view it as a conflict of interest, but I do and will not waver from that." I paused to give him a chance to speak.

It took a few beats, but he eventually spoke. "Had? You and Jacobs *had* a weird set-up?" he seemed stunned.

"Yes, *had*. It's not something I'm prepared to discuss with a colleague, but in the spirit of being honest I shared that. I will also say I appreciate your tasteful transparency," I gave him a tight smile and a gentle nod.

A long sigh escaped his mouth. I knew my words were raw, but it was my truth. A myriad of expressions crossed his face in the span of seconds. Why was this such a big deal for Thompson? I just didn't understand his persistence. Perhaps if I hadn't been Azmir-Jacobsdized, I would've found Thompson's aggression charming. However, I was pretty banged up by my recent decision and cause of leaving Azmir to care.

"I don't agree, but I'll respect your decision and will back down. *But* the minute you change your mind—"

I interrupted, "...Or the minute *you* ditch *Smith, Katz & Adams* as a client, I know where to find you."

He gave a sensual chortled and licked his lips. I could tell he wanted to say more, but I left little opportunity for more to be said. It was an improbable possibility.

When Thompson walked out of my office door, a small part of me wondered if I had made the right decision. I questioned if I should have explored a relationship just to see if things were different and less complicated with him. However, a bigger part of me felt Azmir was my soulmate, if there were ever such a thing. He owned me, mind, body, and soul. And I'd just lost out on him.

Later in the evening, I went grocery shopping to try to stock up the house. I cooked with the blues and barely ate, trying to fight back my tears. I felt so out of place in my own home. The house was quiet and lifeless, so I decided to find music to help fill in the space. I went to my storage closet in the guest bedroom and pulled out a box of CDs I'd collected over the years. That's when I found the CD containing the theme song to my heartbreak: Blu Cantrell's

"*I'll Find a Way.*" I made my way back to the living room, popped the CD in, turned the volume up loud enough to fill the entire room and absorbed the lyrics. She sang the words of my wounded soul.

Blu seemed to sum up my pain in the second verse, but the entire song matched my sentiment. I was prepared to get over Azmir Divine Jacobs, the man who forcefully accessed my world, captured my heart, and had shaken the essence of me, leaving me forever changed.

Those lyrics mirrored my anguish. I broke down *again* in my living room. As much as I wanted to call him—just to hear his voice and to know he hadn't moved on with his life as though we never happened—I could not call or reach out in any way. I'd made my decision and had to stick with it in order to get through the pain that would someday neutralize.

I sobbed and sobbed. I mourned love lost, that which was unexpected and even that which was uncharted and yet undiscovered. I felt pain in every hollowed place deep inside Azmir filled physically and emotionally. I wept, pitying myself for opening up in ways past my emotional limits. I grieved for the impending nights I wouldn't have his lush touch, lighting the torch of my body. The touch I craved and had become desperately in need of. The one that could amend for scores of offenses.

I cried until my abs hurt. *What have I done to myself?* I knew I simply had to ride out the pain and one day it would all dissipate. As much as I knew in my heart of hearts I'd always love Azmir, I knew in due time my wounded heart *and soul* would heal. I did it before...*well kinda*, but this time would be different because we blended our lives and had shared a bed.

In due time this will pass. It would just be hell getting through the first phase of it.

My self-preservation mode was in full effect.

The next morning, I got up and out early to catch my session with Tyler. I'd spent all night debating if I should go considering Azmir paid for his services. I told myself if it came to it, I'd see about taking on the expense alone. Tyler provided results and was worth every penny he required. He worked me over some kind of bad when we sparred. He said it was because I hadn't seen him in over a week and my muscles needed a reminder. I focused my mind and went hard, having a lot of frustration to get out.

When we were done, he praised with an unknowing smile, "You did well, Brimm. Let's see if your man can measure up."

"Huhn?" I asked, confused, and completely flustered by the Azmir reference.

"Divine...he's my next client. You must have left the house before he woke up this morning," Tyler falsely surmised just before taking a swig of his bottled water.

"Oh." I supplied a contrived chuckle.

So, Azmir's in the building?

I was surprised. It was a weekday, and I guess I assumed the possibility of him being out of town on business. I was sure to maintain a swift stride to the showers to avoid running into him. Adrenaline coursed through my veins when I turned the corner, just feet away from the women's locker room's entrance and heard someone greet, "Good morning, Mr. Jacobs!"

"Good morning, Paul," Azmir replied less enthused. My heart trembled at the sound of his silky vocal cords.

I calculated he was maybe a yard away, around the corner. I dashed into the opening of the locker room, praying he hadn't caught my backside. I really wasn't prepared to face him so soon. It made me consider if I should switch around my workout schedule. That idea was quickly dismissed when I remembered Azmir worked out with Tyler at various times of the day, depending on his schedule.

Crap! My life sucks!

I arrived at work and greeted Sharon when I walked through the door. Upon giving me a synopsis of my schedule, she reminded me of our full staff meeting we'd have to host next Monday because the only other conference room large enough to fit the *Smith, Katz & Adams* staff was at headquarters and that room was currently under renovations. I'd volunteered to host, knowing Azmir had several conference rooms next door with ample space. I'd cleared it with Azmir's people weeks ago and suddenly wished I hadn't.

I should have let Dan Smith cancel it until their conference room was complete!

After speaking in limited details about the food for the meeting, Sharon handed me a *Vibe* magazine edition and beamed, "It's the latest issue and I'm sure you know Mr. Jacobs is featured in it, but you can never have enough copies of your boyfriend in a nationally publicized magazine!" She was all teeth and gums.

"Thanks, Sharon," was all I could manage. Of course, she wasn't aware of our split. But then, I never told her he was my boyfriend either. I would decide on my clean up method at a later time.

I had no clue about Azmir being featured in *Vibe*. My curiosity was piqued, so I headed straight to my office and closed the door. The title was **The Top Richest Black Eligible Bachelors**, and Azmir was number two on the countdown. His write up was only about a paragraph like the other mentions, but what stung me was they listed his estimated value at over a half a billion dollars.

Is Azmir worth that much? He's never told me this!

This was personal information being published that not even I was aware of? *I shared his bed for Christ's sake!* Another blow was the eligible part. We'd just broken up just two days ago, and I'm sure this article was written several weeks back, *at least*. He wasn't eligible then, *was he?* The tears started again. It took a minute to get myself under control. So badly I wanted to go back next door and curse him out something painful, but I decided to spare myself the embarrassment. *He hasn't even called!* The lyrics *"I'm gonna make it through the day…"* from my breakup-theme-song came to mind and I immediately shut down emotionally and went about my day.

Later in the evening, I was sitting in Pastor Edmondson's office, listening to him speak about the principles of hope and how it relates to faith. He sat behind his desk while I was in a chair facing him. I was jotting down notes and thought I was doing a good job at keeping up when he stopped abruptly. I looked up to see what was going on. His face was angled toward his desk, and he wore an expression as though he was struggling to hear something faint. I narrowed my eyebrows, confused as to what was happening.

"Rayna, is there something you'd like to share?"

What in the…? We were just here talking about faith, and you turn the corner to ask if I have questions?

Okay…

"Well…errmmm…I was going to wait until you were done to ask you to revisit the concept of the spirit of expectation and how it ties into faith again…" My tone fell because Pastor Edmondson's searing gaze told me we weren't on the same page.

"Put your pad and pen down, daughter." I did as he asked. If I didn't trust him as much as I did, he would have been freaking me. I sat up to give him my undivided attention.

"What's tugging at you?" he searched my eyes. "Is everything all right at work…at home?" My body chilled. I shook my head.

"Do you want to talk about it? Rayna, you know you control

these sessions. If there's something bothering you, let's try to take it on together." Again, searching my eyes, he nodded, asking if I understood. I nodded in agreement. He continued, "It's something at home. What's going on?"

How did he know? I had to quickly decide if I was going to share or lie to keep my personal problems to myself. Solitude had been too lonely, so I went with the former.

"Azmir and I broke up," slipped out of my mouth like melted butter. "I don't know what happened. I don't know what went wrong. I don't know how to pinpoint the issue."

"Did he say anything? Did he lodge a complaint of any kind?"

I thought long and hard about his question.

"He said I don't trust him enough to let my guards down to let him in. I'd just told him I loved him last week after my session with you. What more could I have done?" I was now wide-eyed in bewilderment. Slamming my face into my hands, I exhaled. "I'm so confused. I'm just horrible at interpersonal relationships." I cried and hard.

Pastor Edmondson gave me some time. He handed me a couple of tissues when he came around to the chair next to me and sat.

"Daughter, you're a work in progress. You told him you loved him and that may take some time to sink in for him. You're not horrible, you're human. Rayna, have you shared with Azmir your fear of trust and rejection?"

My head popped up. He continued, "Have you clearly laid it out for him, starting with your mother's neglect during her addiction, then your father's abandonment and rejection of your family and the betrayal of your first love and childhood best friend? Did you articulate how all three incidences, taking place relatively around the same time *and in your delicate adolescent years,* scarred you?"

I shook my head at it all.

"If you want a lasting relationship with this man, you must be transparent about your issues. He needs to know your strengths *and* your weaknesses. This will help guide his approach to you. It sounds as if Azmir is asking you to need him, to trust him enough to make him feel necessary and well-placed in your life. Men need that. It's in our genetic code, how God made us. You cannot ask us to be anything less than what we were created to be. It is simply unnatural. Some of us are more persistent in needing our women to give us that. Azmir seems to be in that group. You have to find a way to give it to him."

"But it's too late." My lips quivered as the tears wouldn't halt. Pastor Edmondson smiled. "I hardly believe that. Just take some time to think about how you could improve on making Azmir feel trusted by you. You never know how things will take a turn in course."

Pastor Edmondson asked if I'd prayed since the ordeal. I was dumbstruck because not at one time had I consider it. *Crap!* I thought I had gotten better in my walk. We sat and prayed for my peace of mind and heart during this learning period of my life. It was a calming experience. I'd just wish it had immediate effects. I knew I was in for the long haul.

My ride home was reflective. The more I tried to consider Pastor Edmondson's words, the more I recalled Azmir had not tried to reach out to me since the night I left the marina. This didn't help lift my self-preservation manner. I turned up the volume and allowed Blu Cantrell's *Blu Is A Mood* to flow through my speakers; because although the blue she sang about was beautiful and positive, the mood I'd taken on during this whole madness was melancholy-blue in spirit. I guessed I could call this a "Blu Cantrell breakup."

I pulled into my driveway with the same song blasting and as I got out of the car, I noticed the same car about two houses up I'd been seeing for the past two days. What made the experience creepy was the tinted windows. *Why?* I made a mental note I would call the cops if the car ever parked closer to my house.

Not thinking much further about it, I changed into my workout gear and took to my dance room where I tried out a few moves coming to mind while rocking to *Blu Is A Mood*. This was the only time I didn't feel pain, when I moved freely and creatively to the jazzy tune. I must have been in there for two hours before assessing I was tired enough to shower and fall right to sleep.

Who needs to eat? Let's rush time by!

The following day was hell and tested my separation endurance. Thank goodness it was Friday, and I could go into a weekend cocoon minimizing the likelihood of me running into Azmir. There was still no word from him, and I held mix feelings about that. What was worse was Sharon handing me a hand-delivered package from someone on Azmir's staff just before I'd gotten in.

Once retreated into the privacy of my office, I opened it to find my *iPad*. I got lightheaded for a brief moment. *Why would he send this to me?* I'd had a wardrobe fit for a troop in his closet, *but he returns my iPad?* I was so baffled. I didn't even power it on, just placed it in a desk drawer and shrugged it off in anger.

This was the first dud of my Friday.

I'd just come from getting a quick manicure and pedicure on my lunch and pulled into the closest parking space I could find near the practice. The sky had cracked over SoCal and the rain was coming down in buckets. I turned off the ignition when I saw Azmir's black Range Rover near the side entrance of the rec center where he typically entered and exited the building. Considering the smoke from the exhaust pipe in the rear, I could tell the truck was running and wondered if he was inside. I waited to see if I could catch a glimpse of him. As I sat there arguing with myself about being a glutton for punishment, I debated making a dash for the building although my toes were exposed in my flip-flops. That's when I saw the side door burst open with two women coming out of the building, holding up umbrellas and laughing excitedly. It didn't take long for me to notice they were Dawn Taylor and Shayna Bacote, getting into the truck.

Seconds later, Azmir appeared behind them, using his raincoat

—he donned so well—to cover his head. *Man, does he drip sexiness in everything he wears?* Brett was on his heels as the four of them piled into Azmir's truck. *What in the...?* Were they double dating? I knew the thought was incredulous, but the searing pain in the pit of my belly felt otherwise. I sat in my car—the car Azmir had given me—and bawled my eyes out *again*.

The rain ran into the following day. I stood at my living room window and watched it come down through the blinds. It was six in the morning, and I had to get over to Adrian's for my hair appointment. I needed pampering to help lift my spirits. Pastor Edmondson's admonishment for my lack of prayer during this break-up rang in my mind. So, before heading out, I fell to my knees. There in my living room; I spoke a few silent words which eventually turned into pouring out my fears, disappointments, and requests audibly through tears. It was very cathartic. When I was done, I washed my face and hit the door.

It was still there. The black sedan with tinted windows was still parked near my house. It was at the same radius, but certainly in clear view. I jumped into my car and sped off to Long Beach City for the salon.

While under the dryer, I'd gotten a ping from my phone for my calendar. I went into the app and saw how some time ago, I'd scheduled a reminder to visit my brother, Akeem. He had visiting hours on Fridays, and I hadn't seen him in months. Considering my current gloomy state, it would be nice to take a short trip over to Jersey and surprise him with a visit, but a projected Friday would be best, insuring a better state of mind for me. I'd just sent him money a week or so ago, so I knew he understood I still had his back, but there's nothing like a visit. I booked my flight, hotel, and car rental there in the salon.

After making the flight and car rental arrangements, I sulked. I couldn't get Azmir out of my head. His smile. His company. His attentiveness. His love faces. His betrayal.

The glimpse of a tall bombshell with long legs, strutting her way to a stylist chair caught my attention. She was beautiful and with warm ebony skin...like Dawn Taylor's. Her strut was powerful, enough to capture my attention and all of a sudden, I could conclude she knew her presence was riveting, she was fully aware of what her catcall walk conjured from unsuspecting people. She wanted to claim the attention of others, of men. I wondered if that was Dawn's subconscious intention as well.

The girl in the salon had long natural hair, still wet and glistening from just having been washed. Her length was nearly to the small of her back. I chuckled, suddenly thinking how Azmir liked my natural length of hair. He made it clear months back by the way he reacted to it, constantly running his fingers through it. He also was very adamant about me not wearing scarves or bonnets to bed. When I explained it could be detrimental to the health of my hair, he had his housekeeper change the pillow sheets from linen to silk. It honestly never bothered me, his possessiveness. To the contrary, it felt good. Comforting.

But not his betrayal. His cheating tore into my chest and jutted out like a ragged knife. I still bled. Everywhere I went, my pain and gloom accompanied me. Just like now. I'd just caught the ebony beauty licking her lips seductively. I suddenly wondered if that single act of enticement would tempt Azmir. Would he find her aggressiveness attractive? Would he kiss her, too?

"Cookie..." I heard in the recesses of my conscious as I obsessively eyed the dark skinned seductress in the chair across the room.

"Cookie, I know the dryer is on high, but it shouldn't have you deaf. COOKIE!"

My eyes snapped up as my trance popped, and I found a restless Adrian, glaring down on me. Adrian was dark himself, rich brown skin with legs just as long as Azmir's. He had sharp European features such as his protruding nose and slender lips. His dark brown eyes were slanted, giving him a bit of an exotic appearance overall. He was gorgeous, just not available to me—or any other woman for that matter.

"Crap, Adrian! I was caught in a daze. You scared the bejesus outta me!" I snapped at him.

"Honey, how many times do I have to call you to call your eyes from Saneese over there. The way your eyes are glazed, you'd think you munched on carpets," Adrian gave me a tentative gaze.

"You're ridiculous," I hissed.

"And you love pickles...like me, Cookie. So, what are we doing with this wild mane of yours?" he asked, raking his long fingers through my untamed tresses.

I chewed the inside of my lips, still unable to shake my gape from the chocolate beauty.

Within seconds, I spit out, "Cut it off. All of it." I didn't know where the emboldened decision came from, but it flew from my mouth, sans the approval from my brain. "Yeah...cut it off," I nodded affirmed.

Adrian must have aged in all of the twenty seconds it took for him to process my request. Though he was as brown as they come, his face was ashen in shock.

"Coooooookie!!! What did that fine ass millionaire do?"

I felt his mention was more of an accusation against Azmir than a question. Of course, it was not up for discussion.

I sputtered, "I have no idea what you're talking about. I've been wanting something new for a while. Something bold...something sexy. It's time," my tone was lofty to help guard the façade.

I didn't want my mask to slip, so my righteous indignation stare stayed glued onto Adrian's.

"But you said your man loved your long and wild mane. We've been training it for months...no weaves...no braids. You said he—"

"...doesn't matter. He doesn't matter!" I caught the jerking of heads in our direction in my peripheral, causing me to lower my voice. However, my glare never faltered. "I'm your paying client.

And. I. Said. To. Cut. It. All. Off!" I lifted a brow emphasizing my instance.

Adrian caught my adamancy eventually. He slowly raised a shaky hand to his mouth for a few seconds, still processing my erratic plans with my hair. He was right; I did say I'd focus on nurturing my hair for the purposes of lengthening it. And that was because of Azmir. But Azmir wasn't to be considered anymore. I almost felt bad about pulling the *who's paying?* card on him. Adrian didn't deserve to be caught in the middle of my love war with Azmir Jacobs—or whatever the hell I could term it.

Adrian dramatically closed his eyes in slow speed, opening them again with newfound resolve. "Okay, Cookie. We'll cut it off something fabulous." He acquiesced with a slow, impassive nod as he reached for my hand to assist me from the chair.

An hour later, I walked out of the salon with the autumn sun kissing my neck. It felt good, bold—new! And I loved it. I needed it. I needed a diversion from my reality. From the pain. Adrian cut and styled my hair an asymmetrical length with one side reaching my ear and the other beneath my chin. He styled it so well, my wavy curls were silky and bouncy, almost resembling a texturized style. I was contented, even if only temporarily. My first anti-A.D. move. And I was damned proud.

Earlier in the week, LaWanda postponed our weekly Bible group study meeting and rescheduled it for this evening. I decided it was best to get out of the house to keep my sanity, so I headed over to her place for a lovely Bible study. The ladies were crass as usual, but a much needed distraction. To my good fortune, no one asked about Azmir. I guessed time does wonders for trivial matters such as shacking with a tall, chocolate, handsome, and apparently rich man.

My fortune continued on Sunday when no one was pressed to sit next to me again. I liked my privacy and keeping a distance between associates. Sad to say, since Michelle's passing, the only person I could tolerate for more than an hour was Chanell with her crazy butt. While in church on Sunday, I laughed to myself, thinking of her and all her outlandish ways. She was truly a delight, and I made a note to call her to see if she wanted to hang out soon. Unless she felt otherwise, she was still a friend of mine. *I had hoped.*

Monday came around very emotionally for me. I'd stayed up the night before crying and menacing over my breakup with Azmir. My body craved him like a drug and my heart mourned the death of his presence. In all honesty, it hurt like hell he hadn't reached out to me. I thought he'd at least try to fight for another chance at *us*. Had he taken on his plan B—Dawn Taylor? Did he finally see what I feared, driving my decision to leave—that we were no good together? My heart weighed so heavy and not to mention, the unnerving throbbing between my legs only added to my blues.

I managed through my workout with Tyler, but not without him noticing my lack of vigor. He didn't say much other than he saw it and wasn't happy with my performance. The remainder of the morning I coordinated the setup of the full staff meeting over at the rec center. They loaned us the large penthouse conference room one floor above Azmir's administrative offices. I had Sharon and the intern running back and forth to set up the room while I saw my morning patients.

When noon rolled around, I was still in with a patient, but was cognizant of the time as I knew the staff meeting had begun. My superiors were informed of my layover appointment and that I would be at least thirty minutes late. I returned to my office at close to a quarter after and sat at my desk. I felt exhausted and melancholy. I scraped together my things, searching my drawers for a writing pad when I laid eyes on my *iPad* Azmir had sent over last week. I'd forgotten all about it and seeing it lying there intensified my blues. My stomach fluttered and my soul felt void. "*I gotta be strong...move on!*" Blu sang in *I'll Find A Way*. I repeated those lines like a mantra all the way out the door.

The lobby of the rec center was flooded with folks coming and going, mostly whisking through to the cafeteria. I'd seemed to be the only body with a leisurely amble in the entry way. I saw young Mark Littlejohn, a front desk receptionist, assisting someone at the desk. He was the same kid who gave me a tour when I was vetting Azmir before I met him. The sight of him made me smile because Azmir would always call him *Young Littlejohn*, endearingly of course. He was a rather short, brown skinned, twenty something year-old, bright-eyed kid. He was always pleasant and extremely articulate. I knew Azmir got a kick out of his size and delivery, hence the humorous moniker. I didn't stop to speak, but brushed past the desk instead, en route to the elevators.

I stood among the large, gathering crowd, waiting at the bank of elevators for the next available car. When I heard the bell alerting its arrival, I wondered if I'd be able to make this trip or have to wait for the next available one. The doors rolled open and to my and all the others waiting dismay, the elevator was packed, leaving room for no one.

And I saw him.

My heart began to race, and my breathing hitched. He wore a meditative expression while engaging some woman who was speaking to him with animation. The sight of him was magnetic and downright breathtaking. His head slowly pushed up and his eyes found me immediately, almost as if he'd sensed my presence. Azmir's gaze on me was sweltering and undeniably arresting. I froze in place. I noticed his lips slowly parting. Before I knew it, the elevator doors started to close, but he leaped forward, catching the door with his hands, interrupting the process. He threaded around a few people, out of the elevator and over to me. I stood there, trying to manage my equilibrium while soaking in his arousing and very familiar scent. He didn't say anything, instead he grabbed me, taking me by the arm and towed me down the hall, opposite of the lobby doors.

I had no idea where he was taking me, but his strides were purposeful. It had all happened so fast. I knew the main gym room, weight rooms, basketball courts and other amenities were there on the main floor, but what else was down this corridor, I didn't know. Before I knew it, he had taken me to the back of the building, returning greetings to at least a half dozen people on the way. I was immediately reminded of the night in the club, after Azmir knocked out my dance partner. He had me flying through the air, trailing behind him. This wasn't that dissimilar.

We eventually stopped at the service elevator. Azmir pulled out a key, calling it to the main floor. In no time, the door opened and he all but pushed me inside. When I looked him in the face for an answer, he wore a scowl as he pushed the key into the control panel and pushed a few buttons, causing the doors to close.

"What in the world are you—" I tried to ask about his bizarre behavior, but he launched at me, covering my mouth with his, hungrily devouring me, and in no time at all, causing a guttural groan I didn't even know was possible to escape me. Azmir's tongue attempted each inch of my mouth as his arm slipped around to the small of my back, pushing my belly into his erection. For the first time in my life, I'd been lain out by a kiss. My legs gave out and my arms dangled behind my limp frame as fulgurate spikes of endorphins ignited delightful feelings of euphoria in his strong arm. We kissed hard, needy, and wild for what seemed like an eternity.

He let go of my mouth and lowered his forehead against mine. Panting, he breathed, "Come home...today. I can't take this bullshit anymore," as his eyes were sealed.

I was momentarily muted. My body was still reeling from the taste of desperation on his lips. "Azmir, I...*I*—"

He grabbed me into his arms and, as I fluidly turned my back to him, trying to break loose, he grabbed me at the shoulder, wrapping his arm across my chest, pressing me into his hard, pounding chest. His right hand searched furiously for the entrance of my wrap around dress and when it did, he quickly found his way down my panties and between my legs to my throbbing pearl. I gasped. I wasn't steady on my feet from the exhilarating feeling of having his trained hands all over me again. My back arched and I grabbed the elevator wall, trying to steady myself as he rubbed and stroked until I could hear the swishing of my well-lathered sex. When his lips and deft tongue touched my now exposed neck, thanks to my hair cut, my body further melted into his lengthy frame. My head swung back, and he rounded my neck with his nibbling. I bit my lip to prevent from screaming. Not only were we in a public place, but I couldn't give Azmir the satisfaction of me losing my mind after the way he had abandoned me.

He worked his finger inside my canal as his thumb deliciously circled my swollen pearl. I felt his head move down until his mouth was to my ear and felt his warm breath rushing through his moist mouth. "I've tried, Rayna. I swear, I've tried to do this your way. I've given you time to fucking return on your own," he pleaded in my ear, adding to my lewd state. "Please, baby, I'm sick without you."

His panting melted me literally and figuratively. I fought to comprehend his words through my libidinous fog, but the allure of his scent invaded my nostrils and somehow traveled down to something in my belly.

I shook my head frantically, "No. We can't. It's. Over," I spoke incoherently, barely catching the collection of saliva trying to seep my wanting mouth.

"You don't mean that. I can't go on like this much longer. Six days, one hundred and thirty hours and thirty-five minutes I've been miserable without you, tortured by your absence and the possibility of you having moved on. Whatever I did wrong I can fix it, I swear…just give me the chance to." His words were tantalizing, and my pelvis danced on his busy hand beneath me. I felt his rock hard penis, poking me from behind and I felt the moisture from my fingers as I gripped the aluminum wall in front of me. I thought I was going to lose my mind.

"Fuck," he growled in my ear. "You're so wet! I've missed you. I've missed this. Tell me you've missed it, too!" He spoke through clenched teeth the way he did when I'd take him into my mouth, and he would try to warn me he was about to come. I was losing my faculties second by second. His deft fingers were diligently at work between my legs. I was close to the edge.

"No. I. Don't. I. Have. Moved. On." I had no idea where that came from, perhaps my will to, but it was so far from the truth.

I felt a smile form on his face from him having it pressed into mine. "Your body gives you away. It's telling me something entirely different, Ms. Brimm." He was goading me. It was confirmed when he used his free hand to strategically massage my breasts through my dress. My misted forehead dipped forward onto the cool silver wall. He ran small circles on my neck with his tongue. And seconds later, I heard him count down, "Eight, seven, six, five, four, three, two..."

Before he could say *one*, my body quaked as my orgasm came coursing through, causing my torso to bow beneath Azmir's towering, brawny frame. I let out whimpers in order not to give way to my threatening screams. Azmir held me tight and still worked his groping fingers on *and* inside of me, dragging out my orgasm until I wailed from sedation and could take it no more. He slowly pulled his fingers out of me and collapsed his back against the wall right aside me.

With a cool and collected demeanor, he licked his thumb and fingers that were inside of me and murmured, "My mother has been in town. I can't keep pushing back dinner with you. I've run out of excuses. Dinner tomorrow at seven. I'll have Ray come scoop you," here was when I caught his Brooklyn twang.

My arms and hands were still splayed against the wall as I tried catching my breath and control of my delicate, trembling frame. "Azmir, I can't," I whispered with little energy to spare.

Unperturbed, he turned the key with his dry hand to start the elevator's ascent.

"You can and you will. This shit is done. Now, I know you don't have time; you're late for your staff meeting. And I have to go call Yazmine to give her a *final* date and time for her first dinner in L.A. with my favorite girl."

How did he know I had a staff meeting? Then I quickly realized since we're using his facility, he could have come across the information easily in a briefing with Peg.

Before I could give a rebuttal, the elevator had come to a halt and the doors parted.

"Your stop," Azmir announced as he continued to lick his fingers as though they tasted of honey.

I was so turned on and ready to go, but I couldn't let him sense it, so I slowly straightened my dress and leaned over to pick up my belongings from the floor before exiting the elevator. I tried my best to maintain a dignified walk out and as I turned to my left, I heard Azmir's deep vibrating voice inform, "You should hang a right."

I stopped in my tracks and did an about face.

The staff meeting was in full swing when I walked in. Jim Katz's eyes landed on me. He then cued Michael Shriver, who seemed to have sped up his presentation on the latest marketing ads, sharing they'd be posted in local publications and billboards. When he was done, Jim stood and announced the impending lawsuit the firm was facing. He gave measured details, likely under the advisement of Brian Thompson's legal team. It made me think of him...Brian Thompson and why was he not present to discuss this himself.

Just then, Jim mentioned more pressing issues took precedence over Brian's appearance for this meeting. He really didn't give much away and that, coupled with my rendezvous in the elevator with Azmir, forced my attention elsewhere. The bottom line was I was not the cause of the lawsuit and wouldn't discuss it any further anyway. My skin felt flushed, and my thighs were sticky, making me switch positions in my seat to find comfort. I could still smell Azmir's delicious scent on me. Thoughts of his big hands being inside me caused my pearl to pulsate all over again. Suddenly, I craved him needing more...much more. My phone pinged, breaking me from my lecherous zone. It was him.

Yazmine has been informed of our dinner plans tomorrow at Maggiano's. Ray will be at your place at 6 sharp.

I was secretly turned on by his forwardness. But he didn't have to know that.

If I decide to come I'll drive. Thanks for the info.

Quite frankly, I wasn't in the mood to put up a front for his mother. What role would I play? Roommate? Former roommate? I most certainly wasn't his girlfriend!

Stop with the resistance. It's over. I could feel his dominant nature come through the text.

I replied, **We're over Azmir. You can't throw me into an elevator, take advantage of me, pull at my conscience of entertaining your mother and expect me to forget all that has taken place to lead us here! I'll think about it and get back to you.**

My phone pinged again. **I'm not taking no for answer Brimm. We can talk beforehand if you like, you name the time and the place & I'll clear my schedule to make it happen but no is not an option.**

Crap! He's not letting this go. I tried my best not to look so distracted in this meeting. Azmir was pushing my buttons—in good and bad ways. There was so much I wanted to say. So many apologies and recent revelations, but it wasn't the right time, nor did I believe this thing with Azmir was a sure thing.

Azmir, I haven't heard from you in nearly a week and you expect me to comply with your wishes of dining with your mother? For what...to explain to her that as your former

"roommate" I can assure her you're a great bed-warmer? I don't mean to be rude but you have to see things from my perspective. Dawn is an issue for me. Heck, Tara is a huge looming issue! I don't think I can do this again.

I readjusted myself in my seat and widened my eyelids to keep from tearing up. Seconds later, another alert appeared.

It was Azmir: **I'll move around my schedule. We'll talk.**

"*When?*" I shouted in my head. I didn't reply because I didn't know how to respond. I'd suddenly become so frustrated and being holed up in a humdrum staff meeting didn't help at all. Nothing the entire afternoon helped lift my mood. I resumed to tending to my patients and putting out administrative fires.

I took the scenic route home, needing to think about this thing with Azmir. Things weren't any clearer or less complicated just because he fingered me in his service elevator...*though it was a nice method of release*. My breasts swelled at the memory of his sweet breath hitting the side of my face. My panties were soaking wet by the time I hit my doorstep.

I didn't see the sedan around, and I was relieved and satisfied with my decision to not call the police. I changed into a cropped sweat suit and sneakers, grabbed Azna's leash and called him out of the door. We took a brisk walk on the beach. Between the emotional tailspin Azmir had put me in and my randy state, I needed the fresh saltwater air. The sun was setting on our way back to the house. Azna's stride slowed, and I knew I'd worn him out. I picked him up and petted him gently.

"I'll fix ya' something nice and warm as soon as we get in," I sang in his ear.

I turned up my walkway and saw Azmir's long legs, squatting on my steps as he sat serenely on my front porch. His gaze had the same effect on me as it did earlier. It excited me internally. I let Azna down and he ran straight over to Azmir, just like a child would do its father. Azmir seemed just as thrilled to see our pup. Azna's tail wagged with frenzy in Azmir's arms. I walked up the steps, next to the two, holding back my smile and noticed two bags behind Azmir; one clearly containing two bottles of wine.

Azmir's dangerous eyes met mine. "You've cut your hair."

He'd noticed, though he didn't make mention of it earlier.

"So, I have," I shot back, not caring about the traced venom.

He didn't like it. I could see it all in his eyes. Though I didn't like his disapproval, I didn't care. I needed a new identity. *And to spite him.*

"Can I come in?"

"Sure. Please." Nervousness was in my voice.

An hour later found us on the couch, working on the second bottle of Pinot Noir and laughing hysterically. Expensive gourmet Japanese food containers were spread across the coffee table and Azna was on the adjacent sofa chair, spread out in slumber.

"Wait! Chanell and Wop? This sounds like a story she'd be sitting here telling me about someone else!" I was in the midst of a laughing fit.

"I know. I swear, I didn't believe it when Petey called me. It was a good thing Petey knew the arresting officer because they would've been in lockup." Azmir chuckled sexily just before taking another sip from his glass.

I couldn't catch my breath. "He was *that* loud?"

"Yes, she was slapping the shit outta him, riding his little ass in the backseat." Azmir shook his head at the image.

"But he's like five foot two and she's easily six feet!" I couldn't stop laughing.

Azmir looked so carefree. I'd laughed with him countless times, but this time it wasn't about me or him, it was at the people in *our* circle, making us connected.

My laughter slowed as I soaked his presence in. He was gloriously masculine—*virile*—and extremely fine. His teeth were so perfect, and his lips were too inviting. The black long sleeved tee he wore told secrets of his chiseled chest and made me recall his abdomen muscles. He sat reclined on the couch, very relaxed and tempting. Suddenly, I wanted him, so bad.

In my haze, I hadn't realized he'd stopped laughing and had locked eyes on me until I heard him ask, "Penny for your thoughts."

His expression told me he knew exactly what was flowing through my mind. But I didn't want to fall prey to his sexual prowess. "Dawn Taylor," I spewed effortlessly in my resistance.

Without a flinch he confidently provided, "Is fully aware you are mine, and I am exclusively yours."

Warmth blanketed my body, and I shivered at his words. *But...*

On a long sigh, I tried, "Azmir—"

"I handled it all wrong. And for that, I've suffered and am truly regretful. It won't happen again." He shook his head remorsefully, his beautiful eyes not on me. "Rayna, I may have gotten you into a relationship that's for the most part unconventional, but you must stop doubting your role in my life. There is no one else, and if that hasn't been clear I only have myself to blame. When I asked you to share my home it was because I'd decided on you and only you. Kissing her was a huge mistake...one of the biggest in my life. You have my solemn promise, it won't happen again."

He was so absolute in his decree. I tried—tried desperately—to take him at each word and suppress every doubt and ounce of fear clouding my mind. I knew the sad reality was he had claimed my heart long before I moved in with him. I wanted something from Azmir, I wanted forever. However, his betrayal with Dawn left me afraid to go full steam ahead.

My eyes bounced all over the place, and I shook my head in confusion. He picked it up and reached over to me, using his index finger to lift my chin.

"I fucked up...but this... This right here." He gestured at the space between us. "This distance between us. My starvation of you—your need for me. It can't go on."

Huhn?

"What need for you?" I asked with incredulity with wide eyes.

Azmir gave a mirthless chuckle and cocked his head to the side, pushing his tongue into his molars before declaring, "Rayna, you're in heat right now. Unless you haven't kept up with your pills?"

I knew he was referring to my birth control pills, but what did that have to do with Dawn Taylor?

"Yeah, and...?"

"*And* you're still on the same cycle. Your period will start tomorrow. I can smell your arousal. I sensed it when I saw you earlier in the lobby of the rec. I can't stand to know you're in need, and I'm not here to satisfy you." Azmir was confident with his assumptions—*well*...facts.

Crap! I hated I had no privacy regarding my own person with him!

It wasn't going down like that.

"Arousal?" I blew air from my mouth in a scoff.

His head swung back in a hearty titter. My eyes stayed glued to him, begging his pardon. Then suddenly, he locked eyes on me and slowly pushed up on the couch, moving over to me, long arms caging me. I stilled, not knowing what he was about to do, but was sure he was testing me. Azmir brought his delectable lips to mine, yet he didn't touch me. His gaze still locked to mine and his eyes were mesmerizing. Suddenly, I heard my accelerated breathing. He touched my lips with his. They were soft and moist.

He didn't kiss me, but spoke into mine, "Tell me you don't need me to straighten you out."

From the moment the first push of breath hit my face, my neck gave out and I staggered, but I regained control. I had to say something. I couldn't let him win.

"I—"

I attempted before his tongue retreated to the back of my mouth, interrupting my words *and judgment*. It was over. My hands moved up to his head and pulled him into me. I stroked the waves in his soft hair, neatly cut into his usual Caesar style. In no time, I was reaching for the hem of his shirt. He helped me take it off and just when I thought I was in for a home run, I felt his undershirt. We managed that one, too. My fingers ran up and down his strapping back.

I moaned at the swift movements of his tongue butterflying in my mouth. He was right, I needed him, so bad that I started removing my own pants and underwear. When I got them to my ankles, I started with his belt. He pushed my shirt up and unlatched my bra to shift it up. His tongue felt so masterful, dancing on my sensitive nipples. I nearly lost my mind. Trying to finish undoing his pants, I unzipped his jeans and went into his boxer briefs to pull him out. I stroked him to express my appreciation of his firm presence, his length and powerful girth. I gave special attention to the large vein running the full length of him and fantasized about my tongue massaging it.

Azmir moaned into my breasts. "You're going to cause my premature undoing. It's been a while for me, too," he droned. "Be easy."

I gazed him in the eyes and realized my mouth was wide opened by the cool air hitting it.

"I can't wait. Give it to me," I whispered and kicked off my pants and panties.

I lifted my sex to the tip of him, finding the right angle for him to enter and once I did, I pushed down on his hips with my lower legs and forcefully met him in a thrust, being sure to take in every inch of his abundance. Azmir's eyes closed and his jaw flexed as he groaned loudly on top of me. I collapsed, separating our bodies, and then pushed back up, bringing him into me again. This time I joined him in moaning. I did it several times before wrapping my legs around him *tighter* and slamming into him repetitively, taking no prisoners. And in seconds, Azmir's body shuddered as he gave way to his orgasm. He fell on top of me, and I kept with my upward thrusts to prolong his outer orbit float.

When he was done, he peered down at me, "Didn't I tell you to take it slow? Got me performing like a fuckin' teenager." I loved when his Brooklyn tongue slipped.

I giggled and ordered, "Sit up."

He maneuvered our bodies so that I was on top of him and pulled my shirt and bra off before kicking his sneakers, boxers, and jeans off. Once properly positioned, I felt his fluids run down my canal, spilling onto him, and I rode him with no holds bar, grabbing the back of the sofa. He felt so good inside me. I was so grateful for his steely erection standing so tall against my swollen walls and wanted to take full advantage of it. Too many nights I'd succumbed to never feeling this again. Never having him again. But he was here, working me over.

He grabbed my cheeks behind me and massaged them in, driving me crazy. He didn't kiss me, in fact, he laid his head back to get a full view of me bouncing on top of him. So badly I tried to keep a straight face and not give away how well he rubbed against that tender spot deep within, but when I took in all of my senses, like my breasts bouncing in the air, the smell of his cologne mixed with his natural body oil and his drunken gaze, my body gave way to my orgasm and my eyes dropped as though I was in excruciating pain. I opened my mouth and let out sounds of a porn star. Azmir pushed me on and off him to intensify my euphoria until my cries turned into whimpers.

He rose and bent me over the coffee table to take me from behind. I still felt his juices mixed with mine on my inner thighs as he pulled my legs apart and entered me slowly. Azmir felt incredible, and I became even more aroused by the way he gripped my hips, it caused heated blood to course through my veins.

In no time, his plunges sped up and, for a moment, I lost my grip on the table. My hand skidded against a portion I was able to catch immediately before collapsing. That's when I accidentally hit the stereo remote, switching on the power. All of sudden Blu Cantrell's voice came crooning loudly through the speakers, *"I'll get over you one day!*" Quickly, I tried to hit the power button to shut it off.

"No...no! We're going to work this song out of your system!" he screamed over the music, and he leaned over to push the remote from my reach. Before I knew it, he started plowing pleasurably into me relentlessly while my heartbreak theme song flowed richly from the speakers. Each time my concentration went to the song, my body's submission to Azmir would reel me back into the reality of him being so deep, making my insides quiver. I felt my orgasm stirring, but it was rivaled by the pain the song was causing to dredge up in my heart again. Tears started forming from self-pity. My mind was at war with my body. It was a vicious internal struggle. Acute pains of betrayal hit my chest as Azmir's strong girth caused flutters in my belly.

"No! Let it go!" he commanded over the piercing tune.

I wanted to, so desperately I did.

"I'm here. Right here...inside of you. I haven't gone anywhere. You feel it....you feel me, here in the flesh," he spoke in between delcious thrusts.

Whether I liked it or not, my body was about to explode. My head yanked back as I screamed Azmir's name like I needed him. The orgasm wrecked my core as I clenched down on Azmir, beckoning him to join me...and he did, forcefully. I felt his body shutter powerfully behind me, reminding of his muscular frame and strong being.

Our reunion didn't stop in my living room. When we were done, Azmir turned off the stereo and tossed the remote on the couch as if he had disdain for the song—as though he knew it had been a part of my coping mechanism while trying to get over him. A song he never knew.

Something hit me.

I dashed over to the front window in search of the black sedan with tinted windows, only I didn't see it. To be sure of my theory, I threw on Azmir's shirt, he looked at me as though I was out of my mind. I stepped out onto my porch and frantically searched up and down my block for it, to no avail.

I came back inside to him, "You're too busy a man to sit and stakeout my home all day, so did you have someone do it for you?" My gape was piercing. I wanted answers.

His contorted expression and busying himself with gathering his clothes gave him away. He couldn't even look me in the face.

"Did you?" my voice louder and sharper than before.

He returned it with a scowl. "C'mon, Brimm, you need to wash that shit off you." He was making reference to the concoction of his bodily fluids mixed with mine. It was now trickling down my thighs. Brooklyn had returned. But I would not be moved.

"I'm not going anywhere until you answer me." I crossed my arms to enforce the statement.

He stood in place, stretching his shoulders and lengthening his spine. "What do you want me to say...that I, like a fuckin' sucker, let you walk out of our apartment at two in the morning and didn't make sure you were safe? That I'd let you go and didn't worry or wonder about your whereabouts? You want me to say I went on as though we never happened?" He paused in his crisp tone. "I'm sorry. That'll *never* happen."

I walked over and stood directly in front of him, intrigued by his truths. "That doesn't explain how you know I played that song this past week. I'm sure your spy didn't include that tedious, little known fact in his reports to you," I muttered.

His eyes went to the floor and then rolled down to me. He didn't want to confess what his eyes had revealed. "I wasn't ready to give you up," Azmir barely managed the words.

My eyes closed in my overwhelming mystification. "This relationship is insane," I told myself—or at least I thought I had.

"That's because I'm crazy about you." He gave a lungful exhale, "Listen, Rayna, I know this is a little intense and it does seem insane, but I'm just trying to hold on to you and at every turn you're trying to get away. I'm not doing that shit no more." Azmir was letting his Brooklyn twang slip a lot today. He wasn't fighting for control of his emotions, something rare. "I gave you space, and I've been miserable. I'll do anything I need to..." His words failed.

I held my reservations but seeing a dominant man in form and command be so ardent about his need for me was invigorating. It pulled at my heart and caused a quickening deep inside me. I couldn't get enough of him. I pulled him back to my bedroom and straight into the shower where I let him wash our reproductive liquids off me, and I returned the favor but added a happy ending when I put him inside my mouth. I worked Azmir over like I needed air to breathe. My hard work and risk of wetting my hair in my small shower paid off when he shot warm creamy fluids down the back of my throat, and I ferociously sucked every baby-making specimen out of him. Back in my bed, he had me clawing the sheets while he bobbed between my thighs greedily, forcing out octaves I didn't know I had in me. Azmir loved tasting me and expressed it every time.

We lay in bed, breathing and talking.

Azmir's dewy skin felt wonderful against mine as I wiggled between my new sheets. He laid on his back while I faced him on my side, admiring his frame.

"How has Yazmine's visit been?"

"Fine, I'm guessing," Azmir spoke leisurely. "She's met Petey, Kid, and a few other people. I took her over to the *Cobalt* and to get her hair done at one of my salons." His voice was deep and relaxed as his eyes were fixated on the ceiling.

"What about the recreation center?"

"Nah. I was waiting for *us* to get it together so she could see where you work while there."

Oh.

"How have things been between you two?" I wanted to know what was going on in his heart.

He exhaled through his nose as he considered my question. "I don't know. I get that she's here and for the most part, her maternal adoration is still there...like she's really interested in getting to know me but... I don't know how to pull her in."

"*Hmmmmmm...*" I measured his words. *That was loaded.*

"Like...there are so many layers, so many underlying factors... and I was already working on *you* and making myself transparent to *you*...but a mother is different from your woman. It's been very complicated."

"Do you want her to know you? Do you want a close relationship with her?"

"I think I do. I just don't know how. This shit didn't come with a manual, you know?" He appeared to be in deep thought about that.

"Well, don't let her read that *Vibe* article. It may scare the crap out of her." I had to go there...I knew it was unnecessary, but that was an issue for me.

His neck jerked and a grin formed on his beautiful lips as his brows knitted. "What is that supposed to mean?"

Crap! "I don't know..." I sighed.

"Did you not like the article?" he turned his head to look at me for an answer.

I shook my head.

"Why?" he asked gently, sounding almost wounded.

"I don't know...it was very personal and invasive." I exhaled and collapsed my head on my pillow. "It stated facts I didn't know about you," I confessed with a moue.

He sat up and turned his body to face me, "What did you not know about me?"

I looked up to see the grimace on his face.

Did I upset him?

"Your net worth for starters. I felt a pang run through my belly when I read the amount. How could I have lived with you and not know you were worth a half a billion?" I caught myself whining.

With a slight smirk and in the calmest tone he informed, "That's actually not accurate."

See! "I knew they over-exaggerated it. Was that Dawn's doing?" I asked dryly.

"Yes. That was her PR firm's attempt at promoting my empire, but the figure is actually slightly underestimated."

My head shot over to his, and my eyes were widened in disbelief. "*Wha*—! Well, if it wasn't correct then—" I cut myself off. "I'm afraid to ask!" I didn't want to pry.

"Rayna, it's okay. *You* can ask. It's not something I want made public for legitimate reasons, but I feel it's necessary to share this with you." His eyes were so genuine.

With my eyes, I gestured for him to spill the beans. He caught my drift and returned to his pillow.

"It's closer to a billion, but as far as the IRS is concerned, my assets and earnings amount to about five hundred seventy-three million dollars, per last year's filings."

You could hear a pin drop in there. I was stunned. Why hadn't he told me this before? It now made sense, how he was so adamant about spending freely on me, the car he loaned me because he never used it, staying in the best hotels, having paid off the posh apartment in *Marina Del Rey*, offering to buy my house. *He's filthy stinking rich!* His fleet of luxury cars, the personal chef, regular security detail—all of these were the fittings of a wealthy man.

"Brimm," he called me from my trance. "Say something," his voice was hard, self-protective. It sounded so familiar—*like mine*.

"*Yu*—you said you don't like discussing it. I don't want to meddle."

"It's not meddling coming from you," he hissed, exasperated.

"What is it then?"

"It's gaining pertinent information. Pertinent information concerning you...your future."

"That's how Kid got his car..." Another thought I intended for internal use only.

"Kid is a long-term friend. I value his loyalty to me over the years. I'm a very private and complicated man. He's understood this and has been very reliable throughout the years. It was an appropriate gift for a trusted friend."

I was stuck.

He turned his head to me. "What did you think I earned before the article? You must have given it *some* thought."

Whoa! I don't think I did.

I started chronicling my time with him. "I don't know...I mean, yeah, you had a *Bentley* with a driver, a lofty apartment on the water...businesses, a personal stylist..." I started to feel silly the more I thought out loud. "I don't know...maybe close to a million... okay, at best two million? In all honesty, I never gave it much thought. I accepted it as all things coming along with your parcel... that it was all Azmir Jacobs. I've never dated a wealthy man before."

"According to you—you've never dated." Azmir was reminding me of the small fact I'd shared with him in our previous conversation in Vegas.

"This is true." I turned back to face him. "I don't know...I feel foolish for not knowing. And...truth be told, I'm mad as hell Dawn knew more than I did," I sulked openly.

"Dawn knows what I need for her to know to grow my brand. The brand that will provide handsomely for you, who will protect my privacy."

What does that mean?

I didn't want to go there. But "there" was somewhere I had to go now that we were back on the topic of Dawn.

"Azmir, you were so incensed about Brian Thompson at the charity ball and in San Diego." I tried to maintain my boldness in the spirit of honesty. "In San Diego—"

He abruptly jumped up in the bed and with a wrinkled nose, *"You didn't...!* Fuck! In San Diego or...since we've been apart." Azmir's body tensed, his pupils dilated, breath hitched, and he formed fists in my mattress. He was scaring me.

"Azmir—"

"When?" he breathed seemingly painfully, collapsing his eyelids, bracing himself for the answer.

"Never!" I shouted. I couldn't believe his presumptuousness.

He visibly relaxed and his back fell into the headboard, causing an alarming thud sound. Azna barked at the foreign noise, letting me know it had startled him, too.

I was offended. He had some audacity to assume a broken temperament when he thought I'd slept with Thompson. "Hypocrisy!" I hissed.

"I know, but it is what it is. Rayna, I can't even begin to think about how shattered...how fucked up I'd be if you fucked someone else."

"I don't fuck!" I shrieked. "Is that what we do? I mean, yeah, we've gone over the semantics, but is that what you believe we do?" He had some nerve.

He gasped, affronted. "No." His tone was soft and defenseless.

"Well, why would you assume I'd *fuck* someone else?"

"Because you said you loved me and *making it* is reserved for me."

"And so are your lips, Azmir! It goes both ways." Anger fueled my newfound courage. "God—do you know how much you've possibly setback my trust issues? Now, I feel insecure in who I am." I looked him square in the face. After a moment, I whispered, "You told me you got lost in the act of her pursuing you with force...that I am not doing that for you. This comes right after I told you I loved you and was in love with you!"

"That was after I'd made the mistake," he clarified, to my relief. I huffed, feeling very annoyed. "Was?" he asked about me being in love with him.

"Azmir, you're in my bed. Give me that at least." He sighed as though *he* was now relieved.

"Rayna, you're not the only one with issues here. Since we've been apart, I've realized I have security issues." He exhaled, "I assume they come from my parents' disappearance from my life so early. When you left the apartment that night, I wanted to run after you, but my pride wouldn't let me do it. Day after day I waited for the miracle of your call, for you to come back to me of your own volition." He stopped his stream of thoughts as though they were too painful to take on. "Let's just say it's been rough. And having Yazmine around only made it that more difficult. How can I acclimate her to my life when the biggest part of it had run away from me?"

His words hit me hard. Was this Azmir's declaration of love for me? *No!* But it was so refreshing, and I realized in this moment it was what I'd been needing from him. No, he didn't tell me he loved me as I'd done him, but I was willing to take whatever he gave so long as it was real. I'd just have to take what he gave in this moment and treasure it. Azmir's ruminative mood also spoke to something deep inside as I felt lubrication between my legs. My eyes darted over to him, alerting his attention to me. I didn't say anything and didn't need to.

"Damn! Brimm, you're insatiable. It's a good thing your vagina will be preoccupied tomorrow. You're trying to wear me out."

I batted my eyes bashfully. I didn't want to be too forward and decided to take the shy route instead by turning my back to him and laying my head on the pillow.

"Oh, no," he droned as grabbed my chin and bestowed a kiss, making me shiver in no time. He scooted over to me, and I relished the poke of his virility into my naked flesh. "No more running, not even in bed," he whispered. His teeth grazed my ear as he murmured, "Moving forward, when either one of us need a moment of truth—for the other to be completely honest and share what's on their minds we need to make that clear. Perhaps a code word."

I tried exercising my brain over my heated body and heaving chest. "Like what?" I breathed out.

"I don't know...something like...orgasm—something I am about to serve up to you." Azmir bit into the piece of flesh just beneath my ear, again reminding me of my short hair, forcing me to cry out as my body melted into him. I decided to humor him.

"Orgasm may be inappropriate to use in mixed company. How about a more neutral term...like..." I tried thinking, but his long fingers were rubbing and pulling my nipple. "...pocket watch. Let's go with pocket watch," I groaned.

"Okay. Pocket watch it is," he breathed into my neck.

My heart was pounding and the throb between my legs had become almost painful.

"Pocket watch?" he asked, I assumed testing it out.

I swallowed hard, trying to fight the heat rising from my belly, "I want you deep inside me. Deep enough to make me forget the pain."

Azmir lifted my leg over his arm and entered me from behind, sending chilling waves up and down my spine. He licked behind my ear and into my neck, further driving me insane. He kept pushing deeper and deeper inside of me and I could swear I felt him in my chest, *near my heart*. I didn't realize how deep this position could place him in me. He started circling my pearl using my juices to lubricate it. It drove me wild.

"I love being inside of you. You're so submissive and eager to take me all in," he whispered so close to my ear and that was my undoing. "You are so beautiful. You were made just for me," he continued his effective narrative.

Within seconds, the fiercest orgasm rippled through my core, triggering my body to violently convulse. Azmir took cue and flipped me onto my stomach and went to grinding into me, thoroughly and hard, stretching out my orgasm, and in no time felt him pumping his warm fluids into me. He growled my name insanely and I fell in love with him deeper. I'd momentarily forgotten about the pain of losing him. Of his betrayal.

The sound of my alarm pulled me out of my dream. It was my usual one of me sharing intimately with Michelle and having her abruptly leave me, promising to return. I irately grabbed my phone diffusing the alarm, seeing it was six forty-five in the morning, and rubbed my face. My short hair was wild in a disarray and my body shivered from being bare underneath a measly sheet.

Why didn't I use my blanket? Then I looked over to the dent in the pillow next to me and it hit me, *Azmir was here last night...in my bed...making love to me, over and over again. But where did he go?*

The last thing I recalled was being awakened by his mouth teasing me between my legs and eventually being underneath him, caught in another toe-curling orgasm at two in the morning. There was no way *that* was a dream. I was still wet...too wet. I looked down and saw the red stain beneath me. *Crap!* My period had arrived.

While in the shower, I marveled at Azmir's timing. He knew my cycle and how I'd be in need *before* today, when my period was due. He was so observant of me, *my body*, it was almost uncanny. *What do you expect of a darn near billionaire mogul?* He knows everything there is to know about his assets and opponents. Though he never mentioned approval of my hair.

Hmmmmm...

That aside, it made me wonder if this was somehow planned, deliberated—if he knew how in days I'd be so sexually vulnerable, it would be the most opportune time to make a move on me. If such were the case, it would only mean he *did* think about me during our breakup. He thought long enough to plan to draw me back in. The gesture was comforting *and manipulative*, but I was now dealing with a new level of blues—those relating to my period. My back ached, and I felt tension radiating from my neck. I knew it would be a rough day to get through, starting with deciding if I would attend dinner with Azmir and his mother.

Azmir's betrayal created debris around my heart, and I'd have to couple that with my monster of a menstrual. It wasn't looking good for either one of us.

CHAPTER 5

Azmir

My eyes shot open, and I smelled her. I found comfort in her warmth, felt the prickles of her short, curly hair poking my face, and I realized it wasn't a dream. I'd had Rayna back in my arms. I couldn't believe she'd cut her fucking hair. I didn't like the bold move, but goddamm if that wasn't my Rayna. She was an extremist. I'd assumed it was a part of her rebellious and independent nature. As much as I hated admitting it, I loved the new look. It turned me the fuck on and had me almost fucking her in the lobby of the rec center when I'd laid eyes on her. She looked like a new woman, stronger than the one I knew. I know that's crazy to think, but she had. I rushed to touch her, to claim her as mine. To remind *me* of who I was to her more than anything.

I'd fucking missed her like mad. Like a bitch, I pined after her in her stubborn absence. The last time I'd woken up, I had to prove to myself she was there in the flesh by making love to her and feeling her detonate from another orgasm. I couldn't get enough of her. I hated to leave her. I could rest in bed with her all day and comfort her from her impending hellish symptoms.

Unfortunately, it was time for me to start my day, beginning with an eight a.m. East Coast Time conference call with Richard, my business partner, followed by my morning workout with Tyler. I tip-toed out of Rayna's room and managed to leave without even a stir from Azna.

I walked out of her place feeling reprieved. I also felt peace, something fleeting when she left the marina. I was happy to have this portion of myself settled. It was the major component of my life, something becoming clear when she left. I could now move on to what I knew best, hustling. Work was the skin to my being. It buffered me and protected me. But even this theory was tested when Rayna turned my life upside down by leaving.

My day kicked off with newfound vigor. The past week had been hell, beginning with being in denial the first two days without Rayna. I thought I was the *Old Divine*, who swore he would never allow a woman to affect his world in a way that could possibly ricochet his work and overall existence. *That's some sucker shit. I'm a man. A man who could survive and flourish with or without a woman.* My experience with Tara's cheating and manipulative tendencies only further intensified this mantra. When Rayna left me, not only was I hit with the revelation of never having been as emotionally drawn to Tara as I thought I'd been, but also that I was in deeper with Rayna than I'd previously known.

My time with Tyler corroborated my theory. He told me, although my stamina was off, my focus had returned. I knew my energy had been depleted during the night before and early morning activities with Rayna Brimm. I was just happy to have my mojo restored.

After my workout, I checked in with Yazmine to be sure she was set for the day before I got into the full swing of mine. She seemed to be excited about finally spending some time with Rayna. I'd been putting her off for some time. She had been in town for only four days, but during our second dinner she asked very dubiously about the beauty I'd brought to New York when I came to see her for the first time since she'd disappeared from my life. I explained Rayna's lead role at the practice required late nights and early mornings, and as soon as she could clear her calendar, I'd set something up. As I sat at my desk listening to Brett shoot off updates and upcoming action items, I fought to suppress my trepidations of her not showing up for dinner tonight.

"Sir?" I heard Brett call out to me.

"Yes."

"The signing with *Mauve* next week. *Bacote & Taylor* would like to know if you'd like to have it here in L.A. or at their headquarters in New York."

Mauve was a brandy line I'd recently partnered with at the coordination of Shayna and Dawn's PR connections. I'd been wanting to invest with a brandy line for quite some time, but never acquired the resources to vet a reputable company in need of investors. *Mauve* was repackaging their brand and was gearing up to execute a new marketing campaign. It was a match made in heaven. These women, *Bacote & Taylor*, were working.

"Let's do it here in L.A. I'm really trying to minimize my travel over the next few months." I had Rayna in mind with that decision.

I knew I had to put in more time with her, making her feel secure in my life. And this wouldn't happen if I was boarding a damn plan every week. I needed to prove to her we were solid. Not to mention, I still hadn't forgotten about Brian Thompson's lurking ass. He was becoming a problem I had to address carefully, yet firmly. He wasn't taking to my niceness.

"Okay..." Brett dragged, as he made notes on his tablet. "And now it's time for the conference call with *Bacote & Taylor*. I'll punch them in." He spoke in his announcer's voiceover as he rose to the phone and dialed a few numbers.

Dawn Taylor answered in her usual professional manner. For the first few moments of the conversation, Brett and Dawn spoke about dates, events, and other details involving my schedule. I checked out, thinking about my conversation last week with Dawn, the day after the Trey Songz concert.

She appeared at *Cobalt*, surprising me once again. She claimed she wanted to see the place to gauge the possibilities of shows and events their firm had planned for the club. She was dressed very seductively in a skirt falling to her knees, a blouse opened in the middle of her cleavage, and sexy ass *Brian Atwoods*. She was trying…too hard. Quite honestly, Dawn was an attractive woman who knew how to flaunt her shit, but she wasn't my type. I didn't want a woman who brought too much attention to her sensual nature. The best thing to do was to make a man believe he had exclusive rights to it, and he had the sole power to bring it to surface.

I was sitting at the bar, having a drink, and talking to my new bar manager, Mike. In the short time he had been with us, I'd picked up on his mild and controlled energy. We could sit and talk about the philosophies of life for hours. I was stressed and needed a midday drink, so after I finished with some paperwork in my office, I came down to the bar. It was always a pleasure and escape from reality to sit and hear some of his life stories and lessons. I got to share a few of mine with him as well.

I didn't notice when Dawn walked in. It was just after two and there were always deliveries being made with maintenance staff coming in and out during the afternoons, so I was never sensitive to the activities of the door. She strolled over towards the bar, locking eyes on me. I didn't say much, just took a swig of my drink, anticipating the nature of her visit.

"Good afternoon, Mr. Jacobs." Her smile was wily per usual, only today I wasn't responsive to it. She stirred up a shitload of trouble in my home the night before, at the after party. Rayna said Dawn was actually crying in the restroom.

"So, it is." I watched her stand just inches away from me, resting her arms on the lip of the bar. "To what do I owe the pleasure, Ms. Taylor?" Even through her smooth cocoa skin, I could see her blush.

"I didn't expect to see you here, actually. I was coming to take a peek at the place to help start drumming up ideas for marketing." Suddenly, her smile deepened, "Seeing you here is a bonus."

Mike, who went back to re-stocking the bar when she approached me, walked back over to us, and with his wise perceptive ways, he lacked warmth when he asked Dawn, "Can I get you a drink, Miss." I had wondered if he had sensed my unease with her presence and had followed suit.

"*Ummm*... Well, that depends...on whether or not Mr. Jacobs here is buying," she attempted to charm with her witty sense of humor.

"Honey, if you're walking in this establishment at this hour to see Mr. Jacobs, I doubt if you're concerned with who's buying." He gave her a stern, paternal glare. Dawn's eyes peeled from Mike and bounced quizzically to mine when I gestured, *I'm out of it* with the pouting of my mouth and took another swig of my drink. She then went back to Mike, who waited patiently for an answer.

"Errrr...gin and tonic...dry, please." When Mike turned to concoct her order, she took a deep breath and turned back to me. "So, did you enjoy your night?" I knew she was referring to the after party.

"Some points of it less than others." I slid my glass back down the bar to Mike. "Hit me again, Big Mike."

"You got it, Mr. Jacobs," Mike called with his back to me.

Dawn gave a nervous laugh. "Now that I see you're here, I am hoping we can talk...privately. Perhaps after you give me a tour."

Mike returned with her drink and didn't go too far to pour mine.

"We can talk here. What's up?"

She used her eyes inconspicuously to motion to Mike.

"Don't worry about Mike. It's his job to hear no evil, see no evil, or repeat it." Her neck snapped at my resistance.

Mike served my drink and went back about his business.

"Well... *Errrr*... I didn't have the most pleasant encounter with your friend."

"Rayna," I chided sternly. She would not disregard my lady and pass her off as a jump-off. This shit ended here.

"Rayna," she settled with, sounding reproved. "And I wanted to dispel any misreporting you may have gotten from her."

"Misreports?" I chuckled silently while staring straight ahead before taking a nip of my drink.

"Yes, she came out of the bathroom stall and walked into a private moment between an associate and me. It was a little emotional, and I can only imagine the impression she got."

"Why are you anxious about what impression Rayna *may* have gotten from a conversation between you and an associate not concerning her."

"*Anxioussss*," she threw my word back to me contemplatively, in a whisper.

I took another sip of my brandy but said nothing to let her know I was awaiting an explanation.

"That's the thing, Azmir." She ran her hand over the back of her neck, expressing nervousness. "I'm still confused as to the nature of your affairs with her. You told me last night she was a roommate, but you didn't say she was a girlfriend or a significant other of some sort. Is there an arrangement in place I should be aware of?"

She echoed Rayna's complaints about my choice of words describing who Rayna was in my life. *What the fuck is up with women being all literal and shit?*

"That you should be aware of? Is this for business reasons?" I asked as I dropped ice cubes from the tumbler into my mouth. Dawn was going to have to come better than that.

"In Connecticut, you advised I be clear with my intentions, so here we go: Are you in a serious relationship with her? Is she a girlfriend? Or are you just fucking her and she's living with you as a professional beard? Is there some arrangement in place?" Dawn barely took a breath in her string of questions. I couldn't decide between being concerned or entertained. "I want to know so I can see how I can gain your attention. And before you ask, I'm speaking on a personal and intimate level." Her eyes stayed upon me as she sipped from her drink, I supposed to help with her nerves.

"A beard..." I chuckled, "Wow! Now, that was unexpected."

She smiled sardonically, "Well, she has a body to die for. Her ass alone would make a nun do a double take. She's always impeccably dressed in designer attire, and I surmised she doesn't work if she can make herself available to you during the middle of the day like she did that day in your cafeteria. I don't think my assumptions are too far off."

Dawn was so desperate for answers, she never paused to gauge my disposition, another character flaw. I couldn't help but laugh. Hard. My liquor had seeped through my veins, goading my sense of humor. She showed her hand too much. Too bad she wasn't mine, or I'd have to coach her on how to hold her cards.

"What is so damn funny?" she laughed along with me, risking the subject of our humor not being the same thing.

"Your newfound ability of avowing." I placed my glass down on the bar. "I appreciate and will adhere to it." I chewed my ice before continuing, "For starters, it may be wise for you to know the nature of my relationship with Ms. Rayna Brimm for professional reasons regarding your firm. As far as for personal reasons, you should know I am not the type of man who's dating options are reduced to entering into legal agreements for professional companionship. My singular tastes and pursuits afford me the opportunity to seek out women with legitimate careers and lifestyles."

Dawn furrowed her eyebrows, "Careers? Oh, so she does have a job? Let me guess, she waits tables at night and runs from audition to audition, trying to catch a break in acting during the day."

She was bold—too bold, and so off target. I swallowed my melting ice. "Not exactly. By day, she works at a physical therapy practice and by night, she keeps me entertained, if not off pursing other tasteful activities."

"She works at a physical therapy office as a...?" Dawn extended her investigational activities.

"...as a lead physical therapist, who manages the practice. Her office is there on the rec property."

She reacted with her eyes. They jumped. *What the fuck did she take me for?*

"Oh! Well, that's good to know. She looks so young. I didn't..."

"She is. And she's also very bright, clearly." I watched as Dawn measured my words carefully. I recalled what Rayna said the night before about not painting Dawn a better picture of our relationship and felt I owed it to both of them. After giving her a moment to chew on that, I continued, "And for the record, I am a private man regarding personal affairs, but my affairs with Ms. Brimm are serious. I need you to know this as we proceed with this business relationship. Our contract is provisory and so far, I'm happy with what you've been able to deliver. Don't allow what is not possible to interfere with your paper." I dragged my gaze to her contemplative eyes, noticing her signature smile. "Don't shit where you eat. Do you understand, Ms. Taylor?"

Her smile was fading. I could tell I'd hit a nerve but couldn't be concerned about her feelings. I needed to clear a path for Rayna, and if that meant it had to be at Dawn's expense, so fucking be it.

"Direct enough," Dawn murmured before taking the last mouthful of her cocktail. "The *Vibe* article you're featured in it hit the shelves yesterday. You should pick yourself up a copy. You look good and read well in print." Her spirit collapsed.

"Indeed." I had totally forgotten about the article until Rayna mentioned it last night. It was good to see their proposal unfold. "If you ladies need a tour of the facility, my executive assistant here can handle that." I could feel her gaze in my peripheral and decided not to give it my attention and possibly open a can of worms. She grabbed her purse and turned her body completely to face me.

She murmured, "Azmir, you stay on this not mixing business with pleasure kick." Dawn let out a soft exhale, "I'll try to play nicely. I am an only child who challenges rejection. I always seem to end up with those things I pursue."

With that, she turned and strutted off.

I took a beat and then called out to her without changing my stance, "I don't want any trouble in our business affairs, Ms. Taylor."

I heard the abrupt pause in her heels against the floors as she considered my words, "It's not our business affairs anyone should be concerned about," she shot back before hitting the door.

It was in this conversation that I'd realized my previous draw to Dawn actually worked against her. Yes, she made it clear she wanted me, but she left nothing for me to desire. Nothing for me to chase. On the other hand, while I enjoyed the chase with Rayna, I needed to feel every once in a while, she appreciated my efforts. I needed to know she wanted my companionship. In all honesty, I wanted Rayna to need me, like I needed her. I was hoping I hadn't fucked up things with Rayna and had hoped to Allah she'd find it within herself to forgive me. If I wanted something solid with Rayna, I had to work with her and give her time to come around.

Damn. I just hoped she'd come around.

"Sir," Brett called out to me, breaking me yet again from a trance.

"Ah, yes. Next week will be fine," I rebounded, recalling the last of their exchange.

"Okay, I'll let your stylist know you'll need wardrobe for then," Brett replied.

"Oh, he finally speaks up?" Shayna quipped. I guess I was that distant from the conversation.

"I'm here, Shayna," I chimed in.

"How are you today?" Shayna asked in her usual southern hospitable tone.

"I'm well. Thanks for asking. I'm pleased about this brandy deal. You guys are blowing me away."

"Well, thanks for that. We have a lot more in store."

"Mr. Jacobs..." Dawn chimed in with her kitten voice, dripping sex appeal.

"Yes."

"*Honey* magazine wants to do a *personal experience* piece with several semi-nude shots for one of their winter issues. They really loved the *Vibe* article and learned you were a boxing enthusiast, which means they know you're physically fit and wanted to see your body. I think we should do this and mention *Cobalt* for marketing purposes."

Did I hear her correctly?

"Dawn, I am a businessman, not a model hopeful. That may be ideal for *Cobalt* but does nothing for *Global Fusions*. I'll have to pass."

Global Fusions was my merger, acquisition, and liquidations firm with Richard. We were growing in lightning speed in this economy. I didn't need any detraction.

"Are you kidding me? With your physique, business ventures, and brilliant mind, we can cause major traffic to your entire brand. Your Google numbers would be out of this world. Just look at Christian Cross. His spread in *Men's Health* demonstrated a significant boost in his cutlery line."

"That's because men don't shop for knives, and I don't have many products exclusively geared toward women. I'll pass."

"Is that a *hold* action item for a future meeting?" Dawn goaded.

"That is a definitive, absolutely, positively, *hell* no." I was firm and slightly annoyed by her persistence.

There was a brief pause. "Okay. We'll work another angle," Shayna assured.

That's when I got a text *from* Shayna, asking for a personal and private conversation with me soon. What a clandestine thing to do given we were on the line together now. It must've had to do with Dawn. I told her I'd be agreeable to it.

The conversation went on for nearly an hour before we ended, and Brett and I moved on to another conference call.

It was a long morning and an even longer afternoon. By five p.m., my trepidations concerning Rayna's showing for dinner with my mother had grown exponentially. I didn't want to reach out to her, not wanting to pressure her or be overbearing considering our time together the night before.

And that had played out so well. That Monday, I was preparing to "run into" her *after* her staff meeting, but when I saw her standing in the lobby waiting for the elevator, I felt several emotions: longing, excitement, hunger, and anger—*she cut her fucking hair!* I couldn't stop thinking about it. I felt a flair of possessiveness and wanted to go fucking caveman and snatch her ass up so I could fully examine what she had done—without my fucking approval! But instantly, her beauty speared me. I saw the narrow structure of her neck, exposing soft caramel skin—skin my fingers tingled to touch, and my tongue twitched to taste. I had visions of running my tongue the length of her ear down to her shoulder. And suddenly, I couldn't resist, I had to make my move.

She gave a little resistance, and I couldn't believe the way I'd practically begged her to let me back in. Rayna was still raw. The shit I copped to in the elevator, and those I shared with her in her bed last night was something I'd never experienced. I wanted to slap the shit out of myself at times for being such a bitch, but I couldn't lie, I hadn't regretted a word I'd uttered. I was simply not accustomed to being so transparent about my inner most personal feelings. Yet, I felt compelled to let her know she meant the world to me.

I'd picked up Yazmine from her hotel. Since her arrival from New York, she always looked uneasy when getting into the *Bentley*. I knew it was a lot to take in, but I also didn't want to make any changes just to suit her. I was content with what I'd built over the years. I'd lived beneath my means for years, and still did to a large degree, so there was no need to recede when she was around.

Yazmine had been pretty refreshing during my suspension with Rayna. We'd talked a lot about our individual lives, and our time apart. She was really laid back, but very discerning, something I didn't recall as a child, perhaps because my mind was not mature enough to catch it. At the dinner table assessing the wine menu at *Maggiano's*, I was nervous. I searched for something to help me bear the brunt of Rayna's absence. I was nervous as hell about her standing me up. I still hadn't heard from her and after a long day, could certainly use her presence.

"Why are you so fidgety?" Yazmine observed.

"Am I?" I responded calmly, or so I attempted.

"Yes, you are. You can try to play that smooth shit with the rest of them, but I'm your momma. It don't matter how long I been up, I know when something's wrong witcha'," Yazmine's accent was thick with her Brooklyn roots and broken idiom from prison, I'd guessed. But no matter how she expressed herself, I still experienced a small semblance of the mother I had once known.

I gave a small chuckle. "I'm good. Just had a long day." I placed the menu down. "How was yours?" I tried steering her away from my truths of Rayna standing me up.

"It was all good. I reached out to Daryl." That caught my attention.

"And?"

"And I told him I was in town and need to kick it wit' him."

I didn't feel good about this because I no longer trusted Big D.

"And what was his response?" I needed to know how he was going to swing this.

"He was shocked as hell! I thought that piece of shit was having a damn heart attack on the phone!" She held her chest and laughed hysterically. Her other hand cupped her mouth, drawing attention to her gold nose ring. My mother had aged. She still had her mildly tinted brown skin, but the bags under eyes told tales of weariness. "We're supposed to meet tomorrow at two...some place called Griffith Park? I knew your driver could get me there, so I ain't sweatin' it."

"I'll send a new driver. I don't want you venturing out alone."

"No problem."

I pulled out my pocket watch and noted it was seven thirty-five, over a half an hour past our reservation time. I knew we had arrived ten minutes late due to traffic, but this was not like Rayna. I had begun to resolve in my mind she wasn't going to show. *Should I have called her to remind her or pushed the issue of having her picked up?* I was wrestled in my thoughts. I immediately became flooded with disappointment.

Yazmine gave me a deep gaze of skepticism. "Are you sure you're okay, beloved."

"Oh, yeah. I'd prefer you not go alone. I know you and Big D have a history and with what we've recently discovered, I don't want to take any chances of a heated encounter," I assured her.

"No. It ain't that. It's something else going on in ya' head." She was right. Her name was Rayna. And she was stressing me the fuck out!

Having succumbed to defeat, I was just about to call the waiter over to start our order when I noticed her enthralling stride over to our table. She was dressed in a black, fitted, long sleeve dress stopping just below her knees, and black suede *Fendi* metallic platform pumps with a black *Fendi* fold-over clutch to match. I knew this because I was with her when it was purchased, just before her birthday, during the summer. I thought the combo was a bit understated, but she said that's why it had appealed to her. It was nice to see her wearing it. Her hair was in the sexy, short loose curls she'd had it cut into. Her jewelry was modest, her makeup was soft, but her lips were lusciously nude against her skin. My dick inflated against my pants.

Just before she reached the table, I rose and took a few steps to meet her. She gave me a nervous smile and was receptive when I went to touch her and pulled her into the curve of my body. She didn't resist. I was so relieved and excited to see her. When we embraced, I heard her breath catch at the point of our contact. In my elation, I pulled her face up with my right hand to plant a soft kiss on her lips, trying to fight the urge to smear her lipstick. Before my lips landed, I felt an electric pull as I inhaled her and when our lips met, I seemed to have shattered into a million pieces.

What the fuck is that?

When I opened my eyes, I noticed hers were open, trying not to give into passion. But I felt her erratic heartbeat in my arms. She smelled glorious in my fold. Her eyes danced back and forth while searching mine. I knew she wondered what the fuck was up with me.

"I didn't think you were going to make it," slipped from my lips in a whisper that could only be heard by her, and I immediately wanted to kick myself for letting it. I slowly released her lower back from my needy grip, raking my hand on the way and could swear I heard a moan escape her.

She looked me in the eyes with furrowed brows. There was so much I wanted to say, so many unfamiliar feelings I wanted to express, but of course this was not the time nor place.

She looked over to Yazmine, leaving my embrace, and greeted, "Mrs. Jacobs, it's so good to see you again," as she extended her arms to indicate she wanted to enfold her.

Yazmine, who appeared to have been watching our private moment, quickly followed suit and rose from the table reciprocating. I watched how they welcomed each other, and both seemed to have been immediately taken. I could see Yazmine's face from my angle. She closed her eyes during their contact, which let me know there was a level of sincerity in her greeting to Rayna.

As they let go, Rayna offered, "I apologize for being so late. Not only was the traffic terrible, but I had to stop at a drugstore on my way. I picked up the phone to text Azmir on the way and saw my battery had died."

"Well, I'm just glad you made it, beloved," Yazmine gushed so forgivingly. "I saw Mir folding up over there. I think he was scared you wasn't gonna come."

As Rayna looked over to me, I noticed Yazmine's eyes stayed on her. Rayna gave me a dubious gaze. I remained impassive, just relieved she'd came. She looked damned good. I'd started thinking of ways I would fuck her later on.

"Oh, I wouldn't have missed this for all the tea in China," Rayna stared me dead in the eyes when she shot back the same line I'd used on her at her job's charity ball when I had first encountered that prick, Brian Thompson.

"Are you okay, beloved? You needed to stop at the drugstore...?" Yazmine didn't skip a beat.

"Oh, yeah," Rayna looked uneasy, almost as if she didn't want to discuss it. "I've had a rough day. Work was, well...*work*. I've had back pains and the like since I woke up this morning. I ran out of pain meds earlier this afternoon and had to pick more up before I got here and suffered my way through dinner. I've been looking forward to finally seeing you again. I'm sorry it's taken this long," she offered a warm smile.

Damn. Rayna's period symptoms never crossed my mind today. She suffered from cramping, bloating, neck and back pains among other symptoms, each cycle. Some months were worse than others. *No ass for me tonight.*

Rayna continued, "I remember my first time out here. I was overwhelmed with the difference in energy from the East Coast.

What have you done so far?" Rayna gave her a soft smile. I was taken by her eagerness to converse with my mother.

"Mir done sent me to the zoo yesterday. The big one in San Diego. Today, I went to see *Hollywood*," Yazmine informed her.

Rayna's eyes shot over to me. "Oh, he took you on the *tourist excursion* as he referred to it when I'd told him I'd never been around town when we first met."

Ha!

She recited word for word from our first "date." Just then, my *Blackberry* went off, when I checked, I saw it was Shayna Bacote hitting me up.

Hey, Azmir. I had my godson's recital tonight so I wasn't able to call but I wanted to reach out to you regarding the reputation and intention of Taylor & Bacote Planning and Public Relations Corp. I've taken notice to Dawn's attraction to you and must admit I've grown disturbed. I hope you don't take that piece of detail to mean we are not a viable firm with your best interest at heart. If there's something you view as a conflict of interest, I hope you'd make me aware of it before dismissing our bid to represent your brand indefinitely.

I knew what she was hinting at. Shayna had an idea of how strong Dawn was coming on. I could tell she didn't want the backlash of it if it came to that.

Thanks for your concern and professionalism Shayna. I've spoken to Dawn about the parameters of our affairs. If a problem arises I'll be sure to give your preemption consideration. Overall, you guys are doing well. I typed back.

The waiter came by and took our orders. Yazmine ordered iced tea, and I ordered a Grand Marnier for me and an herbal tea for Rayna. I could see she wasn't herself, no matter how much she lent herself to pleasantries for my mother's sake.

Shayna texted back. **I'm glad to hear that. But Azmir I need you to know I take my job seriously and I appreciate you took us on when celebrity friends of mine I've known since child-**

hood blew us off and never gave us a thought. This has been a lifelong dream for me so please do me the favor and let me know the minute you aren't pleased with the "affairs" of Taylor & Bacote Planning and Public Relations Corp. Dawn is a unique individual whose determination can be so strong it works against her. She's a dear friend but in business I need to be objective. Give me a holler before you make any final conclusions. Please.

Indeed.

I was taken by Shayna's blatant cry. I was also impressed by her ability to see Dawn's risky behaviors could potentially affect their business. Once again, the essence of Dawn was lurking at the time I was with Rayna. My thoughts were ruminated when I heard:

"Beloved, I don't know how you deal with him being on that phone all the time," from my mother. "You know when I was with his dad, my competition was with the newspaper."

Rayna gave a bellyful laugh. It was so hard she winced. It struck me hard.

"You okay, Brimm?" I asked.

She darted her eyes over to me, oddly causing my erection again. "You know...what comes along with the territory," she muttered uncomfortably. I immediately knew that was code for her discomforts were associated with her period. I knew I could soothe her if she agreed to be with me tonight.

Dinner was pleasant and the conversation flowed well. Rayna didn't eat much of her dinner but cleared her dessert.

She ate nearly all of her assorted dessert tray. I knew this was the time of the month when she didn't deny herself of any sweet indulgences. I loved the way she put food away unabashedly. It made her practical. I needed that.

"I don't know how you eat like that and stay so fit," Yazmine observed.

I wished I could have said *outside of the workouts I put her through, the only other man who worked her body comparably was my fitness trainer*. But that would lack decorum. A rush of yearning came over me like nothing I'd ever experienced. I needed to solidify things with Rayna. I wanted her back in my bed where she belonged. I didn't want to waste any more time trying to let her figure it out. I had the urge to force her hand.

"Brimm, I was telling Yazmine how you so graciously offered up your house in Redondo Beach to her *indefinitely*," I murmured over the table while zooming in on Rayna's eyes, bracing myself for her reaction. Her eyes widened and mouth swung open momentarily. She caught herself and reeled it in. She opened her mouth to say something and closed it again.

Yazmine took notice of all of it. "I told Mir I'm like a stranger to you and know you don't want no stranger staying at your house."

Prying her eyes away from mine, Rayna pivoted in her seat towards Yazmine. "You are no stranger to me at all. You're Azmir's mother. Don't mind me, it's just that we spoke about this so long ago, it's caught me off guard." She turned her glower to me. "We should discuss the details of that over the next few days." She was blowing me off.

"What's there to discuss? The property is vacant," I goaded her.

"It's not empty. I have things there," she scolded me with her eyes and then turned softer ones over to Yazmine. "Things I'm sure you would want removed so you could be comfortable and feel at home." She cleaned it up well, speaking to Yazmine. I didn't stop there.

"Okay, it should only take a day to get your things out." I sat up in my chair and readjusted myself.

"It may take a little longer."

"Why?"

"Because I'd have to figure out where I'd store them."

"Whatever can't fit into the marina, we'll put in my storage space. No biggie." Rayna didn't respond. She was vexed and couldn't determine her next move. I didn't give a damn. She was coming back home.

"Yazmine, have your things packed and ready to go by Thursday. We'll get you in there and take another day to buy whatever personalized décor you'll need to make the place your own before the weekend. Perhaps you can host us for dinner on Sunday," I proposed in jest. That garnered a chuckle from Yazmine, but a blank look from Rayna.

Oh. Fucking. Well.

"You just let me know what you need to feel at home there, and we'll take care of it," Rayna murmured dryly, but with a scent of sincerity to Yazmine.

We were all adults, and Yazmine at best could surmise that I was pushing Rayna faster than she had wished.

"Excuse me, I have to use the restroom." Rayna rose from the table, and I followed suit. As I did, she gave a small smile to Yazmine, but rolled her eyes at me and turned on her heel for the ladies' room.

As I took back to my seat, I heard Yazmine's raspy voice note, "You're in love with her."

My eyes darted over to her. I wasn't expecting that. I adjusted my tie on my chest and abdomen. I gave her the flick of my eyebrows. "Is that what we're calling it?" I was not prepared to go there. This topic had been on repeat in my relationship with Rayna, causing me undue stress.

"What do you call it?" Yazmine came back, wearing a gentle smirk on her face.

I exhaled, "I call it well-placed companionship."

"Is that all you feel is going on between you two?"

"I care about her very much."

"Beloved, what I been watching since that young lady walked into 'dis place is your heart come alive and be on display. You a totally different person when she around. You try to play cool when deep down inside I can tell you burning for her real bad." She giggled, "It's just like when you was ten and had a crush on Otischa from the projects. Every time her momma brought her to

Momma D's you be tense on the outside, but jumpy as hell on the inside." She paused to read my response.

"She's a beautiful and bright woman." Enough said.

"Yeah," she nodded in agreement. "'Dat she is. And you want her living with you. You gon' marry her?"

Yazmine didn't see Rayna coming upon us. But she realized she'd returned when Rayna accidentally hit Yazmine's chair with her purse and excused herself. I rose until Rayna was seated and watched, a little unnerved by Yazmine's observations and Rayna's apprehensions.

"It's currently under consideration," I responded to Yazmine's last question to let her know I wasn't running from the topic. I signaled to our waiter for the check.

Yazmine shot me a nod just before looking over to Rayna and asked, "You okay, beloved?"

"Oh, yeah. I drank a lot of that delicious tea, I had no room left in me for more," Rayna answered with a smile.

Once the check was cleared, we all went out to the wait area of the restaurant where the ladies said their goodnights. Rayna turned to me not knowing what to say. I hadn't told Yazmine about our recent separation. It was in the past as far as I was concerned. Fucking over. Rayna looked at me through her lashes, which told me she was stuck between being upset for my pushing the moving out issue and trying to be polite and play nice for my mother's sake. I didn't let her think too long.

"I'll have Ray take Yazmine back to her hotel and drive you home."

"No, that's okay. You see your mother to the hotel. I'll see you later." I didn't know what Rayna's *later* meant, but one thing was for damn sure: we wouldn't be sleeping apart tonight. And I preferred the comforts of my bed at the marina.

Thankfully, Yazmine chimed in, "No, beloved, you two done had a long day. Y'all go home. 'Dis was real nice and all. I need to go back to the hotel and relax. I'm good alone," she declared with the wave of her hand.

Once again, deadlocking Rayna, and to her dismay. I kissed my mother goodnight, and we parted ways. Rayna and I made our way to Interstate 405.

When Rayna noticed we were exiting off 52 instead of staying on for exit 43 she asked, "Why are we getting off here?"

"Because we're going home, Ms. Brimm."

"I can't stay at the marina, Azmir."

"You can and you will."

"Did you forget about Azna?"

Damn.

I did.

"I'll have Ray swing by to get your keys and then go and pick him up."

"Azmir, that's ridiculous. I'd have to pack some things for him. Besides, I could use an overnight bag myself." Her grimacing gaze seared my profile. I made a U-turn and jumped back on the 405.

We picked up Azna, Rayna grabbed a few things for work the next day, and we were back at the marina in under an hour. I ran her a bath as she played with Azna out in the living room. I was irritated, my mind raced a mile a minute as I sat at the lip of the whirlpool and returned a few e-mails. When the water was done, I set out for the living room to grab Rayna.

"Ready?" I asked her, interrupting her playtime with the pooch.

Rayna's head shot up and the smile...the pure, unadulterated, and natural glow of her smile caused a tremor in my chest. It slowly dissipated while she looked my way. *Damn.* She rose to her feet, but not before giving Azna a final rub and mirthful giggle. I waited for her to continue back down the corridor.

She maintained a few steps ahead of me, but when we passed one of the bedrooms, I yelled out, "Hold up."

She arrested her stride and turned her head for answers. I turned the nob and opened the door, prompting her to enter the room. She slowly ambled toward the door and once she arrived, she craned her neck to take a peek. Once she caught a glimpse of the room, her mouth collapsed, and her eyes fluttered. Rayna stepped into the room holding her face. She looked around to observe the bars attached to mirrored walls and angled her head to the ceiling to see the high fans. Her eyes darted to the floor to observe the hardwood sprung material. She eventually transferred her gaze over to the two flat screen televisions mounting either side of the room and then she landed her attention on the stereo operating the surround sound speakers, suspended on the walls throughout the room. It was her own personal dance room. At the marina. With me.

She stood speechless for a while. I needed to know what she was thinking. I had to know what she was feeling. But I gave her time to process what this was.

"Azmir...it's..." Rayna whispered.

"Your own dance room. Here. At the marina."

"But...why would you go through the trouble?"

"It's no trouble at all to make you feel comfortable here, in *your* home. I don't want you to have to want or need for anything that isn't here with me. I want you here. Permanently."

Rayna covered her eyes, taking long minutes to settle her emotions. I was sure it didn't help that it was that time of the month for her anyway. I waited patiently. I would always wait for her to adjust to me.

Later, I bathed Rayna and gave her a full body massage to help with her menstrual symptoms before we drifted off to sleep. In our bed. Rayna didn't speak much. I figured I'd given her lots to think about and didn't want to disrupt her flow. And besides, I'd said all I needed to say.

Rayna

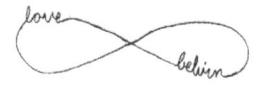

The next morning, I dropped Azna off at my place in Redondo Beach. I needed to be sure I wanted to try again with Azmir before falling into the same peculiar arrangement that got us into this estranged place we were in. I took off to work and went about my day as usual.

My appointment flow at work was normal and all of my morning patients were familiar, but what wasn't was my inability to get Azmir's betrayal out of my head. The visual imageries of him taking *her* face into his mouth drove me crazy, and wondering how she liked it threatened upheavals of bile from the pits my stomach. I couldn't shake the fear of upcoming events when they'd be left together *alone*.

At one point during my third appointment, I had to abruptly leave the room, requesting my PTA to take over. I barely reached my desk before the tears streamed down my face. Breathing became painful and the more I recalled Azmir's sweetly making love to me a few days ago, I couldn't help but see visions of him on top of Dawn Taylor.

It starts off with a kiss for everybody.

My thoughts led to more questions fueling my curiosities. And before I knew it, I was sitting behind my desk and had Googled Dawn Taylor. An impressive number of hits filled the page. One link catching my eye was her *Facebook* page. I clicked on it and saw it was open to the public. I'd only known a bit about *Facebook* from my brief tutorial with Michelle the day she came to the office to show me how to set up a page for the Long Beach City office. That day, I looked up Azmir only to learn he didn't have one at the time, but the recreation center did. Immediately, I called on the recollection of Michelle's guidance.

Dawn was an avid poster. She had a personal page aside from her PR firm's fan page. After spending less than a minute on her personal page, it was painfully obvious she was crushing on a man, a man who fit Azmir's description. She'd post random things like:

Oh, 6 foot 4 inches of dark chocolate glory...
Take a chance on me, trust me to market your story.
I can lead you to places your half a billion can't afford you...
Take a trip with me into erotic gateways that only I can fit you through.
You say things are too complicated and she makes it impossible...
Take me on like your body told me how much my touch was critical.

This bitch is insane. My hand clenched the mouse, almost cracking it. My heart sped, colliding into my chest.

I clicked on *About* and saw her relationship status set to *"It's complicated."* I went back out to her timeline to see frequent postings, asking her friends to "like" *Cobalt*'s page, the rec center's page, and *Mauve*'s page and a few more names I didn't recognize, like *Global Fusions*. But what I did know was the first two were a part of Azmir's brand. When I came to the picture of her and Azmir at some event last week, I became lightheaded and needed to recline in my office chair to secure my equilibrium. I gripped the chair handles to help steady my head spin. Rage pumped in my veins, and I saw red when I glanced over at Dawn's crooked smile.

I'm not sure how long I sat there; I lost track of time and

reason. My phone buzzed and it was Sharon, making me aware of my next appointment. I took a minute to gather myself then pushed myself out of my office to face the remainder of my day.

After lunch, my phone pinged. It was a text from Azmir.

At the airport. I have to make an emergency trip along with my attorneys up to Canada. Rich's daughter was in an accident earlier today so I couldn't defer this to him. I'll be back as soon as things get settled. I trust you and Azna will settle back into the marina seamlessly. Call me once you do.

I didn't respond. I didn't know what to say. I felt the push in his words about settling in at the marina. I knew I had to soon tell him it wouldn't be happening. Him being in Canada gave me some time to think of just how I would.

I thought about Yazmine and wondered if she had packed her things up and was awaiting my call to have her move into my place. I also thought of Chef Boyd showing up to the marina to cook for an empty apartment. All of the inconveniences of me not being forthcoming strangled me at the throat. I challenged myself to let it go and to think about me first. It was Azmir who'd cheated. It was him who wouldn't set the record straight with his delusional PR stalker. I would let him work out all the nuances of me not moving back into the marina. Hopefully he'd do a better job than what he did with Dawn Taylor.

It wasn't until later when I sat alone in my living room, working on charts that I decided to pen Azmir a letter to hopefully explain my plans. I opened a new e-mail and started typing away.

Azmir,

I received your text and hope you were able to resolve your issues in Canada. I know it must be difficult having to change the course of your plans unexpectedly. Unfortunately, I'll be adding to that.

Azmir, I will not be moving back in with you. I apologize in advance for the inconvenience this may cause in planning Yazmine's living situation. It's just that no matter how hard I

fight to forget, I can't let go of your betrayal with Dawn Taylor. It was an eye-opener and I feel it's not totally your fault. You have emotional needs apparently I'm not meeting, which is probably why we haven't taken on a formal relationship. As much as I am working on my deficiencies, I cannot expect you to wait on me to heal what ails me internally. I am damaged and it's not fair to you at this point in your life when things are going so well to have to baby-sit a woman who's so broken she can't assist with your needs. Dawn's presence reminds me there are other women who are more than willing to give you what you need while you wait on the glue to dry as I attempt to piece myself back together. Hopefully, we can take some time next week to discuss me returning your car and the things you've gifted me. Except for Azna. I wouldn't survive losing the only two beings connected to my heart.

Please know that as much as you may hate me, I hate myself for fooling the both of us into thinking I could love you the way you needed to be loved. I appreciate all you've done to make me feel whole and alive in my otherwise motionless and empty existence. I want you happy more than I want to continue to risk hurting you and at the end revealing those very things you were waiting to surface in me were actually improbable possibilities.

Take care.

I owe you a debt of gratitude far beyond what I deserve.

Rayna

The next two days came and went. My period and its symptoms relented and dissipated, much to my relief. I was still very blue, but miraculously still in motion.

On Friday, I met with Brian Thompson to discuss the impending lawsuit against the practice. He needed to brief me on the details of it and what to expect in the upcoming weeks from the preliminary hearings. I couldn't believe how quickly things were progressing. And to my surprise, the PTA who had been transferred to my location two weeks prior was at the center of it. Apparently, he was transferred to me as a legal strategy when he was accused of sexual harassment by one of the interns at the Orange County location.

Naturally, I was livid and asked how ethical it was to put other staff at risk of the same harassment Wayne Tanner was being accused of. Thompson did his best to explain the procedure was standard and other tactics were being considered to protect all parties involved. We spoke extensively about the situation, and it added to the mountain of stress pressuring the levy in my world.

When I peered up to check the time, I noticed it was well after two in the afternoon, and I was starved.

"Thompson, I'm sorry to be rude…"

"Shit. I didn't realize how much time had passed. I hope I didn't keep you from seeing patients."

"No. Not at all. It's just that I'm hungry. I've been moving so much over the past few days, I've been neglectful in nourishing my body." I gave a sheepish smile. I could be so "valley," something I'd often accused Michelle of.

"I could use a bite myself. Why don't we go grab a late lunch? There's a new spot at *Marina Pacifica* I'd love to check out."

I stilled at his invitation. It had always been a red zone for me. I never had to think about the answer, just how to formulate a no. Until today.

Thompson snorted, "It's just lunch, Rayna. I'll even let you pay if that'll make you feel better."

I exhaled into laughter. His proposal was actually attractive. "My stomach won't allow me to say no. Let me clear it with Sharon, and I'll meet you outside."

The biggest, most endearing smile crested upon Brian's face. It was as if he'd won his first sports championship as an adolescent. It also felt good to let down my guard, and I looked forward to a simple lunch date with someone low-key.

The lunch date turned out to be all but simple. My marred judgment to order a cocktail was the first strike. I was so wound up and knew I didn't have any more patients for the rest of the day, so I used that to make it okay to order a second. Brian followed suit and enjoyed *Patron* pomegranate cocktails, an odd drink for a man in my opinion. The ambiance of the restaurant on the water was familiar. It was the backdrop to many of the dining excursions Azmir had arranged for us, only I wasn't with Azmir. I was with Brian Thompson, laughing mindlessly at the candor of his feelings for the higher ups of the practice.

"Jim Katz has no balls. He allows Dan to take risks all the time leaving the practice so damn vulnerable. And *he's* a fucking pathological liar. You know that Dan Smith is lying through his teeth when his nose turns red."

I balled over in laughter. I knew that crimson nose so well. "Even the lumps on it turn a special shade of pink!" I spat out.

"Oh, so you know the infamous indicator, too?" he cackled as he put his glass back down on the table.

"Yes, Michelle put me up on to it my first week of interning with the practice."

"Shit. I wish I'd had someone to give me the heads up before my first sit down with an opposing attorney."

We laughed hysterically as we covered a myriad of topics. It was nice to escape reality, even if only for a couple of hours. It afforded me the opportunity to meet *another* Brian Thompson, one

I needed at this point in my crazy world. I was relieved to have safety and a carefree environment conducive to my emotional state at this time.

Somewhere, mid our third drink when the waiter was clearing our plates, Brian muttered, "This has been my dream for the past two months."

"What?" I sighed, catching my breath from my last laughing spree.

"Seeing you this free to laugh around me. To see a new smile upon your face, one that I affected." His gaze into me narrowed as I experienced the sincerity in Thompson's eyes. If he was kicking game, he had me believing him.

"Well, thanks for the laughs." I took a sip of my cosmopolitan. "Considering the past couple weeks I've had, it feels good to laugh."

"Your smile compliments your cut. It's beautiful by the way. It unleashes your femininity." Thompson's tone stopped short of a growl.

I could tell he was measuring his coquetry. For some reason, I was pleased he, not only noticed my new change, but approved of it, something I doubted Azmir did. Azmir was extremely fond of my natural mane. He even loved it more when it was wild and unrestrained. Humbly, I brushed the back of my neck, something I'd been making a habit of because it was exposed. I felt empowered.

"*You're* beautiful," Thompson continued. My brows furrowed at his openness. "Not that you haven't always been, but this is a new side of your beauty I wasn't privy to before today. I feel honored, and now I'm jealous." He didn't break his deep gaze when he lifted his hand to drink from his martini glass.

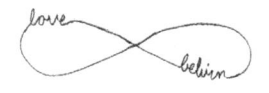

Brian and I made it back to the practice just before five p.m., and through my inebriated fog, I saw people taking to their cars, ending another workweek. I noticed Brian's smooth dash around his sleek white *BMW 750* to open my door. I was careful to stand gracefully considering my state. Once out, I leaned into the car, giving him enough room to close the door. I wanted to thank him for a nice afternoon outing. I'd likely be heading out after clearing my desk.

Thompson's smoldering eyes were drunken with strong desire that couldn't be mistaken. When his mouth came into my face, I knew what he was doing but didn't have the speed of mind and-or the coordination of body to move clear out of the way of his tempting lips. I felt the heat from his tequila fragrant breath and braced myself when I was abruptly hit with the realization that it wasn't Azmir's familiar brandy mixture. But it was too late.

"YOU MUST HAVE LOST YOUR FUCKIN' MIND!"

The frightening shriek rang familiar and had my legs quivering in my pumps. My movements were slow thanks to the four cocktails I'd downed at the restaurant, but eventually I was able to turn to see Azmir's onrush towards me and immediately felt him toss my limpid body away from the car. Panic settled in when I couldn't stop flying and then I felt the arms of someone else. I looked up to find Ray's long arms surrounding me, breaking me from my near-cement collision.

Thompson flew into a rage. "What in the hell do you think you're doing, Jacobs? She doesn't belong to you anymore!"

Azmir's seething eyes left mine before he looked over to Thompson, and I saw red in them. They were droopy and told stories of his lack of sleep, restlessness, and something darker—*fury*. He was draped in a wonderfully fitted two-piece dark gray suit with a hint of a gloss exposing his deliciously crafted thighs, and his dress shirt was untucked with the first few buttons undone. The stubble in his face couldn't go unnoticed. While the look flawed on most men, it wondrously made Azmir's look edgy and sexy as hell and turned me on to an end. My strong, commanding, virile mogul was exhausted, and looked at me with such ferocity it terrified me. In a flash, I saw pain and betrayal in his eyes oddly giving my drunken state a boost of courage.

"Who do you think you are, making a scene like this?" I fired away.

Azmir's face scrunched as he walked closer to me suspiciously. It was deathly frightening. I didn't know what he was capable of, because I'd never seen him this angry...with me. That's when I saw Thompson rushing Azmir, and before I knew it, he swung his fist and hit the tip of Azmir's chin and seemingly without much impact.

Fearing Azmir would be caught off guard and harmed, I screamed, "Nooooooo!"

Azmir, unfazed by the minor blow due to Thompson's inaccuracy and lack of strength, maintained his amble towards me.

"Are you... Have you been drinking?"

I didn't know how to respond to his question. His revelation made me feel exposed and that somewhere along the way I'd allowed my drunken state to show. His scowl effectively forced me off my balance and farther into Ray's hold. Angrily, I snatched away from him, trying desperately to give a façade of dignity.

"What is it to you, Azmir?" was all I could think to retort.

Azmir reached over to me, causing me to flinch, and with tender care, wiped my right eye.

"You let her...fuckin' did this to her in the middle of a workday?" Azmir yelled over to Thompson.

That's when I saw Thompson, again launching toward Azmir, "Don't fucking touch her!" he screamed violently and hit Azmir in the back of his head.

Again, Azmir didn't recoil. It was as if Thompson's efforts were from an errant toddler.

Hoarsely, Azmir ordered to Ray, "Take her to the fuckin' marina! I'll be there in a minute!" Brooklyn was definitely in effect.

When Ray gently, yet firmly took me at my shoulders, he urged, "Come on, Ms. Brimm. Let's go."

"No! I'm not going anywhere!" I screamed at the top of my lungs. "Azmir, I don't belong to you. I'm not one of your many assets!"

Calmly and with gentle tugs, Ray begged, "Ms. Brimm, please. We're causing a scene at your place of business."

Huhn?

I turned to see at least a dozen people gawking at the events taking place. Then what should have been my initial fear in a sober mind had arrived. At least a half a dozen of brawny and treacherous looking men suddenly started closing in on our cipher and zeroed in on Thompson like vultures to its prey.

"Give the word, Divine!" the thick one with his shirt already removed vowed, flexing his chest muscles, nearly drooling with harmful anticipation.

Azmir, without looking at them, raised his left index finger in the air. The gang stopped in their tracks. "Legal Eagle," Azmir spoke firmly. Even through my drunken state, I presumed it was cryptic for *lawyer*.

He then looked over to me and roared, "You stay the fuck put until I get there!"

That's when Ray practically lifted me in the air, pulling me away from Azmir and Thompson. I wanted to scream and to pull from Ray's grasp, but before I could sway my body, I saw Azmir walk into Thompson's person with his head cocked to the side, saying something not audible. I couldn't hear what Thompson said in return either but saw when he took another jab at Azmir. It was caught effortlessly midair. After he grabbed Thompson's fist with lightning speed, he struck him square in the face twice, causing blood to squirt from Thompson's face before his legs gave out and he collapsed on the ground. Azmir stood over him, still speaking as if Thompson was in any condition to respond.

Thompson's body was sprawled out and motionless on the

concrete. Just like the guy on the dance floor with me last summer, Thompson didn't see his doom coming. Azmir was a quiet storm, unassuming and I believed that's the way he wanted to be reputed. As Ray placed me in the car, I heard Azmir's voice raise as he repeatedly asked him, "Didn't I fuckin' warn you to stay away from her?"

It tore at my chest to see Azmir so angry and in acrimony while I was being hauled off, unable to calm him. Thompson was laid out on the ground, bloodied without Azmir even breaking a sweat.

I sat on the sofa back at the marina with tears streaming down my tightened and stained face. In the past thirty minutes, I'd cried so many tears—some had dried, making tracks down my trembling cheeks and others fresher, tasting of bitter regret. Guilt had settled in while I rewound time and replayed it over and over again in my mind. My chest heaved in my blouse violently, my diaphragm was hyperactive with spasms. My quivering lips were moist from the warm breaths rushing through my mouth. As my cosmopolitan high came down, I couldn't believe the many lapses in judgment leading me to this agonizing place.

Was Azmir arrested? Was Thompson hospitalized? Will this ruin Azmir's image? Will I have a job? How will I deal with his impending hatred of me? I couldn't begin to piece together a plan of resolve after this.

Was it worth it?

The plan was to sit. And wait.

Ray had kindly walked me to the door and let me in. I didn't have my keys. Azmir had snatched them from the ground after they'd dropped from my hand when he pulled me from Thompson's fold. I couldn't go home to check on Azna. He needed to be let out and fed, *he can't call for help. Will Azmir call from the county jail?* He wouldn't call me; he has handlers for that. The cogs of my mind wouldn't slow.

Will Brett be calling me with the news? Perhaps Dawn Taylor. *Oh, god! What have I done?* My fretful thoughts wouldn't halt.

I jumped and swung my body around when I heard the door snatched open. Azmir's lengthy physique forced through the door frame, cupping Azna in one arm while carrying two duffle bags on his other shoulder. I immediately recognized them. They were the same ones I'd packed from here when I left him last week. His eyes seized mine right away. I steeled.

He dropped the bags from his shoulder and let down Azna, who didn't run over to me. Instead, my little fur ball ran toward the back of the apartment, possibly looking for his old toys. Azmir sauntered past me and over to the bar there in the living room, near the waterfront view of the picturesque marina. He snatched a tumbler and poured a half a glass of brandy and in seconds, drained it before going for another. Seconds felt like hours anticipating his next move. The silence was deafening, but my throat was constricted, and fear gripped my liberty to speak. He emptied the second glass of amber juice and slammed it on the bar, spewing mumbled profanities. My sweaty hands clawed the sofa.

He set his fixation out on the marina and with a calm voice feeling like a roar in my heart, he asked, "Do you want Thompson?"

My eyes widened and mouth went dry as I parted my lips. "No," I spoke with trembling cords.

"Well, why the fuck would you get drunk with him during work hours?"

I didn't know how to answer that. I didn't have to.

"What do I have to do?" he asked with a frightening even tone.

I didn't understand his question. With a deep swallow, I attempted to wet my throat.

"Do...?"

His head jolted over to me infuriatingly. "Do! What do I have to do to make you feel safe again? What do I have to do to get you to forget about Thompson and...and Dawn...and to get you back to understanding here is where you belong?" His breath gave out and his fist rose to his mouth. I knew there was no way around this conversation.

"Time," I submitted just above a whisper.

Azmir slammed both fists into the bar and all the bottles on top leaped in place and met the bar top with a clash on their way down. *"FUCK TIME! YOU DON'T KNOW WHAT TO DO WITH IT!"* His vicious shout in his Brooklyn tongue vibrated off the walls.

My head flew back into the sofa and wind came crushing through my mouth audibly. There, was that frightening side of Azmir I'd guessed laid dormant. I couldn't believe I'd caused the resurgence of it. I'd uncovered the rage.

"In all my projected thoughts and plans of aging, never once did they include scraping at the meat of my nails..." he glanced down at his hands, and I shivered at the visual. "...to keep a woman in my arms, at my side, in my home, or in my bed. Never once did I think she wouldn't feel I was good enough to hold on to."

His words plummeted my heart in double time. My throat closed up. I couldn't breathe. "No, Azmir. It's not like that," I whimpered.

His scowl darted back over to me. "The hell it ain't!" he scoffed. "You run every chance you get. You run!"

"It's not like you have no culpability in this," I bravely murmured, offended by his summary of things.

"FUCK DAWN!"

"YOU WANTED TO!" I jumped from the couch and dug my feet into the Persian rug, seething at his audacity. "You can stand here and lie all you want, but I know you—I know your sexual temperament. You wanted to fuck her, just like you wanted to fuck me after our first kiss," I charged back at him.

He cocked his head to the side, pushing his tongue into his

molars and walked slowly over to me with revelation in his eyes. "Is that what you were going to do? *Wuh*—was that your plan? To take him home and fuck him?" His brows were furrowed, masking the deep stirring of his wrath as he searched my eyes for the truth.

"*I*—I would *never* stoop so low. I can't believe you asked me that—"

"You let him kiss you! If I hadn't come out there looking for you to return, you would have—" he turned in disgust at the thought. "Gah!" He tramped back toward the water's view with one hand on his hip and the other in the air as he swung it aimlessly and so hard, I jumped.

What did I do? Would I have kissed Thompson back? Am I even attracted to him? I mean, he is an attractive man, but does he even catch my attention? Or was my behavior retribution for Azmir's betrayal? Had I allowed my pain and angst from his kissing Dawn to push me to behave so reckless? That was it—that was my motive!

"You kissed her," I murmured.

"And you let him kiss you!" He shot back with his gaze steady on the marina and his voice with a sudden tremor. "When I saw his lips touch yours... I felt a pain spike my dick as if that motherfucka' tried to yank it from my body. He tried taking something that is attached to me!"

Tears pooled my eyes and my throat choked out, "Well, I'm glad you know how it feels."

Azmir's head swung around, and his eyes pierced through me like a sword. Before I knew it, his lean frame jaunted over to me, and his hand cradled my head as his mouth covered mine. His tongue pushed through my lips as his strong arm pulled me into him by the small of my back. The brandy...the stench of auburn juice I'd come to appreciate, hit my nostrils, surging through my brain, alerting of a familiar fragrance and suddenly every cell in my body came alive and hypersensitive to his scent, touch, and sight.

He reached down, ripped off my blouse and tore the zipper of my skirt. His touch was so abrasive, but my body responded to it so well; I needed it. I needed him. To cleanse me, my mind, and inoculate my body of every memory of another man's touch. And I wanted him to. I wanted him to free me of everything preventing me from loving him the way he needed me to—because I knew I needed him.

His head bowed and from my chin to my eyelids he licked every stained tear from my face. My breasts felt so heavy in my bra and my breathing was uncontrolled. His tongue traveled down to my neck, and I pushed his head into me, clawing my frustrations at him, my insecurities of his adoration for another woman. My chest heaved again, and tears began to pool *again*. I collapsed my hands to my side.

"No. No more shutting down." Azmir looked down into my eyes and growled, "*No...*"

He dropped to his knees, desperately pulling down my panties and yanked my leg over his shoulder. He flickered his wicked tongue into my valley. I was already aroused, already slickened, so wet I feared remnants of mother nature lingering. But Azmir's groans spoke endorsements of the flavor he craved. He took me at the hips and pushed my sex into his face as his deft tongue shoved into my canal. My spine shivered as I held on to his shoulders, reveling in the sight of me, standing in the middle of his living room, wearing nothing more than a bra and having Azmir Jacobs on his knees before me, beckoning my orgasm. What woman wouldn't die for this? How many would pay anything to be in my thigh-high hosiery right now. *Especially Dawn Taylor.* At her name crossing my mind, my eyes shot open, and I froze, but not before my body started to quiver from Azmir's tireless efforts below.

"Let it go! There is only me and you. It has always only been me and you," he declared from beneath me, and I could see lasciviousness start settling in through his slanted eyes.

And after just three more feather-light flickers of his firm tongue, my orgasm overtook me, tingling my nipples and warming the pads of my feet. Azmir's groans intensified my ascension into an outer orbit realm. I felt him lifting me from his shoulders, into the air. I landed on the sofa. My heart pounded through my chest as I tried to come down.

He plopped down next to me after removing his jacket. His head flew back against the sofa and his eyes closed, scrunched as though he was in pain. I knew it was from what my reckless actions had caused. *Is he having second thoughts?* My heart wanted to relieve him just like he had just done me. Provide momentary reprieve. In spite of my ill-actions, he still wanted me, he was willing to take a chance with me, just as I was right after I'd learned of his kiss with Dawn?

I jumped to my feet in front of him and fell to my knees, frantically unbuttoning his shirt. It was ridiculously tedious, but I was on a mission.

"I need you to tell me, Rayna. You haven't told me since you left me," he growled. His voice was low and hoarse.

My eyes shot up to him, but he didn't open his, just remained reclined and defeated. I made my way to his belt and then the waistband of his slacks. I tried yanking down his boxer briefs along with his slacks, but soon discovered I needed his assistance. Much to my relief, he slowly lifted his lap so I could pull them down. Not able to get them down to his ankles after being caught with the loveliness of his beautifully erect, glistening, and throbbing appendage, with rash effort I pulled him into my mouth, deep, desperate, and greedily taking relentless draws of him. With a need down deep in my belly, my tongue rolled over his head in lightning and firm speed, summoning drops of his fluids to quench my emotional thirst. I applied gentle chomps and moaned at the appreciation of being in Azmir's lap instead of any other's, inhaling his sensual musk from his private area. I yearned for it; I needed it.

His spine became fluid, so he attempted to sit erect in his seat, and I relished the roll of his abdomen muscles as his belly lurched. He moaned angrily and I could, too, sense his hesitation. His haunting thoughts of Thompson and me being as intimate in any way.

He wouldn't open his eyes when he slurred, "Tell me."

With two determined fists, I jerked him, beckoning his juices into my mouth, my belly. Badly, I wanted it to wash me of the despair I felt from coming so close to losing him. *To Dawn?* I stroked and pumped and swirled and sucked with hollow jaws. When his back coiled and slammed into the sofa, I knew he was ready. In desperate anticipation, I repositioned myself on my knees to prepare to catch him, every ounce of his sweet juices.

"No—*ahhh*!" he bellowed, and I went into a frenzy, drawing him in and pulling him out of my mouth until the first squirt of his specimens hit the roof my mouth, causing me to grind my pelvis in the air below him. I was so turned on, I moaned on every morsel from him. It was so much, and I was eager to catch it all, filling my belly until he stilled beneath me.

When he peered down at me, I saw vengeance, it was in the snarl of his lips and the cocking of his neck. He reached down to me and with his thumb, smudged a drop of his semen escaping my lips, over my mouth, back and forth, lubricating my swollen and pounding flesh. He used the same smug look he wore in San Diego. It hurt.

"Say it. Tell me."

My heart crushed in my chest and tears chased down my face. *Why is he doing this to me?* Then it hit me. I never saw him kiss Dawn Taylor, but he saw Thompson with me. He had a visual to haunt him possibly forever, I'd only had my imagination.

"Fucking tell me, Rayna!" he yelled.

I sat there on my knees, trembling through tears, and lied to him through a shaky whisper, "I don't know what you want me to say."

He growled. Frustrated, he stood and lifted me to my feet. Then he stepped out of his shoes, pants, and boxer briefs with a penetrating glare. Circling me like a predator, he completed three hundred-sixty degrees.

Azmir lifted me into the air, forcing me to straddle him and walked us into the dining room where he forcefully pushed the decorative place settings to the side, breaking a glass and plate on the far opposite end without flinching.

He laid me out on the table and with the same deadpan glare he muttered, "I will make you scream it."

My legs trembled and even with the acute pain flashing through my chest, I couldn't speak and give him what he was asking for. Once he realized I wouldn't speak, he stretched my legs as far as they would go and with a swift plunge, he rammed into me. I yelped in pain at the fullness of my belly. Azmir could be brutal and my memory of it was crisp. He began pounding me with fury and after moments, cocked his head to the side. Azmir was sending a message. He wasn't going to let up until I gave into him and did as he asked.

I was scared out of my mind yet refused to forget about his betrayal. It hurt and I was pleased to share the sentiment. As conflicting as my feelings were, it pained me to take revenge on the man I loved. The man who hurt me.

His thrusts were delicious, but we were warring here, and I refused to let him break me. That was until he cleverly angled his hips, dipping his knees so he started to rub fiercely against that sensitive spot deep inside my womb. He pumped furiously until my body bowed from the table, giving into a violent orgasm coursing through my stubborn frame, shattering me into pieces. I bit down on the insides of my lips to keep from screaming out insanities of pleasure. His glare suddenly turned satisfying because he knew he was breaking me down, thrust by thrust.

Azmir pulled me from the table and flipped me over without a moment for me to register the movements. He pinned me to the table and lifted my right leg to the chair next to me and started plunging into me. My face suffered from spasms at his fullness. My body tendered to him in spite of his rough handling. Azmir knew it, he was greatly skilled at the art of sex. His hand traveled to the apex of my thighs, and he massaged my pearl with nearly as much speed as he plunged into me from behind. I was losing my mind, trying to control the pleasure spiking through me. My upper torso slammed into the table when my arms gave out on me. Azmir hooked me at the shoulders with his arms and lifted me to his chest, taking me, maliciously tantalizing my body.

"I need to hear it," he forced through my ear as he rested his face against me limp neck.

"Ah...ah...ah...ah!" flew from my lungs as I shuddered in his arms from another brutal orgasm.

Damn my overly-responsive body. Damn Azmir and his practice of sexual manipulation!

I felt a smile forming on his face against my cheek.

Screw you, Jacobs! My head bobbled as he held me from behind.

"I can do this all night," Azmir hissed then he turned me and lifted me onto himself where I straddled him. My body was weak, undulated from two near-death orgasms. Inspiration hit when Azmir entered me again—still strong, still erect. He was going to sex me into submission. I didn't think I could endure another orgasm. My body could receive no more pleasure. I was drained and overly-satiated. I could take no more.

"Azmir," I begged over fatigued pants.

With his left hand, he snaked my fatigued body and with his right he cupped my face forcing me to look at him. Through heavy eyes I saw his determination. A shiver of fear ran through me.

"Tell me and I'll stop," he murmured softly, but with caveat.

I was too weak for a poker face. So, I collapsed my face into his neck. He anchored me from my shoulder and started his upward thrusts. It wasn't long before I felt the warm impressions from his presence inside of me. Not too soon after, the quickening started flashing in my core. He was so deep and felt so good. Even without my participation of will, he pleasured my body.

Fear struck. I knew another orgasm was nearing. "No. No. Stop. Right now...stop!" I whimpered.

My body couldn't take any more excitement. It was torturing. It was control. I thought I was going to pass out again. This wasn't passionate love making between two consenting partners. It was torment and a vicious battle of wills. It didn't matter what my mind could perceive, my body gave in. I choked in tears as my orgasm ambushed me and my body convulsed inside of Azmir's strong chest and arms. I was losing it. Losing my mind, body, and now will.

"I LOVE YOU! I LOVE YOU! EVEN THOUGH YOU BETRAYED ME. LIKE A FOOL, I STILL LOVE YOU! I WILL ALWAYS LOVE YOU, AZMIR!" I howled from the pits of my belly over the last stretch of my orgasm.

Never in my life had my brain been so mis-wired and detached from my body. The experience was surreal. I hated him in this moment. Hated his strong-willed nature, hated my need to be dominated by him in order to express myself. Hated myself for being so weak and in love.

Azmir exhaled audibly. He started to plunge harder and deeper, he held me to his chest so strong and possessively. He pumped into me insanely until his erratic breathing finally told me he was ready to climax. In an instant, he laid me back down on the dining room table and pulled out of me with sharp withdrawal and I lay there in disbelief as I saw hot, rich semen shoot from him onto my body. It wouldn't stop. The first of a series of squirts landed on my chest, nipping my chin, then my upper abdomen. Azmir's body jerked with every gush. Another round landed on my lower belly and finally the last of it hit my pelvis, stretching down to my sex. As I watched each spurt and its landing, my gaze went between it and Azmir's empty eyes.

When he was done, there was arctic silence so startling, I cried. I was laid out on the top of Azmir's dining room table with my legs hiked beneath me, looking at his extracts splayed across my body, weeping at the despondency swathing his existence. *Where did he go?* He was not my Azmir.

My sobs grew vocal, but he was unfazed. He reached over me and once again, smeared his semen, this time over my chest, breasts, rib cage, belly, and finally my vagina. His touch was course and devoid of affection. He was marking me, branding me like some animal. He didn't have to say it. It was understood. This was his response to my delayed obedience. To my betrayal.

He sauntered off into the living room and pulled on his pants. Seconds later, I heard the slamming of his office door.

The tears wouldn't stop.

Azmir

I was fucking pissed! Sitting at my desk, breathing erratically, I wanted to punch the shit out of something. I tried to collect myself, center the rage surging from my gut to the surface of my being. I watched her on the surveillance monitor. Still spread out on the dining room table, still sobbing uncontrollably. As much as a small part of me wanted to go and console her, I couldn't summon the compassion to do it.

Fuck! I smeared my semen on my lady's face and her body, marking her like some fucking caveman. It felt good. *Dominion.* She looked so bruised. So raw. *So tamed.* The only time I can control Rayna is when my dick is buried in her—or my tongue. This shit has spun out of control, my world was off its axis. I'd forfeited my control over it for a woman who runs from me at every turn.

I jolted from my chair when she moved, watched her like a vulture.

Rayna better not try to make a dash out of that door, or I swear with everything I have, I would drag her little ass back in here by the roots of her hair if I had to.

Caveman is right.

Shit! What is this?

I knew what it was. She had acquired my heart, and I needed to possess her. *She is fucking mine. All of her!* Every inch of her hair, every cell on her precious body.

I watched as she sat up on the table and observed my sperm plastered from her chest to her thighs, my seeds coating her torso. The sight of it made my dick rock hard. Animalistic, I know—and incongruously, I didn't give a fuck. This—this was what she did to me.

Rayna stumbled from the table, trying to find her balance. I had her legs pinned up so high, I needed to reach the depths of her. She'd feel the echoes of my dick for days. *As she should.* I watched as she wobbled feebly into the living room, collecting her things. My fingers gripped the sides of my chair and my tense shoulders leaned forward, ready to lunge out of my office if she fucking touched that doorknob. My heartbeat accelerated and I felt the perspiration misting just above my eyebrows. She was not fucking leaving me. No way. Not again.

I sighed of relief when she turned right, toward the back of the apartment. *All praises be to Allah for her good senses.* She stopped at my office door. I couldn't believe I was in my office, watching this shit go down as if it wasn't my life. She was feet away, at my door, contemplating her next move as I watched her raise her fist, prepared to knock. Within seconds, her arm recoiled, and she cupped her mouth and cried silently.

Again, I fought to comfort her, to lift her in my arms and pour my shredded heart out to her in hopes of her understanding my position and the need for her to be patient with me and ride this shit out. But I didn't. Visions of Brian Thompson's cock-sucking lips reaching hers riled up my inner G who didn't do comfort. We defiled, destroyed, and took what we want.

Every time I replayed the image of him reaching for her face, I felt sharp pains in my dick. I wanted to kill him. I considered it as I cocked the shit out of his face, aiming for his lips. The lips that touched my lady. If I could've thought of legal ways to kill him and pay my attorneys my entire fortune to preserve my freedom so I could be with Rayna, I would have. He let her get drunk and tried to fuck her. I knew that would've been next. I'm a man. We fuck our prey, and he'd been patiently waiting for the right opportunity. If I had not been there, at that very moment when they returned. If I had not made a turnaround trip. Had not told the pilot to keep the plane juiced. Had I not believed her letter, attempting to terminate *us*. It would have been his cock inside her, and this would have played out a lot differently.

FUCK!

The first officer on the scene was a former employee of mine, who asked me to leave the parking lot immediately and contact my attorney, which expedited my trip home to deal with her. To make sure she hadn't run again. This had been the cycle of my life; I fuck up, she runs, we fuck, she stays. But this time was different. She ran to the arms of another man. *How do I deal with this?*

Rayna turned on her heel and headed to the master suite. *Wise decision.* Her loud sobs down the hall tore my heart from my chest. *But I'm a G.* I just sat there, feeling it justified and my growing problem solved. She'd complied. My dick got hard again. *Fuck!*

Control was a dangerous addiction, but it was even more hazardous when its fleeting. Suddenly, I felt the need for another swig of brandy. I needed to relax. My phones' constant ringing snapped me out of my trance. I wasn't surprised when I saw damn near fifty alerts. I knew people were calling about the incident in the parking lot. My assistants, attorney, and PR team.

I just needed to get to Rayna first. So, when I left the scene, I shot over to her place, washed the remainder of Thompson's blood from my hands then scooped Azna and some of her clothes and toiletries. She would not be returning there to stay. It was clear to me Rayna didn't know how to handle time apart.

I took some time to return the calls, starting with Chesney, my spitfire attorney, giving him a run down on the situation. He, in turn, called my public relations people. I knew Dawn and Shayna would have much preferred hearing from me, but I had other people to reach out to and in all honesty, everything they needed to know could come from Chesney and his legal associates. I reached out to Petey with the details of my next move with Thompson and then called Brett with instructions for the staff, particularly those who were out there in the parking lot. I asked him to expect a media briefing from Chesney's firm as to how to address the media and/or Thompson and his legal team.

I sat and contemplated and analyzed and designed and schemed until I was satisfied with my stance and plan. By the time I reached the master suite, I could tell Rayna had showered and washed her hair before getting into bed. I showered and met her there. It didn't take long for me to fall into slumber.

I lunged from the bed. My body was heavily perspired, and my heart was raced and banged against my chest. I recollected images from my nightmare. My head swung over to find Rayna, and I saw her resting peacefully as her, *now short* hair was tidily in place on her pillow. I knew it would take some time for me to adjust to not having her long, wild mane splayed in my bed or in my face. Or my lap.

Desperate to feel her warmth, I lunged down and kissed her. My lips moved hard and swift as I grabbed the back of her scalp, urging her to awaken. I needed her. New visions of Thompson's mouth over Rayna's and her receiving his, just outside of her bedroom, at her place in Redondo Beach caused me to shiver as I tried to catch my breath. *She walked him into her bedroom!* Rayna eyes shot open, and her lips hardened.

"Brimm," I called out to her to let her know I was in need of her.

I wanted to calm her. My tongue swooped into her mouth as though I was wiping away any traces of another man. *What the fuck am I doing?* The Thompson shit had crept into my subconscious and manifested into my dreams. For the first time in my life, I was physically shaken. I rolled her over onto her back and lowered my boxers to enter her. Her breathing accelerated. I put the head of my dick into her warm folds.

"Azmir. I'm sore..." Rayna panted.

"*Shhhhh...*" I beckoned. I couldn't stop myself. "I'll take it slow."

I could feel her juices with the tip of my cock. She was always ready. I took my time working her in. I had to feel her, had to claim her. Possess her. Rayna was warm and the more I stroked, the more inviting she'd become. I felt her tensing underneath me, and I buried my face in her neck to hide my guilt. To shield my barbaric nature. As much as I knew it was wrong, I couldn't fight the impulse to do it.

What the fuck!

I felt the warm tear running from her left eye when it traveled down to my forehead. I knew right away she was crying, but I couldn't stop. I angled my hips to be sure to hit her most sensitive spot. Within seconds, she shivered. I kept working her to work Thompson out of my head. I was alive inside of her. I felt that dominion while inside of her. And when she bowed off the bed and gripped my back preparing to come, I pumped harder until we climaxed together. In my heart, I swore I would never let Rayna go again.

CHAPTER 6

Azmir

The sunlight was bright on the other side of my lids, but I wasn't ready to awaken. It had been a long night. One quickly turning into morning. As I started to recount why such was the case, I recalled the horrendous events regarding Rayna.

Rayna!

My torso leapt in the air, and I frantically searched the bed for my fleeting woman. Shit! She wasn't in sight. I made my way out of the bed and did a quick scan over into the sitting room. No Rayna. I made my way over to the balcony, perhaps she was getting some morning air. She's done that quite often. The view is to die for she's said. But the door was locked, which means there's next to no chance she's out there. Still desperate, I went and gave a cursory glance anyway. No damn Rayna.

By now, I was perspiring—my fucking mouth was going dry, and my heart was trembling. I made my way over to the bathroom. The door was wide open.

Shit!

"Rayna," I called out, not recognizing the pathetic anxiety in my cry.

Nothing. No Rayna. Next was the closet. Only that was empty, too, as I walked in one door and made my way out of the other. *This had to be another nightmare.* Now, I was sprinting out of the room and down the corridor, giving quick glances into each room including her dance studio.

No fucking Rayna!

What's that?

I smelled...turkey bacon and...something familiar. *Is Boyd here on a Saturday?* I headed straight into the kitchen through the dining room instead of the living room. She must have sensed my presence or heard the duds of my footsteps nearing because she damn near jumped in my direction. Her eyes drew large, and her beautiful lips parted. I'd startled her.

I realized I must be a staggering sight for her to see. Fuck, I was out of breath and sweating out of control. I brushed my face with my clammy hands and let out a forceful exhale. But we didn't speak. I wasn't sure about her, but I hadn't a fucking clue as to what to say after the events of yesterday. Last night. This morning. Hell, I'd fucked my girl into folly—for hours!

Rayna stood there, suspended in the middle of the kitchen, wearing a black, silk robe with colorful flowers dispersed throughout. She was holding a spatula. There was so much behind her eyes. Anxiety, exhaustion, wariness. *Fear?* Was she afraid of me? I wouldn't hurt her. *Had I hurt her?* I mean, I was vexed—goddamned livid. Still was. But I would never hurt my girl.

The mixed aromas were flooding my olfactory lobes, bringing my attention to the display of food on the marble counters, stove, and island. There were pancakes, waffles, home fries, biscuits, sausages, gravy, and a fruit salad spread over the counters. On the stove, there was turkey bacon frying. I knew it was turkey because Rayna knew swine didn't make it through my front door; coincidentally, so did my chef. There were two saucepans on low fire on the stove, too.

What in the hell was all of this? *A parting feast?*

"Pocket watch," I muttered, remembering our code word for honesty.

"Old-fashioned oatmeal, grits, and turkey bacon. I didn't know what you wanted for breakfast, so I made every breakfast item available in the kitchen."

Rayna must have seen my eyes travel to the stove and assumed I was asking about the food. That was good information, but I needed something with a little more substance in terms of insight. She remained still, her fearful expression still lingering.

I shook my head. "What are you feeling?"

Her eyes danced. I could tell she was processing my request for her to open up, something she found difficult. I stood in the same position for what seemed like hours, not finding the ability to even fucking breathe. This was do or die. So much had taken place over the past twelve hours...hell—the past week. My actions with Dawn and my reaction to Thompson could fucking make or break us. I couldn't handle losing her, but I had to admit to myself the impending reality of our relationship. I so desperately needed to know what was going on in that pretty little incommunicado brain of hers. My mind wasn't yet fresh enough to anticipate her needs. I made my attempt.

Finally, she moved! She pivoted and shut off the burner for the bacon and removed it. I took a hard swallow. Somehow, I realized I'm standing in the middle of my kitchen, wearing just my underwear. I hadn't thought to put anything on even my damn feet.

Rayna turned back towards me, but her eyes didn't follow. She'd trained them to the floor or something below and gave a deep exhale. My chest tightened and my body tensed, preparing for a physical blow from her words.

"Since I left Jersey for *Duke*, do you know how many times my father reached out to me?" she murmured. I didn't have an answer for that. As her eyes finally reached mine, she let out another shaky breath. Rayna jerked her neck, another technique she used when edgy. I found myself holding my breath.

Finally, she continued, "Everyone believes zero because I've never shared how he called me during my first semester of grad school. I got excited." A mirthless smile formed on her beautiful face. This was news to me. I thought the bastard fucking forgot all about her. "I thought I'd finally have my moment. Finally have closure on his reclusive neglect. I was wrong. He asked if I'd taken my mother's wedding rings with me when I left for North Carolina." Rayna snorted, "Can you believe that? He said the set belonged to his grandmother and he needed it to propose to his girlfriend. He said they were expecting a baby and asked about another heirloom; my christening necklace…something that was purchased for me when I was an infant. My dad said he figured I didn't need it anymore and it would be generous and responsible of me to turn it over to my new baby sister."

Fucking prick.

"I never told anyone." Rayna softly shook her head. "How do you tell people that not only did your dad up and leave you, your mom, and siblings without looking back, but his one opportunity to speak to you after the pain he'd caused, and he requested sentimental heirlooms from you to bequeath to his impending family? How do you rebound from being told that you were not good enough to be loved by the one who created you? If you're not good enough for him, then who else would want you?"

She gave a rueful smile. I wanted to launch and console her, but I knew my touch recently hadn't been as delicate as she needed in the moment.

"It was almost like being on a conveyer belt—the ones I used to see in *Woolworth* as kid—or a carousel, displaying product. Being picked to love then cherished, taken care of…made felt special. Then out of nowhere being determined useless, damaged…and having your owner go back to the conveyor to return you and pick again for your replacement." Rayna shook her head, clearing it from the image she'd just articulated. I stood, witnessing her forlorn gaze as she went silent again. I felt helpless. If only I could hold her. Soothe her.

Her eyes shot over to me and after a beat she murmured, "You kissed her. *You* picked *me*. I didn't come knocking on your door. I was fine just getting by, flying beneath the radar. *You* selected *me*, took me off that carousel, wined and dined me...made me feel like nothing in this world mattered to you but me." My heart tore as I saw Rayna's eyes redden. She was trying to fight the tears. She didn't want my pity, just my understanding. I fought to remain in my stance. "Then you saw my flaws. My damaged heart. When you saw a different prospect...fresh and glistening, you threw me away and selected her as your *new*." My nose flared and chest expanded at the revelation of her analogy. "You kissed her. You chose *new*."

My breath caught, like a blow to the fucking gut. That's not what I'd been feeling at all. That's not what was happening between Rayna and me. Not what happened between Dawn and me. If I could only get her to see that. I couldn't find my voice to speak. She made me live her fears, her pain from the moment she learned I'd kissed Dawn.

"My father may have manufactured my body, but you mended my heart; manufactured a spirit in me that was new." The first single tear dropped. Before I could garner the strength to raise my arms to console her several streams followed as she tightened her lips.

"You are no different," she whispered through tears.

Fuck!

"I see your wounds..." I barely recognized my voice, could hardly hear it over my racing heartbeats. Shit, I was finally able to speak. "...your imperfections and I will buy the whole damn factory to repair your flaws just enough for you to let me own *all* of you. I choose *you* as my *new*, flaws and all. Always, Rayna."

Rayna sucked in a deep breath. Surprised by my proposal, her eyes widened, and diaphragm rose. "No. No...you don't mean that. You don't know what you're saying." She cupped her mouth and nose with her hands, then brushed her tears from her eyes. "You had the stamina to try when we started out, but it's clear I've exhausted your patience." Her eyes bounced back and forth as they projected low. "Azmir..." she shrieked. "What if I woke up in his bed this morning instead of yours because I chose to get drunk to handle my pain. How would we have—"

Rayna covered her mouth and I jumped to her, grabbing her before she could utter the words. I wouldn't lose her.

"I wouldn't allow you to. I'll fight for us. Always. I'm here. You just have to trust me, Brimm. Let me in."

Rayna melted her frame into mine and cried out, "Azmir, I'm so sorry!" I felt her fragile body tremble in my arms as she sobbed into my chest. "I swear I will do anything to fix this mess I've created. I'll do anything." Her head popped up in search of my eyes. Her eyes were wide, and her expression was haunted. "Is Thompson going to involve the police? Will you be sued? My god, what did I do?" I could tell she was now fearing the possible consequences of yesterday. I didn't want her to be concerned with that. I just wanted her to decide if she wanted me, if she desired a future for us.

"Well, first things first," I looked around the kitchen at all of the food she'd prepared, wondering what we'd do with most of it. "We eat. And then we meet with my people to discuss how to handle the public backlash of it. We'll let my well-equipped attorneys sort out the legal matters."

"It can't be that simple. Are you sure you don't want me to call Thompson to try and smooth this over. I'll do—"

"You have no reason to even speak to Brian Thompson unless it is work related. Are we clear?" I hated to flip from being caring to caveman so quickly, but until I could get that mutherfucker as far away from her, I needed for it to be understood there will be no more interfacing with the prick.

"*Yu*—yes." Rayna's eyes fluttered in embarrassment. Her mind registered this was not a request, but a command. It was nonnegotiable.

Rayna

Azmir's tone was definitive. I saw it in the twitching of his jaw. It was hard to process a demand, but considering the mess I've caused, I thought it best to acquiesce to his decision of steering clear of Thompson outside of the parameters of work. I still felt I needed to square things away with him. I was responsible for making him feel I was available to him on some level yesterday when I thought it was true. Therefore, I had to undo the mistake.

But for now, my focus needed to be on repairing the debacle I'd made. I'd seen Azmir in a manner I never wanted to revisit. He was so angry. His disposition was inflamed as he plummeted into me on the dining room table. The sweat seeping from his wrathful pores burned with disdain. For me. It terrified me. I didn't want to feel that level of contempt again. He attempted to make amends for it this morning by making love to me, but even then, I saw the fear in his eyes. I could feel the restlessness in the stride of his hips, they were less confident in their drive into me. He was afraid. Afraid of what, I hadn't quite figured out yet, but it was felt. My efforts at finding a rationale of all of his actions led me here to the kitchen for manic cooking.

After eating all we could fit in, I asked, "What are we going to do with all of this stuff, Azmir?" He wiped his mouth, indicating he was done as well. "I can't believe I cooked all of this food. What a waste of your money. I'm sorry," I sighed, now feeling even more frustrated with myself. "If you can tell me who to write the check to, I'll pay for the next round of groceries."

Azmir didn't speak as he reached for the wall phone from his seat and dialed a few numbers. I waited, wondering what in the world was he thinking about instead of the wastage issue at hand. "Yeah, Manny. I don't know who's all on duty, but Rayna has cooked for an army and there's a feast in my kitchen for anyone interested. Yeah. I'll leave the door unlocked...help yourselves. Just lock up when you're all done. Yeah. No problem. Indeed." Azmir ended the call.

I waited for his next set of instructions. I felt so fragile. Like a trained dog, I was afraid to move out of turn.

Azmir could sense it, as his next words were, "Next is a hot warm bath for the morning beauty." *Huhn?* That was unexpected. His tone was firm, but his direction was endearing. His eyes bore into mine as he uttered, "I've desecrated your body. My Neanderthal behavior over the past fourteen hours were brutal. I need to make nice with your heart as well. I can't have your mind and body's natural inclination not yielding to me after recent activities. I need to care for you."

My pulse raced, and I slowly dropped my eyelids. Even after sleeping with Azmir for months, I was still taken by his attentiveness to my body. Yes, he'd handled me with little care, but the more I thought about him branding me with his creamy essence, the less angry I felt. I was not sure if that was his intent: to make it another sexual excursion in our relationship. But I was secretly—and surprisingly—turned on each time I thought about his scorching liquids against my skin.

Does this make me sick?

"I won't do that again...unless you ask me to," Azmir's stern tone interrupted my ruminative thoughts. My gaze rose to meet his knowing eyes.

"*Wha*—huhn?" I felt my heartbeat increase and my mouth went dry, immediately embarrassed by the prospect of him reading my thoughts, something he'd done accurately in the past.

"It was not intended to please you, rather to level you and to serve as a reminder as to who you belong to. I was extremely...irate and acted with very little thought, but there was rationale. I'm sure you were affected by it. But if you liked it, maybe it's something we can do again...only under better circumstances." His penetrative gaze seared me. My mouth hung open in sheer shock. "Did you enjoy it?" He eyed me with caution, lasciviousness gleaming from his smoldering eyes.

Did I?

I hated the circumstances, that was for sure. Hated his soul was missing when he handled me intimately. But I wasn't sure there was anything Azmir did to me sexually causing me to feel uncomfortable or leaving me anything short of wanting it again. Wanting him again.

How do I tell him this?

Abruptly, Azmir shook his head, clearing his mind of the direction my answer could have taken us. "No. Don't answer that. It doesn't need to be addressed right now," his tone sobered. "I've overworked your body, and I'm sure your mind. Right now, I assuage and then we get ready for our luncheon meeting with *Taylor & Bacote.*

"*Taylor & Bacote?*"

"Yes, Rayna. We have to meet with my public relations team to manage the aftermath of yesterday. It's not something I can ignore or wait to play out. With my status and Brian Thompson's legal savvy, I have to position myself offensively just in case."

Unable to speak, I was frozen in my seat. What would I say anyway? *I don't want to meet with the woman who is at the root of this problem? There's no possible way she could help map out a solution when she was, in fact, the problem.* This couldn't get any messier. How would I survive this season of Dawn Taylor? I had no clue, but quickly decided to keep moving forward. I wasn't prepared to lose Azmir. I'd made the decision sometime last night. I would not forfeit whatever it was we'd been growing here.

True to his word, Azmir ushered me to the master bathroom and ran me a glorious bath in the Jacuzzi. He massaged me, limb by limb. He made nice with my body all right, my heart was a different matter. Something a calming bath couldn't settle. We talked and slowly readied ourselves with dressing for the meeting. On the drive there, I pondered on so much. I wondered what Azmir was feeling. Was Thompson badly hurt from Azmir's lightning speed jabs? Was Dawn having a laugh at my expense? And how badly did she anticipate me screwing this up with Azmir so she could sink her claws into him?

When we entered the upscale restaurant, my nerves started fraying immediately. I didn't know why Dawn represented such a threat to me, but she did. And it was clear she had some fixation with Azmir. Azmir gave his name and the hostess, who couldn't get enough eye-time in with him, directed us to our table right away after informing, "Your party has been waiting on you, Mr. Jacobs. This way," with a husky tone.

Ughhhhh!

This wasn't kicking off correctly at all. Azmir took me at the small of my back, and I followed the tall brunette to a secluded area. Right away, Dawn and Shayna's eyes were upon us. Shayna rose with a polite plastered smile, while Dawn remained seated along with the sinister sneer on her lips, but her eyes registered something entirely different. She actually looked shocked.

Azmir pulled out my chair, inviting me to sit before he greeted Shayna with a brief hug and Dawn with a handshake. Once everyone was seated, I noticed the uneasy expressions from both Dawn and Shayna. I felt out of place. Nervously, I brushed the back of my neck with my hand and glanced over to Azmir for guidance.

"Well, we didn't expect you here, Rayna," Dawn informed very perky in her tone, dripping righteous indignation. "After yesterday I thought you'd be somewhere...recovering from yesterday's events."

Already, her fangs were out, ready to attack. My heartbeat sped up and my body silently trembled. I wasn't expecting her to come with it so soon. I didn't want to engage in a war with her at this sensitive time in Azmir's and my relationship. I tried to quickly center myself and play ball. I couldn't let her back me into a corner. Not now. Not ever. But I had to move with tact.

"I have. And now we're here. What do you have for us in terms of managing the chaos? It is your job, you know."

Azmir grabbed my thigh from underneath the table before speaking, "Dawn, Ms. Brimm is here because this situation involves her. If we're talking strategy, I'm sure it encompasses her. Here's your opportunity to address her directly, but with diplomacy."

"Sure, Mr. Jacobs. This is what we do," Shayna spoke up, clearly attempting to soften the blow dealt by her partner. "Ms. Brimm, we don't mean any harm at all. In fact, it's important you are here. There should be solidarity between you two. This is what we need to calm this matter." Again, it was clear to me there wasn't a shared agenda between the two regarding Azmir. Her words didn't do a lot to ease my nerves, but I appreciated the peace in her actions.

"Okay. First things first, are you two together...or will you remain together after yesterday's event?" Dawn forged ahead with her *Kill Rayna Dead* campaign.

It was the best and the worst question to ask. Azmir and I didn't have a title. Therefore, we've never been *together*. All we've had was an intimate relationship. This was the only thing I was sure of.

What do I say? How do I respond? I was slipping and slipping fast. I didn't have an answer.

"Nothing has changed between Rayna and me," Azmir spoke firmly and in all of his CEO mien. It was his trusted strong and deliberate intimating tone working each time he executed it. "Rayna and I have spoken extensively over the past eighteen hours, and we agree nothing has changed in terms of our status. What took place yesterday was nothing short of a misunderstanding between Rayna and her overzealous colleague after a few drinks over a late lunch."

Dawn's mouth dropped. Even I was surprised by Azmir's affirmation. He was unwavering in his summary of the situation. Shayna's eyes were popped but stayed glued to the document before her. She slowly raised her pen to record his comments.

"Wow. That's rather firm, Azmir," Dawn mentioned.

"Oh, my position regarding my personal life is very firm, Ms. Taylor," Azmir retorted. "And with that being said, I believe the etiquette for the nature of this meeting is for you to reference me as Mr. Jacobs and to her as Ms. Brimm. I am paying you, not the reverse. I expect the utmost formalities when dealing with matters of business. Are we clear, Ms. Taylor?"

The table grew quiet. You could hear a pin drop. Dawn's crimson lips were parted in shock. As much as I wanted to, I couldn't gloat in her discomfit. There's nothing funny about being at the end of Azmir's wrath.

"Y-yes, Mr. Jacobs. Of course. I apologize for my lapse in professionalism." Dawn shook her head in an effort to clear her brain. I watched raptly as she took a hard swallow, a fortifying move to regain herself. "Well, now that that's out of the way, why don't we discuss strategy. Huhn?" Dawn's eyes ascended, agenda anew.

Azmir gave a firm nod before muttering, "We should. It is, by the way, what I pay you for." The mocking in his tone was gentle yet couldn't be ignored.

"Okay..." Dawn breathed out, obviously taken by his crisp response to her. "...well, we've mapped out a plan which will include addressing the inquiry from calls coming in from the magazines and bloggers you have established relationships with. They've heard about the incident involving Mr. Thompson and want details. Here's how we'll handle them..."

Dawn continued with the strategy, and Shayna filled in when it was her turn to speak. Though I listened fixedly, the tension looming over the table was palpable. No one was relaxed, not even Azmir, no matter how collected he appeared. This was going to be a long road ahead. Having to deal with the likes of Dawn Taylor would make the journey that much more arduous.

It was a Saturday evening, and I'd just returned from visiting my brother, Keeme, in Jersey. I'd caught a flight out first thing Friday morning and arrived just hours before his allotted visiting time. I would have returned right after, but Azmir insisted I stay overnight to recoup from the long flight. I remember Michelle scolding me about not staying for a few days, and I wouldn't relent. But now that I was with Azmir, I agonized over being separated from him for even one night.

The past couple of weeks had been so intense, but slowly I'd adjusted to being back at the marina. In my most candid ruminations, I'd admit I so enjoy seeing Azmir every night and waking up to him every morning. He'd made my life so adventurous and settled at the same time. I honestly hadn't felt so at home since living with my parents as a child. Azmir's apartment was far warmer and more welcoming than my own house in Redondo. I cherished that.

I would never compromise my commitment to my brother, so I complied with Azmir's wishes and stayed overnight. I also lied and told Azmir I was going to visit Chyna again. He offered to send

Chanell, but I declined, reminding him I am a very private person and would prefer not giving people privy to my family life. I had to remind him of how difficult it was divulging parts of my life to even him. He relinquished after I conceded to staying one night.

I missed him before the plane took off. We usually found ourselves in a passionate lovemaking session prior to either of us traveling, but he'd become so preoccupied with work I didn't see him before leaving for the airport.

Tonight, there was a big show at *Cobalt*. It had been talked about on the radio and advertised over the internet. Even bloggers were posting about the precedence this scale of event would take. There was a very popular R&B artist touring who agreed to make *Cobalt* a leg in their schedule. This particular artist drew other big wig names as well, so it was sure to be a night of celebrities at the club. I'd heard very little from Azmir since my plane arrived in L.A. I sent a couple of texts but decided not to call.

I ran to the high-rise to quickly shower and dress. I swear, since being with Azmir I felt like I lead the life of a celebrity. I was constantly traveling, always having clothing delivered to me, or at a boutique, buying pieces for upcoming events. Shoot, I now even had personal shoppers and makeup artists, vying for signed contracts with me. It could all be overwhelming, but I constantly reminded myself that my life was now anew, as it included the business mogul, A.D. Jacobs.

I selected a *Rebecca Taylor* cheetah print mesh daisy dress with long sleeves and a low neckline. It fell inches above my knees. I paired it with my above-the-knee, black *Christian Louboutin* boots. I accessorized with oversized gold hoops and flashy bracelets and kept my makeup mild with simple smoky eyes and nude lips. As I gave myself a final look over in the mirror, I felt a singe of excitement travel up my spine as I imagined seeing Azmir. I couldn't wait to get him home tonight. You would think after his cannibal antics following the Thompson incident, I wouldn't think about being with him for weeks to come, but as much as his behavior still haunted me, I had my need of him.

I decide not to take the *S550* tonight, but instead I grab the keys to his *SLS*. I swear, this man had more cars than he could drive. I have to admit, every once in a while it was fun playing with Azmir's toys. When I arrived at the club, as usual, there was a line wrapped around the corner. I headed into the private parking lot and showed my face to the club's parking security. He nodded his head in approval and directed me in. I parked next to Azmir's *750* and felt another chill zing through me. I went in and headed to the hostess to find out where I'd be seated. She had security escort me over to the V.I.P. section where I saw lots of familiar faces, Petey's being one.

"Oh, shit! Sup, Rayna!" he greeted, exposing all of his teeth.

"Hey, Petey! Great seeing you. You're looking like you've slimmed down a bit," I charmed.

He gave a goofy laugh warming my heart. Though I still held my reservation about his orchestration at Kid's party with Dawn Taylor, I'd easily learned to love Petey. He was very devoted to Azmir, which went a long way with me. I greeted Kim who has grown on me a lot as well. When I met her, I could hardly get her to muster three consecutive words and now she's my favorite chatter box—second to Chanell, who was there as well, dancing in her seat.

Then my eyes somehow met those of Dawn Taylor's. As much as I wanted to question her being here, I knew I couldn't. This was a big night and the first of *Bacote & Taylor's* work with *Cobalt*. Azmir prepared me earlier on in the week, saying Dawn would be around more often than usual as their marketing strategies would be launched over the next few months. I had to decide if I wanted this thing with Azmir to work, I'd have to bear the brunt of her presence and exposure to Azmir. But the decision wasn't met without apprehension. What helped me arrive at my decision was how he'd never changed his password to his cell phone records, subliminally saying he had nothing to hide. Either way, seeing Dawn did something to me. It was a reminder of who my *cleanup lady* was. There was always something behind her charming smirk. Just like tonight. She gave a knowing smirk as her way of speaking. I responded with a firm nod.

Mark and Eric were there with their ladies. I couldn't keep up with Eric and his wife, NaTasha's, status. The last time I saw them they could stand no more than three feet within each other. Tonight, NaTasha couldn't keep her hands off him. And clearly Eric loved it, as he was beaming from ear to ear.

"As always, it is a pleasure, Ms. Brimm. You are a joy to look at as much as the sun on a new day," Eric lightly flirted. I could tell he was taken by me, but he never crossed the line. It was like having a seven-year-old have a crush on you. He was harmless in his puppy love.

"Why, thank you, Mr. Garrity. As it is with you and your lovely wife," I returned.

"When is that berk of a man going to end his vainglorious ways, make you an honest woman, and put your sea of admirers out of their misery?" I suppressed my laughter in order to not make him feel uncomfortable. I so enjoyed Eric's didactic vernacular.

"*Hmmmmmm...* I have no idea. You're his bestie. Surely you have an idea of where his mind is, more or less his heart," I returned.

"Hey, where *is* he, by the way?" Mark chimed in as he greeted me with a small peck on the cheek.

"I'm not sure," I mumbled with narrowed brows. I'd just assumed he was there. He told me he'd be here, so I was sure he had been. "He's probably up in his office. I just got here. I'll ask Petey," I offered just before making a beeline for Petey.

Petey confirmed Azmir was in the building. So, I moseyed my way over to Chanell who was never short of an entertaining story. We chatted for about twenty minutes or so before the emcee began announcing the opening act. Certainly, Azmir should have been down here by now to watch the show. He'd told me how much he was looking forward to tonight.

I glanced over to Petey, subconsciously wondering where Azmir was. I soon discovered he clearly had the same thoughts because he was looking over at me and motioned he had no idea with his hands. I excused myself from Chanell who was just telling me about her last street fight with a girl over the latest love she had been involved with. *Never a dull moment with this chick.* Gotta love her.

I walked toward the entrance of V.I.P., and passed Petey on the way, telling him I was going upstairs to look for Azmir. I walked down on to the main floor where security was waiting, unbeknownst to me, to escort me to wherever I was going. It was weird, but I did get moved through the droves of patrons quicker. I stopped at the elevator and that's where I parted ways with my armor.

When I arrived at the third floor, I saw someone manning the receptionist desk. A young, chunky Caucasian woman who sported a jet-black boyish haircut with over-sized black, plastic framed glasses and conspicuous lip and nose piercings. I'd seen her around a time or two. Clearly, she knew who I was from the way she respectfully nodded as I passed by her.

"Is he in here?" I asked, walking towards Azmir's office.

"Uhn-huhn," she eagerly and politely confirmed. Once at the door, I knocked. I didn't want to just barge in. No matter what Azmir and I had going on, he was a respected businessman first.

"Yeah!" Azmir barked, sounding annoyed. My eyes bulged and lips pouted rapidly in response to his curtness.

With apprehension, I slowly opened the door. I never attempted to be overly-familiar with him in his places of business. As I walked in, within seconds, I made eye contact with him. He was sitting behind his desk with his back straightly aligned. Azmir, while as gorgeous and alluring as ever, looked stressed, very rigid. He visibly registered my identity and immediately appeared relieved. A strong exhale escaped his mouth. I'd guessed that meant he was happy to see me. All tension left my body. I closed the door behind me.

"Hey..." I greeted with concern.

"Hey yourself. I've been trying to call you for the past thirty minutes. I was beginning to worry," he was partly scolding me. "Come here," he gestured with his hand and a loose and rapid wave of his arm. He wasn't wearing his typical coochie-creaming smile or panty-snatching smirk. I was concerned.

I pulled out my phone to check it as I walked over to him. Sure enough, I'd missed three calls from "*A.D.*" I held up my phone, showing him. "We're all downstairs waiting for you. I know you've been excited about tonight!" I say with sheer excitement. Even I'd built up anticipation after experiencing the energy from down there.

Azmir pulled me into him until I collapsed on his lap. He wrapped his long and comforting arms around me. In a natural response, I pulled my arms around his neck. He buried his face in my neck. His breath against my skin brought those trustee currents through my body. A sensation I tried extremely hard to fight off, feeling it being inappropriate. Something was wrong.

"*Heeeeeeeeey,*" I whispered. "What's wrong?" I pulled his head up using my index finger under his chin so I could look into his beautiful face. He softly exhaled again, and I was overtaken with yet another current as his breath hit my face. My eyes closed to let it pass.

What in the world does this man have on me that causes my body to respond so lasciviously to him?

He quickly caught on to my reaction and, in response, Azmir gazed at me with a slight squint in his eyes.

There was a knock on the door.

"Yeah!" Azmir barked again.

The receptionist girl opened the door, and I froze. Azmir and I were in a somewhat compromising position. I squirmed in his lap, prepared to get up. He gripped and pinned me to him, messaging me not to move.

"Yeah, Molly?" Azmir inquired of her presence. I then noticed Molly was a cute, young, stud girl. She wore pinstriped slacks with a chain in the belt loops and a white, short sleeve T-shirt. Her classic black and white *Converse* sneakers were sloppily tied, and her multiple piercings and forceful husky voice sealed the deal.

"Mr. Jacobs, Ms. Taylor wants a word with you," Molly muttered, and before Azmir could answer, Dawn swung her head of bouncy curls into the doorway followed by her small frame draped in a red fitted, midi-length, full sleeved dress, matching her lips. When she noticed me and registered my position on his lap, Dawn suspended her motions. She then quickly caught herself and retracted her steps outside of the doorframe.

"Oh, I didn't realize you were preoccupied. I'll just wait until you're done," Dawn offered apologetically, it seemed, and disappeared out of the frame. I could tell the last thing she expected was seeing me perched in his lap. I felt a twitch of victory deep down inside. Azmir never uttered a word to Dawn.

He really was in a foul mood.

"Is there anything else, Molly?" he bit out.

Molly pivoted a little closer into the door frame. "*Uhhh...* Yes, sir. My shift is over. If you don't mind, I'm gonna go downstairs and enjoy the festivities while I give the fax from New York City time to come through, sir." She was asking to be dismissed for the day only to continue work later—non-mandatory I ascertained.

"Indeed. Lock the elevator. If anyone needs me, defer their needs to Kareem or Tracy," Azmir gruffly requested. "Goodnight."

This was so not like him.

"Sure," Molly humbly returned with a nod before closing the door behind her.

I turned my head back to him and murmured, "What's the problem, Jacobs?"

He placed his forehead against mine and shook his head.

Once again, I lifted his chin to search his eyes. He, in turn, studied mine. The next thing I knew, he slightly leaned his head in a familiar manner—something he does when he was prepared to orally embrace me. As his face approached mine, I was ready. I followed his aggressive kiss with great welcome. My hands found their way to his head as our tongues engaged in a sweet dance. It lasted for an eternity and in no time, I was caught up.

Azmir grabbed me by the waist and lifted me onto his desk. He pulled my feet up to the armrests of his desk chair. My heels hook onto the handles. He pulled back from our embrace. My eyes were dancing at the suspense. *What is he doing?* He buried his face into my crotch and gave a long and hard inhale with his eyes closed. When they opened, they're drunken with clear desire. I sat there with my hands stapled to his desk, watching him, and I couldn't help but to be turned on by this. Azmir reached for my panties and pulled them down and over my boots. Once off, he balled them in his fist, lifted them to his nose and inhaled again.

"Damn, I've missed you," he whispered, seemingly much to himself.

My mouth dropped and opened simultaneously. I was delighted in lust. He carefully placed my panties at the end of his desk. I watched his every movement in slow motion. Next, he threw his face in between my thighs. He licked, stroked, grazed, and dipped his tongue and masterfully dragged his teeth the full length of my valley. My body reclined and hands gripped the back of his head. Azmir was on a mission, and for some reason, I detected I'd little to do with what was behind this sexual fury. But in this moment, I didn't care what the cause was. I was pleasured by him using me to remedy it. He was taking it out on my body in a way bringing us both bliss and relief.

I experienced a transitory touch of reality and was reminded of being spread out on his office desk. Typically, this would bring a halt to my randy state, but it had the opposite effect on me just as it had a few months back in his office at the rec. I felt my inner freak being unleashed as my body trembled at every swipe of his deft tongue.

In a rapid move, Azmir scooped me off the desk and lowered me onto his lap. He was entering me, and I was left to find my balance. My legs were aside his upper arms, and his hands were planted on my hips. Azmir was in. Deep. He lifted me and let me down onto himself for his pleasure. I gripped his shoulders, keeping him arm's length as I took in all of his fullness. He was buried so tightly I felt him pulsating inside of me. I let out a stifled moan. His breathing grew distressed.

"Rayna...you mean...so much...to me. Stay with me... Stay forever," he managed over my lunges onto his lap.

Unable to focus my eyes, I tried to look deeply into his...unsuccessfully. I gave up. He knew, in this condition, I'd agree to anything with him. My head was clouded, filled with erotic expressions of A.D. I heard the sounds of his firm length slamming into me, and the slapping of my anterior flesh meeting his hard thighs. The cords in Azmir's neck bulged, telling of his forceful pushes and pulling of my heated frame.

"Yes...yes, baby... I will!" I assured.

Eventually his hands made their way to my lower back as he slammed me into his lap. At this point my body tightened, and I was overtaken by his diligence...by his strength, pushing me down and lifting me up...and his promising words. I was there. I was ascending. My body convulsed as my joints stiffened in orgasmic readiness. I bit my lips together as not to scream in his office.

"Yes, baby girl... Let it out," he sung just before he joined me in my outer orbital float. Azmir grunted his pleasure against me as his face collapsed into my breasts and I welcomed him.

We sat there for a few seconds catching our breaths. As I was being cast back down from orbit, reality settled in. My Azmir wasn't himself. What was that all about? I wanted to help and comfort beyond lovemaking.

"Hey, what was that all about?" I whispered warmly.

Azmir grabbed my face and slammed his lips into mine, demanding my tongue, which I offered up with little reservation. His tongue took long draws into my mouth, sweeping the entire reservoir—greedily. I grabbed the back of his head to balance myself in an attempt to keep up. He was communicating something, though I was quite sure it wasn't *to* me, it was through me. I allowed him and relished in his abrasiveness. Azmir eventually withdrew and brought his forehead to meet mine. We sat this way for a moment before he lifted and whisked me into his en suite bathroom where we cleaned up in private. When I was done, I watched penetratingly as Azmir brushed his teeth. He took notice of my gaping as he rinsed his mouth.

He wiped his mouth dry and lay his towel on the wall rack. I squinted my eyes at him in playful annoyance. He snorted and reached down to passionately kiss me. He rested the side of his lengthy body and his head against the frame of the bathroom door and smirked. *There's the panty-snatching smirk.* I folded my arms in my abdomen, messaging to him I was not letting up.

Azmir let out a brief sexy chortle, "Brimm, it's nothing in particular. A man with my level of responsibility can grow weary from time to time and need to blow off steam. It's just the nature of the business. Your being gone, and...shit—me seeing you in this dress and boots—it brings it all to a head," he murmured as he leaned down to plant a wet kiss on me.

I smiled and took him at his word. Frankly, I was glad to be his method of release. "Okay," I acquiesced. "I like you discharging your frustrations in—I mean, on me," I muttered salaciously.

He showered me with soft kisses around my face. "Good. Because I'm not done. I have more ammunition to unload," he shot back as he continued to lay the soft kisses down my neck.

"You need to refresh your lipstick. I've smudged it. And I want to smudge it again when we get home. Let's go say goodnight, Ms. Brimm."

Downstairs, the second act was finishing up on stage. She was a young female with a jazzy resonance to her sound. I'd heard this cut on the radio. It was nice to put a face to a voice.

As we approached his friends, just about all the men in V.I.P. rose to greet Azmir. He quickly dapped all of them before announcing to Petey we were leaving. I was reading Petey's expressions and could tell he'd asked Azmir if everything was okay. I guessed me staying at bay didn't help. I stood near the velvet rope. I knew I had washed up, but I would die of horror if anyone had an inkling of what had just taken place upstairs in Azmir's office. I knew standing like this made me look awkward, but I didn't want to risk anything. Besides, Azmir made it clear we weren't staying, and it was final. I waved goodbye to everyone and realized the ladies were too preoccupied with the show to care. We left *Cobalt* under our own agenda.

Hours later, back at the high-rise, Azmir and I are laid out in front of the fireplace wrapped in sheets after hours of lovemaking. I was in euphoria after the expressions of love we'd just exchanged. We were talking and laughing, which was what I appreciated about our chemistry. Azmir and I laughed together. We talked about varying topics such as politics and pop culture. I guess anything was easier than discussing our pasts.

"Nah. My jokes are Kevin Hart type funny and yours are like...Tommy Davidson!" Azmir noted, mildly laughing.

I gasped with furrowed brows. "And what's the difference between the two?"

"Hart is *pee your pants* funny and Davidson is just silly...*desperate for a laugh* funny," he informed, and we both laugh.

I was on my back wrapped in expensive Egyptian cotton sheets feeling delightful against my skin. The fire was burning calmly, and it created a romantic glow in the room.

"I'm thirsty. You want something to drink? Wine...brandy?" Azmir offered as he wrapped his waist in sheets, to my dismay, and headed into the kitchen.

"Juice will be fine. I'm thirsty myself. You've had me perspiring since we walked through the door! I need to rehydrate. I think the nightcap should've come before the smashing," I playfully chastised.

With his eyebrows narrowed and eyes squinted he quipped, "I'm sorry. I didn't get the impression I was imposing." Then he took a few moments to consider what I'd said before admitting, "Okay, so maybe you didn't have a choice in the matter," with a bashful smirk.

Azmir came back with tall glasses of juice for the both of us and handed me mine.

"In all seriousness, are you okay with my moms staying at your place?" Azmir asked. Yazmine had been at my place since the day after the Brian Thompson fiasco. I didn't fight with him as he made the call after leaving the debriefing with the *Bacote & Taylor Public Relations'* team. I knew better than to argue with him.

"Oh, yeah. At least the place isn't just there decaying. I mean, the week or so I was there was rough for the first few days. I tried to make myself comfortable, but there was still no life there. I think it's a great idea. She seems to be comfortable. I saw she's put up photos on the walls in the living room already."

"She just came off a twenty-plus stint, and it's like she was in a time warp. The décor in there is so Brooklyn nineteen-seventies," Azmir noted ruefully. I couldn't help but laugh.

"Well, if she wants, I can get her a new mattress. It's weird having her on the same one I've smashed her beloved son on," I shared in jest as Azmir's phone went off. This time it was his *iPhone*. As soon as he answered it, his *Blackberry* went off. Because it was so late, I wondered who was calling.

"Peace-peace," he greeted in his thick Brooklyn accent. It always amazed me how thick that New York twang was in so many of his pronunciations considering he'd lived in Chicago and L.A. since there. I was actually turned on by it. Even Jersey girls can't get enough of New York men.

"Where?" Azmir roared into the phone as he gathered his sheet around his naked waist again and went into his study in search of something. I sat up alarmed. Here we go again. I'd just forgotten about the mean and cold Azmir I'd gotten a glimpse of in *Cobalt* earlier, now he'd returned.

He came back into the living room with his laptop. "What's the address again?" he growled into the phone. Then he typed on the keyboard. After a few seconds, he informed, "Yes. She's here. Let me holla at her and get back to you. Yeah." He hit a button before tossing the phone to the other side of the sofa.

I sat on the floor in front of the fire, in silence as he viewed whatever was on the laptop. I thought I'd heard Caribbean music, but why would he be listening to anything related to that? It ended and he placed the laptop on the glass coffee table and snapped, "What the fuck is this, Rayna?"

Flushed with bemusement, I looked at him and immediately to the computer screen as a video played. It was a low quality recording, clearly from a mobile phone showing a woman giving a man—apparently very dark skinned man, judging by the shade of his penis—fellatio. You couldn't get a full view of the female, but there was footage of the male who spoke with a thick Caribbean accent. The videographer was a female and rooted the fellatio-giver on.

Then—*What the fuck! Is that Michelle in the background, periodically licking the man's balls and the base of his penis.* She appeared to be drunk and silly. She was cheering the female on as well. It hit me like a ton of bricks: the other girls were Britni and April! I could make out Britni's voice, pumping them up. *Yup!* That was definitely Britni, which could only mean that the woman going down on the guy was April. Again, you see Michelle dip in to pleasure the man with licks and groping. Tears began to flood my eyes.

"Where did you get this?" I asked, aghast.

"It's all over the fucking internet. This shit has gone viral!" Azmir shouted.

I mumbled, "Oh, my god, Michelle." Bile ascended from my belly as a gag; I then quickly cupped my mouth. After managing it back down my esophagus, I tried to regain my breath. The tears began to drop uncontrollably.

"Was this what you guys did in The Bahamas before I got there?" he hissed.

My eyes flew up at him as he was hovering over me. I realized he thought I was there with them.

"Azmir," I was unable to hide my defensiveness. "You don't think it was me recording my best friend degrading herself, do you?"

He gave me a callous glower.

Wait a minute. Oh, no!

"You think it was *me* giving another man head on the vacation *you'd* paid for?" I theorized slowly.

His eyes softened, but not by much. Azmir maintained his daggered gawk.

"Azmir, I swear on everything I have, I was not there when this was shot. I didn't even know this tape existed until a few seconds ago," I shared in all candor.

"Lady Spin released it earlier on the radio show she webcasts. She's saying it's a tape of Divine's girl, giving a native head on the vacation he paid for her and her girls," he quoted with still a hint of accusation in his tone.

"Azmir, I didn't hang out with them the whole time out there. I told you before that trip those bitches were not my friends," I spat, trying to prove to him I was telling the truth. "If you recall, when you showed up, I was alone. They had gone out earlier in the night, and I stayed behind!"

"Well, why the fucking tears when you were watching the tape?" he barked.

"Because I see my *dead* best friend giving head to a stranger in her wake! Can you imagine how fucked up this is?" I screamed while bawling my eyes out.

He stormed his way towards the bedroom. I collapsed into the couch, crying uncontrollably. Seconds later, I heard Azmir tread into his office.

My heart shattered into a million pieces. I couldn't believe people were viewing my dear friend this way. *How many people have watched it? Has it hit her family? Does Erin know about it?* So many questions flooded my mind. Images of her from the recording wrung my heart dry. *Why would Lady Spin release such damaging footage? Is she that bruised over Azmir? Did she have to drag me into it?* She had to have gotten the tape from Britni who knew damn well I wasn't there. *I knew I was going to have to put that bitch over my knee!*

Lord, I know I've been working on my temper and language, but there are just some trifling ass people who will bring you back!

After I exhausted all of my thoughts, I saw it was after two in the morning. Azmir was still holed up in his office. I was too emotional to face him. I showered and cried some more in there, allowing the water to cascade over my tears. I began to think about how Azmir all but accused me of being the woman in the video. *Does he think so little of me?* I tried to convince him it wasn't me.

I won't again. He'd have up take me at my word or not at all.

That night, I decided to sleep in one of the guest bedrooms. There was no way I would sleep in the bed of a man who believed me to be a harlot. Azna followed me, trotting down the hall to the second guest room.

This room was dark and modernized with smooth brown walls and mahogany hardwood floors. The king sized bed was mounted on an ivory platform with a high headboard and was covered with a chocolate brown text-tiled quilted comforter resembling small concrete blocks trimly stacked on top of each other. There was an off white chaise placed catty-cornered against the walls of the room with brown and ivory throw pillows neatly placed on it. Over the bed, a dark brown jeweled chandelier hung. The poster sized artwork displayed on the wall appropriately blended with the jazzy motif and the flat screen television mounted to the wall added practicability to the room.

Although I knew he'd hired an interior decorator for this place, it once again reminded me of Azmir's impeccable taste. He approved and even designed much of the swanky and prodigiousness. This man's genius and creativity knew no bounds. As I lay on the firm mattress, I realized how luxurious it was, like the one in the master suite. But nothing compared to that one because it was where Azmir lay his head at night and the linens smelled of him. No one had ever slept in this bed, not even Mr. Jacobs himself. My thoughts went blue again, and I fought them off to finally find sleep.

I was sitting down in an outdoor dining area at an amusement park. I looked across to find Michelle, looking her usual preoccupied yet beautiful self. I don't know what we were chatting about, but she was assuring me everything would be okay.

"Na-Na, you know everything is going to work out in your favor at the end, right?" Her smile was bright while eating her frozen yogurt. "You just have to be patient and wait for things to fall into place. You worry too much about what you have very little control over," Michelle declared as she took a heartfelt laugh at my expense.

The sky was the perfect shade of blue, as the sun didn't give too brutal of a shine. Kids were carelessly playing in the background, wondrously taking in all the youthful spectacles of the park.

"I gotta go now," she chirped so casually.

I was unable to speak in this dream. I could only listen. But I was visibly upset at the announcement of her departure. She took notice and cheerfully declared, "Na-Na, you'll be fine. Girl, you know I'll see you later! I just have to send the letter off before the post office closes." Her smile was warm.

While her reassurance was intended to calm me, it had the opposite effect. I started to tremor in agitation to my muteness. There was so much I wanted to tell her and ask her, too. She packed up her things to go and shook her head in confusion as if I had been overreacting. She stood to leave, and I watched her throw her trash in the can and walk away. I got up to try to run to her, but no matter how fast I ran, I couldn't catch up to her. She never looked back. I tried calling out to her, but nothing came out. I ran and ran and ran for Michelle, but never got to her.

I was awakened from the dream. I looked around the room and took inventory to recall where I was. I then realized I was not in bed alone. The fragrance smelled familiar. I looked over to find Azmir stretched out over me, sleeping quietly. *How long had he been here?* I looked over to the nightstand at the digital clock. It was nine-oh-three a.m.

I jumped up to get out of the bed. I had hoped I wouldn't be late.

Azmir stirred, trying to collect himself. "What's the problem? Where are you going?"

From my peripheral he looked a little dazed and confused. I was surprised he'd slept so late. His body was on a timer. I guess he stayed up much later than I had last night.

"Where else would I be headed at this hour on a Sunday?" I asked wryly as I stepped into my slippers. I hadn't forgotten his nasty accusations from last night. He gave an affronted reaction. I walked out of the room to head to the shower.

I checked myself out in the full body mirror in the walk-in closet of the master suite. I had to be sure I was not revealing too much for church. It was not about what others may perceive of me so much as it was what I was putting out. I didn't need to stick out in church in terms of appearance. My mother constantly pounded it into my head as a child. As I headed for the door, I saw Azmir coming in from walking Azna. He closely observed me with a flexing jaw, but I ignored him and gave Azna a playful massage before walking out the door.

During my ride to church, I realized Azmir had once again broken a piece of my heart. I knew there was no such thing as a perfect relationship and the people involved hurt each other from time to time. This was one of those times for Azmir and me. He didn't believe I wasn't the woman on camera, giving a total stranger head. He also showed no comfort for my heartache of seeing my dear friend joining in. How insensitive could the most endearing man on the face of the planet be? As I was pulling into the church's parking lot, I forced the frontal section of my mind clear. I needed to cleanse spiritually. I could think of Azmir later.

Just after the benediction, Pastor Edmondson got up to make his announcements and acknowledge special guests, a Pastor Green and his family, visiting from a church in Anaheim. I was surprised a pastor would dip out on his own Sunday morning worship to attend another's. Then Pastor Edmondson mentioned it being his birthday, and he was honored Pastor Green and family would be joining him and his family for dinner to celebrate. This was nice, I thought.

I could tell Pastor Edmondson was in a rather sentimental mood. He even announced the recent engagement of Pastor Green's son. The church went up in applause. Pastor Edmondson turned around to where Pastor Green and other dignitaries were seated on the altar and asked Pastor Green the name of his soon to be daughter-in-law. It was a rare display of their personal lives considering this was a fifteen-thousand-member church. Our services were televised so there was little time to go off the program like this. I thought it was a refreshing change. It seemed like a personal moment for Pastor Edmondson, and because I had grown so fond of him, I didn't mind sharing in the moment.

Pastor Green said the name of the young lady who would be marrying his son, but because he wasn't mic'd most couldn't hear him. Pastor Edmondson turned back to the crowd and announced, "April Miller. April Miller, would you mind standing?"

My head started spinning at the possibility of seeing another April Miller this morning. As did the other parishioners, I twisted and turned in my seat to locate the woman. She was actually two rows in front of me. She stood, wearing a bright green two-piece suit and a matching wide brim hat with ivory stripes encircling it.

She faced straight ahead at first to address Pastor Edmondson before turning around to wave to those of us behind her. When she did, my body flashed cold when I realized it *was* April Miller! The church was still clapping as she implemented her pageant wave to them. I was surprised when her eyes locked with mine. She gave me a surprised and enthused wave. I seriously doubted if my reaction and excitement mirrored hers.

After service was over, she quickly made her way to me.

"Hey, girl! What are you doing here?" she asked as if church was the last place she would expect to see me.

"I attend this church. And I see you're an advent goer as well," I returned with full on sarcasm.

She caught on to my attitude quickly. "Can we talk outside?" she asked. But before I could agree, we were interrupted.

"Ap, we can exit in the rear," a light-skinned brother with sandy brown hair informed as he approached her.

"Oh, Gerald! This is my friend, Rayna, I've told you about. We went to school together in North Carolina," she tried to say with mustered excitement.

"Gerald Green. It's a pleasure to meet you. I rarely get to meet any of April's long-term friends," he smiled warmly and extended his hand. I immediately took notice of his beautiful green eyes. They're befitting of his name.

"Pleased to meet you, Gerald," I replied.

As we exchange pleasantries, Pastors Edmondson and Green walked up on us.

"Hey, son. We're headed out now to make our reservation," the senior Green shared. He was short and had given several of his features to his son.

Gerald smiled. "Yes. I was coming to grab my fiancée. She's here catching up with an old college buddy." He regarded me politely.

"Dad, Pastor Edmondson, this is Rayna. I'm not sure if she's a member here—"

"Brimm. How does it go there, Rayna?" Pastor Edmondson greeted me warmly. "Rayna here is my daughter in Christ. I know her very well. I am pleased she's attached to this fold," Pastor Edmondson informed the small crowd that had now gathered around me. He had his hands on my shoulders like a father would his daughter. Though I hadn't realized he viewed me so dearly, it felt good to be connected. I patted his right hand on my shoulder. He'd always tried making me feel welcomed.

"If you don't mind, I'd like to walk Rayna out. I'll be right out as soon as I see her to her car. Please?" she asked politely. *Whoa? When did April develop etiquette?*

After taking two glances, one at me and the other at her, Pastor Edmondson insisted, "The birthday boy here consents. We'll meet you 'round back." He spoke with a smile expressing his words were final. "Rayna dear, I'll see you on Wednesday?" he confirmed by way of a goodbye.

"Until Wednesday," I bade. And we turned toward the entrance of the sanctuary.

"Rayna, I'm sorry. I had no idea!" was April's response to my news of the released video. I was appalled by it. We were beside my car, discussing recent events.

"April, I was hoping for more than a weak apology. Not only is Azmir's reputation on the line, but so is my word and professional image as well as Michelle's memory." She grimaced before she turned and gazed off into the distance with a forlorn expression. "April, you know I wasn't there!" I plead.

"Rayna, what do you expect for me to do—go hold a press conference, admitting it was me on my knees, giving a total stranger head?" she snorted in aggravation.

"So, it's okay for Azmir and me to suffer when we had *nothing* to do with it. And what would Michelle think? Are you...kidding me?"

She paused to consider my words. Within seconds, I saw the tears she'd tried to fight back. A car approached us from a short distance and beeped the horn. We turned to see it was her fiancé and his family.

My sharp, life-threatening gaze didn't leave April's face as she processed my words.

All of a sudden, she grabbed my hands and clasped them in hers, gently and kissed them in humility. It was then that I noticed the tattoo on her right hand in the area between her thumb and her index finger. *That's the same one from the video.* I guess I'd never paid April much mind. She was Michelle's cousin, not my friend. At best, she and Britni were occasional associates.

"Rayna, I am so, so, so, so sorry. I can't do it. I have so much riding on this right now," with widened eyes boring into me, she admitted while gesturing to her impending family in the car behind her. "I swear if there were something I could do without jeopardizing this, I would. I pray it all works out for you and Azmir. I can honestly understand the pressure of chasing down love. You understand, don't you?" Her eyes were filled with tears.

I jerked my hands from her grip and called on every bit of decorum I possessed to not haul off and slap the taste out of her mouth. She'd just told me her life with her fiancé trumped what I had with Azmir. And she didn't even acknowledge Michelle's disgraced memory. Who needed enemies when you have shallow, faux family-friends like the one who stood before me?

I gave her the exact response Azmir would have as my parting words, "Indeed," and I turned to get in my car.

My dignity had been challenged and although it prevailed, I felt I owed her at least a nudge in the forehead for her selfishness. I was once again confronted with the familiar feeling of loneliness. I was in a place all by myself. Azmir doubted me and my only redeemer just told me she wouldn't help. I cried the entire way to the marina. I didn't understand just how I'd gotten back *there*— with my back up against the wall.

One thing was for sure: I would not be living with a man who all but accused me of being a whore. I couldn't get past it. He was accusing me of behaving like a slut on the vacation he'd paid for. I had fallen in love with him by that time—*and I told him!* My feelings were doubted along with my reputation and—*here again*—dignity. There was no way we could go any further in this relationship if he obviously didn't trust me.

Before I knew it, I was pulling up to the high-rise at the marina. Once inside, I headed straight to the bedroom and started pulling my clothes into a cheap suitcase I'd purchased from doing a bit of unexpected shopping while out on the East Coast during my last trip. I knew I wouldn't be able to take everything, but I tried getting as much as I could in there.

As I was tossing in underwear I heard, "What the fuck do you think you're doing?" I jumped and nearly fell on my behind, startled.

It was Azmir in a dark blue sweatsuit. His towering body was poised in defensive a manner. I'd seen him like this. It was becoming all too familiar now. *Does he feel he can address me like this because he believes I'm the one on the video?* A sharp pain ran through my chest.

"What does it look like I'm doing?" I asked, out of breath.

Wow! Didn't realize I was expending so much energy doing this.

Azmir went to say something but used his fist to muzzle it. He threw his arm against the frame of the walk-in closet's door and gave a distressed look. It was time for me to go. I didn't want a showdown. I'd barely zipped up my little piece of luggage and rolled it out through the other entrance of the closet. I passed Azmir as he rested the back of his head on the door frame.

"Rayna, you're not leaving," he informed calmly. Too evenly. I maintained my stride to the door. He started on my trail.

"Yo, you're not fucking leaving!" he yelled at the top of his lungs, frightening the crap out of me. It stopped me in my tracks.

I turned around, facing him, "You will not view me as some type of whore and think I'm going to live here and tolerate it. I don't have to put up with this...and I won't!" I tried to keep it as clean as possible. Although I'd given up profanity a little while ago, I was struggling here as Azmir was the second person I'd wanted to cuss out today in four different languages.

"Rayna, you're not leaving! Give me this!" Azmir demanded as he attempted to snatch the suitcase from me. He could've taken it clear from me, but if he had, it would've been a more volatile nature. By him trying to release it from my grip, the cheap luggage burst open and most of the contents spilled onto the marble floor, there in the foyer.

I lost it. I fell to my knees, wailing out of control. I didn't know what was more upsetting, this emotional tug of war or the fact of it being hard for me to control my emotions around this man. I didn't understand what it was about him causing me to too often become so unraveled in his presence, sexually and emotionally. *Why do I cry so much? What was I doing here?* Just twenty-four hours ago things were so peaceful. Is this what relationships were really like? I was at such a loss.

"Wait...baby... I didn't mean to make you cry," he murmured apologetically as he wrapped me in an embrace. Azmir lowered himself down on the floor with me, trying to provide consolation.

"Azmir, I swear, that was not me! I was not there! I wouldn't lie to you! I told you and Michelle those girls were not my friends. I would have never asked you to invite them out there. It wasn't something...I particularly enjoyed. I know this hurts your image as you're starting to become a public figure. But I swear, I knew nothing about that event or recording," I attempted unintelligibly. My body was shuddering uncontrollably.

"I know. I've been an asshole about this whole thing," he

muttered while burying his face in my head. "I'm sorry, baby. I went about this thing all wrong," his words were spoken softly.

"It wasn't me! I swear... I wasn't there!" I once again declared, sobbing into his arms.

"I know it wasn't you," he murmured.

What?

I peered up at him, still unable to control my diaphragm from my crying. "You know?" I asked through tear-filled eyes.

He eventually gave a slight release from his tightened grip. "Yes, I know. I told you I've gone about this all wrong," Azmir paused in exasperation, trying to find the right words. "I let my manly pride get the best of me. After watching the tape for the second time and really studying it, I noticed the tattoo on ol' girl's hand," he informed while looking me square in the eyes with the most sincerity. "Plus," he continued, "...the technique she used was not your style at all."

I jumped, tossing my head back to get a clear view of Azmir who was wearing a placid expression. And out of nowhere a belly full of laughter exited my mouth. I belted out the biggest cackle. Azmir eventually contracted the infectious humor himself and let a mild chuckle escape. I bolted over backwards, laughing uncontrollably.

"Seriously, her grip was all off compared to yours. She ain't deep throat that shit at all," he jeered in attempt to extend my humorous state. And succeeded.

"Azmir, I didn't have any technique until you arrived somewhere during that trip," I squeezed out over laughs.

"Goddamn right. Your only mastered techniques were customized for my stick and mine only." His lush lips twitched up into a charming smirk as he watched me laugh myself into hysteria.

Somewhere in the midst of my laughter it hit me. "Is that why you came to bed with me last night?"

He shrugged his shoulders. "Part of the reason. The other was because no matter how much of a blow it would have been to my ego, in all honesty, I was not prepared to walk away from you yet. We were just heating up at the time...not exactly committed like now," he murmured, studying my eyes. "I panicked, thinking you'd ran off. I was so relieved to see you were in the guest bed."

My body froze at his words. No matter how many times he said it, I could never get used to his genuinely gratifying words. It always amazed me how articulate he was because Azmir embodied so many personas. He'd go from street thug to corporate CEO in a moment's notice. I sometimes wondered who he really was. Maybe he was his true self with me?

"I just don't want to turn into a burden or something you learn later on you really don't want. I'm not trying to trap...or use you here," I explained as my diaphragm slowed and tears ceased.

"Baby, you're gonna have to trust me to tell you I don't want this, *if* that time comes. Don't do it for me because you will always get it wrong and try to run prematurely. I don't want you to leave. How many ways can I say this?" he implored.

I sighed, trying to weigh his words. "Well, where do we go from here?" I asked. Between the Brian Thompson fiasco, Dawn's lurking presence, and now this scandalous tape, I was at a loss.

He snorted after a brief pause, "For starters, let's put your things back where they belong, or Louise will lose her mind when she gets here tomorrow." I let out a giggle at that. Azmir's cleaning lady could be a bit fussy at times. More often than not, I couldn't blame her. She was constantly picking up our clothing that seemed to trail from the front end of the house all the way back to master suite. I guessed I'd be pissed, too, if I had to pick another woman's cheekies from the kitchen floor and balcony.

Azmir continued, "Then, we go get something to eat. A brother's been starving. You stormed outta here without fixing me a dog biscuit this morning, and you don't have anything ready to cook for dinner. I'd been waiting on you to get in from church. Of course, not expecting what I got." He was referring to my failed attempt to leave. "I made us reservations at a place on the water. We can go there, and I can fill you in on my talks with my legal team."

Legal team? Why were we involving them in?

He must have correctly read my expression. "Brimm, this is defamation at its best. Lady Spin spewed lies vindictively. She knows damn well that ain't you in the video. I'm sure Britni handed it over to her, co-conspiring. She marred the image of your dearly departed without thought. You're a professional and shouldn't be subjected to this fucking harassment. I'm going to find a way for her ass to pay. My people have already been in talks with the radio station."

My eyes were locked down towards my knees as I tried to process Azmir's fury.

"This is all too much to take in," I pinched the bridge of my nose, trying to slow down the millions of things running through my head. Azmir seemed to have been so concerned about me, but I was afraid of what this could do to his brand.

He rose from our kneeling, proffered his hand to assist me in standing, "We take it one day at a time. Isn't that what you Christians sing about in your hymns?" His lips curled up into a smile.

What is it about this man I trust implicitly?

CHAPTER 7

Rayna

The next morning, I was awakened by the annoying sounds of the alarm clock. I jolted and tried to jump up to snooze it. Only, my body was mounted just inches from the bed.

What in the...

I looked up in search of my restrained hands to find my wrists cuffed to the bed. Between the noisy alarm and the frustration of not being able to collect my arms, I grew distressed. I finally look over to Azmir's side of the bed. He was peering down at me in humor, watching me squirm. Suddenly, I was relieved, but expecting an explanation.

"What is this all about?" I demanded.

He placed his *iPad* on the nightstand as he wore the most lecherous smirk. To say this was the last way I thought I'd wake up this morning wouldn't be saying much at all. He reached over me to quiet my alarm and took a sharp exhale as he ambled back to the bed. My belly clenched as I watched the columnar muscle cords of the sinewy wing of his back hover above me. His white *Calvin Klein* boxer briefs were inches below his rippled abdomen, and I wanted to run my tongue beneath the band of them. He planted a wet kiss on my lips.

Crap! He got me again!

He smelled of mint, which meant he prepared for this while I was asleep. He apparently had the time to cuff me, too.

What is this all about?

"Ms. Brimm, you look even better cuffed awake than you did while you were asleep," he observed.

I gave him an expression of bewilderment, though I knew where he was going with this. As much as I tried to fight it, I was getting turned on by the second.

"I woke up just after dawn from a nasty dream," he murmured as he pulled the comforter from my waist, down to the foot of the bed. "I don't want to rehash it, but I must say, it consisted of you leaving me yesterday," Azmir was speaking in the most even tone —somewhere between contrite and salacious. I couldn't choose. He ran his fingers softly up and down the side of my abdomen. I shivered.

He continued, "I've expressed to you I don't want you to leave. This includes my side and my home. So, I wondered, *'How can I get through to her in a manner she'd understand?'* Then the thought came to me, *'Chain her to the bed for the rest of her days,'* but that, of course, has legal implications. So, I thought of a milder version. I thought I could cuff you and remind you of why you should stay. Make sense?" he asked, expecting an answer.

I nodded my head in agreement.

"Good," he affirmed, flashing that panty-snatching smirk. "So, I am going to start now, understanding I have a good half an hour before you need to be showered, fed, and out of here to make it to your workout session on time. Okay?"

I enthusiastically nodded, again. I was so ready, I'd already started squirming.

He began to kiss me passionately, causing my brain to pound in my head as electric pulses coursed my body, setting fire down deep. His tongue was fierce, igniting all my senses. Before I knew it, he began his descent down my body, landing at my breasts. He teased my turgid nipples torturously by sucking and deliciously tugging at them, pulling them to a near painful length. It was spicy pleasure and an erotic visual. He stayed there, working them over, sucking, sparring with his trained tongue and kneading my breasts thoroughly. My head swung restlessly from side to side. My pelvis thrusting in the air, desperately wanting friction of the A.D. type. But he lay at a forty-five-degree angle, torturing me with his adept mouth. I felt the rising in my belly. He pulled at my nipples with his lips, then teeth. I lay twitchily as I watched and heard his tongue slap against my flesh. My toes curled into a ball as my body tensed in preparation.

I tried to fight the urge, but I could no longer.

"Ahhhhhhh!" I yelled and then my body collapsed seconds before convulsing over the mattress. I couldn't feel anything but rippling waves of pleasure as an orgasm swept through my body. Never in my life had I obtained an orgasm from sole activities to my breasts. It was clear by his expression that Azmir was precipitating it.

He stilled to crack a smile and then continued his oral deeds as I thrust my hips in the air, wishing it was upon him. This was air humping at its best, something I hadn't done since high school. Azmir knew what he was doing. His tongue moved with agility around my belly, causing it to lurch from unrelenting oral persecution.

Man! If my hands were free, I'd push his head down below.

"Are. You. Getting. The. Picture. Ms. Brimm?" he asked between kisses down to the juncture of my jumpy legs. My panting was out of control. I was so ready for him. Again. With a heavy tongue, he traveled from the top of my pubic hair line to the opening of the lips of my sex.

He stopped.

No!

"Ms. Brimm, this is the best time for sex of any kind for you. Do you know why?"

What the..! A pop quiz at a time like this, Jacobs?

Still heavily panting, I quickly whispered, "No."

With his smile still present he answered, "Because you have a full bladder. Not only will your impending orgasms be first-class, but my thrusts will feel more intense to you. Are you ready?"

Orgasms ending with an "s"? I felt my muscles clenching again. *Oh, I am so ready!*

"Bring it on—PLEASE!"

Azmir chuckled, further spinning me out of control. *Is there anything he can do to turn me off at this point?* In no time, he started skillfully lapping his tongue into my canal. His clever tongue was weighty this particular morning and it was what I needed. I think he somehow knew that. Having my hands above me made the experience more erotic and tantalizingly pleasing at the same time.

"Damn, Brimm, you taste so good in the morning," he growled with such desire, bringing about mass lubrication at the apex of my legs.

I wish I could touch him. His head...his shoulders...

"Let's hurry up. We don't have long," he reminded me and went straight to my throbbing pearl as he caressed my thighs hovering over his ears and head. I flexed my sex at him back and forth and up and down, feeling perspiration gathering on my forehead. He reached up to my nipples and skillfully massaged them, and not too long after, I became undone. Heat coursed through my veins as I splintered into tiny little pieces beneath him. I cried out, shuddered, and my body jolted every which way imaginable.

Holy cow! He was right: this is more intense.

I guess I'd never considered it. It was more intense than the first one.

It went on for so long. He held me at the waist to keep me still until I was done. Once my whimpers were silenced, he rose and pulled down his boxer briefs. His erection vaulted out, prominent as ever. It looked so inviting. He stroked it a time or two, well aware of the torment he was putting me through. Swiftly, he reached over me to unhook me from the bed. I was slightly disappointed because I'd enjoyed the brief erotica. Azmir was never short of freaky. My one hand was still cuffed, so I had to be careful as to how I moved because the cuffs were heavy and could hurt me if I was not mindful. He sat me up so that I was facing him and checked my wrists.

"No marks. Good. If this were the weekend, I'd try something that would definitely bruise you, but you have to go to work," he muttered, mouth twisted, and brows knitted. I'm not sure why, but his words piqued my interest, and I found myself a little disappointed. "I know you like to ride on top, but I wanted to see how you performed when slightly restrained," he murmured, kissing my neck. He had so much passion in his eyes as he lifted my slip over my head. I was now naked. He made his way to my lips, and I tasted myself on him. We taste good together. *I am so aroused.* I moaned through my nose as he cuffed my hands together behind me. I heard the clicking as he adjusted it to size of my wrist.

How did I sleep through this earlier?

I didn't care. I wanted this so bad.

"If you need my help to grind, just ask. Okay?" he whispered chidingly in my ear. I eagerly nodded in agreement.

He lifted me onto his lap as he sat on his legs. He was so strong. So virile. I was in awe as I stared into his most alluring eyes. His long lashes were piercing, and his smooth coco skin was so inviting, but I couldn't touch him. As he guided me down onto his wide length, I groaned. His eyes never left my face. He felt so good filling me. Right away, I unsuccessfully tried thrusting because my self-control had fleeted.

"*Uhnt...uhnt,*" Azmir reprimanded, heeding me. "I'm not all the way in," he informed through clenched teeth. This told me he was enjoying me as well. With his arms draped around my back, he hooked one of them on my shoulders to anchor me.

"Ah!" I cried out. The pleasure was indescribable.

"Ready," Azmir informed me.

I began going to town. I thrusted and flexed every which way, trying to find my balance. I couldn't. He felt so good buried in me, but he was inconsistently hitting my most sensitive spots in there. I needed a rhythm but couldn't get it without the use of my arms.

Azmir, stilled, looked me in my eyes, and mouth, "Just ask," he reminded me in that husky tone of his I knew well. I was panting in my frustration of feeling like I had an internal itch but couldn't navigate my scratcher.

"Please!" I bit out with deep exasperation.

He pulled down on my shoulders and pushed me onto him and then off. Oh, I loved the way he used my body as if it weighed two pounds. It was effortless. He did it for a few seconds before I caught on and then went for broke. I began plowing into him like a mad woman, feeling electrical pulses traveling through my spine. He moved his arms to hold on to my hands behind my back while kissing me wildly on my shoulders, neck, and breasts.

"Azmir! Oh my...Azmir!" I screamed. My insides were on sensory overload, and I tightened at the core to grip him internally.

"Rayna, you're such an enthusiastic lover," he choked out in a gruff over our pace. "You see...this is why you can't leave." At those words my eyes pried open. I could see the determination in his eyes, the hidden retribution for my stubbornness.

In this moment, I knew I was exhausting him mentally, my resistance wearing on him. But how long before he broke? I didn't want to think about that. I wanted to focus on his workings of my anatomy. He felt incredible. "You feel it. Don't you, baby? There it is," he droned accurately because somehow, *he knew*. He knew I was on the brink of an orgasm. Azmir was so in tune with my body he could accurately predict it.

I let it go, singing the letter "O" with more meaning than I thought it had.

Azmir pulled me closer to him. "You won't leave?" he asked with anxiousness. Desperation.

"No... No!" I screamed in torturous pleasure as my orgasm was still in full swing.

"Tell me, baby. Tell me you won't leave me—*ever*," he demanded through clenched teeth and with urgency in his tone.

"Never. I'm never leaving you. I swear, Azmir!" I meant every word of that proclamation. I felt it in every corner of my body as I was coming down from my orgasmic high.

Azmir had taken over the thrusting and it felt inconceivably delicious. "Good...because I plan to give you the world. I'm gonna make you so happy, Brimm. Do whatever I have to. I'm gonna make you my—" his declarations were interrupted by his ravishing orgasm. He held my limp body so near to his as he writhed beneath me. It was as if he needed to become one with me. I felt the goose bumps sheathing his tense body.

I was absolutely spent. We sat in this position until we both finished collecting ourselves.

I couldn't get his last sentence out of my head. *He's gonna make me what? Happy? Proud? His wife?* He'd already said happy, so he had to have meant his wife. *Am I ready for that? Am I worthy of that?* I don't want to move things too fast. It was enough that I'd been living with him. I was still adjusting to that. My eyes paced the wall behind Azmir as my thoughts ran wild.

"You okay?" he whispered against my neck where he buried his face during his climax.

"Yeah," I breathed, trying to mask my bemusement.

Azmir reached for the key to free my hands from the handcuffs.

"Ah!" I cried. I hadn't realized my shoulders were locked into that position. "Try explaining that to Tyler this morning," he teased.

Azmir took my hands into his and lifted them gently to his face to inspect damages. He sighed in relief when he noticed no bruising. He kissed them and for once he wasn't looking me in my eyes. This was strange for him. It played on my suspicions. *Was Azmir hinting at a proposal?* I had to confront this head on.

"Azmir?" I called to him, though he was two inches away and still rock hard inside of me. I tried to capture his diverting eyes.

"Yes, baby," he answered while still planting small kisses on my hands and wrists. It was distracting.

"What you said earlier? Or what you were trying to say—"

Crap! What am I trying to say?

He grabbed my face in his hands and kissed me slowly and tenderly. This was dangerous considering he was still strong inside of me. He broke our embrace.

"Ms. Brimm, we have lots to talk about, but now we must start our day. If we stay here like...this..." He gestured to me on his lap, "...we'll never leave. Boyd should be out there by now, waiting on our orders. I have my session with Tyler, an insane number of meetings and a dental appointment this morning," he muttered, lifting me off his lap, causing me to wince. He was evading my questions.

"I have to shower." He kissed me my shoulder then left the bed for the bathroom.

After washing and dressing for the gym, I walked out into the kitchen. Azmir was there at the breakfast table on the phone and his *iPad* at the same time. He was always working.

"C. Boyd!" I call out as I always did when seeing him in the morning.

Chef Boyd turned to find me, "Ms. Brimm, you look like you're ready to run a marathon this morning! What can I fix you to help with that?" Boyd asked playfully as Azmir eyeballed me until I sat at the table with him. I could tell he was ending his telephone conversation.

"I'm starvin' like Marvin! I think I'll go with Belgium waffles with your wicked blueberry sauce," I requested.

Azmir shot me a sharp gaze. "I wonder what Tyler would say about that."

I wasn't sure if he was serious or not. In fact, I wasn't sure I was picking up the warmest of vibes from him at all, which was weird considering our time earlier.

I returned his glower. "If you won't tell about my breakfast, I won't tell him about your kinky fascination with restraints this morning and how it's the cause of my feeble shoulders and wrists." I knew it wasn't necessary, but my words were out there before I could weigh them.

Azmir raised his eyebrows as soon as he knew where I was going and before I was done. His neck extended forward, and he cut his eyes toward Chef Boyd, who was within earshot. I didn't care. We were all adults. *Shoot, he knew I live here.* He'd followed Azmir to my place in the high hours of the morning. *He knew we have sex!*

Azmir didn't seem too pleased about me alluding to our intimate life in front of his staff. I didn't want to piss him off, especially after our superb lovemaking this morning. Then it dawned on me: Perhaps Azmir was feeling vulnerable about his nearly slipped confession of wanting to get married. I'm not accustomed to seeing him in an insecure state. I bet very few get to sit in the seat I'm theoretically resting in now.

"Any meat or sides with that, ma'am?" Boyd asked, surely trying to cut the tension in the kitchen this morning.

"Turkey bacon would be nice. Thanks," I replied with less zing in my voice. Azmir had just knocked me down a peg. His eyes were still glued to me, though now he held up his paper with both hands over the table. I rolled my eyes at him. *Yeah, he was in a foul mood—again…but it was so unnecessary.*

Out of nowhere, he quietly reached for my hand over the table. As I turned my attention back to him, his eyes softened. He turned my wrist up still in search of markings. *They were actually on my breasts.*

We ate our breakfasts in silence. Azmir had his usual egg white omelet with spinach and tomatoes and turkey bacon. Boyd's presentations were most exquisite.

As we were finishing up, Azmir broke his silence. "Don't forget to clear your schedule for our meeting with the attorneys this afternoon." I nodded and am once again reminded of the looming quagmire I'd been thrust into—we'd been thrust into.

Over a romantic dinner on the water yesterday, Azmir shared how his legal team was eager to take this bull by the horns and had begun reaching out to all parties involved, including my practice. I questioned if I was ready for the day as I cleared the table, preparing to leave.

Over in the foyer, Azmir and I were leaving out at the same time. This didn't always happen. I was still thrown by his mood. It was like he'd been sulking since our morning expedition, and I was not all that certain why. But I had bigger fish to fry; getting through the day lying ahead, so I brushed it off.

At the front door I yell to Boyd, "Thanks for breakfast, CB. It was great per usual. Can't wait for dinner!"

"It's my pleasure, Ms. Brimm. Hope I can pull it off again for dinner. Have a great day!" he returned while busying himself in the kitchen.

"Make it a good one, Mr. Jacobs, sir," Boyd bode.

"This evening, Boyd. I'm looking forward to it," Azmir replied with his lips petulantly set into a grim line. I thought it was strange, as Boyd prepared our dinner in the morning. He was only contracted to show in the morning for two meals. I usually warmed up dinner he'd prepared in the mornings when I got in at night. But again, I shook it off due to impending issues.

Azmir peered down at me with an intense gape. "It's going to be a trying day, I'm sure, Ms. Brimm. You'll get through it," he murmured, giving me words of encouragement.

Mood changer!

Initially, I resolved to say nothing, just tried to read his mood. But I couldn't help it. This communication thing he constantly summoned went both ways. "What were you trying to say earlier—"

Azmir cut me off with a tender kiss as he grabbed my backside, pushing me into him. He did all of this while taking a sharp inhale through his beautiful nostrils. His kiss took my breath away, and my pulse surged. It was promising and calming all at once.

Still staring deep into my eyes, he murmured, "We have lots to discuss."

But what does that mean?

I didn't ask. Clearly, he was not ready to answer.

∞

I rode into work without incident, and my workout with Tyler went well. I'd been enjoying the way my body was sculpting. It had been just a few short months, and I was more impressed with my body than I had ever dreamed possible. Now, Azmir wasn't the only one with a killer frame. I'd stepped my game up. I showered and dressed at the rec and made it into the office by eight twenty a.m.

After speaking with Sharon about my schedule, I got my day started. The morning sped by as usual. However, my thoughts of my morning with Azmir played in the front of my mind. *Marriage? Me?* I couldn't come up with why I wasn't suited for this particular institution, but it was honestly something I'd never thought about since being a kid. Until now, I hadn't come across a man capable of taking my dreams that far. I mean, after our time in Vegas, I knew I wanted to be with Azmir forever, *but marriage was an entirely different bird.*

After finishing up with my midday client, Mrs. Ginn, I quickly scarfed down a bite to eat from the kitchen. Azmir had the cafeteria from the rec deliver various menu items to us several times a week. He paid for it, and my staff always expressed their gratitude whenever he came over.

I walked over to the rec and was confronted by my favorite nemesis, Old Lady Peg. She had warmed to me slightly over the months, but it was clear she didn't want to get overly-friendly.

"He's finishing up a meeting. You can go right in—at least, that's what he said. It seems quite rude to me," Peg remarked. I fought the urge to roll my eyes as I made my way over to Azmir's office and knocked on the door. I didn't want to barge in.

"Come in," Azmir barked. I turned to Old Ice Queen Peg who rudely gestured for me to walk in as if I were a child. Once again, I ignored her and stepped inside. I saw there were several people in Azmir's office and all eyes were on me.

Once Azmir saw me, his eyes went into a priapic slant, and we were suspended in time before he breathed, "Ms. Brimm," as he searched for the time on his pocket watch, all flustered.

Once it registered to him it was nearly two in the afternoon he announced, "Well, that's my time, all. I expect those newly implemented reports in forty-eight hours from now. Should there be any further questions, forward them to Brett. And if you think by doing that you're off the hook, God bless you because he's hell on wheels about these new standards. They're his baby. Good day, folks," Azmir announced far more cheery than I left him this morning.

I walked over to him as his staff all stared at me, trying to decipher the look he gave me moments ago. It was either that or they were wondering *who was this woman who had the authority to inter-*

rupt an A.D. Jacobs meeting? I tried to lock my eyes ahead toward Azmir as he exchanged a few parting words with Brett who politely greeted me.

Azmir's eyes traveled over to me like a child in wonderment. "It's nice to see you. Breaks up the monotony of the day," he murmured in a manly and husky tone. It was arousing.

"You act as if we weren't scheduled to meet at this hour," I replied in an effort to end his flirtatious attempts.

I could hear Brett, who was just inches away from Azmir, speaking into a wire, say, "Mr. Jacobs, conference room C is ready for your meeting with Chesney and his team now." Azmir nodded and continued eyeing me from head to toe as he reached for his suit jacket.

"Ready?" he asked. I shook my head with a smile, and we headed up to the conference room.

Once seated at the table I asked, "How did your dental appointment go this morning?" I wondered where his dentist was located. Was it in Marina Del Rey? Unlikely, because he was new to that area. Was it here in LBC? Was that a personal question? *Ewwwwww!* I was tortured by my personal thoughts.

"It was...discovering," he chuckled to himself, looking deliciously gorgeous doing so.

"What's so funny about discovery?" I asked as we were trying to keep our voices low.

Azmir leaned into me, "As she cleaned my teeth, she admonished me about my food choices this morning." He tried to contain his private amusement. I was confused. I recounted what he had for breakfast.

"Was it the spinach?" I asked.

He shook his head. "A little stringier." Azmir cocked his head to the side, bringing my attention to his mouth when he pushed back against his molars.

My eyebrows furrowed, trying to catch on. At the same time, I heard people entering the room behind me and Azmir cut his eyes to them, waving them in.

I was looking at him searching for an answer. Putting me out of my suspense, he murmured, "Hair."

Hair? What hair?

He quickly pointed to my lap with his eyes and nodded his head. Within seconds it registered.

My pubic hair!

"Oh, *shhh*—!" I trilled, successfully keeping myself from sputtering profanity. My eyes bulged at him, and he flashed a panty-snatching smirk before turning his attention to his guests.

"Chesney!" Azmir greeted with great cheer and familiarity in his tone to a slender Caucasian man matching his height. It was his attorney, Chesney, I presumed as I stood to greet him myself. His eyes locked with mine from the moment he laid them on me, looking beyond Azmir. It made me uncomfortable. I didn't know if he was reading me or undressing me with his eyeballs.

Chesney was followed into the room by his associates who seemed familiar with Azmir, too. Azmir finished up his hellos to them and then proceeded to introduce me. "Chesney, as I'm sure you've figured out by now, this is the illustrious Rayna Brimm. A very special friend of mine."

"I see. Are we using that title now?" Chesney taunted without a smile. He continued to study me for a moment, looking me from head to toe before exercising a wide contrived smile and announcing, "Ms. Brimm, I'm Edward Chesney of *Chesney's Law* located in Glendora. I am A.D.'s—I mean, Mr. Jacobs' attorney. I handle civil legal matters for him amongst other akin items," he shot out quickly and cunningly removed his smug smile. He gestured to my seat, "You may sit."

I looked at Azmir who was wearing an odd smile not quite registering to me yet. But I had to motion to him regarding Chesney's introduction by way of shooting him a look of bewilderment. Overall, his aura was weird. Azmir glanced at me for a brief moment before returning his attention to Chesney who had not stopped gaping at me diverting his sight down to his shoes now.

"Ms. Brimm, Mr. Jacobs here is not only one of my prized clients for...*obvious reasons*, but he's also one of my favorites. Do you know why?" he posed a question.

I shifted in my seat, growing uncomfortable and gave him a blank stare.

"I see. Well, it's because he makes my life and therefore my job easy by doing one simple thing, which is keeping me informed—on everything!" He paused before continuing. He was now pacing the room from the opposite side of the conference table.

"You see, Mr. Jacobs is sure to share with me every detail of his life that can cause risk. Risk to his name, risk to his brand, risk to his reputation, and risk to his wealth. My job is to protect his wealth and I'm *damn* good at my job, Ms. Brimm," he emphasized the "m's" in my name while towering over me, leaning on the other side of table.

I squinted my eyes to chase off his very imposing gaze.

"I see," Chesney continued. "Back to Mr. Jacobs and his skillful ability to disclose. Yes!" He tossed his long index finger in the air as if he'd just found his way back to his lecture. "He's really good at divulging pertinent information. For instance, I know you manage a physical therapy firm next door for *Smith, Katz & Adams Sports Medicine Center*. I know you earn roughly sixty-seven to seventy-two thousand dollars annually—*which is grossly underpayment for the role you play, coincidentally...*"

I darted my eyes to Azmir, wondering how he knew how much I'm paid. I'd never shared that with Azmir, which I guess is why I had to calm myself. Azmir shrugged, gesturing he was just as much surprised by this information as I was.

Chesney continued with his monologue, "Okay, enough about you. I know during January of this year, Mr. Jacobs endowed you with an extensive *Louis Vuitton* luggage collection. I know it was part of a ploy to get you to vacation with him in Mexico. *Some expensive woo'ing in my opinion but...*" He held his hands up, femininely, in defense. His inflections were killing me! "...every man goes about charming in his own way," Chesney paused again, gauging my reaction before continuing. "Let's see. I also know you and my client now cohabit *and a little off my advisement.*"

I narrowed my eyebrows at his audacity.

"Oh, yeah!" he confirmed, responding to my reaction. "If I had it my way you would have signed a cohabitation agreement, highlighting every agreed upon detail, down to bathroom usage, *but...he denied my request*—something he always does as it concerns you, Ms. Brimm," Chesney informed me while giving Azmir a cold gaze.

"E," Azmir warned.

"Okay. Okay. *Okaaaaaay,*" Chesney placated very dramatically. In fact, this whole production was melodramatic. I couldn't help but to wonder about his sexuality. He had several feminine traits, but that doesn't guarantee anything now-a-day.

"Where were we?" Another dramatic pause, "*I see.* You see, Ms. Brimm, there are very few things I *don't* know about my client. I know his tastes and his preferences. For example, I know you're wearing lace panties of his gifting. And narrowing down his preferences, they are either *La Perla* or *Victoria's Secret*. Narrowing down his color preferences they're some variation of white, pink. or black," he shared while peering me dead in the eye.

That forced me to look at Azmir, who now looked uncomfortable as he was readjusting himself in his seat, but still said nothing.

"It is not my intention to belittle or embarrass you this afternoon, rather to orient you to the culture of my practice. Mr. Jacobs has generously retained me on your behalf and my firm has already begun our work in investigating said individuals. I would just like to stress to you full disclosure. This can get *reeeeally* ugly depending on if or how much the radio station backs this young lady who released this provocative video, claiming it *starred* you.

With what we've uncovered, along with Mr. Jacobs—*astounding discovery*—we have a very strong case. I would just hope you are just as forthcoming a client as your...boyfriend here." Chesney cut his eyes at Azmir.

What the...

"I plan to pursue this vigorously. You are now just as much of a client as Mr. Jacobs here. We have secured a meeting with your higher-ups over at *Smith, Katz & Adams Sports Medicine Center* for six this evening. I hope you don't have dinner plans," he paused before asking, "Do you?"

Oh!

He was waiting on an answer from me.

"Oh! Seeing you know so much about me, I had assumed you were going to answer the question *for* me," I hissed.

He gave an arrogant chuckle. "No, dear. But I do endeavor to know more about you...*considering you don't seem to be going anywhere anytime soon.*" Yet another pause. He raised his index finger to his temple. "Yeah, and about that! How *do* you feel about prenuptial agreements? *Just by chance...*" he asked, drawing into me again.

I gasped. *Is Azmir's attorney asking me about marriage after my incident with Azmir earlier this morning? Is this confirmation?*

"Ed!" Azmir fired off another warning shot.

Chesney shook his head, unsuccessfully attempting to retract his previous question. "Bad timing...*bad timing*. We can revisit that at another time."

"Chesney, what do you need from Ms. Brimm now? I'm sure she's still on the clock and has patients to get back to. And then I'd like a word with you," Azmir took over.

Finally!

Chesney shook his head again in exasperation, "My associate, Whalus, over here will take a full statement and ask a few standard questions. The sooner you answer, the quicker you can resume your workday," Chesney sulked.

This must mean he's in trouble. Good!

I stayed behind for about a half hour to consult with Chesney's team. I even had to give full disclosure about how I came to run the Long Beach City practice. I hadn't thought about the details of that story in so long but provided everything to the best of my memory. When that was over, I returned to my office to finish up my day.

I met Chesney and one of his associates at *Smith, Katz & Adams Sports Medicine Center's* headquarters later in the evening. The meeting was extremely brief. I was pleasantly surprised at how amenable Dan Smith was to not suspend me or take any disciplinary actions until they had indisputable evidence showing I was involved. Brian Thompson did most of the speaking while Dan Smith looked preoccupied. He mentioned he was mortified Michelle was on the tape and would do anything within his power to bring all those responsible for leaking it to justice.

It was weird seeing Thompson there. I could still see the healing bruises on his face. As much as I wanted to discuss his fight with Azmir, I knew this wasn't the appropriate time or place. I was surprised he hadn't broached the subject yet himself. I also recalled Azmir's request of me steering clear of Thompson. Azmir and I were still rebounding from the event, so I'd managed to obey his firm request. I guess it was something I'd have to wait out.

Rayna

On my way home, I longed for my bed. It was later than usual, so I hoped Azmir had warmed dinner in my wake. As I walked through the door, the aroma was delightful. The lights in the kitchen were on, and I could hear the clashing of dishes ringing from there.

I placed my briefcase on the bench in the foyer when I suddenly saw a woman of Asian descent walking past. "Oh!" she gasped while holding her chest.

I must've given her the look of death.

Who in heaven's name is this?

"Ms. Brimm! I'm so sorry! We didn't know you had arrived," she flashed a nervous smile to move past our frightening introduction.

"I'm Kim. Mr. Jacobs is out on the patio awaiting you." She extended her arm toward the patio.

Warily, I walked over to the balcony, passing the kitchen where I could hear Chef Boyd working the stove on the way. Soft music was playing as I walked out to find Azmir on the phone. I quickly noticed the dinner table for two set up with an ivory tablecloth and chairs with white covers. The fresh white lilies were resplendent with their black bulbs bursting from the center. The utensils were displayed in a formal manner with two forks and spoons and a knife. If I didn't know better, I would have thought I'd just walked into one of the five-star restaurants Azmir takes me to. There were gorgeous white lights trimming the balcony, creating a romantic ambiance. What was this for? My eyes darted back to Azmir who was still heavily engaged in his conversation.

"He bought how many shares? Is this something we'd still want to get into? Yeah? Uh-huhn. Well, let me sit on this and get back to you in the morning. Nah, man. I can't rush this one. Something doesn't feel right to me."

He turned to find me waiting in the doorway. His expression changed as did the mood in his eyes. While keeping his gape on me he continued, "I gotta go, Rich. Love's home. Yeah. First thing in the a.m.," he assured before ending the call.

With his eyes still fixated on me he greeted, "Good evening, Ms. Brimm." He didn't smile, but there was still that sparkle in his eye. And not to mention, the lights of the marina bouncing off the water, reflecting a warm glow against his skin.

"Hungry?"

"I was before stepping into all of this." I gestured the romantic set up with my hand. "I see we have guests." I was asking for an explanation when a young male waiter, with honey blonde hair and the most piercing green eyes, wearing a black chef coat, came out with two bottles of wine. He didn't speak. Azmir acknowledged him by asking me to take a seat.

"Join me?" he asked, pulling out a chair. I strolled over to him and sat. He scooted me to the table and took his seat. Once we were sitting, the waiter approached the table. "Good evening, sir and Ms. Brimm. I am Chaise, one of your waiters for this evening. May I offer you a drink? Tonight, we have a red, a two thousand-five *Chateau Lafite Rothschild* and white, a two thousand-seven *Sassicaia*.

Azmir chose red, and I followed suit. As Chaise poured into our glasses Azmir asked, "So, I hear your meeting with the *Smith, Katz & Adams Sports Medicine Center's* heads went well. How are you feeling overall?"

"Tired. Annoyed. Happy to be done with my day." Azmir looked affected. "Is Chesney always that intense?" I asked.

Azmir snorted, "You should've seen him the day I evaluated his law firm for services. You would've thought he was putting me on his payroll. Intense is an understatement. But he's superior in his work."

"Well, I can assure you the good bosses of *Smith, Katz & Adams Sports Medicine Center* weren't expecting the flair of Chesney." We both giggled at that.

"So, are you going to tell me?"

"Tell you what, Ms. Brimm?"

"Tell me what's going on with you. Your missed announcement this morning during our love session—"

He gave a sly smirk and interrupted with, "That was something to write the heavens over, wasn't it?"

I blushed and maneuvered in my seat while trying to inconspicuously return to my point. "Then your foul mood this morning at the breakfast table. And this afternoon during the meeting with Chesney and his associates. You were...subdued."

He tilted his head to the side and asked, "Subdued. *Hmmmm... Really?*"

I nodded as I took a gulp of my wine. Kim came out with crab bisque soup and bread. I started attacking it immediately. *Oh, my!* It was sooo good!

Azmir took a moment to think.

"Here's the thing, little girl," he began and it kind of turned me on. Azmir reached over his bowl of soup for his wine glass and took a quick sip. "It's no secret I have difficulty gauging your moods and gaining your ultimate trust. It has been my daily goal to get you to trust me totally and completely. Once I do, I can take you places you've never dreamed possible. But until then, I'd like to start physically taking you places."

That was loaded, I thought to myself as I tried to follow his conversation.

"Let's go away," he proposed softly.

Go away?

"When?"

"Soon."

"How soon?"

"Next week—soon."

Boy, was he straightforward. Could I do that? Did I have the time from work?

"Brett has already checked with Sharon. She said you can expend a few days at work with fair notice."

Really? So, it's that simple! You can simply go over me and have my receptionist check my availability?

"That's a little intrusive, wouldn't you say?" I asked mildly.

Azmir shrugged, "That was the purpose of synching our assistants, was it not?"

Technically, Sharon wasn't an assistant. She was the office receptionist. She was only at my disposal more than other PTs because I headed the practice.

"Look," Azmir broke my ruminative thoughts, and I noticed him placing his glass back on the table. "I don't mean to intrude. I would simply like to take you away."

I finished my glass of wine and Chaise came out. "Refill, Ms. Brimm?"

"Please, Chaise," I forged a polite smile.

Azmir's eyes shot up, "Done already?"

"I told you; it's been a long day." I exhaled as Chaise poured me another glass.

"So, what's going on with Tara and the baby?" I asked. I don't know where the question came from, but I put it out there. And after I did, I was glad because it sounded like the most responsible thing to do. I mean, our future laid in the balance of the paternity of this baby. *Or did it?*

"She's still dragging her feet on the test."

"Sounds daunting."

"Sounds hood rat-ish to me," he returned, clearly frustrated by it all.

"Would you want full custody?"

"Rayna, for the millionth time: that is not my baby."

"I'm just saying if—"

"End of story," he pronounced with a slight raise of his voice.

Before I could think of a response, though I was not sure I would have had one after that outburst anyway, both waiters came to collect out bowls and serve the main entree.

They sat stainless steel salvers with covers before us and

opened them simultaneously to serve broiled salmon with a cream lobster sauce, asparagus and red potatoes.

"Boyd's presentations sure were always elegant! This smells amazing. Did you pick the menu?"

Azmir gave an affirmative nod. "In hopes of you delighting in it. Do I have your approval?"

My mouth formed a wide and annoying smile I couldn't get rid of. I tried so much, I ended up laughing at myself.

As Azmir was sorting through his plate, he caught the infectious amusement as well.

"Someone has had one glass of Rothschild too many," he sang.

His smile appeared, and I couldn't ignore how gorgeous this man was. His teeth were perfectly aligned, and his nose was nicely proportioned to his face. His eyes were seizing even when they weren't on me. I often wondered if he knew how good looking he was. I took notice of other women checking him out, but I would never make a big fuss over it. He wasn't something I possessed. But I questioned how he regarded himself.

"You know, you're an extremely good looking man?" The alcohol was definitely making me more brazen than usual.

He stopped with the fork in his mouth. *Lucky fork.* He pulled it out and looked up at me. "You don't say!"

I nodded and grinned like a little schoolgirl.

"Do you get that often?" I asked just before sampling my fish.

Mmmmmmm! Delicious.

He took a sip of his drink. "Actually, I don't. But it wouldn't mean as much as it does when it comes from you."

I didn't believe him. Every woman I knew had commented on his features. Did he really expect for me to take him at his word?

"You're being modest." Suddenly, I was feeling so bashful I could barely look him in the face.

He smiled embarrassingly. "Ms. Brimm, if a pretty face can't get a woman, I'm seriously...madly pursuing to go away with me, what good is it?"

"That face has gotten you in the most private of places with this lady. What's more intimate than that?" I was flirting and it felt so refreshing.

He raised an eyebrow, "My tongue got my face into those private places, Ms. Brimm. I don't know what else you think did."

I giggled.

Boyd came to check on us. "My compliments to the chef! Delicioso!" I cheered as I clapped my hands.

"Boyd, you've outdone yourself, my dude. This is off the chain," Azmir praised the meal.

"Thank you, Mr. Jacobs, Ms. Brimm." Chef Boyd humbly bowed his head towards me, using professional grace. "I'm glad you've enjoyed it so far. I just wanted to check up on you since Kim and Chaise are inside putting the kitchen back together. I hope you've left room for dessert, Ms. Brimm. I do believe we have one of your favorites this evening."

I dubiously glanced at Azmir, who gave the most intense gaze with a slight squint in his eye.

Turning back to Boyd, I softly returned, "I can't wait."

Okay, Ms. Brimm, I'll refill your wine. And is there something I can get for you, Mr. Jacobs?"

"If you can, get Ms. Brimm here to agree to come away with me, I'd go to bed with the widest smile because my goal of the day would have been met."

I gasped, "Azmir."

"Water would be nice," Azmir retracted in jest.

"If I may, Ms. Brimm, I've come across lots of people in my line of work and rarely do I find what's embodied in Mr. Jacobs. He's a hardworking man who's fair and generous. He's very narrowly focused. If he wants you...give him the honor. I doubt you'd go wrong."

Azmir's beautiful mouth formed an infectious smile I couldn't ignore.

"Did he pay you to say that CB?" I teased.

"Not at all," Boyd chuckled and then turned to Azmir, "Your water is coming up, Mr. Jacobs," and then turned on his heel.

I took a sip of my wine, still eyeing Azmir with great suspicion. I murmured, "Only under one condition."

"Anything," he shot back.

"You let me cuff you."

He stilled in his seat, furrowed his eyebrows as he licked his lips and sucked in the bottom one when he was done. He brought his eyes to mine, "I don't know if you're ready for that yet, do you?"

What? "Why not? What's the worst that could happen?"

"You may take advantage of me. You know—" he was interrupted by Kim, clearing our dinner plates, making room for dessert. Chaise immediately followed her with Azmir's water.

Once they were gone, I asked, "Like what?"

He chuckled, "I don't know… Like you having me restrained and screaming like a little bitch." I took note of his Brooklyn accent.

I tilted my head to the side and squinted my eyes. Chaise had returned with our dessert. Crème brûlée.

"Oh, wow, Azmir! How thoughtful!" I jumped up and ran over to his seat to grab his face and plopped a juicy one on his lips. He wanted more. I could tell by how long it took for him to open his eyes. I stood, bent over him smiling salaciously.

"Girl, you better stop playing. You gotta give a brother due warning before you come over here with that after talking about cuffing me," he whispered.

I couldn't help it. I had to tell him, "Azmir, baby, you can take me anywhere you like. I am so happy to have you in my life. I think I'm a pretty lucky girl—dare I say, blessed?"

He looked troubled by my introspection. He moved in and gave me the softest kiss as he squeezed the small of my back if it were possible. *What's biting him?*

"Let's finish dessert. I want to give you another round of

training with the cuffs before handing over the key." I felt butterflies in my stomach as I sauntered back over to my seat.

The crème brûlée was to die for. Chef Boyd really knew his craft. We sang our praises to him and his team as they walked out the door. I tried to hide my yearning to have Azmir all to myself. He held me by the waist in his pelvis as we saw them out the door. I'd soon discovered Boyd owned his own restaurant. He worked part-time for Azmir to earn extra cash for his twin daughters' college tuition. Kim and Chaise were waiters from his restaurant. This explained the odd hours. I wondered how much Azmir paid him, though I'd never ask.

Boyd shut the door behind him, and I turned to Azmir, placing my palms flat on his hard chest and asked, "So, what now?" I couldn't help my giggle.

"You really wanna know or would you rather be surprised?" He smiled at my giddiness.

"No surprises for me, Mr. Jacobs," I flirted as I turned back to tease him with the softness of my rear.

He bent down and whispered in my ear as he nibbled on it so softly and sensually, "We go to our room and strip down naked so I can acquaint myself with your third hole."

I gasped, speaking in a louder tempo, "What do you mean *acquaint?*"

Azmir turned me around and gave me the sexiest deep gaze dead in my eyes. I felt my lubrication immediately. "I'll take it slow and won't move a minute before you're ready, but let me prep it," he hummed in my ear. And that's all it took for me to be fully intrigued. He led me to the master suite where we explored a new level of intimacy.

I was on my way back to the office, and on my drive, I was still settling my mind on my trip to a swimwear boutique Azmir arranged for me to visit. We were scheduled to leave for our excursion the following day. Apparently, the proprietor was an old acquaintance he wanted to support in her new venture. Tanu was extremely hospitable and knew her craft. From the time I walked through the doors until I said my goodbyes, she was very attentive. Her pieces were exclusive and included all types of appealing fabrics and designs. I had no idea there was a market in bathing suits, but after seeing them in great variety I'd been enlightened. She recommended several pieces based upon my size and shape and after being put through the scrutiny of trying on, literally tiny straps of material, I could honestly appreciate Tyler's tough regimens at the gym.

I surprised myself by selecting a few sheer cover ups minus breast coverings in the ensemble. Azmir wouldn't tell me where we were headed, but he did advise we would be surrounded by water and have privacy. He also ordered Tanu to not discuss the prices with me and simply bill him. Once again, I was uneasy about his exorbitant splurging on me. I fought off feeling like a sycophant as I walked out of the boutique. The bathing ensembles were exquisite, I had to admit.

I left the bags in the trunk as I went into the building. Sharon was at her desk and informed me of a visitor in the conference room.

"Oh?" I wasn't expecting anyone.

"Yes, he's a detective and was insistent on waiting for you," Sharon shrugged her shoulders as she whispered over her hand, holding the phone from the call she was on.

I mouthed to her, "Okay," as I headed to the back. The only thing I could think of that would bring law enforcement here was either matters from my PT assistant being arrested earlier in the summer or the Wayne Tanner lawsuit underway. On my way, I dropped off my purse and slipped on my white work coat.

I opened the door to the small conference room to find a middle-aged, brown skinned man with eyes full of charisma. His belly was slightly pronounced, and his head completely bald and shiny. His smile was disarming and slick.

"Rayna Brimm, sir. How may I assist you, Mr...?" I attempted as a means of getting a name.

"Ms. Brimm. I finally have the pleasure of making your acquaintance," he muttered, flashing a sinister smile as he rose from his chair. "You've been such a focal point in my circle. It's nice to put a face to a name, or better yet an energy. And a quite lovely face at that. It makes a little sense now."

"I'm sorry. I don't quite understand." He gave a chuckle, but I quickly gathered it was at my expense. "You, sir, are?" I asked with a little more blitz in my tone.

"I'm Darryl Harrison. You are... What terms are you kids using nowadays?" He squinted his eyes while rubbing his chin. "*Fucking*...a young man who's like a son to me. Divine."

"Azmir?" I murmured.

Was this about Azmir? Was this Tara's father? Why was he here?

"Ahhh... Is that the reference of your relationship?" he snorted in a revelatory manner. "I came here expecting to see you in an administrative assistant role of some sort, but I've underestimated my son. I've taught him well," Harrison announced boastfully. "He loves the high sharks. I wasn't prepared for an educated and...*well-ranked* professional," he shared, referencing my position at the practice while surveying the room. "But I'll speak to you in terms you're better conversant with in spite of your academic and professional accomplishments.

My eyes were glued to him. I had no idea where this conversation was going, but what I was quite sure of was not liking the end result. I braced myself.

"Rayna dear, we have a problem. See, your presence in Divine's life has created a bit of a...rift in my family. And I am very protective over what's mine," Harrison narrowed his eyes to emphasize his sentiment. "I lost my wife this past spring, and she never got the opportunity to meet our granddaughter, Azina." He gave a short yet hearty laugh while searching his breast pocket and pulling out his mobile phone, "I'm a proud Pop-Pop. You have to see this gorgeous little angel." He tapped the phone several times before a picture appeared. If he was about to show me a picture of Azmir with Tara and that baby, I was prepared to lose my bladder and the bile from my stomach simultaneously, on the carpet where I stood. But it wasn't.

Whew! Instead, it was a candid shot of a newborn child.

He flashed the phone toward me, "Isn't she a precious little thing?" He shook his head in admiration as he put the phone away. This man was really full of melodrama. I wasn't prepared to speak yet, so I remained silent. I wanted to know why he was here.

"I see you were bright enough to rise from the ashes of the projects in New Jersey and despite your humble up-bringing, was formidable enough to go to school and obtain a lofty and stable career here," he waved at the room again. "But just as I imparted into Divine, I did the same for my little girl. I told her when she was a tiny ol' thing to only end up with a man who can provide for her and her children...and well. Now she has a little girl...just like her. And so soon her family is in a disarray." Harrison set his glower on me, "I can't have that in my legacy. Remember, it was I who told her how to choose her man." He paused while searching the corner of the room. "Well, she did that. Not only did she choose well, but she chose a man of my sculpting and mentoring, honey. It doesn't get any better than that. Divine is young, calculating, intelligent far beyond what he's credited for, collected, connected...and rich, something I'm quite sure you're aware of." He shrugged his shoulders. "I get the allure."

He was taking this too far and taking too long to get to the point of him showing up at my job!

"The point of your visit to my workplace, Mr. Harrison?"

He hiked his brows, "That's Detective Harrison to you, sweetie!" he hissed.

Excuse me?

I froze in place. Where was this going? I was getting upset and feeling threatened. It was only a matter of time before I would go off.

He continued, "I'm here to start repairing my family. As you can imagine your presence in it has caused a bit of trouble. A man in my line of work has many resources stretching far and wide considering I began my career on the East Coast, coincidentally where you're from. It's my job to discover things…less than favorable things people want hidden. For instance, an Akeem Brimm who is a resident of *Caldwell* prison. I know who he is and why he's there."

I lost my breath. My body stiffened like a board.

Did he just mention my…

"Yeah, baby girl. I know all about J-Boog and O, and how your little fast ass was at the center of the shooting of that innocent little girl. Just like you're at the center of my little angel's family."

Breathe, Rayna. Breathe!

"But I think I can help. The lawyer you have working on his appeal can use a little help from my people out there. I can have him freed in a few short months. It only takes a couple of calls on my part. The discharge paperwork would take longer. I can even throw in a…let's say, sixty grand to help with your moving expenses back home to Jersey." He paused to catch a reaction from me. I couldn't believe what was happening. He continued, "You're young, smart, and determined. You can stay in your field out there and start all over. Hey… You may even find someone better than Divine. He's a very complicated man with demons you would never believe."

Harrison evaluated my process again. I remained stoic, giving nothing away. I slowly started to regain my wits.

I can play chess, too.

"Now, I know he's all up your ass—and by the way, I know it's a juicy one to have," he droned lecherously. It was most incestuous. "He's never home. Every time I drive by his car is never there. I'm sure he spends romantic nights at your place on Redondo Beach." I raised an eyebrow. "Yeah, I know where you live. You're just a block away from the water." A devious smile crest upon his face. "You must think you're living the California dream. From the dirty East Coast projects to the Pacific beach. I get reports of his car being there nearly every night, which surprises me because he's a workaholic. But I get the new pussy syndrome. It'll pass." Grease was dripping from his tone.

Detective Harrison stood and gathered his jacket as he was preparing to leave.

My turn.

I brought my hand to my nose and snickered.

"You find something funny, young lady?" Harrison's tone was extremely intimidating, but I wouldn't fold.

"Yes. You're far less impressive than Azmir describes you."

He jolted his head back as to demand an explanation.

"Well, you're very melodramatic. What man your age comes into a woman's—virtually your daughter's age—place of business, interfering in their daughter's love life? Then you flash my receptionist your title to get back here. That has to be misuse of your limited authority." Now, it was Harrison's turn to raise a brow. "Yes, limited. I've done nothing wrong. You're investigating me, and quite inconclusively might I add. You have some nerve," I ended as he casually brushed past me towards the door.

With a grimacing expression he vowed, "They'll be married within a year. A year! And you? You'll be left with the designer shoes he bought and fucked you in your appreciation of him." He gave me a slick and wicked grin again, attempting to call my bluff. Harrison went for the door handle and retorted, "Sweetheart, you have seventy-two hours to take me up on my offer." Another dramatic pause. "If you should choose not to, thinking I'm a fucking joke, tell Divine about our little chat today and get his take on my detailed investigation," he murmured too close to my ear before exiting the room and closing the door behind him.

I stood suspended in the same position for nearly ten minutes until I was paged over the inter-office P.A. system. I tried making sense of Detective Harrison's surprise visit, still feeling the lingering of his disgusting gritty presence in the air. That man was cunning, but I had a strong suspicion he was also desperate.

love ∞ believe

Once the sessions with my afternoon clients were complete, I sat in my office finishing up charts, but struggled with keeping my focus from running over to the various things Harrison had said.

They'll be married within a year. A year! I heard the echoes of his sentimentalities loud in my head.

Is that true?

Azmir never gave me the impression he had flights of fantasies to marry Tara. He told me she wasn't suited for that level of commitment. *Well, those were things he told me.* How true it was, only he knew. But why would he lie?

Then he begged me to move in with him. To my knowledge and by way of his own admittance, they never lived together. And speaking of which, Harrison said he had reports of Azmir's car being parked at my place nights at a time. When he's not being chauffeured by Ray, Azmir drives his Jeep *Wrangler* or his *Range Rover*. Rarely did he drive his cars. Which car was Harrison referring to?

Then it hit me like a ton of bricks: Harrison was not very much in touch with Azmir! First of all, he'd never spent nights at a time at my place. Secondly, I'd been living with Azmir for nearly two months now and sleeping next to him every night unless he was out of town on business. Yazmine was staying at my place and didn't have a car similar to any of Azmir's. Harrison lied by manipulation.

My thoughts were interrupted by the office phone ringing.

"Hello?"

"That's what I thought I'd hear you say at least two hours ago. Where are you, little girl?" Azmir's silky voice flowed through the phone, stammering my heart.

"Eh... Hey, you," I mustered as I looked for the time. It was nearly eight p.m.

Geesh! Did I really let the time get that ahead of me?

"Are you coming home, Ms. Brimm? I wasn't aware of you having church service this evening." He was expecting an explanation.

I closed my eyes and took a long exhale. With as much confusion as this man had caused today, it was nice to be sought after by him. "Azmir, I'm sorry. I let time escape me. I've been working on my charts, trying to clean them up since I'll be away for a week. I didn't want to get behind." This was partially true.

"Your dinner is getting cold," Azmir advised softly. *Focus, Rayna. Focus!* Though he didn't intend to, the tone of his voice spoke to my libido.

"Well, what doesn't get done by eight twenty, won't get done until I return. I'll be there soon."

"If I call there at eight thirty and get you, don't bother driving. I'll have Ray bring me to get you. I mean it," he threatened.

"Deal," I agreed, relieved he couldn't see my face heating up.

And we disconnected.

After being snapped out of my trance, I looked down at my progress on the charts. Only two more to knock out and then I could leave with a cleared desk. I completed them and then headed over to the marina.

I couldn't shake my conversation with Harrison on my drive. So many things he said just didn't add up.

Even over dinner, I couldn't escape the echoes of his voice. He was creepy. What was even more upsetting was Azmir could tell something was going on.

"You've barely touched your steak. Boyd would be offended," Azmir phished for my thoughts.

"The filet mignon is really good. And the béarnaise sauce sends it over the moon. I'm just really exhausted. I didn't plan on working as late as I did. And I still have more packing to do."

His intense gaze told me he didn't buy my story, but I wasn't ready to divulge the truth quite yet. I just wanted to finish up my packing and go to bed.

"What time should I be ready in the morning, again?"

"We ascend at seven sharp, so we should leave at six fifteen," he replied, maintaining the interrogative gaze. Even that was sexy as all get. *My goodness!* Was this man even capable of making an ugly face?

I dismissed myself, saying that I needed to finish packing. He rose from the table with me, as he always did, being polite. I knew he was burning a hole in my back with his gawking, but I had to keep a straight face until I was out of his presence.

As I packed, I wondered why I was even going on this trip. If Azmir's heart wasn't totally with me or our relationship, why should I go through the motions of vacationing with him? Was he really just out sewing his oats with me when his heart had actually belonged to Tara? Also, if Harrison knew about my past, he could easily call my bluff and tell Azmir. I didn't like the idea of that creep having privy to my past that not even Azmir had. For heaven's sake, he described Azmir as some helpless puppet under his control. That stung my conscience. If Azmir found out about Akeem from a source other than me. it could be devastating to our friendship.

Once done packing, I decided to do the only thing I could think of. I retreated to the shower and prayed. I prayed in silence, hard and long. I'm sure I was repetitive, but I wanted my requests clear and known. When I stepped out, I had resolved to telling Azmir a piece of my past.

As I walked back into the bedroom, I saw Azmir lying in bed with his perfectly sculpted chest wondrously bare, watching *ESPN*, one of his favorite pastimes. I eased over to the bed, pulled back the comforter and glided in.

He looked at me, this time more relaxed in his gaze and asked, "You good?"

I thought about his question for a few. Then I finally found the courage to say, "No."

The next thing I heard was flicking from the television being shut off. *That was apt.* Azmir looked over to me, giving me his undivided attention. He murmured, "Pocket watch."

It's now or never, Rayna.

Action!

"Azmir... Playing spades with the cards up...all trust." I gulped in air as I was sitting on my legs, facing him in the bed. *Five-four-three-two-one.* "I have a brother, just a few months older than me, who's incarcerated back in Jersey for murder. I don't want to discuss the details right now, but I can say I've been paying his attorney fees for quite a few years now. We've been pursuing an appeal." I ended there, unable to think of anything more to disclose.

He lowered his gaze to the comforter on the bed, I'm sure confused and definitely taken by surprise. *Say something, Azmir! Please!* I don't know what I was expecting him to say. I certainly didn't think he'd go berserk, but I anxiously awaited a reaction.

"Do you need money to help with the attorney fees?"

What?

"No. God, no!" I was taken aback.

"Sounds like you need a new lawyer. Is that what you're asking for?" he asked, clearly bemused.

Seriously?

"Azmir, I don't need anything from you. Just for you to know, that is a huge part of my life I keep extremely private. You're only the second person who knows." I was at a loss for words.

"Is that why you visit Jersey?"

"Yes. To see Akeem and replenish his commissary."

"Only him?"

"Oh, God...yes! Only my brother."

"Is that the reason for such short trips?" He was catching on, attempting to make sense of the bomb I'd just dropped on him.

Was he asking if I had some type of jump-off back there?

"Yes. The trip last summer, when you came out, was the first for something other than him. I'd learned my father had passed and my sister asked for me, something she'd never done. And I went to see about her and my grandparents, again, something I'd not done since leaving." The lids to my eyes collapsed as I recalled the horrific event. I hated talking about anything relating to home or my past. "And for some odd reason, I went to check on my mother: another first for me, too. Had to visit old demons, so to speak," I shared the last line with a forlorn giggle in an effort to disarm his doubts of my odd story.

"I'm sorry to hear about your loss," he murmured before a long pause. Then, "I didn't know you had an older brother...didn't know you had a sister until I found you out in Jersey."

"I know...because I don't discuss them. And I'm still not ready to." I looked him in his eyes as a way if asking permission to re-seal my box of secrets for that moment. His ruminative expression tugged at my heart. He grew silent.

"Azmir, say something," I murmured.

"I'm not sure what to say. You've made it clear that you don't care to discuss more than you have. So, I have to make do with what you've given." He then shifted towards me, "Rayna, is there something detrimental, illegal, life threatening—or anything of that nature in your past that I should know of? Remember, we're playing spades with the cards up...all trust."

My heart rate increased as I pondered his question.

Death maybe, but not in a present tense.

Ummmmm...

"No."

He gave me a deep, intense, and purposely emphasized gaze into my eyes. I swear I started to perspire where I sat. He was intentionally intimidating me...sending a message to my conscience. I now had an idea of what his staff experienced under his tutelage.

Here we go.

"No," I repeated.

"Then go to bed. We have to be up bright and early." Azmir exited the bed.

I lay there, staring at the ceiling, trying to think of what could possibly be going through his mind. I knew he was in his office, his favorite room in the house. He spent more time in there than he did even in his bedroom. The man functioned on very little sleep. Oddly enough, he'd been sleeping increasingly more since I'd moved in. He had gone from nearly four hours to five and half hours nightly. This was progress in my book.

My stream of thoughts carried over into my dreams. I didn't know if I were sleep or awake until a little after two in the morning when I turned over to no Azmir. I sat up on my arms and didn't even see Azna in the bed. This alarmed me. *Is he upset with me?* My conscience told me if the shoe were on the other foot, I'd be pissed with him, so be fair. I got up to see if he had fallen asleep at his desk. In my foggy state, I tip-toed down the long corridor where I could see a light glaring from his office. Yup, he was there. When I looked in the room, I saw him there on the phone and looking on the desktop. He noticed me right away.

"Hang on, Washington." He turned the mouthpiece of the phone down in his neck and asked, "Everything okay?" with a look of concern.

"Errr... Yeah. Just a little odd waking up at two twenty-two in the morning to an empty bed." He looked up at the clock and seemingly realized the time.

"Now you know the feeling." His smile was forlorn as he referred to my working late a few hours before. "Where's Azna?"

Azmir pushed against the wheels of his chair to scoot away from the desk. And although he was too far away for me to see, he pointed to his lap to answer my question.

Hmmmmmm...

"So, it's a man's world?" I asked in jest.

He flashed that panty-snatching smirk. The currents flashed through my body. My smile disappeared and I suddenly felt guilty and desirous at the same time. After the bomb I'd laid on his lap earlier, he still had the capacity to smile.

I paced over to him on a mission. His eyes never leaving mine and once I arrived to him, I bent over and kissed his soft lips. I couldn't stop there. I wanted to taste his lips and I did. I sucked softly as I held the sides of his face. Reluctantly, I slowly let go of his bottom lip. When I opened my eyes, I saw his, though filled with priapic readiness, were open. I wanted him so bad, but under the circumstances knew not to push my luck. I decided to collect Azna and return to bed. But as I went to scoop him, I accidentally rubbed against Azmir's strong erection. Subconsciously my eyes shot up to him. The cool air hitting my gums from the strong release of his lungs told me my mouth was open. Azmir's eyes were heavy with need.

Does he want to take it there as much I do?

His body was telling.

"Go back to bed. We have to be up in less than four hours. I'll be there in a minute," he murmured, trying to gain control of the situation.

With a broken ego, I obeyed and returned to bed. It took a minute or two for me to doze back off because I had to ignore the throbbing between my legs. I accepted it as punishment for my delayed disclosure.

What a day...

CHAPTER 8

Rayna

Several hours later, we were pulling into a large lot I would soon learn was an airport in Hawthorne because Azmir had chartered a private plane for our trip. Ray retrieved our luggage from the car, and Azmir assisted until aircraft's staff came over to take them from him.

"Mr. Jacobs! It's a pleasure to see you this morning. Ms. Brimm, this way," he looked at me with a huge, welcoming, and professional smile. I returned the gesture.

"Jim," Azmir greeted in return then held the small of my back to point me in the direction Jim was leading. He looked preoccupied, but I didn't know how to address it. So, I didn't. Azmir was wearing denim jeans with a graphic T and track jacket. I had on a maxi dress with a cropped jean jacket and a scarf draped over my shoulders. I wasn't sure of what to wear, as I still had no clue of where we were going.

We immediately boarded and were introduced to our aircraft staff which included a flight attendant, who I could immediately tell was taken by Azmir. This happened often and I never tripped. There were times he caught on to his admirers as well and was embarrassed. But today, he was so internally engrossed, he never took notice. My heart sank.

The airliner was sophisticated. Too rich for my blood. I'd never flown on a private plane before. It made me wonder how often had Azmir. The plush ivory leather seats and benches were oversized for comfort. They were very fitting for a man of Azmir's height and frame. The carpet was a rich tan shade, giving off a pristine feel of the luxury aircraft. This thing was huge and could fit over a dozen people. In the center of the cargo area was a forty-two-inch flat screen television. To the left of the television area was a workstation with a desk and phone. At the far opposite end was another television mounted on the wall, only smaller. *Who needs all of this?*

I turned to the man who'd arranged it. Azmir's sullen disposition had me afraid to talk to him. I just didn't know what to say. Through my peripheral, I observed him as he sat back and adjusted himself in his chair.

The captain announced himself on the P.A. system, gave our expected arrival time, and the temperature of our destination. I quickly did the math and estimated an eight-hour flight. Coincidentally, the captain announced an eight-hour travel time mere seconds later. *Crap!* My suspense was on overdrive. *Where are we going?* He addressed us by name, making it difficult to forget we were on a private plane. I was thoroughly impressed. Azmir seemed indifferent and more concerned with getting some shut eye.

Catina, the flight attendant, came over and handed us menus. I was surprised to see there were exclusively breakfast items listed. Suddenly, I felt Azmir's hand on my right thigh, patting it gently. Without looking at me he shared, "We're in for a long flight, so get comfy. Order when you're hungry. I'm gonna catch a few Zs. Order something for me when you're ready. Surprise me," he gave an adorable yawn before turning over and falling asleep.

The flight was long and provided too much time for my muddling thoughts of Harrison's visit from the day before. He'd mentioned my presence causing a rift in his family. As I sat reclined next to this...Adonis of a man, I couldn't help but to wonder where exactly I stood in his stratosphere. I mean, I'd moved in and now what? We cohabitated until we grew tired of each other. *Will he get bored with me?* Then, I thought of Azmir's possible proposal. If that was, in fact, what he was contemplating, he sure hadn't produced anything—not that I was terribly disappointed because I was not sure if I was any more suited for marriage than Azmir believed Tara was. But when I thought of him being with someone else, making love to them, singing their name in ecstasy, calling on them to come home at night after work, flying them on private planes like he was with me right now...I felt sick.

Oh, I just didn't know!

One thing I could empathize with was the loss of Harrison's wife. Tara's baby came at such an awkward time, and the paternity issue must take things to another level. For the first time in a long time, I didn't know what to do. One thing was for sure, if Harrison's objective for coming to see me was to get inside my head, he had succeeded. What if Azmir wasn't mine after all? What if I was simply the *"in the meantime"* chick? I felt an insurmountable sense of anxiety coming over me. My heart rate increased, mouth went dry, and I felt wet everywhere. Panic began setting in. I felt my body jerking.

What was this!

"Rayna!" I heard my name.

"Goddamit, Rayna. Wake up, baby! Are you having a nightmare?" I opened my eyes to see Azmir looking spooked. He and Catina were hovering over me as I tried catching my breath.

"I'll get her some ice," Catina announced before scurrying off.

"You okay?"

I scanned around the bright room to recall where I was. Once the environment had settled in, I nodded my head. Catina had returned with a cup of ice, I assumed to help cool my body temperature. I was drenched in sweat. Azmir looked so concerned and worried. I didn't know what to say, but clearly saw I had to say something.

"Must be the altitude," I managed a chuckle. He exhaled. "Don't forget this is my first time in this type of aircraft. How much longer do we have anyway?" I asked in diversion.

"The captain just announced about two hours," he muttered with his eyes shut and fists balled. I couldn't fight. I had none in me. I needed him to know that, so I leaned into him, forcing his embrace. After no time he pulled his arms around me sighing and saying, "Ms. Brimm, you're concerning me," before kissing me on the top of my head.

For the remainder of the flight, I struggled to keep all thoughts of Harrison at bay. Azmir challenged me to a game of chest. Catina offered us lunch, but my nerves were still settling and didn't leave room for much of an appetite, so I declined, and Azmir followed suit. Instead, we opted for light snacks and cocktails. By the time we landed, I'd felt more relaxed and ironically Azmir appeared the same.

Once on the ground, the captain announced our arrival in Tahiti. *Oh, my!!* I gasped and looked over to Azmir who looked as pensive as he always did when trying to surprise me. "Azmir, I've never been to a Polynesian Island before! This is a girl's dream!"

He gave a nod and mirthless chuckle as he cleared his tray area so we could disembark the cab. On our way out, the captain and co-captain were awaiting to bid goodbye and thank us for choosing their airline. Azmir was mildly gracious while I was awestruck by the entire experience now.

We arrived at our hotel and in traditional Polynesian fashion, we were escorted to a large, luxurious overwater bungalow. We traveled a ways from the reception area of the resort to a secluded portion of the property where there was a lot more privacy than the other bungalows. The water was breathtakingly blue and clear. So transparent, you could see to the floor of the ocean. Our front view was in a private groove, allowing us to see miles of water ahead. It wasn't until we traveled to the back of the bungalow that we saw other dwellings in the distance. Azmir did ensure privacy. This was really exclusive.

The bungalow sat two stories high with the bedroom on the top floor. The first floor had a full kitchen, fairly large living area with oversized sofas, and a plasma television mounted on the wall. There was a billiard room off to the rear of the house as well as a laundry closet, dining room, office, and powder room. The front of the house opened up to the water. There was a walk-out balcony leading to an in-ground pool, and inches away from it was an outdoor dining deck you had to walk through about four to six-inches of water to get to.

Azmir had shared we'd be surrounded by water. Shoes weren't very necessary for this trip. In fact, we shouldn't be needing many clothes either. This was heaven on earth. It was so serene, I took a few seconds to give God thanks for His creation. It was divine and... So was Azmir.

"Does it meet your satisfaction, Ms. Brimm?" Azmir called out to me as he stood in the main doorway with the property manager. Talk about customer satisfaction. What complaints could I have thus far?

I nodded my head and Azmir turned to him. "Jack, you have the lady's satisfaction and therefore my approval. We're good." He politely shook his hand. Jack turned on his heel to leave. Azmir joined me on the outdoor dining deck and stood beside me, admiring the view.

"Mr. Jacobs, you're making it very hard for the man coming after you—you know." I was partially serious, considering Harrison's heeding.

"Actually, I'm trying to make it clear there won't be any after me," Azmir retorted matter-of-factly and without skipping a beat. "Let's go get cleaned up for lunch." He turned to make his way back inside, and I was right on his heels.

Lunch was at a restaurant in the water. We sat with our feet immersed in the gorgeous aquamarine colored water. The air was fresh and the wind gentle. The entire island had an ambiance, which could not be orchestrated without nature, no matter how exclusive a place it was. *This was how the other half lived.* I was in awe.

"How's the fish?" Azmir asked as I was busy taking in the surroundings.

"Delightful. How's your chicken?"

"Pretty good. The glaze is the kicker."

"Have you been here before?"

Azmir sipped his iced tea before answering, "To the islands? Yes. To Tahiti? No."

"Oh," I wondered if he'd wowed other women with this majestic landscaping.

"Was Tara with you when you visited the other island or *other islands*?" I asked just before stuffing my mouth with sea bass. I knew I was pushing it.

Azmir's eyes shot up to me. He slowly lowered his fork back down to his plate, "I've traveled very little with Tara. A bit of Europe and the Caribbean. So, no... No Polynesian Islands." He looked affronted.

"I was just curious is all, Mr. Jacobs." It was my turn to be affronted.

"It's not your curiosity that concerns me, it's your sudden interest in my former relationship."

Crap. He was right. I never pried. I'd always felt it was useless information...until now. The truth of the matter was I loved this man. I loved him and wanted all of him, his present, future and past. I didn't care that it wasn't plausible. I wanted it all. With him. I never wanted anyone more than I wanted him. I couldn't help but feel a zap of jealousy whenever the idea of another woman presented itself, particularly Tara, who—according to her dad—was in position to spend the rest of her life with Azmir. Suddenly, I had lost my appetite. I motioned for the waiter to order a drink. A real drink.

"How may I help you, ma'am?" asked the sandy brown haired, tall, and slender waiter. His tan was to die for.

"I'll take a rum and coke."

I looked over to Azmir whose eyes were glued to me. I could tell he was surprised by my selection.

"Make that two, please," he ordered, and the waiter excused himself.

"So, what made you choose this place?" I didn't skip a beat. I had to know.

He gave me a deep gaze as he cut into his chicken, clearly annoyed. But I didn't care. What did I have to lose? Either he was going to be with me for a long while—*whatever that was*—or I had very little time left before he'd rejoined sides with his long lost love, Tara. And the clock was ticking. Moving forward, I wanted to savor every moment with him.

"Well, I'd learned it was an exotic island years ago. And coincidentally it's known as the island of love. Plainly put it's beautiful... just like you and what you represent to me. I wanted to share a destination with you, one new to the both of us. Luckily, I chose correctly." He flashed the first smile he had in twenty-four hours before going back to his food.

"I think it's more than luck. This is what you call a blessing. To experience all of this glorious seascape..." I muttered as my voice trailed off. I was overwhelmed.

Our drinks arrived.

I took a sip and inhaled a bank of fresh Pacific air. The cocktail was strong. This must be a man's drink. Good! I needed to lose my grasp of reality. Heck—for all I knew, this could be the last of former reality.

Azmir took a swig of his beverage as well and then went back to his food. He didn't look up very much and it dawned on me he was offering less conversation than he typically did. After gulping my drink once more, I confronted him.

"You're upset with me."

He looked up with his long lashes as he chewed his food. "Justification doesn't escape me; do you not agree?"

I knew automatically he was referring to my abrupt notification of Akeem. "But I was forthcoming...notwithstanding good timing, but still a noble act in my book," I argued.

"*Ahhh*... Timing. Not such a novel concept, I don't believe. Don't you think that would be something you told someone— *hmmmmm*... Once you realized you've fallen in love with them?" Azmir hissed, now giving me his full attention.

"The sarcasm in your tone hasn't gone unnoticed." I swallowed another mouth full of my rum and coke.

"Again, justifiable."

"No," I shook my head as I swallowed my gulp. "No, it isn't justifiable if you don't have the decency to reciprocate. Let's not act as though you've been the most forthcoming in this...relationship either—" he interrupted me.

"Relationship." Azmir cocked his head to the side as he furrowed his brows with incredulity. "You don't even know how to term what we have. Newsflash, Ms. Brimm, when two people are living together and fucking monogamously, it's safe to call it a relationship at the very least," he spoke swiftly, harshly, calmly and quietly.

The audacity!

"Oh, no! Do you, 'Mr. Experienced In This Arena,' realize you've not once told me you loved me or are in love with me? But, yes, you did ask me to move in." It was now my turn to cock my head. "How could that not confuse me?"

There was a brief pause as Azmir tended to his plate again.

"I give you orgasms. Love is far less complicated a task," he sharply shot back.

What did that mean? I wasn't quite sure of where he was

going, but by this time my tipsy state was upon us. It was all or nothing.

"Really? Well, let's see the next time I allow you to *give* me an orgasm. Just like you so eloquently illustrated back in San Diego, it's not as fun of an experience if it isn't shared."

Azmir dropped his eating utensils and motioned for the waiter. He ordered two more drinks and asked for the check. Within four minutes, we left the restaurant with fresh drinks in tow.

We traveled back to our bungalow and as soon as we arrived, Azmir stripped down to his trunks. When he pulled his white T-shirt over his head, I caught a glimpse of his chiseled upper torso. The muscular cuts in his back were artwork. Every muscle group was well defined. Azmir's chest was bare, but the sexiest trail of hair on his abdomen led down to his pubic area. His trunks set perfectly on his hips. He was upset with me and here I was, giving in to my lecherous thoughts. What was more odd was I'd just told him I wouldn't succumb to another orgasm as if I could control my body under his tutelage. He was far more versed with it than I was, even at my age.

I watched as Azmir jumped into the water from the deck and then I decided to go upstairs and put on one of Tanu's special bathing pieces. I had a sudden urge to seduce Azmir. Now, clearly intoxicated, I felt like I had something to prove. So, I choose this particular one-piece with a strap around the neck and the cloth formed like seashells around the breast. A sheath of cloth ran down from the connector of my breasts to my pelvis with brown straps wrapping around my hips, leading into a thong on my backside. It was really something to behold, though I was extremely insecure about this number. It exposed my butt marred with stretch-marks, something I'd had since I could remember. It was the big booty curse as it occurred when my backside expanded as a young girl.

Tamu shocked me when she said not to be concerned about it. "*Azmir Jacobs is a booty man. He doesn't care what graffiti is painted on it, just as long as it is soft and natural. Trust me, Rayna, I've known him for a very long time."* Her confidence in Azmir's tastes challenged mine until she all but told me she was a lesbian. I didn't know if I should have been relieved or concerned about being indecent in her presence. I decided to leave it alone.

Once downstairs, I took notice of the well groomed bar in the corner of the living area. I decided to make us drinks and take them out to the deck.

When Azmir came out of the water, I was resting on a float in the pool, laying on my front. He stood over me on a partition, gaping as he sipped on the drink I'd made for him.

"Enjoying the sun, are we, Ms. Brimm?"

I pushed up against my arms and glanced up to see him standing there wet and sexy. I think I'd dozed off. I'd overdone it with the alcohol.

"Come swim with me."

"I'm not that great of a swimmer," I used to blow him off.

Azmir jumped into the pool after saying, "Let's see how good you are."

He splashed water on me as I screamed. When he emerged, he grabbed me, snatching me off the float. I yelped in sheer shock. I couldn't believe he was doing this. Azmir commenced to dipping me in and out of the water. All of a sudden, he pulled me into him.

"Show me how you swim."

I extended my arms and legs and paddled with my head above the water. My body moved a few yards at a time. "That's some pretty girl swimming. You have to put your head down and go under."

I stopped, feigning righteous indignation, "That sounds like something you do." Okay, now I was flirting.

Azmir gave a sexy snort. "Let you tell it, I won't be *allowed* any acts to bring you pleasure."

I shrugged my shoulders and murmured, "That is correct...and serves you right."

Azmir halted in movement and in the next beat, took me by the hand, and led me inside the bungalow. In the main doorway, he kissed me so freely and meaningfully. I returned the favor, only mine with fury. I had something to prove. He could not control my heart and body only to return to his true love. I was in charge of my body from this night on, or so I challenged. He reached behind my neck to release the tie in the string holding the clasp of my bathing suit. Slowly he peeled it off from my breasts down to my feet, taking in every inch of my body. All I could think was, *Yeah, this is what you'll be missing.* As he rose, he made contact with my eyes as if he was communicating something to me without words. Well, I was too. I'd put out a challenge just a few short hours ago. One I had every intention to make good on. His erection was piercing through his shorts.

"Let's go upstairs," he muttered softly, and I could tell he was inviting me to lead him, so I went first.

As soon as I crossed over the threshold of the door, he grabbed me from behind, wrapping his long arms around my belly pressing me against him. He bent down to my neck and started licking down into my shoulder. A groan traveled up from my belly and exited my mouth. His lips were so soft against my skin. His right arm traveled down to my inner thigh slowly, and his hand gently rubbed over my sex. My body started to shiver. It had been days since we last made love and for this reason my body was hypersensitive. I couldn't give him total power. I had to regain control.

I quickly turned around to face him, bringing his head down to mine before throwing my tongue in his mouth. Azmir always tasted so sweet. He seemed to maintain the perfect amount of saliva in his mouth and never transferred much of it into mine. I enjoyed our oral dances. My hands fell to his waist to undo his swimming trunks and once they were on the floor, his underwear followed. I grabbed his length into my hand, stroking him back and forth. He moaned.

Yes. I was in control.

Or so I thought because the next thing I knew, he picked me up off my feet, into a straddling position and carried me over to the sofa chair in the corner of the room. He sat me down close to the edge of the seat and spread my legs eagle style. While hunched on his heels, he observed me while licking his lips as a dog salivates. All the while I could hear the breeze from outside, flowing into the open room. The opened doors of the veranda were bringing the outdoors in, adding to the licentious atmosphere.

Before I knew it the warmth of Azmir's mouth was over my most intimate parts. His tongue was strong and flexible as it was in search for my ultimate pleasure. Not long after, I found myself grabbing his head as my panting took over. He felt so good. He slipped two fingers inside of me and circled them over and over, and I was prepared to lose it. *Oh, no!* I had to stop this. I gripped the handles of the chair and scooted back. When his head came up, I lunged at him, taking him by surprise. My mouth met his as we spread out on the floor. An involuntary moan escaped as I tasted my juices in his mouth. I was so aroused.

I planted kisses from his mouth down to his neck as my hands searched for his pleasure tool and once I found it, I slowly mounted myself on it. My walls were a bit tense, but in no time, they remembered him and made room. Even working through the tightness was deliciously pleasing. Looking down to Azmir who was biting his bottom lip turned me on even more. He grabbed me by the waist to help fit him in. Then I started to ride him, and as I did my insides went wild. I felt him so deep and so did every wall of my canal. My breasts clapped together and against my chest, and the reverberation aroused me so much I found myself moaning out loud. It was almost a cry because I felt I was losing. I didn't want to give in, but I was lost in his libidinous orbit.

"That's right... Come for me," Azmir grunted, subpoenaing my orgasm. That slapped me back to reality. *No way.* I jumped up and off him. With pure virile athleticism, he bolted forward and on to his feet, wearing an expression of confusion.

"Did I do something wrong?" he asked, but not in his usual gentle manner. I shook my head as I panted, and my body hummed in excitement.

"Well, then you mind telling me what was that all about?"

I paused.

The pulsating coming from between my legs was so strong—violent even, and it spoke directly to Azmir. There was almost a twitch in his eye telling me he'd suddenly got it. He knew I was holding back on him. I felt weak in will, but believed I needed to remain true to my cause. I didn't care how petty it was, it was a matter of principle.

I squeaked, "You haven't told me you love me." I felt reduced as I spoke and could hear my defeated tone.

Azmir's face balled in frustration? Anger?

"Rayna, do you think you could keep yourself from me? I will bust ya' young ass!" he declared in his thug rhetoric before taking me at the waist and lifting me in the air where I was once again straddling him.

He entered me and using my hips, he grind into me. With each thrust, I could feel my myself lubricating. I tried to squeeze my internal walls in an effort of gaining some control. Wrong move! I felt my orgasm coming on. *No!* I tried to maneuver in a manner to let him know I wanted to get down. After a few seconds, he got the hint.

As soon as I landed on my feet, I dropped to my knees taking him into my mouth. *Yeah, I'm gansta! Two can play this game, Jacobs.* I went at him ferociously, pushing him all the way to the back of my mouth as I looked up at him, showing him who was boss. His face read disbelief, but he didn't push me away. I stroked him with both my hands until I heard him moan my name.

He groaned again, "Damn, Rayna," so slowly and sensually.

It drove me insane, and I kept pushing him deeper into my mouth. Then I heard a growl-like belt come from him and the next thing I knew, he had lifted me in the air and carefully tossed me onto the bed. I landed on my back, and he opened my legs and descended on me, dipping his head down between my thighs, taking a swift lick against my sex. I was so sensitive there my body jolted. He was mad and on a mission.

He pulled me by the legs toward him and entered me. Before resting upon me, Azmir placed my legs on his shoulders, and I knew he meant war because he was going deep. His hips started flexing and he slipped his tongue in my mouth. It was mind blowing how his tongue was so gentle, yet his thrusts were primal. I loved every bit of it. Every time he plowed into me, he took me higher. I moaned in anger and pleasure as he took command of my body as he always did. It somehow just didn't seem fair.

"Rayna, baby, I need this. I need you to come for me. Please. I need to satisfy you," he groaned.

I lay there, staring at him with my mouth sealed shut. Something came over me, and it wasn't exactly my very impatient orgasm. It was my concession. I knew I was losing. I knew I had taken on a battle with Azmir I couldn't win. A tear flowed from my right eye, and I opened up my mouth to breathe. When I did, my orgasm came like a tsunami, and my body convulsed as the tears sprang out.

"No, don't cry—" Azmir managed before he was overtaken by his own orgasm. His hard and lengthy body shuddered on top of me, forcing me to endure his full weight, and I enjoyed every moment of feeling him lose control over me. And inside of me.

When he was done, he swiftly scooped me into a bear hug with my back against his chest. He kissed my neck and held me close, so close I could feel his heart rate relax.

I felt betrayed by my body and conquered by a man who didn't even love me. How could something so good leave me feeling so empty? This had to stop. I don't think I've ever felt this low with Azmir, and I never wanted to again. What a way to start a vacation in the middle of paradise.

We lay there skin to skin for nearly an hour. My head spun and my heart bled. I was out-of-my-league-in-love with this man who suddenly I felt so disconnected from. What was even more strange was he had to have felt a change in me—in us as well, over the past day or so, but was still here with me. I had lost control of myself. Something had to go. Maybe Harrison's visit was a gift and a curse.

I drifted off and apparently so did Azmir because he jumped at the sound the doorbell ringing. After rising from the bed dazed, the bell rang again.

"*Shit.* Dinner!" he exclaimed as he bolted out of bed going for his swimming trunks. He ran downstairs. I slowly rose from the bed and found my way into the shower where I tortured myself even more about the potential end of my life with Azmir.

I made my way downstairs to find two people in the kitchen. I dashed into the small office where I found Azmir on his laptop.

"Who are those folks in the kitchen?"

He turned around to me and chuckled, "Chefs. I didn't bring you out here for you to cook. I had to tell them it's okay to let themselves in. So be cognizant of that during mealtimes." He searched my eyes. "You look tired."

"So do you." I didn't know where we stood after our copulatory standoff earlier.

He rubbed his eyes with his thumbs, "A little. I'm gonna hit the shower. Dinner should be done soon." Rising from his seat, he kissed me on the forehead before leaving the room.

We had dinner outside on the dining deck, under the Polynesian skies. My mood had improved slightly, but my dismal thoughts loomed. After dinner, Azmir had arranged for us to attend a show, but we were both exhausted from the travel, so we agreed we'd postpone the show to get some rest.

The next morning, we were awakened by the ringing phone. Azmir unhooked his arms from my resting body to answer it. He didn't say much and quickly got off.

"Brimm, you have a scheduled spa treatment on the water in twenty minutes. No bra is needed."

I took a minute to process his words in all my grogginess. "I didn't arrange for that."

"I did. Now get up. You don't want to keep them waiting," Azmir ordered in his morning groveled voice that liquefied my insides.

Fighting it off, I slowly stood and realized just how off kilter my body was. I showered and threw on a wraparound dress, minus the bra as Azmir had so effectively passed along.

When I arrived downstairs, I realized I had no idea where this would be taking place. Before I could go back up to ask Azmir, he belted from the bed upstairs, "Just out back on the beach."

My massage was serene and relaxing, just what the doctor ordered. Azmir was incredibly thoughtful. The full body massage was for ninety minutes, and the foot was for forty-five. It was heaven on earth. Just as in The Bahamas, the sounds of the open air added to the milieu. With every muscle being relaxed and kneaded over, I thought of it being at the expense and provision of Azmir. *How could a man who puts so much thought into me have only one foot into our relationship?* Maybe Harrison had it all wrong. Besides, he had quite a few facts off, especially about Azmir spending *endless* nights at my place. But he was correct about Akeem and his record.

Oh, the agony!

After my spa treatment, I returned back to our bungalow where I found Azmir knee-deep into work in the living room. As soon as I walked through the door, he put his finger up resigned to being caught working again.

"Washington, you're being paid to know, not guess or assume. Is that the best you can give a man paying you the salary I am? Do you know how many quality professionals are in your line of work with relatively half the pay? I don't have time for internship-level antics. I fucking need deliverables—yesterday."

I headed up the stairs to change my clothes. I wanted some air and had to see the surrounding locales. I threw on a silk one-piece dress wrapping around my neck and exposing my entire back. When I returned back down to Azmir, he was at his laptop and jumped up when he saw me. He was still on the phone. "Hold on," he snapped.

"I'm going into town. I shouldn't be long."

"If you give me a minute, I can go with you." He pointed to the phone, "I'm sorry. Something went wrong back at headquarters that needs to be rectified," he shared apologetically.

"Oh, that's fine. I can use the alone time to sort my thoughts. You need anything?"

Did I really just say that?

Azmir gazed at me, trying to find a crack. I maintained my poker face. I wasn't ready to divulge Harrison's consternate visit.

"Here," he snarled before turning toward the safe there in the office and retrieving a wad of cash. He placed the crisp bills in my hand, not offering it but forcing it instead. "Take your phone."

I gave a polite smile before leaving. Even in his irritable state, he was alluring.

The market I visited in town was vibrant with natives selling their goods in an open outdoor hypermarket. Vendors sold everything from fresh produce to island specialties, to beachwear, to souvenirs. I marveled at the handmade figurines created by the locals. How beautifully carved the ornaments were and delicately engraved the jewelry was. I was in heaven in no time. I sampled the food, absorbed the music, and noted the ethnic beauty of the islanders.

At one end of the crowded market was a small group of people, giving a show of live music and dancing. This, of course, captured my attention, and I found myself captivated, studying their techniques and counts. I sat there for a while, very entertained and reprieved with peace.

I rested my feet, admired the energy, and let my mind run free with random thoughts, and those not so indiscriminate. I thought of Michelle and how much she'd enjoy this, even more than I was. She'd enjoy the carefree atmosphere this place provided. That was Michelle, a natural free spirit. I think I was the only thing in her life keeping her attached to a reality not agreeable to her free-styling nature. Guilt swept over me and once again, I was hit with the unpleasant revelation of being a burden to her.

"*I'm improving, Shelly. I'm going to make it worth your investment in me,*" I whispered to myself, hoping she'd catch the power in my decree wherever her free-flowing spirit rested. Suddenly, I regretted not inviting Azmir. I would have so loved for him to share this explorative moment with me.

As I was taking in all the retailers and merchandise, I got a ping, alerting me of a text message. I looked to find Azmir informing me of dinner reservations in an hour. I wasn't aware of dinner plans, so I scurried along in the tent before heading back to the bungalow.

When I arrived, I saw Azmir swimming in the waters below the house. He really looked like quite the athlete. His arms extended out like fins, motioning the water for movement. His back stayed perfectly aligned as it flowed over and into the water. It made me wonder if that's what he looked like when he's over me, making love. *Wait!* Does he make love to me? He did say we're two people who are living together, *fucking* monogamously. A pain struck my heart at the thought. *Is that how he really termed it?* Perhaps Harrison was right. Out of nowhere, I felt tears prickling down my face. I jumped at the realization and flew upstairs to the bathroom, not wanting to be seen by Azmir in this state. I felt then I had to tell him how I felt.

As I was in the shower, I asked myself, *What exactly can I tell him? That I want to breakup?* I mean, breaking up was for people who were in bona fide relationships, not those who were just "fucking." More tears. *What would my life be like without Azmir?* Exactly as it was before him: dull and uneventful. I couldn't care less about his money. His attention, thoughtfulness, and artful lovemaking was far more valued by my heart. He made me feel kept far beyond what his money could do. As I wept, I uttered a silent prayer, asking God for strength and to cease my wrestled mind. In my heart, I knew whatever the outcome of this thing with Azmir was, I'd survive it.

I heard Azmir outside in the bedroom, fumbling around and decided to finish up in the shower and fight to suppress my tears.

Dinner was on the beach, underneath the setting sun tonight. The view was breathtaking as Azmir held my hand, walking me down to our secluded gazebo on the sand. We walked to a private table under a tent made with white sheer curtains tied to every spoke. There were about twelve in all. It was very exclusive. I noticed the other patrons were yards away with just umbrellas covering their tables. Under our hut, the table was set for two with a white linen tablecloth and chair covers.

Azmir walked me over to my seat then took his next to me. I was taken and didn't try to hide it as I looked over at him. He gave nothing away as he observed me as well. Two men came over to us almost immediately. One was dressed in wait-staff attire and the other in a suit.

"Mr. Jacobs, I'm glad to see you and Ms. Brimm have finally arrived. I am Aata, your host for tonight. And your waiter will be Ihu, here," he pointed to the waiter who nodded politely. "We're going to start you off with drinks and your hors d'oeuvres will be out momentarily," Aata informed before turning on his heel as Ihu remained and poured champagne into our flutes.

When the waiter left, Azmir turned to me, "So, how was your massage, Rayna."

I was spun back into reality and caught off guard at him calling me by my first name. This typically happened when he was angry with me, or during sex—if then.

"Very nice. I really appreciate the gesture. In fact, let me take the time to say thanks for this entire experience. It's truly one of a lifetime, Mr. Jacobs."

Azmir's eyebrows narrowed. I heard the build of sadness in my own voice. I felt like I was saying goodbye already.

"My pleasure," he muttered puzzled. "And your expedition in town?" he asked while the waiter was placing our hors d'oeuvres before us.

"That was beautiful. I thought of how nice it would have been had you come," I admitted as I gazed down at the spring rolls and duck kabobs looking quite delicious. Azmir served me first and then himself. I bit into a spring roll and my taste buds were all manic from the artful culinary experience occurring. I looked over to Azmir and something hit me.

"Do you eat fast-food?"

He gave me an unwilled, sexy gaze as he finished swallowing his food. "Where did that come from?"

"Well, when I think about it, I eat very well with you. And the fact that I've never seen you eat drive thru before. Not to mention you have a chef."

He didn't break his gape as he shared, "I haven't had fast-food in quite a few years. Maybe three or so."

"Why?"

"I got sick for the umpteenth time after eating at my last fast-food restaurant. I went to the doctor to learn my aging body no longer responded well to those types of foods."

Hmmmm... Interesting.

I continued my line of questioning, "So is that the reason for Boyd?"

I was now super-intrigued. He continued looking at his plate as he considered my question. "It took some time to readjust my life, so I'd have the time to sit for a meal. My doctors stayed on me about lifestyle alterations. Things started taking shape in my life, and I finally made the decision to hire a cook."

"Things? Such as?"

He snorted. He wasn't used to me asking questions and neither was I, but I had the sudden urge to learn more about this man. "Such as me working primarily at the rec and building my team there, ending my former relationship, finding a new place, and meeting you."

Wow. I couldn't deny how good it felt hearing myself included in his new and improved life.

"Your positive changes have seeped over into my life. I do eat better, obviously, and your personal trainer has given me the results I've always dreamed of."

"You look amazing. You always have, but there's nothing wrong with change," he uttered slowly, causing those electrical-like currents to flash through me. I muzzled my libido. I couldn't afford to slip into an intimate situation with Azmir. I needed to let him know we needed a change.

"Speaking of change, I'm sure you've taken note of mine over the past couple of days."

He nodded. "Yes, Ms. Brimm, I most certainly have, and I haven't been too pleased about it."

Whoa! Talk about direct.

Our dishes were being cleared for the next course. I was antsy and hoped he couldn't sense the fidgety movement of my hands and legs beneath the table. I waited as Aata cleared the table and Ihu placed our hot plates in front of us. I continued with my introspect, feeling it was do or die.

"Azmir, I've lost my footing here. You know I'm on a journey of repairing my deficiencies...and knowing my place in relationships is important to that process." I got stumped at my words but knew I must forge ahead as I gave a deep sigh, "I guess I've been feeling a little insecure about our relationship." I thought about what I'd just said and thought to clarify. "I mean, I'm not demanding anything by saying this, but more...definition would be appropriate, I think." I was feeling reduced because I couldn't find my articulation. It didn't help that Azmir was looking at me *and* the waiter *and* the food as he ate and listened. He still hadn't responded. *Is he leaving me hanging?* How do I rebound from this?

"I got you," is all he retorted, and I was furious. He wouldn't have found that response from the Washington guy he was chewing out earlier acceptable. So why should I? Once again, I fought back the tears.

"Try the Mahi-Mahi," Azmir suggested as he brought a forkful to my face. I cleared the contents of my mouth and then rinsed it down with pinot before tasting his fish. It was mouthwatering.

"Succulent," I muttered sardonically. He wasn't getting it. I wasn't getting through to him.

"That's how I would describe you."

I gasped. As much as it was flattering, if Azmir thought he could placate my concerns by way of flirtation, he had another thing coming!

"Yeah, about that..." *Five-four-three-two-...* I did my count and braced myself. "Sex with you doesn't help my tumult state. It furthers my bewilderment."

"So, what are you saying, Rayna?"

"I don't know... You know..." I looked down at my plate, trying to unravel my feelings. Looking out at the water, I noticed the sun had finally set and darkness was fully upon us. That's what my mood had settled into—a dark place. "Maybe we should slow that part of our relationship down...just until we're at a place where we both are comfortable and want to be."

Azmir laughed and did so unapologetically. This went on for

nearly two full minutes. He eventually dropped his fork and knife and sat up in his chair.

"Are you going to finish your food?" he asked calmly with a trace of a smile on his lips. Lips I was finding very hard to ignore right now. *I had to be strong I can't think about food right now.* He snapped his fingers to call on the waiter.

"I'm sorry the humor in that missed me," I hissed.

Ihu arrived.

Azmir's eyes were glued to mine as his smirk quickly disintegrated into darkness, and he leaned into me and growled, "You cannot and will not ever deny me of you. I can have him empty this table, close these curtains, and I'll throw your ass on it and have you for dinner instead," without a flinch. It was similar to the look he gave Brian Thompson that night in San Diego. Once again, I was face-to-face with the dark side of Azmir. His eyes were cold, and I could feel my goose bumps rising.

"I'll finish my food," I squealed petulantly. I was at a loss, now even more so.

Azmir spoke to Ihu in almost a whisper. It was clear he didn't want me to hear. I knew I'd pissed him off. I'd just hoped he wasn't going through with his threat. I didn't think I could've survived that. Azmir the CEO was as present as ever. This man could surely switch it up lately. This time he was doing it to me. How could I blame him with all the attitude I'd been giving him. Justified or not, he didn't know. And the bottom line was, I didn't know how to tell him.

Azmir went back to eating his food in silence as did I. Something deep down inside told me I needed to calm down, that my worries were unfounded and self-inflicted.

Minutes later, once we were done eating, Aata visited the table and asked Azmir, "Mr. Jacobs, would you and Ms. Brimm like to retreat to the open beach lounge for dessert or would you prefer it here?"

I had no room for dessert. I was stuffed and frankly preoccupied. Azmir gazed at me and slowly requested, "Open beach, Aata."

"Okay, great. This way please, sir, ma'am."

Azmir and I rose from the table, and I was gestured to go ahead of him and follow Aata. We walked down a few feet, west of our dinner tent to the most awe-inspiring lounge on the beach I'd ever seen. Continuing with the white linen theme, there were sofa-like seats arranged in an "L" shape with an oversized coffee table in the center. All the furniture sat on pine-wicker bases, giving a homely feel to it, except the seaside view reminded you of being out in nature. Lights burned by way of tiki torches and a bonfire in the sand, all of this illumination creating the most beautiful glow against the sand, water, and moon.

I must have been stopped in my tracks by it because Azmir whispered in my ear, "Let's go and have a seat."

I turned toward his voice and looked up to see the glow bounce off his chocolate skin. Trying to calm myself, I continued my stride towards the display. We were seated and Aata left us to ourselves. I couldn't help my gawking at the entire scenery. This man's romance had no boundaries. How did he know how to court me so well? It further fueled my frustrations with our relationship.

"Why, Azmir? Why for me?"

With a trace of irritation on his face he snorted as he sat back to find comfort for his long torso on the sofa. He murmured, "You have no clue, do you." He phrased it with incredulity rather than in a question form.

"As a matter of fact, I don't. This is what I was trying to say earlier. I'm so confused here," I muttered lowly.

Aata returned and was accompanied by Ihu. They were carrying stainless steel salver trays. Aata had two and sat one down. Azmir was biting his thumb nail. Could this night get anymore odd?

"Mr. Jacobs, Ms. Brimm, your dessert selections tonight," Aata informed then looked to Ihu who uncovered his tray. "In this selection, we have your traditional American favorites; apple pie, caramel bread pudding, sherbet, chocolate lava cake, carrot cake, crème brûlée, and key-lime pie." I noticed Azmir's attention was elsewhere as he gazed behind the sofa with his arm resting on the back of it.

Aata then removed the cover from his tray and continued with, "Here, we have our traditional Polynesian favorites such as haupia pudding, pineapple tortes, kulolo, banana guava pie, Lilikoi chiffon cake, and an assortment of bars."

Aata's attention turned to the third tray sitting in the center of the table before me. He didn't raise the cover, but touched it and Azmir, out of nowhere, expressed, "Rayna Brimm, your gift of friendship has been far beyond the scope of anything I can reference." He leaned into me, "You said I've never told you I loved you and you're right, but not because I don't. It's because love is a phenomenon I've survived without for so long that when it slapped me in the face a few months back, it staggered me. It took some time for me to adjust to the force of nature, and clearly, it has caused you a bit of confusion." Azmir squared his shoulders and cleared his throat.

"So here it is Ms. Brimm, I love you. I've loved you since the moment we sat in the bleachers at the *Lakers* game at the *Staples Center* last spring, and I watched as you informed your girlfriend of your whereabouts." My breathing caught in my throat. Between the aquatic backdrop, the romantic ambiance, and the powerful words pouring from Azmir's lips, I questioned whether I was in a deep sleep and in a captivating dream. I remained quiet as he continued, "I fell in love with you the night we had to rush to the hospital to see about Michelle during your first visit to my apartment." Azmir's long lashes descended, closing his eyes as if he were removing a mask and it was difficult to be this vulnerable.

"I haven't told you because I didn't know what I was feeling. I guess you could say I denied it. Hell, I was in denial for over a month until I realized I was experiencing '*Brimm withdrawal*' and set out to find you in Jersey. I'm no religious man, but I do come from love and therefore honor the institution. My parents embodied it, well and clearly." He exhaled deeply. "I want you, Rayna. I want all of you. I want to complete you and have you back me. I want to give you my children to carry and birth. I want to protect you and provide for you until the day I die." He cracked his signature panty-snatching smirk, expressing amusement, "There's a lot about this shit I don't know… But I think I'm in good company because yo' ass don't know shit about it either. Please do me the honor of carrying my surname, sharing my world, and becoming my life-partner. Please marry me."

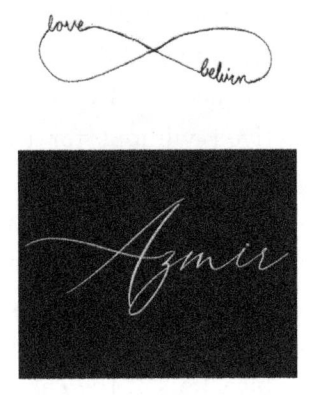

love believin

Azmir

    Aata opened the third tray holding the five-carat emerald cut diamond engagement ring. I was nervous as hell, hoping she'd approve.

    She was still, mouth opened in collapse, frozen in time. I could throw a pebble in her mouth and make the shot.

    Rayna, you've been out of character for the past two days. Don't do this, baby. Don't say no.

    I turned to look at Aata, "We're gonna need a minute here."

    He and the waiter excused themselves as I maintained my gaze on Rayna.

"If you don't like it, we can go for something bigger. I know you're not a flashy—"

"You wanna marry me?" she asked, still looking shell-shocked.

What an odd question. "Yes, sweetheart. I want you to be my wife." *Why is that such a difficult concept?*

"But...but...I thought you didn't..." she muttered before her voice fell off.

"I didn't what?" I asked forcefully.

"You didn't love me!" she rushed out before silently bawling her eyes out.

I took a minute to gather my thoughts. *How much does that word weigh in gold?* Damn. *Did I fuck this up by taking so long to tell her?* I grabbed her hands from her face and cupped her chin with my other hand.

"I'm sorry... I didn't know. You're not the only one with deficiencies here. Baby, you're special to me. You have been since you came into my boardroom. I had no idea what awaited me. I was so intrigued by your allure, and as much as I told myself to leave you alone, I kept pursuing you."

Rayna peered at me with desperate eyes. She thirsted for my truth, and I tried giving it to her to the best of my articulation, which was very difficult as a man. But I felt I owed her that seeing I was constantly begging her to open to me.

I massaged my eyes in exasperation—not of her, but of the need to chronicle my feelings. Perhaps I was failing her by not expressing them enough. *Shit. How could I get her to see?*

I closed my eyes and moaned, "Rayna, baby, why do you think it took me so long to touch you? It took me so long to eat from the forbidden fruit purposely—well, until I couldn't hold out any longer." Well, that was part of the reason.

She snorted. *Humorous?* Good. Now we were getting somewhere.

"You say that as if you had a choice," she clapped back.

"Trust, I could have had that ass months before I finally tasted it."

"I beg your pardon?" she pouted beautifully.

"Ms. Brimm, I could have fucked you on the table that night at *Mahogany*. Shit. I'll put up fifty stacks that I could have had that ass in Puerto Vallarta."

"Mr. Jacobs, you're far more confident than I took you for."

"I speak facts, Brimm." Her body language and response confirmed what I'd already known. "Anyway... We're getting off subject." There was no need to argue about something I'd already owned—I owned it, Rayna's pussy was mine.

Suddenly epiphanized, I stood from my seat and stationed myself over her before lowering my body on to one knee. Her eyes widened in total disbelief. I was desperate for her to understand just how austere my motives were. I grabbed the ring, lifting it from its gripping position inside the box and brought it to her hand. Her mouth swung open as her body trembled from jitteriness.

"For the third time, Rayna, will you please put me out of my agony and agree to my hand in marriage?"

Within long seconds, she nodded her head over and over with manic enthusiasm. For the first time ever, she gave me an immediate response. As I picked her up from the sofa and swung her in the air, tears fell and her nose ran, racing the tears down to her mouth. I motioned for Aata to bring tissues. He was there in a nanosecond.

She cried out, "Oh my god, Azmir, I didn't know you wanted to marry me! I didn't know..." We'd gained an audience because out of nowhere I heard an outburst of applause. The live band began to play a festive number a few feet away.

I wiped her face, trying to hide my relief and my laughter. She was rarely this vulnerable. This raw. I just wanted to relish in it. But I knew there was something behind her doubtful expectations of me. I'd just have to work toward dispelling any reservations. I had never felt so happy and accomplished before in my life. And although I knew I wouldn't be complete until the day she actually became my wife, I'd felt a sense of satisfaction unrivaled.

Rayna grew conscious of the attention from the crowd. I knew she didn't like attention on her, so I whispered, "Let's go back to the house where we'll have more privacy."

After I signed for the bill and we thanked our well-wishers, we left.

Rayna didn't want to turn in right away, so I ran inside to grab a blanket and then we stole a spot on the beach, next to our bungalow. The area was mildly lit and very secluded. The water was calm and the breeze generous. We sat next to each other in silence, I assumed, both trying to reel in our thoughts about this next step. I was very much sure about my proposal and had put a lot of thought into it, but there were still a few reservations I held on to myself. Much of which came from not knowing much about Rayna's past.

I had my hands in a few pots, trying to learn more about her, but I'd totally missed the low-down about her brother. I spazzed out on Washington, the head of my private information's team. He wasn't even near that discovery. Before leaving I'd learned the nature of his stint, but I was still waiting to hear why Rayna had kept it from me and why in the hell was it something she didn't want to talk about. Washington's career hung in the balance of this intel. I was fully prepared to fire him and had already had my assistant working on other investigative firms. Shit. Even he knew I was prepared to marry this woman and she revealed this just days before I hit my knee. It wasn't a good look for him. And for me, whatever made no sense made no money.

"Hey, what's troubling you? I've said yes," Rayna teased.

Even under the dim light of the moon and that of the stars I could see Rayna's beautifully tanned skin. "This sun really works well for you. Your bronzed complexion is out of this world, girl."

She gave me a shy smile and leaned her head on my shoulders

bashfully. "Thanks, Azmir," she murmured. Then Rayna let out a slow and labored exhale. While gazing at the water she shared, "I don't know how you could be so assured of...me—even after my news on Friday. I swear, Azmir, sometimes I don't feel I deserve you, let alone your confidence in me," she ended her last words, searing me with her eyes.

"Are you committed to me and only me?" I asked.

"Yes."

"Will you always protect me?"

"Of course," she spilled breathlessly, almost sounding affronted.

"Could you love me forever?"

She immediately answered, "With everything I have. Even if this doesn't pan out," she vowed while raising her ring finger donning her engagement ring.

Even she was taken by the brilliancy of it.

"This is exquisite, Azmir. I'm in awe," she whispered.

"I wasn't '*assured*' you'd like it. Wasn't sure if it was big enough..."

She interrupted me by grabbing my face and kissing me, filled with passion. Her hands found their way to my head not too long before she slid on top of me. I was with it—all of it. Without removing her tongue from my mouth, she shifted her dress to straighten it, so her skin lay directly on my lap. My jimmy expanded in the favorable attention as she grinded on my lap. After a brief time, she rose from my wanting lap slightly and shifted to undo my linen pants, tugging at them.

"You wanna do this...here?" I asked, breaking our embrace.

With desire in her eyes and heavily panting, she looked to her left and then to her right before nodding her head ferociously. And I lifted both our bodies to allow her to pull them down enough to expose my strongman. My hands found their way under her dress to her ass, and I rubbed it in great anticipation. *Fuck!* Rayna wasn't wearing any panties.

She lowered herself onto me with an opened mouth and moaned, "*Ahhhhh!*" as she slowly slid onto me. She felt so warm and was unbelievably wet.

With her arms astride my shoulders, she plowed into me smoothly. Her lips softly nibbled on my neck, jaw, and lips. Rayna's lovemaking faces would have me deliver prematurely if I wasn't careful. I kissed her neck as she bent backwards giving me full access. Suddenly, I heard, "Azmir, this thing...between us ain't about money. I'd take you mind, body, and soul without your bank account."

It was music to my ears and totally captivating. I felt in that second my decision was affirmed. I'd made the right choice in asking her to be with me forever. There were certainly doubts, but they'd always be there. I'd just have to take a leap. Her words were intoxicating and unexpected. She always used her body to tell me what was in her heart when her mouth couldn't.

She lifted and dipped on and off my lap. I was overcome when she called my name out in ecstasy. When I felt her juices melt down onto me and her walls clench my cock, I couldn't hold on to it anymore. I exploded inside of her with stifled whimpers.

We stayed there, wrapped around each other like a vine well after we were through. I felt so connected to Rayna. So resolved to my destiny. I could have stayed there in this spot, holding her for days.

Rayna finally lifted her head. "My mood has been crappy," she admitted, ducking her chin like a child. I gave a small laugh and nodded my head.

Seconds later, she spoke again. "Azmir, Harrison came to visit me on Friday."

"Come again," Suddenly, I didn't trust my ears.

Her eyes met mine and she muttered, "Detective Daryl Harrison came to my office on Friday...after I left Tamu's boutique. He was waiting for me."

"What did he say?"

"A lot. He threatened to expose the truth about my brother to you, and then he bribed me with money to disappear. He said I was interfering with his family. He said once you're done with me, you and Tara would be married within one year. He said a lot of things, which is why..." she began fumbling with her new ring, I guess reflecting on the grim possibilities.

I couldn't believe what I was hearing and didn't think her information would slow. Why was she in the habit of fucking keeping pertinent information from me? I'd hurt people for much less. This shit was wack as hell!

I went to lift her off me as I demanded, "Why would you wait so long to tell me this shit?"

She rose and with eyes widened. "Azmir, I—I've been trying to piece all of this together in my mind—"

"It ain't for you to fuckin' piece shit together! It's for me!" I yelled enraged. I saw blood as I pulled up and tied my pants. "From now on if this shit gonna work, you can't keep a muthafuckin' thing from me. I am a fuckin' man! I provide protection. I *put* shit together. Fuck piecing! Do you understand?"

"I'm sorry," Rayna's voice cracked.

I was not about to be moved by tears. She'd crossed the line and had been making a damn fool out of me. I went for my phone and punched a couple of keys.

"Peace-peace."

"Peace-Peace. It's the god."

"Salute, Duke." Petey greeted.

"Hit Big D. Tell 'em his fuckin' retirement package is now null and fuckin' void. Tell 'em all bets are off with the seed, too."

"You sure, Duke?"

"Crack, his bitchass ran up on my girl at work. His ass just got into a war he wasn't anticipating," I growled low, hiding my fury.

"Whoa!" I know he was taken by my ire. I was never out of character. I always discharged with a firm demeanor. But shit, this was an entirely different circumstance from anything I'd ever experienced. "I'm on it, Duke."

"Set up a meet with Santiaga and Paulio. D's ass is getting cut the fuck out starting this second. He just made this shit personal."

"Indeed," Petey hesitated. There was a pause. I huffed.

"Duke, did you do it?" he asked, referring to my impending proposal. I glanced over my shoulder to Rayna who was again toying with her ring, only now with trembling fingers and looming doubts.

"Done deal."

Petey exhaled and it surprised me. He never showed emotion.

"Yo, god. Let that be your focus, Duke. Big D will be dealt with when you touch down. That right there is what's important for now."

Once again, I looked at Rayna who was now looking at me with remorse in her eyes. My guilt started setting in. I had to get used to this level of intimacy. Suddenly, and ironically, I remembered Big D schooling me on love. He'd said several times in the past, *the woman who wins your heart will forfeit your control of your universe.* Damn. That fucker was right. I was caught between a rock and a fucking mountain.

"Indeed," I agreed. "Peace-peace."

"Peace-Peace, Duke."

D made that visit testing my chin. He was gauging my commitment to Rayna. If I ignored it, he would believe I didn't give a shit about Rayna. If I react, he would know where my heart is. Shit just got real. D's days of pawning me were over. His depravity knew no bounds.

"Let's go," I hissed to Rayna.

We headed over to the bungalow in silence. Once we were in, I told her I had to check my e-mail. I sensed her standing by the door of the bungalow until I walked in the office and slammed the door.

I checked in with Washington and he had given more information on Rayna's secret about her brother. His charge involved a third dude from her projects. Some kid named Omar Brown. Washington informed me a little girl was killed in the crossfire among other facts, but nothing he'd come up with so far was secretworthy. There had to be more if Big D thought to bribe her.

See, D was infuriated because I'd shut him down after learning about his role in killing my father. My agreement with him was that we'd end our business in the same timeline originally planned, but I wouldn't cut him out of any money considering he was damn near broke from his gambling bug and blowing dough on pussy. This man had run through millions over the years. It was still unbelievable to me. I assured him that after these next couple of months of me washing my hands from the game, we'd go our separate ways. I knew it didn't rest easy with him. Couple that with me having done the same with his daughter. I never told him the full truth and apparently neither had Tara. I was going for a full makeover in terms of my loved ones. Those two opportunists never loved me, but they did love what I was able to profit them. *Game over*. But clearly, Big D didn't want to bow out gracefully.

Rayna had no idea what was going on. She'd been caught in the crossfire. This shit had nothing to do with her, but I couldn't have her thinking she could keep things from me. She was my blind spot. I understood I'd brought her into my convoluted world blindsided, but she had skeletons in her own closet I was trying to work with.

I could hear the water running through the pipes and into the tub upstairs. She was preparing to take a bath. I'd guessed I needed to relax, too. I had really spazzed on her. This was supposed to be a celebratory getaway, not be plagued with issues from that selfish, manipulative fuck. I swear my feelings for D were turning malevolent. It challenged my new path in life, but I swear if he ever came close to Rayna again, I'd kill him.

Rayna had looked so broken out on the beach. I knew I needed to change the course of our vacation. I didn't want to leave early, and we had several excursions planned for the following day, so I needed to assuage the situation.

I walked into the bathroom where she was laid out in the tub. And upon entering, she swung her head to me and innocently searched my eyes, trying to assess my mood.

"You're still wearing your ring," I attempted to break the ice.

"You want it back?" her eyes shot up and body tensed in the water.

I shook my head. "No. Besides it's no longer mine. You now have the headache of keeping up with it. It cost me enough to get it here secured and on your finger. I don't want the stress of that anymore." I was being honest.

She held it up slightly, savoring in her new reality yet once again. She looked proud of it as she smiled.

"Can I join you?"

"Oh. Please do." Rayna anxiously agreed and scooted her body up in the oversized tub. I like baths but could never found comfort in one since I was about twelve or thirteen years old because of my height. In all of my homes I've had special sized and shaped tubs installed. In hotels, one of the many reasons I preferred suites was because they typically came with Jacuzzis or whirlpools.

I stripped my clothes and descended behind her.

"The water feels good. Spicy." I pulled her back to rest her body on my chest. We engaged in peaceful silence for minutes long. I exhaled and closed my eyes, relishing in a private and intimate moment with Ms. Brimm.

"You were livid. I don't want to get used to seeing you that way. Are you still?"

"I was. I'm calming as we speak," I opened my eyes, deciding to receive her conversation.

"I'm sorry. I didn't know the protocol. You told me he was your mentor, so I measured his words perhaps...too deeply," Rayna murmured as I ran the sponge over her arms.

"Detective Daryl Harrison is no longer my mentor. He hasn't

been for some time. For all intents and purposes, he's simply Tara's father." I needed her to know this moving forward. She remained quiet, and I could tell the cogs of her mind were working.

"What was the agreement about Tara's baby?"

"*Huhn?*" I stopped washing her shoulders.

"When you were on the phone, you referred to *the seed*."

Oh.

"I agreed to help Tara out until the paternity situation was cleared."

"Help how?"

"Take care of the hospital bills and doctor fees for the baby."

"Would you do that?"

"As a parting deal; it was a steal."

"That's some bargain."

"It's all strategic," I divulged, being partially honest and hoped this conversation's end was near.

Rayna snorted. "He does know you a little, I see."

"Why do you say that?"

"He said you were strategic and calculating."

"That I am."

"Oh," she replied contemplatively.

"Turn around. I want to wash your legs," Rayna swiveled around in the whirlpool to face me.

I grabbed her legs one by one to wash them. She started off tensed but eased up in no time. Once I was done, I nibbled on her toes, causing her writhing movements in the water.

"Stay still," I playfully scolded.

She tried but could never endure the pleasurable sensations. Even her eyes gave away her sheer delectation. After some time of doing this, we couldn't make it out of the tub before sex occurred. I had her ass hanging halfway out of the whirlpool, screaming my name. Lovemaking was something I was becoming very acquiescent to, particularly because my acts of *smashing* appealed to Rayna, we brought the two together.

This could actually work.

The next two days in Tahiti were a huge contrast to the first. Rayna and I indulged in parasailing, jet-skiing, canoeing, and horseback riding. We ate great food and made love every day, several times a day. We shared in laughter and playful moments. Rayna was back. I did everything I could think of to help her shake whatever insecurities she had about my commitment to her. The last thing I needed was a weak link in my strong chain. I needed her confident in what I was proposing. I had only wished her girl, Michelle, could have been around to celebrate this next step with her.

Our return home was bitter-sweet. I hated leaving paradise and being in our bubble as she termed it, waking up to Rayna in open air and lying down in the same. But it was nice to know we were on the track to a new life together.

As we were seated on the plane, waiting to take off, Rayna looked over to me with a half a smile and a slight moue.

I lifted her chin with my index finger to engage her eyes. "Hey... What's that all about?" I asked.

"We're leaving our Eden," she puckered her lips and sniffled to gesture a desire to cry.

"We'll always have Tahiti," I sang.

She reached over and rubbed my cheek in adoration. It was consolatory.

"I freaking love this!" she exclaimed, referring to the wildly grown stubble. It had taken over my face since we'd arrived. That immediately gave me an idea.

"Good. Because I'm not cutting it until you give me a date."
"A date?"
"Yes. A wedding date."
"Oh." Rayna smiled and ducked her head embarrassingly.
"Well, what date do you have in mind?"
"Oh, no, Ms. Brimm. It's obvious that you weren't expecting

my proposal and therefore I am not strong-arming you to the altar. You'll have to do it on your own volition."

Her eyes opened wide, giving me an affronted expression. I knew Rayna. She needed to be given a push to make a decision involving trusting another individual. In this case, I was asking her to enter into a lifetime institution, the biggest trust and commitment proposal of them all. I believed she was agreeable to it but needed a little motivation to take the next step.

"I'll just wait miserably until you come around," I continued to taunt her.

"You don't think I want to marry you?" she'd become argumentative instantly. I didn't want to fight about it but egged her on.

"I hope so, but... Time will tell," I murmured as I adjusted my pillow in my seat to get comfortable. She sat erect in her chair, at a loss for words when I turned my back to her.

You can lead a horse...

CHAPTER 9

Azmir

The sound of my *Blackberry* ringing snapped me frantically out of my sleep, ejecting me from my pillow. Veered between torpor and alarm, I glanced around the room. Rayna stirred in the sheets but appeared still very much asleep. I reached for the alerting phone.

"Peace. Peace."

"*Errrr*... My name is Detective Timothy Ames, and I'm looking for an Azmir Jacobs." Why was *One Time* calling my cell at this hour?

"I'm sorry, what is this in reference to?" I asked as I picked up my *iPhone*, prepared to dial my attorney.

"Mr. Jacobs, I'm sorry to have to call you at this hour to inform you there has been an act of arson at your residence."

I regarded the bedroom around me. *There's no fire. Is this some kind of joke?*

"Mr. Jacobs? Are you away on vacation? How soon can you get down to the Pasadena PD so we can discuss this?"

"A fire at my home on Farmingdale Drive?" My senses had begun returning. I felt Rayna sit up in the bed.

"Yes, sir. How soon can you be here? Or I can meet you there."

"Give me under an hour. I'll meet you at the house," I disconnected with the detective and swung my legs out of bed, still somewhat languished.

"What's going on?" Rayna groggily asked, grabbing my lower back. I paused, trying to process what had just happened.

"Supposedly a fire at one of my properties. I'm going to check it out."

She gasped, "What? Oh, my god!"

I turned to her, patting her leg, "Go back to sleep, I'll be back as soon as I get a handle on it."

Rayna started making her way out of the bed, causing Azna to jump from the edge to the center of the mattress. "No, this is awful. I'll go with you!"

"Rayna, baby, it's nearly three thirty in the morning. There's no way I'll have you out at this hour. If I need you, I'll call. Rest," I demanded.

She recoiled her legs back into the bed, making it clear she'd caught on to my adamancy. I kissed her on the head and left for the john. From the bathroom, I called Petey who, in turn, called Kid. They both agreed to reporting there. I was dazed, still adjusting from our return from Tahiti the evening before.

When I pulled up, the firefighters were still out there, hosing down the rear of the house and a couple were walking through the front area, I guessed making sure nothing was ignitable or combustible and possibly confirming there were no bodies in there.

The fire was pretty bad, all that seemed to have been left was the frame and my fireproof safes. My breathing hiked as I grabbed my head.

Petey walked up on me, "*Shiiiiiiiieet!* What the fuck is this?" He wore gray flannels, a hoodie, and his bedroom slippers. His face was still wrinkled from recent sleep.

"Yeah," I sighed. "This is some bullshit," I muttered, watching strangers walking all over and through my property.

"Tell Kid and them to get the tools needed to unbolt the safes and take them over to my warehouse down in the Watts. There's storage space there for them."

"Mr. Jacobs?" I heard my name being called and turned to find Detective Ames. I recognized his timid voice.

I turned to him and watched as he approached us. He looked at Petey, but we didn't do introductions, so I didn't even acknowledge him, and Ames quickly got the message.

"*Errrr...* Is this your primary residence?"

"No." I was interested in seeing where his question was leading.

"Do you rent this out to anyone or have someone living here?"

"No."

He scratched his head contemplatively. Petey and I just watched, giving nothing away. "*Ummm...* That was the fire chief I was just talking to over there, and he's saying he'll need a couple of days to come to a full investigation, but he can say with little revelation this was an act of arson. Some sort of explosive bottles were thrown into the front and rear of the house through the windows. This being said, do you have any idea who would want to harm you or your property?"

"I've no clue."

"Well, here's the plan. I'm going to let them conclude their investigation before I come in and do mine. In the meantime, I'll need you to come by the station to answer a few preliminary questions that would help me discover the person or persons responsible for this. Here's my card. I'll look forward to your call."

He handed me his business card. "How long do you think it took for this place to crumble? I'm curious about the level of malevolence here. Could they have been unoccupied kids who knew the house was vacant, or do I need to hire a security team?" I asked in jest, but slightly sincere about wanting to know how badly someone wanted me dead.

"Considering the methods taken to burn it down, this is seriously malicious."

"Indeed," I nodded. "We'll be in touch, detective." He took my pro-offered hand and gave me a brief, but firm shake.

By this time, Kid had walked up. Ames took off toward the back of the house, and I turned to Petey and Kid. "What's the streets saying?"

"It's ya' rapper boy," Kid murmured. I knew right away he was referring to D-Struct.

"How sure are we?"

"'Bout seventy five percent." Kid's head rocked left to right in his estimation. "My cousin going over to his old baby mutha's later on. They friends. She told her he came through there a couple of hours ago smelling like gasoline, asking to shower and shit. I'll have more on that in a minute. Yo, D, man, if it's that dude, he need to close his eyes tonight. He can't live no more."

"If it's son, he might get sniped by one of 'dem youngin's trying catch Divine's attention. It's gonna be a bounty on his fuckin' head," Petey muttered.

Petey was right. This shit wasn't looking good for ol' boy.

"Kid, y'all good on those safes in there?"

"Yeah. Son pulling them up from the floor now. Let me go check up on him." Kid headed back inside the house despite the firefighters urging him not to. It was my shit, and I damn sure wasn't about to let such personal items stay there in an opened charred house.

"You want me to call Kip?" Petey asked.

"Yeah, but see if he can lay low until this place is empty. I don't want the officials to know about the surveillance out here unless it's necessary."

"You got it, Duke."

Petey walked off to make the call to Kip, a surveillance

specialist I'd contracted years ago to protect my properties. You almost forget about him until an incident like this when you need him. Footage of the property should be stored and that should pinpoint the perpetrator, if not, point us in the right direction. My gut told me Big D was behind this in some way. He didn't like my cutting him off and therefore wringing him dry. You mess with a man's money, he'll eventually get desperate and make risky moves. I stayed there for about a half an hour before I decided to head out. The ride back to the marina gave me time to think and plan.

She lay there with the house phone and her cell laying on my pillow, I guessed for easy access if I had called. I looked over to the time on the nightstand to see it was six forty-two.

Taking her by the shoulders, I nudged her, trying to ease her back into a conscious state. "Brimm. Brimm, baby," I murmured. From her shoulders, I shoved her body several times before she had actually awakened. Her tired eyes were red as she tried to focus them.

"Azmir! I'm so glad you're back. I must have dozed off. What time is it?" she asked, rubbing her eyes.

"It's nearly seven. Get up. I got your favorite old-fashion oatmeal from the deli around the corner. I don't want it to get cold."

She took a few moments to collect herself and strode into the shower.

∞

Back out in the kitchen at the table, she took a seat next to me and I opened up her steaming oatmeal. Her yogurt and fresh fruit sat adjacent to it. I rose to put on the kettle for tea. As I filled it Rayna asked, "Well?"

I knew it was coming. We needed to talk, which is why I didn't serve this to her in bed like I typically did on a weekend morning if I didn't want her to cook. I took my seat next to her and opened my *to go* container holding my vegetable omelet.

"Well, it's bad."

"How bad?" Her eyes were glued to my profile as she licked the smudge of yogurt from her thumb. Rayna looked adorable in her boy shorts and matching thin camisole.

"Pretty bad. Nothing salvageable besides a few safes I had there."

"Where is the house? I know you said you'd just bought this apartment recently, but did you stay at that house before living here?"

I cut into my omelet, prepared to dig in. "Pasadena. Yes. It's where I lived prior to moving in here. I had lots of things there I'd been meaning to have packed up, but never got around to it." In all honesty, I'd been so wrapped up in Rayna, nothing from my past seemed important to rush into here, not even clothes.

"How did the fire start?"

On the way home, I prepared for this disclosure. Although the detective had given me a preliminary cause and the investigation was not conclusive, I had to take this seriously.

"I'll know for sure once they get the investigation underway, but they're smelling foul play."

She stilled and I grabbed the small of her back.

"Before you ask, I'm not sure if these were errant kids who knew the property was vacant or something more serious. But I want us to be aware of all of the possibilities."

"Azmir, you don't think someone would try to hurt you, do you?" Her eyes were drifted afar as she conjured horrid thoughts.

"I'd like to hope not, but I have to be honest with myself and know I've made a few foes along the way in my journey. I have a lot at stake and much to protect, and that includes you. So, I need to make you aware of a few changes that will be implemented until this issue has been resolved." Rayna's eyes diverted back to me, and I knew I'd had her full attention.

"First, this is our home and we're fully protected here. The security features of this property are stellar. There are three guards on the grounds at all times and the building is equipped with monitored surveillance. We have a security alarm system, which can be accessed here at the front door and in our bedroom. I don't think it's necessary at all, but should you need to take an extra measure, feel free to use them. The concierge has been instructed to call before bringing guests up. We don't have visitors, but in the event that we do, if they do not get approval from us when they call up, no one will be allowed up here." I took a break to make sure I wasn't going too fast for her. I was growing angrier by the second having to explain this to my lady.

"Are you getting this, Brimm?"

Still a little dazed, staring off into the distance, she nodded her head.

"Okay. Those things are virtually in practice now or, like the in-house security system, can be employed when needed." I turned to take her hands, "The biggest change would be muscle. I know that's not been something you've been very keen on with me, but you've tolerated it. Right now, until all of this shit has been sorted out, I have to assign detail to you—"

Her eyes enlarged. "What!" she barked.

"I know," I ducked my head in sympathy. I understood this was a lot to take in, but it had to be done. "I know it sounds foreign for you to need your personal security, but it's non-negotiable and I swear it will be an accessory you'll easily forget in no time at all—trust me. But between Darryl Harrison popping up on you a couple of weeks back, Spin and her antics, the Thompson fiasco, this fire, and the announcement of our engagement, you're exposed to people who meant nothing to you just a few short months ago. I need you safe and with peace of mind."

She shook her head in disbelief.

"Right now, I need cooperation. Rayna, all I could think while standing there watching my burnt home being hosed down was *what if I'd had Rayna with me here?* How close to that being my reality had I not happened upon this place some time ago." Rayna remained steeled in her seat. "Baby, when you presented in my boardroom, I was living in that house. Yes, I had this place, but it had only been an escape haven for the period of my breakup with Tara. I'd only had a bed here. You were my motivation for having the place furnished. Shit, I hadn't even made love to you when this place was being filled."

I interrupted my rant, at a loss for words. I was losing my breath, trying to explain to her how close a call this was.

"But Azmir—"

"It's final. You'll have assigned muscle at all times when you're not with me. While you're working, they'll keep their distance, but get it in your head that their presence will be felt at your job. They'll blend in with the wallpaper. As this investigation progresses, so may the details of your security." I stood from the table, feeling the loss of my appetite, and I wasn't about to argue about what had been decreed in my mind. "I have some calls to make. I'll be in my office."

I left my love there processing my words.

Rayna

It had been two days since Azmir hit me with the news: from now until the unforeseeable future, I'd be followed by security—and not just any security, my detail was professional. I learned yesterday he went to the extent of contracting with a private company employing former governmental agency security and they carried weapons.

Imagine my surprise when yesterday, as I prepared for church, not only did Azmir get dressed along with me, but insisted on attending. I was followed all throughout service by a large, stiff red head man in an all-black suit. It was intolerable. It was odd enough having Azmir, a self-proclaimed Muslim, sitting next to me, stiff and squarely poised himself. But to be followed by my personal security to the ladies' room was the most embarrassing thing I'd had to endure in years. All the women gaped oddly at me and ogled Azmir for the duration of the service. Once it was over, I made a beeline for the door before Pastor Edmondson could call for me. I couldn't explain my varied company in morning worship.

And then this morning, I had to ride into work with Azmir and Ray with our security in tow, two cars behind. Who in the hell were we, Barack and Michelle? I didn't express my disdain and total confusion about this debacle, trying to respect Azmir's decision and accommodate his lifestyle, but this was too much!

This morning before we began seeing patients, I had to hold an impromptu mandatory staff meeting and inform my team from here on out there would be security on the grounds monitoring, per the advisement and loan of the recreation center. I threw it all on the rec because there was no way I was prepared to discuss my personal life with my staff. It was humiliating.

Once my day was done, I jumped back into the *Bentley* with Azmir and Ray and headed back to the marina. As soon as I laid eyes on Azmir, I could tell he'd ended his day with a session with Tyler. He wore a soiled sweatsuit. We rode in silence. Other than him grabbing my hand once we pulled off, we had very little interaction. I had forgotten he was there. I thought to myself maybe if I had the heart to express my feelings about this to him instead of holding them inside and suppressing them, I wouldn't be so wound up. I'd said very little to Azmir since his announcement of this insanity. He didn't press me either. He had seemed so preoccupied, I'd assumed from the fire.

We walked into the apartment and Azmir headed straight to the shower. I was right on his heels but went to the walk-in closet to discard my work clothes when I heard the phone ring. Azmir had state of the art technology at the marina, which included a telephone system streaming jazz music at every station and utilized several ringtones. This particular ringtone indicated a call from the front desk downstairs. I answered and could hear Roberto speaking in a distinct murmur.

"There's a Tara Harrison down here. She's been waiting for over an hour for Mr. Jacobs. I explained to her when she arrived, he was unavailable, and she said she knew and would wait."

What on earth is Tara doing here? How does she even know where he lives? Does she have stalker tendencies like her father?

This was all becoming too much for me. I felt like I was going burst of frustration. Tara picked the wrong day to show up unannounced, and I was prepared to show her.

"Send her up, Roberto."

Within seconds, I'd hatched the perfect plan of introduction. I flew into the closet and pulled on my short peach silk robe and the matching slippers. I ran to the door, unclicked the lock, and left it ajar before cantering into the kitchen to prepare the dinner Boyd had cooked earlier, which coincidentally would have been my normal routine had she not shown.

In minutes, I heard the door push open and a little strange noise from that end of the apartment. I was sure to slam a counter drawer or two to indicate someone was in the kitchen.

"Wow! This is some place," Tara shrilled excitedly in her valley girl twang. "Damn, Mir. Is this the type of swanky bachelor you've turned into? I mean, you've always done well, but this is fancy as shit!" she tittered as she admired the contemporary decor of the apartment. I could appreciate her reaction; the apartment was really something to behold.

The place was enormous, but I could sense she was making her way to the kitchen. I could also hear a squeak as she neared. I just kept hitting pans and clicking the cabinet doors to lure her into my direction. I adjusted the top of my robe to expose my cleavage. I wanted to appear as at home and informal as possible. My heart pounded from my jumpy nerves, hoping my plan would work.

Stay in the shower for a few more minutes, Mr. Jacobs. I knew after late day workouts he liked to sit on the shower bench at home, under the parching cascade, and it seemed like today was one of those days. *Perfect!*

"Is this a *Claude Monet?*" she gasped. I could still hear those odd noises growing louder and sharper as she drew closer. I could now hear she was rounding the doorway of the kitchen, "This place is magnificent! I can't believe you did this—" her speech was halted at the sight of me. I couldn't hold my suspense any longer, the noise was killing me, so I took a few steps closer until we met. And I froze once I caught a glimpse of her as well. But it made sense at first sight of her. Tara was with her baby...in a stroller. *Why would she tote her baby here for a surprise visit to Azmir's?* I quickly regained myself. Baby or no baby present, I was prepared to play ball.

"Surprised?" I asked with wide eyes and a Cheshire cat's smile. "I was prepared to offer you a glass of wine, but I see you're... *With child.*" I carried a sardonic tone with a matching faux smile as I held a tray topped with three glasses of wine.

Tara's feet looked as though they were nailed to the floor. *Score!* She was clearly knocked off balance by my presence.

"Azmir must have forgotten to mention you coming by this evening or else I could have prepared for you and your baby," I threw the infant a smile of acknowledgement as I referenced her.

"Are you planning to stay long...because I can throw something together?"

Tara, suddenly, had a sway in her neck, "Azmir didn't tell me you spent so much time over here. Had I known, I would have been sure not to show during your assigned time." Tara's wit was always on point.

"That would have been a little difficult for you to do considering *I live here*." At the raise of my eyebrows, I conspicuously whispered my last three words.

Her eyes nearly popped out of her head at my words. *Second score!* To say she was taken aback wouldn't properly describe her reaction.

"Don't worry, Tara, you're in good company with not being up to date with Azmir's world. Apparently, your father knows very little about the inner workings of his life as well. But I'm here, and I'll be glad to acquaint you with every detail necessary to illustrate you have no place in it," I maintained my smile.

Tara's eyes darkened, but her voice remained pleasant, "And you do because he lets you spend the night? You have a lot more convincing to do than just standing here in your stay-over robe and slippers."

The baby started becoming agitated, forcing Tara to tend to her, "Oh, Azina. It's alright, princess. Mommy's here," she sang in her maternal vocals as she picked the baby up. She no doubt wanted me to catch her daughter's name and deep down inside it was a gut blow, but I had my game face on and was facing a gridlock in score.

The doorbell rang, and I jumped to it, remembering Azna was being dropped off from his grooming appointment. Another service the property assisted with.

I took Azna from the arms of Roberto, thanked him and closed the door. There was still no signs of Azmir, leaving time on the scoreboard. I carried him over to Tara.

"Oh, a doggie. How cute. I didn't know Azmir was fond of animals," her wry statement screamed of sarcasm.

My smile was as broad as a billboard. "He bought him for me," as I petted Azna. "Tara, maybe Azina would like to say hello to Azna," I smiled with my eyes, trying to keep from laughing at her haunted expression. She was offended and I was glad.

And yet another score!

"You named your dog after him, honey? How pathetic," she laughed, and well it seemed.

"Oh, sure! I find naming a dog he *gave* me after him far more appropriate than a baby he *didn't* give you."

Her smug was clipped. Tara took off her gloves, "Listen, bitch. You have no right speaking about my child or anything between Azmir and me. You may be his new little piece of ass, but we still have undeniable and irreversible history."

I scoffed, "New little piece of ass? I guess you weren't made aware of our recent engagement." As I extended my hand I informed, "Azmir can be so modest. But you still should have heard. I was there when he shared it with all of his closest friends," my eyebrows furrowed. As bad as I wanted to laugh at the lack of a poker-face Tara was capable of issuing, I had to stay focused on her next move; I knew it was coming.

"What the fuck?" Azmir belted from the foyer a few feet away. Both our heads swung to him. He was topless, wearing basketball shorts and black ankle socks. His splendid frame was hard to ignore. This couldn't have played out any better if I had planned it from start to finish.

"What the fuck are you doing here and why do you have..." he gestured toward the baby. His tone wasn't of his CEO mien, neither was it raised as to involve emotions, but it was sound and crisp. It was also clear that he was just as dismayed by her visit as I was. At this point, he had even intimidated me.

"I didn't know you had company," Tara hissed in my direction.

"That doesn't answer my question. How'd you even know

where I lived?" Azmir was livid. I could see it all in his face as he approached us in the living room. I put Azna down on the floor. Even I was heavily awaiting this answer.

She cut her eyes to me, and I could tell my presence under Azmir's wrath made her incredibly uncomfortable. But seeing we were both indisposed drew a picture of private boundaries she'd clearly crossed.

"I heard about the fire in Pasadena and wondered if you weren't still living in *that* house where you could be. So, I did some digging around and came up with this address."

"Digging around? What type of answer is that? You know what..." He raised his hand to cancel out his previous question. "How about we get back to why you're here?" He didn't stand next to me, instead he was adjacent, placing himself in the middle of Tara and me, but I still had clear view of her.

"If we *must* do this here..." she repeated, stealing a glance at me. "I thought we could talk about why the money has stopped. I didn't receive anything for this month, and I have bills due." Tara didn't resemble the strong, confident, and colorful woman who had confronted Azmir and me last summer at *The Grove*. Instead, she looked all of a twelve-year-old child who was embarrassed and in need.

This all boiled my blood. I absolutely felt nothing but enmity for those who pulled on and relied entirely too much upon Azmir's wealth. No one seemed to have sowed into him, other than her father and even that had changed according to Azmir. Azmir said he was helping out financially, and I had wondered why but didn't deem it appropriate to ask.

"I take it you haven't spoken to your father?" His face was agitated.

"Why should I? This arrangement is between the two of us."

"But made between your father and me," Azmir pushed out a long exhale as he gripped his head with both his hand. You could see all the muscles in his back bulge reflexively. My heart bled for him. Suddenly, I wanted to kick Tara's ass for upsetting him. I wanted to call on my inner b-girl and drag her across the apartment by her hair. I still had it in me. The only thing making me think twice was her baby being present. With calm in his voice, Azmir observed, "You brought the baby to play on my conscience. How fucking incredulous," He'd just been smacked with the revelation.

Oh, wow.

"Tara, you have to go. I can't have you barging in on my personal life like this. Please don't stop by again. I don't live alone and don't think it's fair to her to have to deal with reminders of my past. If you need to contact me, call my cell or my office."

I saw the tears rushing from their ducts and Tara's face reddening. A ball gathered in my throat. I felt uncomfortable for her until she screeched, "Azmir, could you at least let me know what to expect with the money so I can take care of my mounting bills?"

That's it!

"Why can't you just hurry with the paternity test so the payments will either be justified or permanently suspended!" I shouted to Tara before turning to Azmir and asking, "Why must you carry a load we don't even know is yours?"

"Not now, Rayna," Azmir warned, calmly.

"Don't know?" Tara perked up and giggled as I watched her mood go from sullen to excited within a second's time. I didn't understand how or why. Just seconds ago, I felt sorry for her. "How did you phrase it earlier?" Tara furrowed her brows and tilted her head, feigning a pensive state. "*Oh!* I guess *you weren't made aware* the test was taken, and the results were revealed weeks ago. Azmir isn't the father, but he's been helping out with things until I get on my feet."

My neck jerked involuntarily, and I saw Azmir's eyes close in exasperation.

"What?" I demanded.

"Tara, get the fuck outta here!" Azmir ordered in his Brooklyn tongue through clenched teeth then paced over to the door. "And if you really want to know about money, go ask your muthafuckin' father," his voice had slightly hitched.

Tara didn't say another word. She didn't have to. She'd won. She placed her baby back in the stroller and with a trace of a grin, made her way to the door. She didn't turn to look at Azmir before he slammed the door when she stepped over the threshold. He stood there, facing the door with his hands resting on his waist.

Suddenly, I realized my breathing was out of control and my body had tensed. I felt like I'd been hit with a bag of bricks. Azmir was caring for a child who was not his *and* her mother, who tried to trap him into believing it was his? He'd lied in Tahiti. He had agreed to take care of Tara and her baby *indefinitely?*

Was Harrison correct about their bond?

Why was I now feeling like the outsider Harrison tried to convince me I was?

I stood there for what seemed like an eternity, trying to make sense of it all. In my periphery, I could see him turning around, but before Azmir could utter a word, I headed toward the bedroom. I went straight to the closet to throw on a pair of jeans. As I reached up to grab a pair off the shelf, I felt his hand snatch them from my grip. Looking up, I saw his heavy eyes.

"I don't need this shit right now. Let me explain," he spoke with flared nostrils and out of breath.

"Explain? Explain how you were going to marry me and secretly take care of a woman who cheated on you and fucking humiliated you in front of your peers by getting pregnant by a wanna-be rapper?" Azmir's forehead wrinkled. "You think I didn't know? I do!"

Frustration flashed across his face. "Rayna, you don't know all the details of this story. Let's sit down so I can explain them to you."

"Fuck you, Azmir! Apparently you don't mind allowing people

like Tara and her father make a fool out of you, but I don't take well to it being done to me at all."

I looked up to go for my jeans, but his hand was still laying on top of them. Beyond frustrated, I peeled off my engagement ring and slammed it into his chest. "You can give this to her to pawn for more money. I'm sure it will get her enough money to buy *you* time to get over me because I am fucking out of here!"

He grabbed the ring and I saw the fear in his face. He shook his head, "No. You're not running. Not over something that means nothing to me. Not right now. Not ever!" his voice grew.

"Move, Azmir!" I screamed, nearly to top of my lungs, feeling my tears flooding the sockets of my eyes. "Move!" He wouldn't budge. He just kept shaking his head.

"Move!"

"No! You're not leaving! She doesn't fucking matter. That money wasn't significant. I can fucking wipe the shit from my ass with it! It won't happen again," he declared.

I don't know where the audaciousness came from, perhaps from my rage, but the next thing I knew I had hauled off and punched Azmir in his mouth. His head swung from the unexpected blow. Fear pounded in my chest. *What in the world did I just do? What is he going to do?*

When he turned his face back to me, I flinched internally, in disbelief of my anger. But I was ready for more. I was eyeing the vase sitting on top of the island there in the closet. If he made one move to hit me, I would make a dive for it.

Azmir's face was balled, and his grimace was fixated on me. We were both out of breath, waiting on each other's next move.

"Got any more?" he muttered.

I was caught completely off guard by his question—his reaction. My eyes danced back and forth, trying to read his, to find his level of anger. Before I knew it, he'd lunged down at me, covering my lips with his, gripping my face to his, using his large and strong hands. He tried forcing his tongue in my mouth as I sealed my it shut by squeezing my lips together and tried to break away from his impossible clamp. I bit his lip and while he winced, Azmir didn't let up. He was determined to have me participate in an oral embrace, but I was too angry with him. I banged my fists into his ironclad chest, trying to deter his grip, but to no avail.

He hooked my body with his right arm, gripping my ass while his left arm cradled my head like a baby. My body was tense, ready for a physical attack. I was straining against his tall and hard frame. He found his way underneath my robe to my panties and rubbed me so intently, so greedily. I was weakening from failed attempts to break from him and eventually crumpled from defeat. His tongue entered my mouth and swirled and swirled, furthering my weakened state. My breathing vocalized as he invaded my mouth. I could taste faint traces of blood ejecting from me biting his lip, but I still couldn't stop him. He unfastened my robe and as he tried to push it off, I mustered the strength to tug it, holding it in place. With force, Azmir yanked my robe completely off. He lifted me in the air, forcing me into a straddling position where I could feel his strong erection on my way up to his waist. I was angry and didn't understand his aroused state.

"I need you, Rayna. You can't leave me," he forcibly whispered to me, out of breath as he walked me out into the bedroom.

I pushed and screamed, dragging my chords, "No! No! You want me to need you like everyone else and I refuse." Azmir shook his head vehemently, rejecting my summation of his crazy world. "Put me down. I'm leaving!"

He walked into the bedroom, near the bed. I was still trying to force him to ease up from his impossible grasp. He held me so tightly to his pounding chest. I could hear him closing a drawer but didn't have the room nor energy to even turn to look.

"Let me down, Azmir. Give me my space!" I squirmed in his arms.

"No. No space. Just be here with me," he offered softly, walking back to the closet, but this time to the other doorway where he stopped underneath. I heard metal clinking above me, and when I looked, I saw the handcuffs he had used on me weeks ago. He let me down so my feet touched the floor but held on to me with one of his arms.

"What are you doing, Azmir? Are you crazy? Are you going to do this every time we fight?" I was horrified at the turn of events in my day. He was suddenly scaring me.

"Are you going to *run* every time we fight?" he spat back mordantly.

I couldn't believe it when he was pulling my arms into the constraints, one by one. Once he forcibly lifted my left arm up to throw the other cuff over his pull-up bar, I knew his plan for my other hand. I tried like hell to fight him, but he was too strong, it was pointless, and I didn't want to risk scraping my hands against the metal. I shouted and screamed helplessly.

"Relax before you hurt yourself!" he demanded as he pushed the last cuff in, to adjust it to my wrist size. He stood back and let out a deep breath. I watched as his shoulders sagged. I was winded, firing off all types of nastiness.

"Do you know how insane this is? This is all types of crazy! You think I'm going to want you after this? I'm calling the cops!"

With my hands, I lifted myself from the bar and swung my legs aimlessly, trying to widen the distance between us. With ease, he caught my legs, one at a time and dropped to his knees, pulling my lower torso into an embrace. Here I was, in only my bra and panties, breathlessly crying my eyes out.

I didn't possess the stamina needed to keep up my resistance. Azmir buried his face in my abdomen, breathing forcefully into my bare skin. The front of my thighs strained against his naked chest and his fraught hands were plastered to the back of them, skin to skin. *What is this?* I couldn't fight anymore. I needed a reprieve. We stayed in this position for a while, panting hard and hearts racing until I felt his face lift and his lips trace from the side of my abdomen to the center of my belly. He started off slowly as he licked and kissed me desperately. My abdominal muscles jumped at each movement of his skilled tongue. With one hand, he began tugging at my sky-blue lace boy shorts.

"No! No!" I was all breaths with no force behind my pleas.

Devastated.

Shattered.

That one hand managed to pull my panties off, licking maniacally at my belly. My body went from fight to acquiesce, betraying me. I went nearly limp but for the possibility of the cuffs cutting into my flesh. He freed my legs, bringing his hands up to my back, slow and steadily, caressing me. My body began convulsing. I felt him prying my legs open with little resistance; I was so exhausted from fighting, but I didn't want intimacy. It just wasn't right.

"Azmir! I can't—" I panted hoarsely.

Before I knew it, he'd lifted my hips in the air, placing them astride his broad shoulders while planting his face at the apex of my thighs. My body bowed at his deft tongue lashing each and every way until it found its way to my pearl, causing me to lose all control. Azmir's tongue was forceful, strong in its swipes. Each lapping communicated his state of mind. He was desperate. He wouldn't stop his oral rage. As much as I tried to will against what my body was inclined to do, I was powerless. I felt it build from within, pleasure brewing. There was something very arousing about his kneeling posture beneath me, poking and prodding at the most sensitive place on my body as his strong arms cradled me carefully. It took no time at all for my orgasm to explode inside of me and all over his face. I was struggling, trying to catch my breath from the violent orgasm ripping through me.

Azmir pushed from his feet and rose against my body, "I love you so fucking much, Rayna. More than anything ever before in my life," his voice was hoarse and raw, searing through my heart. He pulled up my chin, forcing his tongue in my mouth, devouring me. I could barely breathe from his primal hold.

Azmir grabbed me again by my hips, lifting me higher in the air this time as he entered me. He took no time planting himself way deep. I maintained my grip on the bar as he plowed into me. Suddenly, I got it, he was claiming me, marking me *once again*. I was being reminded of how beautiful we are together and how much we shouldn't be apart. And we were. Beautiful. Together. But I couldn't take the externalities, the invasions of my world—our world. *Tara, her baby, and father have to go!*

I felt him unhook my bra and could feel my breasts bounce in the air. He was pulling out all stops, proving his point. He brought one of my breasts into his mouth, sucking and licking with no particular rhythm. I pushed my lips together, trying not to give in to the overwhelming sensations of his plunges. He felt so determined and familiar as he pulled me onto him and pushed himself into me. He worked with great vigor to break me.

"Come, Rayna. Don't fight it!" Azmir commanded through clenched teeth, sweat sprouting from his beautiful milk chocolate skin.

I shut my eyes because I didn't want him to see the tears springing from them.

"Stop fighting it!" he growled in my ear before pulling my short hair back from the roots to raise and lick my neck. He accelerated his speed, pushing me over the edge. My eyes shot open, and he pumped even faster, causing me to scream mindlessly. I'd lost majorly. To Tara and now to Azmir. My orgasm crushed every bit of resistance I had. Azmir followed me with shaky legs and promises to love me forever. Spent and totally sated, I collapsed on his shoulder. We were motionless for some time.

From the brisk dip in air suspension, I could tell he was reaching for his shorts because not too long after, he uncuffed me from the bar. I fell into his capable arms, and he pulled off my loosened bra then carried me into the shower, sitting me on the bench while he turned on the water. When he walked back over to me, he inspected my wrists for bruises and spewed profanities underneath his breath. I just laid there lifelessly, observing it all from an outer-body experience.

Azmir positioned my shower cap on my head then lathered my scrub with liquid soap and washed me from neck to toe. My body was still weakened and throbbed from earlier episodes, so he supported it as he rinsed me. He sat me back on the bench to quickly clean himself. After drying me off, he covered me in my white plush housecoat hanging behind the bathroom door. He carried me in his arms over to the bed, pulling the covers back and gently laying me down. He went into the closet and walked back out seconds later, wearing fresh shorts and a T-shirt.

He made his way over to the wall adjacent to the end of the bed, turned on the television and murmured, "I'll be back in a few minutes."

True to his word, Azmir returned two commercial breaks later with a tray of food. The aroma caused my stomach to growl as I lay there exhausted, fully spent, and physically and emotionally depleted. He placed the tray beside me and fed me eggplant parmesan, pasta, and merlot until I could eat no more and declined. My arms throbbed viciously from being raised over my head for so long. He lifted an eager Azna onto the bed, who quickly found his space of comfort and fell asleep. When Azmir left to discard the food tray, I realized I couldn't take the throbbing stiffness or sleepiness anymore, so I stretched out my arms and legs, lowered myself in the bed and succumbed to siesta.

I don't know how long after, but I could feel him slipping into the bed behind me, pulling off my housecoat and when he was done, scooting over to spoon with me. I had then realized the television was off. I slipped back into my coma, but not before feeling the trail of passionate kisses he endowed from my shoulder to my neck. I was too tired and fatigued to make sense of it.

My eyes flickered open to the soft night lights of the marina casting through the curtains of the bedroom. I felt soft lugging at my body but was too much in a fog to immediately catch on to Azmir summoning my body from sleep. He was rubbing my breasts and breathing into my neck. I looked at the clock straight ahead and saw it four sixteen in the morning. It seemed as though I'd just shut my eyes for the night. Seconds later, he was mounting me. My thighs opened to him instinctively. He found his way into me via his finger, making sure to awaken my canal.

It didn't take long as I heard, "You're so wet. So ready."

He pushed himself inside of me, communicating his regrets and apologies. It was like slicing through smooth butter, my body had just welcomed him in despite the late hour. My stomach spasms started from the unrelenting pleasure of his lazy thrusts. His stride was strong, slow, and purposeful. Even at the inconvenient hour, he took his time working me. His pulls were gentle, his plunges less. His ragged breathing was rhythmic in my ear and his grasp of my torso was needy. Azmir was making love, meek and gentle. His body trembled with trepidation at every plunge. He was afraid. Frantic, even over his thrust.

Out of nowhere, I began to cry again. The tears wouldn't stop. He felt so good on top of me, pushing his love inside of mine, trying to once again become one with me. He commanded my body from scent alone, *but this...* We were so connected. *In and out, in and out...* he stroked me gently with his elbows buried in the mattress aside my ears. Azmir's tongue chartered my mouth hungrily as if on a mission. He made sweet love to me as I lay beneath him, bruised and vulnerable. It not only stimulated my body, but it also sent my mind on a flight.

All this time, I felt he was leading me on my journey of self-discovery and motivating me to seek out my purpose and push my demons behind me. But in this moment, I felt I didn't know who guided who—who was sent to help who. I'm not sure it mattered because I knew I needed him. I needed him just as he professed needing me. I had nowhere to go. Yes, I'd had my home now occupied by his mother, but it wouldn't have been any more of a home had it still been vacant. Azmir was where my home was. More than the abundance of space this apartment provided; he was every bit of the substance that made it a home—my home.

I still didn't get it all. I was still confused about so much. But one thing was for sure: my incredible, magnetic, and most powerful connection to this man. I felt it in my heart, and somehow in my body, as he penetrated me. My legs started to stiffen.

"I feel it, too," he whispered hoarsely in my ear, excitedly. "Please don't fight it. I need to feel connected to you. I need you with me. Come with me like you love to do."

Azmir's invitation was so heady and difficult to resist. My previous tears of confusion turned into that of bliss as I felt the growing detonation in my belly and came all around him. He spilled into me, potently. Hot, virile, translucent liquids squirted, invading my womb. Azmir's chest beat violently against mine as his silken skin lay dank against to mine. His body shuddered over me, not withholding any emotion or sensation he felt as he climaxed hard. He relaxed his six-foot four-inch frame on top of me, not wanting to break our enfold. Azmir's desires didn't need to be communicated using words. I knew he was begging me not to leave him over this recent discovery. To be with him forever.

When my alarm went off a few hours later, Azmir lay splayed, partially on top of me as I lay on my stomach. He was so possessive and insecure in his subconscious. I reached over to turn off the clock and proceeded out of bed to start my day when I caught a glimpse of the glare from my hand. I squinted my eyes at my engagement ring. He must have slipped it back on while I was asleep.

Azmir was making it abundantly clear he didn't want a break, or interruption of our relationship. I looked over to him, surreptitiously stealing a view at his sleeping profile. Azmir was gorgeous even in his sleep. His position resembled a male model on the cover of a magazine. It was difficult at times to believe his pulchritude, it was remarkable. Then when you factor in his physique and stature, he was damn near unbelievable. *Could I maintain this man?* He could have any woman he wanted, but he was here petitioning my lifelong commitment. A pang ran through my belly, forcing me to retreat to the bathroom.

In the vanity mirror, I observed the bags underneath my reddened eyes as I sat there, taking inventory of all the reasons I should have called out of work for the day. When I tried pulling at my skin to stretch the bags, I noticed the sadistic bruising on my wrists. *What in the?!*

Those handcuffs.

Azmir's brutal handling of me.

My unrelenting combativeness.

Our chemistry.

It made me question what Azmir and I were doing in our relationship. I learned he was financially supplying the welfare of his ex-girlfriend and *her* child, I reacted to it and somehow woke up to bruised wrists and a sore body, feeling pain—inside and out. *My god, even the sex was violent.*

After finishing up, washing, and applying much needed makeup, I went into the walk-in closet and picked up my phone to text Tyler. I had to cancel my workout session with him. There was no way I could explain the bruising and my overall feeble state.

I stood in the closet in a black midi skirt I thought would be easy to pair a top with. I frantically searched for a long-sleeved blouse to match. One not too formal for workwear. My unbearable frustration was nearing again from last night when Azmir walked up on me.

His appearance—vast, masculine stature always caused my breath to stagger. He was bare from the waist up, wearing his black basketball shorts and black ankle socks, sipping a cup of coffee with one hand and handing me two jewelry boxes with the other.

"I ordered these up a few weeks ago, but forgot they were in my office with other deliveries I haven't had the chance to go through yet. They should help today."

His eyes bore into me, begging for words of comfort and approval of the state of us, but I had nothing for him. I took the boxes, examining the designers' names on them, feeling anger stirring inside again. Azmir remained standing there, towering me, imploring with his eyes. He was back to his calm and resolved self, almost as if last night didn't happen. I still needed my distance from him. I just needed time to think about *exactly how nauseatingly crazy last night was.*

"Boyd has arrived. What would you like for breakfast?"

"I'm not sure. I don't have much of an appetite," I murmured raspingly.

"How about your usual?"

"I guess." *I mean...really?*

"I'll tell him something lite." Azmir got the memo. I needed space. He couldn't cut his gaze of my wrists and it made me uncomfortable. I lifted my free hand, running it over the back of my neck. Simultaneously, his mouth collapsed as his eyes widened at the revelation.

"Are you going to make your appointment with Tyler this morning?" I could tell by his tone he was urging me to cancel.

"I've already sent him a text canceling. My body is too sore," I nearly choked out on a cry.

Azmir grunted profanities, much to himself as he let out an angry breath. "I'll have Brett make you an appointment for the spa. We can go right after work today."

We?

"I have counseling after work, so I'll need to drive myself today." *Are you going to offer to attend my session with me, too?*

His eyebrows furrowed immediately. He didn't like my cold tone. "No. That won't be necessary. I have a meeting with a bank this morning in Culver City and will be back at the rec after lunch. That'll be plenty of time to think about how you'll get to counseling," he commanded, heading out of the closet, leaving me to the boxes.

One held a *Évocateur Museum Capriccio* cuff bracelet. It looked about six inches wide and was mostly black, decorated with music notes and gold trim. It was beautiful and most certainly ideal for covering Azmir's animalistic indiscretions.

In the other, was an *Auden Lunar* cuff. It was designed with black beads inside of gold brass rings. Both bracelets were beautiful and miraculously came at the perfect time. They were both bold pieces I would have never typically worn together, but I needed to mask my wrists, and this was my only option. That Azmir sure had exquisite taste. After considering the color in the bracelets, I selected a champagne and black, horizontally striped silk sleeveless blouse. I was relieved to have found a solution.

Breakfast was odd. We ate with much discussion between Azmir and Chef Boyd, but very little talk amongst Azmir and me. I was anxious to get to work and away from him for a few hours. So excited, once we pulled into the rec's parking lot, I let out a quiet sigh of relief.

When the car stopped in front of the practice, I grabbed my briefcase and turned, prepared to exit when Azmir pulled me into an impassioned kiss taking my breath away. I didn't want it, but per usual, my body readily accepted it. When he pulled back, I noticed the slant in his eye. It wasn't attributed to lasciviousness and his usual undeniable desire, but stress and anxiety instead. I knew I was responsible for it, and it made me wonder if he had gotten much sleep the night before. I told myself I didn't have time to be concerned with that. I needed to be mentally ready for my workday.

I didn't want to acknowledge his caveman behavior. Couldn't express how much it frightened me. So, instead I turned again to leave the car when Azmir took a firm hold of my thigh and decreed, "Don't run. If you do, I swear with every fiber of my being, I will employ *every* resource I can afford and deploy *every* recovery professional I can find to locate you. That is my fuckin' word, Rayna."

I had no words to retort. There was something dark and honest in his eyes locking to mine, expressing sincerity of each word he spoke. My mouth dropped in sheer surprise and my ability to speak fleeted me. I heard Ray open my door and felt a sense of relief like none other. I finally got out of the car with his heated gaze still upon me.

With each step I took towards the door of my practice, the idea of escape grew more and more enticing.

XXX

THANKS

Thanks again for taking a chance on this love story! Please join us in the finale of this love journey, **Love Redeemed**!

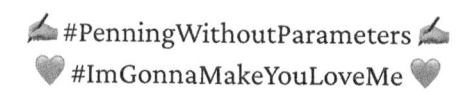

✍️ #PenningWithoutParameters ✍️
🩶 #ImGonnaMakeYouLoveMe 🩶

www.LoveBelvin.com

NEXT UP...

LOVE REDEEMED

from the *Love's Improbable Possibility* series

Available now!

~LOVE ACKNOWLEDGES

Love's Promoters: Thank you to all of my family, friends and L.I.P.'ers for your assistance in promoting the L.I.P. series. Juaquanna, Angela, Karmen, Tondi, Zakiya, and other #TeamLB members, I alone couldn't do it. We have a journey ahead but are on the right road because of your efforts. Special thanks to Brandy of ***Momma's Books*** for your tireless resources!

Marcus Broom of DPI Designs: once again, thanks for your talented artistry on the L.I.P. covers.

Tanya Keetch - The Word Maid: Thank you! Thank you! Thank you! Great feedback and catches! Feels like we've come such a long way from **Love Lost** in terms of the flow of the books, right? What a journey with these characters. I love it!

In-house editors: Zakiya Walden of **I've Got Something to Say Incorporated**. Keep bossing Love around. It pushes me towards a greater me.

Tina V. Young: Thanks so much for helping me comb through this baby for a good cleaning. I'm sure we'll do it again. LOL!!

MDT: Thanks for being about that LB life. Another one for #TeamMKT!

To my **Master**, my *Jireh*, my **Rohi**, James 1:17. My gift belongs to the Gifter.

~OTHER BOOKS BY LOVE BELVIN

Love's Improbable Possibility series:
Love Lost, Love UnExpected, Love UnCharted & **Love Redeemed**

The Letter *(from Michelle to Azmir)*

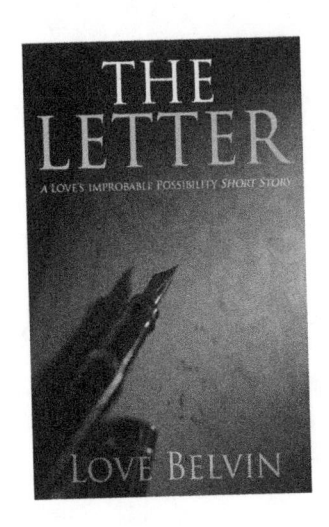

Waiting to Breathe series:
Love Delayed & **Love Delivered**

Love's Inconvenient Truth (Standalone)

Love Unaccounted series:
In Covenant with Ezra, In Love with Ezra & Bonded with Ezra

The Connecticut Kings series:
Love in the Red Zone, *Love on the Highlight Reel, *Determining Possession, End Zone Love, Love's Ineligible Receiver, *Pass Interference, Love's Encroachment, & *Offensive Formations (*by Christina C. Jones)

Wayward Love series:
The Left of Love, _The Low of Love_ & The Right of Love

Love in Rhythm & Blues series
The Rhythm of Blues **&** *The Rhyme of Love*

The Sadik series:

He Who Is a Friend, He Who Is a Lover & He Who Is a Protector

The Muted Hopelessness series:
My Muted Love, Our Muted Recklessness, & Our Reckless Hope

The Prism series:
<u>Mercy</u>, Grace, & The Promise

Low Love, Low Fidelity (Standalone)

~EXTRA

You can find Love Belvin at www.LoveBelvin.com
Facebook @ Author - Love Belvin
Twitter @LoveBelvin
Goodreads: Love Belvin
and on Instagram @LoveBelvin

Join the #TeamLove mailing list on my website to keep up with the happenings!

Made in the USA
Middletown, DE
25 April 2025